Praise for The Gates of Heaven Series

"Lakin's clever retold . . . tales as she continues The Gates . . . fantasy series makes one miss them as a vehicle for instructing the young."

—*Publisher's Weekly*

"The Gates of Heaven is the series that introduced and converted me to the fantasy genre."

—**Glynn Young,** Faith, Fiction, Friends

"The Gates of Heaven promises to be one of the best fantasy series to come along in quite some time. One of the signs of this potential is its ability to hook you into its world at page one and leave you saying, 'just one more page' or 'just one more chapter.' That has happened to me before with C. S. Lewis's The Chronicles of Narnia, J.R.R. Tolkien's *The Lord of the Rings*, and Susan Cooper's The Dark is Rising sequence. Now C. S. Lakin has done the same with The Gates of Heaven."

—**Jonathon Svendsen,** Narniafans.com

"Much richer and deeper than traditional tales from fairyland . . . what Lakin does so well with her fairy tale is to provide images which remind us of what God has done for us."

—**Mark Sommer,** Faith, Fiction, Friends

"Lakin has masterful control of the writing craft, developing her characters and drawing the reader to see the world through their eyes."

—**Phyllis Wheeler,** *The Christian Fantasy Review*

D1603429

THE HIDDEN KINGDOM

A FAIRY TALE BY
C. S. LAKIN

LIVING
INK
BOOKS
Winning Worlds Reading

The Hidden Kingdom
Volume 7 in The Gates of Heaven® series

Copyright © 2015 by C. S. Lakin
Published by Living Ink Books, an imprint of
AMG Publishers, Inc.
6815 Shallowford Rd.
Chattanooga, Tennessee 37421

Print Edition	ISBN 13: 978-0-89957-907-8
EPUB Edition	ISBN 13: 978-1-61715-446-1
Mobi Edition	ISBN 13: 978-1-61715-447-8
E-PDF Edition	ISBN 13: 978-1-61715-448-5

First Printing—June 2015

THE GATES OF HEAVEN is a registered trademark of AMG Publishers.

Cover designed by Chris Garborg at Garborg Design, Savage, Minnesota, and Megan Erin Miller.

Cover Illustration by Gary Lippincott
(http://www.garylippincott.com/).

Interior design and typesetting by Reider Publishing Services, West Hollywood, California.

Edited and proofread by Christy Graeber and Rick Steele.

C. S. Lakin welcomes comments, ideas, and impressions at her websites: **www.cslakin.com** and **www.gatesofheavenseries.com**.

Printed in the United States of America
20 19 18 17 16 15 –LSI– 7 6 5 4 3 2 1

To my gracious and merciful God,
who prepared a kingdom for us all from
the founding of the world.
Tantummodo crede.

PART ONE

With a sweep of her hand, Alia opened the filigree curtains that shimmered with vibrant creamy light from the three moons lifting off the distant horizon as if taking flight. Her breath snagged as she stared and let the beauty of the moment drench her soul and fill her with gratitude. She had stitched into the curtains the Ganari crystals she'd found three centuries ago in the Caves of Calani, on a world whose name she had long forgotten, and the pale-blue light caught in the facets and spun rainbows around the room, which had been her intent when fashioning them for the nursery.

"Ooh, Momi! Pretty!"

Alia smiled at her son tangled in blankets with dozens of stuffed animals snuggled around him—his audience that often listened in silent, rapt attention to the imaginative tales he told with a flourish, as only a five-year-old could do. But tonight Aron had insisted she tell him a story. The glittering crystals already forgotten, he waved her over to his bed with an impatient flick of his hand.

With spangling moonlight crisscrossing the floor and spilling onto the bedcovers, she sidled up to Aron and kissed the top of his head.

"Ugh!" he said, smearing the kiss.

Alia chuckled and ruffled his unruly hair. Aron settled back against his pillows and pouted. "Are you going to tell me a story or not?" He *hmphed* and gave her his stern look, which only made her heart flutter with love.

She had forgotten the sweet moments like these—it had been so many years since she'd last had a child. And she hadn't thought she'd want any more. It was hard enough keeping track of them all, scattered through three galaxies—the children, and grandchildren, and great-grandchildren, numbers and names beyond her ability to remember them all. In eternity's slipstream, not just time but family blurred into a fluid dance of life and motion and experience. Death, loss, suffering—gone now so many years that the former memories were wisps of images void of emotion. Like the tailings of a dream long forgotten and out of reach. Perhaps that forgetting was the greatest gift bestowed upon them.

Now, every day was filled with renewed wonder, this new century in this new world so much more special as she saw everything for the first time through her son's young eyes. No truer words had ever been penned than those written in the Book so very long ago: "He has made everything beautiful in its time. He has also set eternity in the human heart; yet no one can fathom what God has done from beginning to end." No matter how far-flung across the universe, no matter how many millions of years might pass, humans would never learn all there was to know about this precious and puzzling thing called life.

"Momi!"

Alia turned at the sound of Aron slapping the covers. "All right, sweetling. What story do you want me to tell? And do you promise to go right to sleep afterward?"

Aron nodded with vigor, pulling Big Pig and Puppy into his orbit, arming himself with attention. "I want the story about Sherborne. The last one—about the magic land and the mean gripins."

Alia smiled. *Gryphons.*

"And the wizards. Don't forget the wizards!"

"Of course not. What's a fairy tale without wizards?"

"Momi—and the fairies!"

"Oh, yes. I won't forget the fairies. It is a fairy tale, after all."

As Aron wiggled in anticipation, Alia glimpsed the moons' steady rising, the crystals in the curtains glittering like stars against the deep-violet night. Their family had been among the first to settle this world, and like so many times before, Alia and her husband had woken from the twilight sleep and emerged from the solar-wind-powered ship as if being reborn on the first fresh morning of creation.

She looked out at the vanishing horizon and pictured the countless ships sailing like dandelion seeds on the wind, lighting on unexplored planets in unnamed star systems. How do you populate an infinite universe? One planet, one person, at a time.

One story at a time.

For, what was life but story?

"But it's true—right, Momi? A true story. All of it."

She smiled sweetly at her inquisitive son. And what was story but truth forged in lies?

Story was what beat at the heart of the universe. Without story, there would be nothing but the emptiness of space. Life was story.

Alia turned to Aron and laid her hands on his small ones. "Yes, sweetling. It's a true story, although a very old one. But we mustn't ever forget the stories."

No, we must not. If we do, we forget who we are, and *why* we are.

Aron yawned, but his eyes glinted in moonlight, and shadows moved like dreams across the lace of the curtains.

Drawing in a breath full of story, Alia began.

"Once upon a time, there was a powerful wizard who lived hidden among a brave and noble people and who married and had three daughters and used magic to protect them from the evil rampant in the lands around them—"

"Sha'kath!" Aron hissed.

Alia frowned. "Are you going to let me tell this story, or do you want to tell it?"

Aron pinched his lips shut and shook his head. She waited for the wiggling to stop.

"However, the threat of evil grew so great, the wizard had no other choice but to use magic to hide the people of the great ancient kingdom of Moreb, and so, when Sha'kath was not looking, a great rent ripped the ground open, and all the frightened people of Moreb fled underground—"

"Far, far underground!" Aron chimed in.

Alia chuckled at his excitement over hearing the same story over and over. He never seemed to tire of it, reminding her of God's delight in repetition. For every day, in constant and perfect patterns, galaxies and planets and moons repeated their orbits, and on many planets, day and night, summer and winter, never ceased. As if God alone had pure childlike delight in his creation and said to the sun, "Do it again. And again!" Never tiring, never losing the wonder.

She understood now, looking at Aron, why God wanted all his creatures to be like small children. It was the path to joy.

"And the wizard, with great magic, formed a beautiful kingdom far below the earth's surface in which all could live—man and beast alike. And in time, the people forgot they were underground. They forgot the real world above, and the centuries drifted by, and the wizard watched and waited, ever alert. For although the people lived in safety and peace, the wizard knew it was only a matter of time . . ."

Alia let her soft words trail off as the quiet rhythmic breaths puffed out of Aron's mouth, as his head slumped against Big Pig's plush cheek. Carefully, she extricated herself from the arms and animals and got to her feet.

She stood by the window, the three moons now cresting the dome of night in tandem, and let out a sigh.

She remembered back to those years, those centuries of smuggled peace and prosperity. Remembered how her power had gradually waned, the artificial light dimming more and more until she'd nearly lost hope of sustaining them any longer. She recalled the hard choice before her—to let her people wither and die in darkness or do the unthinkable—abandon their land and return to the surface to face whatever they would find there. But then, unexpectedly, the door to the secret room, long sealed, opened. And the choice was made for her.

No, she would never forget. It was her task to remember. Her duty.

Her promise.

If humans had learned only one lesson from the thousands of years of evil and suffering, it was this.

Never forget the stories.

ONE

THE MAT of dry silver leaves crunched under Meris's feet as she tromped along the winding path to the spring. She loved this part of the woods and this time of year, when the shimmering round leaves of the quaking firth trees rang out like tinkling chimes, filling the hollow with glitters of song. The fireflies were thicker here, drawn to the music and adding their own tinny, high-pitched shrilling. As she set down the heavy clay urn, they circled her head in a flicker of bright light that rivaled the pale dome of pink sky overhead—although the sky seemed awfully dim this morning, and the wind colder than usual.

She brushed the fireflies aside along with the strands of hair that had fallen in her eyes, but they drew near again in laughter, dancing about her ears and tickling her. Her sisters called them fairies. Abrella used to tease her when she was younger, saying they watched her and reported everything she did. No doubt she'd made that up to taunt her and to keep her out of trouble, but Meris knew better.

She placed the urn under the cascade of water tumbling down the side of the mossy rock face that fed into the shallow creek. The air sparkled with water droplets that settled in a web over her hair and on her cheeks, smelling like lilac and wild roses. She watched the creek as it wound through the woods and cascaded into a gulley—one of her favorite places to play, where the deer liked to nibble the bright-blue grass and watch her as she made up songs on her woodpipe. She'd used the excuse of fetching water to get out of the house, hoping to run up the hills with the deer, but now she heard her mother calling her name. Another spoiled morning!

If only Abrella's wedding day would arrive—then she could be free of all these tedious chores. Why her sister had to have such an elaborate wedding puzzled her. Abrella and Delon had known each other since birth. Their families practically lived next door to each other. Delon was like a brother to them, but for some reason Abrella had suddenly become enamored with the big-eared, clumsy boy and had to wed him. And after marrying, they planned to move into the cottage across the lane. It all seemed rather uneventful.

But maybe that was why Abrella was turning it into an event that would be talked about for years. And being that she was the Lord Na'tar's eldest daughter, just about everyone in the kingdom would be coming to the great hall for the ceremony and celebration. Well, at least Meris would get to see her older brothers, who lived in the far reaches of the kingdom, where they mined precious metals. She missed them and their playful teasing. Sapha and Abrella were poor substitutes for entertainment, with their lack of humor and trivial concerns.

Weddings were rare events, so Meris guessed the whole idea may have developed out of boredom, or the need for a break in routine. But Meris never tired of routine. She liked nothing better than to spend every day the same as the day before—wandering the hills with the deer, playing in quiet pristine pools of deep-green water, making up songs on her woodpipe while the fireflies sang along. She felt little need for human companionship, as her deer provided her with both company and entertainment. She loved watching them chase each other across the meadow, nipping and teasing, and sleeping huddled together in the tall grass they pounded flat with their little hooves. Sometimes on warm balmy afternoons she lay with them, her head on a deer's flank, listening to their soft even breathing as they napped. On occasion she would fall asleep as well, although she rarely needed sleep now that she'd grown to her full size. But it had been many long months since she'd enjoyed such pleasant weather.

Her name rang out again and she bristled. She grabbed the urn overflowing with sweet water and hefted it under her arms. The fireflies swarmed her again, making it hard for her to see her way.

"Please, move!" She stopped and scowled, sending out intent in a cresting wave. The fireflies backed away, and their song quieted. "I don't mean to be rude, but you'll make me trip."

A waterfall of silver leaves drifted down on her. She tipped her head and looked up. The fireflies swarmed the tree, giggling as they broke the fragile stems that held fast the last stragglers of autumn to the branches.

"All right, that's enough!" Her shout sent them ricocheting off the tree and into the woods, leaving a balm of quiet. She shook her head and took a quick look around, worried someone might have seen her. Someone being Sapha, her younger sister. If anyone would give her away, Sapha would. And she didn't want anyone to know about her strange ability.

Abilities, she thought, as she approached her cottage. She hadn't understood how odd she was until the first few curious remarks and stunned expressions. After that, Meris took care not to reveal what she could do. What would her mother say if she knew? What would her father do? She didn't think she'd get punished, but since trouble always seemed to latch on to her, she didn't want to invite more.

Through the window she could make out Abrella standing on the bench, turning this way and that in her wedding dress, her mother kneeling and fussing with the hem.

Meris pushed open the door and set down the urn.

"Ah, there you are, Meris," her mother said, her face buried in ruffles. "There's a bolt of lace trim in the cellar, on the far shelf. Would you get it for me?"

Meris caught Abrella's stern gaze, which sealed her decision to be an obedient daughter and do as she was told. Her mother's tone of voice implied there was disagreement on just how the dress should look, and Meris had no interest in joining in on the debate.

"I could just grow an inch and that way you wouldn't have to redo the hem, Mother," Abrella said in all earnestness.

Her mother cocked her head and gave a pinched smile. "Then you'd be as tall as Del, and that would never do." She bit down on a few straight pins and realigned the hemline. "Besides, raising the skirts and adding the lace will look so much better. Trust me." She added, "And I really don't think growing your hair to your waist for the wedding is a good idea. It will only get tangled up and be difficult to pin up."

Abrella put her hands on her hips. "Oh, Mother—"

Meris slipped out of the room and headed for the cellar stairs as the terse discussion faded to a dull murmur behind her. Through the open hallway window she heard her father chopping wood with his axe in steady rhythm, and the sound was comforting to Meris's ears. She loved the aroma of the cedar logs stacked alongside the back of the cottage, and the soothing crackling of a blazing fire in the hearth. Soon the nights would grow cold and frost would lace the windows, and the deer would spend more time sleeping in the dell. Then she and her sisters would begin planting the winter garden and another year would end.

She peeked into Sapha's empty room; she must be off playing with Del's sisters—who were just as young and nosy as Sapha. However, they never seemed to get scolded for all the eavesdropping they did, and that hardly seemed fair.

Meris opened the door at the end of the hall and stared into the darkness. With a quick glance, assured no one was nearby, she summoned fireflies. Why waste her time lighting a torch? Within seconds, a swarm gathered about her head, emitting tiny sparks of light.

"Brighter," she whispered, then pointed down the set of wooden stairs. Soon she could make out the cellar in the harsh light, and as she took the steps two at a time, the fireflies winged about her head, the hum of their busy wings loud and boisterous. She sent a dozen along the far shelf as she stood on the bottom step, their spotlight illuminating the various jars and stores her mother kept in this musty space.

"There—that must be the lace Mother wants." She made to move, then stopped as an idea came to her. She glanced up the stairs and listened, but she heard nothing other than the fast beat of gossamer wings and the pounding of blood in her ears. A strange sensation came over her, one she had been feeling more and more often in recent months. She knew it had something to do with her abilities, and it was an unsettling feeling. As if unnamed things were rattling inside her head, making her limbs stretchy and weak. Perhaps they were only growing pains, but she was afraid to tell anyone. What if her mother claimed it was just her overactive imagination? What if no one else ever felt these things? Surely someone would have told her, or mentioned them if they had. No, she dared not tell anyone. And certainly not about the strange things she'd been seeing lately—things no one else saw. Like the way Elder Webble's face had changed into a black crow's—with a crooked beak and beady eyes—while he stood speaking to her father last week at the great hall. The sight had shot a pain to her gut, and she'd almost dropped the platter of muffins.

As she remained still on the bottom cellar step, she bit her lip and concentrated. How had she done this just yesterday by the lake? She'd seen a pretty green rock resting on the shallow ledge underwater, but it had been too far to reach. And she hadn't wanted to go for a swim in the chilly morning breeze. So she had . . . just *asked* the rock to come to her.

Meris stared at the bolt of lace and willed it to move, but nothing happened. She shushed the fireflies' giggling, feeling her face flush hot in embarrassment. If Sapha saw what she was doing, she would think her daffy. And if Abrella saw her, there'd be no end to the chastising. But it wasn't silly. Whatever the reason she'd been given these abilities, she needed to master them—before they mastered her. Surely they must serve a purpose, and no doubt they'd come in handy on occasion—if she could just figure out how they worked, and why.

The fireflies quieted at her command and backed away, their lights dimming, but Meris could still see the lace on the shelf. She gritted her teeth.

Come to me . . . come . . .

The bolt of lace wiggled. Encouraged, Meris called again, and this time it rose lightly into the air, kicking up a soft cloud of dust.

She heard footsteps in the hall, and her breath caught. With a severe look to the shelf, she blurted out the words in her mind, *Now! Here!* The bolt of lace flew through the air and smacked into her chest, causing her to grunt in pain and surprise. The fireflies dispersed in an explosion of fluttering, making for dark corners and cracks in the wood-plank walls. Meris wrapped her arms around the bulky bundle just before it fell to the ground.

"There you are—what's taking you so long? And why are you down there in the dark?"

The sharp edge of her mother's voice in the hallway cut Meris to the quick and choked her throat. She turned and hurried up the stairs, her arms extended.

"Sorry. Here." She thrust the lace at her mother, who shook her head with a scowl and briskly walked back down the hall.

Meris drew in a deep breath, and tears welled in her eyes. Why was she so emotional? What was wrong with her? Usually her mother's irritation barely bothered her. But today feelings of anger and resentment were pushing up out of her heart like the tenacious weeds in her garden. Maybe before her mother could find more chores for her to do, she should run to the dell and find her deer. At least they wouldn't scowl at her.

She turned and looked back into the dark chasm of the cellar. Fireflies emerged tentatively from their hiding places and flitted around the room as if waiting for instructions. The ache in her stomach reminded her of the collision with the bolt of lace. She had done it—made it come to her. Was it her intent that had summoned it or her burst of emotion? Or both? She needed to figure this out and gain better control. Or else she'd end up bruised and sore from her efforts. Weariness nibbled at her composure.

"Just go," she told the wiggly lights. "Leave me alone."

Meris climbed the last steps and closed the cellar door behind her. She walked over to the bathing pool in the atrium and splashed the warm mineral-rich water on her face, clearing away any trace of tears. After popping a few bubbles that shimmied to the surface, she decided to get her woodpipe and head to the dell. A glance through the window at the bright-pink sky told her it was almost midday. That would give her plenty of time to play, maybe even compose a new tune, before she and her family had to eat supper and go attend the weekly council meeting at the assembly hall. The plan lightened her mood.

She enjoyed watching her father officiate in his robes at the meetings and listen to the complaints and needs brought forth for his consideration. Her father was a kind and gentle man, and Meris loved his big hugs and the way his smile lit up his face. Although, he hadn't been smiling much lately, and Meris suspected it had to do with the dome.

He hadn't said anything, but Meris knew the worry and fear of the people of Me'arah weighed on his heart. Rumors of doom and peril were passed among her neighbors in hushed undertones. Never before had the dome of light that shone over them—faint and soft for night and bright and vibrant during the day—faltered. But the alarming facts showed the light was waning. Gradually, yes, and it could be many years before it became a real concern, but Meris knew her father was concerned now. She'd heard her father speak to her mother late at night in whispers in their room. Meris smirked. Sapha wasn't the only one who eavesdropped.

She had often gazed up at the sky wondering about the source of the light. Where did it come from? Fireflies and flames gave off light and heat, but the light overhead shone as if pasted on the sky. What made it dim and brighten? As far as Meris knew, the Me'arans had always marked their days and nights, as well as their seasons of planting and harvesting, by this fluctuation of intensity. The dome was brighter for more hours during the summer, giving off heat and making the flowers and vegetables and trees grow and flourish. In the winter, the dome darkened and the climate turned cold, but the seasons and cycles had always remained constant. Until recent months.

But what could be done about it? And what danger did it really present? Was the world coming to an end?

Meris shook off the tingling of fear crawling up her back and headed for her room to get her woodpipe, and sweater—in case the wind kicked up. As she passed her father's den, though, something caught her eye.

She backed up a step and looked into the room, not seeing anything amiss. The easel in the corner showed a half-finished painting of her mother. She smiled. Her father loved to paint but he was hardly talented, yet he would be the first to admit it. He painted because it helped him relax after a difficult day at the council. Meris thought maybe he should tackle some other, less difficult subject, like a flower or a piece of fruit.

The walls were adorned with some of his more successful attempts at art, alongside the many drawings Meris and her sisters had done over the years. She walked over to a simple sketch she had done of two deer when she was much younger, smiling at the silly lines and funny expressions on the deer's faces. On the long, low table sat a piece of wood she had carved into a cat. At least *she* knew it was a cat. Surely no one else could tell. But her father had gushed with love when she'd given it to him for his two-hundredth birthday.

She thought her father must be the oldest person in the land, but he looked no older than Delon's father, and *he* was not much more than one hundred, if Meris was remembering correctly. Her father had once explained that the Na'tar line of lords tended toward longevity, and that their families also enjoyed living long, healthy years of life.

Meris frowned. *But if the dome's light faded away, none would live, would they?*

There had to be an explanation. Someone, somewhere, must know what the dome's light source was. Only then would they know if they could fix it. You had to know how something worked before you could fix it—her father had taught her that when she was a young girl. He often took things apart and put them back together again to show her. But the dome of heaven was not something one could take apart and analyze. It was vast and unreachable. Not even the fireflies could ascend to its boundaries, if there were any. It appeared that the dome went on forever, without end. How could anything go on forever? It boggled her mind. And why was it called the dome anyway? What did the word mean?

Endless, irritating questions flitted around in her head, but unlike fireflies gave no light to help her see how she could help. Again, something caught in the corner of her eye, and she turned her head. Her gaze landed on the door in the far corner of the room.

A chill danced across her neck as she stared at the door that seemed to beckon her. But why? She'd barely noticed the forbidden door in years. She and her sisters had been warned never to touch the knob or go inside. They'd been told that since they could understand speech, and so over the years the door had become practically invisible. But now it glared at her as if on fire.

She knew she was *seeing* something, plagued by this strange sight that would suddenly alter the way she perceived things. Only last week she had been watching Sapha as she washed the breakfast dishes, and Meris saw a shadow cross her face. It frightened her, but it passed quickly. Yet Meris knew it had been a dark thought in Sapha's mind. Not much later Sapha had gotten into a fight with her best friend, Hally, accusing her of taking something.

Lately Meris would look in a person's eyes and their whole face would change for a brief moment, showing an entirely different emotion than the one they really portrayed. And somehow Meris understood that what she had seen in that momentary flash was their true heart. Was this a gift or a curse? Did it have something to do with the Na'tar lineage? She'd never heard if any of her fore-bears had such sight. It only made Meris think something was very wrong with her.

She studied the door, and even the thought of touching it made her tremble. She should leave, now. If her father found her in here, even looking at the door, he would be furious. She could only imagine the punishment he'd mete out.

Yet, her feet would not obey. She drew closer. The door was made of simple wood planks. The knob was of metal, but there was no keyhole. Odd. Was it truly locked, then? If so, how?

With a shaky hand, she reached out and touched the knob. It was icy cold to her touch, but nothing terrifying happened. She gave a nervous chuckle. What did she expect? That the door would splinter apart?

For the first time in her life, Meris wondered what was behind the door. Never had she been at all curious, but now her need to know what lay behind it grew to a great compulsion. Squelching the tirade of warning voices in her head, she grabbed the knob and tried to turn it, but it only jiggled unresponsively.

She stepped back and looked over her shoulder. The house was suddenly quiet, as if waiting and watching expectantly to see what she would do next. For she had decided exactly what she must do, without question.

Something important was in the room behind this door. How Meris knew, she would not be able to explain. And she had no doubt she would be pressured under threat to explain why she disobeyed her father's strict edict. But she couldn't think about that now. She had to know what was behind the door. Once, long ago, her father had said the room contained things from ages past, secret things that had to be preserved, that had been entrusted to the Na'tar, generation after generation.

Perhaps the past held the answers to the future. How could it hurt to look? Maybe in that room was what the Me'arans needed more than anything else.

Hope.

She would be remiss if she walked away. Maybe she was meant to open the door, for clearly it was locked without a lock. No key in this kingdom could open such a door.

But Meris knew in that moment that she didn't need a key. And she knew she wasn't crazy. There wasn't anything wrong with her. She had just caught up with her destiny, that was all. This strange sight she had, the unusual abilities—perhaps she had been given these for this purpose. Maybe she was meant to uncover the secret to the dome and save her kingdom.

Or maybe she was just making excuses, hoping they would help her stop shaking from head to toe.

Before she could talk herself out of it, Meris softened her gaze. She stared at the door, letting the need to open it run wild across her bones. Like a herd of deer, the need trampled her fear underfoot and squished it. She reached out her hand, filled with intent that surged from her fingers in a cresting wave.

"Open," she commanded in a voice that swelled from a deep place in her soul.

The door obeyed.

TWO

IN THE WANING afternoon light, under the undisturbed bright-blue skies of Elysiel, Perthin, king and Keeper of the sacred site, wished he had imagined the terrifying beasts that had flown overhead the day prior. Their horrifying screeches still rang in his ears.

Gryphons, the ancient ghost had told him. Minions of the Destroyer.

Sha'kath.

He had spent the night searching the annals of the kingdom but had found nothing to shed light on this threat to his cherished kingdom. Nothing about a destroyer, about anyone called Sha'kath. Nothing about these fearsome beasts called gryphons. But he could little afford to wait for doom to show up on his doorstep in full force—whatever form it would take. He needed answers. And help. But from where?

In all these years of his ruling Elysiel, he had never had to seek outside the boundaries for anything. He had traveled on occasion to Tolpuddle, his humble childhood village, and the great seaside capital, Paladya, but that had been long ago, when those he knew and loved were still alive.

He turned to face the towering slabs of crystal, hoping they would come alive again as they once had and give him guidance and insight by showing him the future. He rested a hand on the one before him and felt its smooth uneven surface cool under his palm. Nothing. The quiet peacefulness of the day seemed a brittle and ephemeral patina layered over his worries, which stirred like a restless sea beneath. He knew he should address the people, for he sensed their concerns and heard their many troubled thoughts. He had vowed three hundred years ago upon accepting the crystal scepter and appointment as king and Keeper that he would keep Elysiel safe from harm. He had every intention of keeping that vow, and that was why he wore the boots King Cakrin had given him so long ago. But where should he tell them to take him?

"Where do I go?" he said aloud, wondering if the ancient king, Daedan, would appear to him as he had yesterday. But when the mist coalesced, Perthin saw it was King Cakrin, and the sight of his predecessor comforted him. Cakrin had become much like a father to him over the years, although that was perhaps an odd way to view a ghost. But Perthin greatly treasured the wisdom and encouragement Cakrin imparted to him, and the wise one's counsel had never steered him wrong.

"There is a man called Kael," Cakrin said in a breathy voice, his shape wavering before Perthin like heat waves on the plains on a hot summer's day. "Like you, he is both king and Keeper. He is the first and the last, the beginning and the end. He holds the key to the gate of heaven."

Perthin studied the ghost's face and wondered at the bemused expression. "What do you mean? What key?"

Cakrin's form blew apart in the breeze that kicked up from the plains below the rock ledge. Perthin waited, his impatience growing. Daedan had told him the gryphons meant doom if something wasn't done to stop the Destroyer.

Cakrin's shape reappeared at Perthin's side. A gentle smile arose, but to Perthin it seemed wistful. "The fullness of time is upon you, young king. The time of the end."

He felt as if he'd been slapped. "The end of what?"

"Everything comes to an end."

The harsh words brought a bitter taste to his mouth. His heart hurt at the thought of Elysiel gone. No, it couldn't happen. He wouldn't let it.

"How can you say this? How can you just . . . float there and predict Elysiel's end so calmly?"

King Cakrin drew closer and peered into Perthin's eyes. "You, too, are the last king. The last of the long line of Elysiel's kings chosen to protect the sacred site."

"What? There will be none after me? No heir to take the scepter, to bond with the land?" A horrible lump lodged in Perthin's throat, and tears sprang to his eyes. He could not bear such terrible news. Surely there had to be a way to prevent this inevitability. The future was not fixed; the crystal had not shown him any sign of Elysiel's end—not even once in three hundred years. So why was Cakrin telling him this? Was it to spur him to act? To stir up his determination? Perthin grunted. It hardly needed stirring. He would do anything to stop this Sha'kath from ravaging his precious kingdom.

"Where is this king—Kael?" if Cakrin had mentioned him, then hope must lie with him. Cakrin said he was the key. Key to the gate of heaven, but what could that mean? Years ago his mother had told him there were seven such sites in the world, but all were called gates of heaven—*sha'har sha'mayim*. Were there, then, seven Keepers? What if they banded together? If they were united in purpose against the Destroyer, could they perhaps stop him?

He gritted his teeth. Why wouldn't Cakrin tell him what to do?

Cakrin's doom and gloom brought a scowl to Perthin's face. But the ghost merely studied him, saying nothing. Perthin had never felt such exasperation before. He let his anger crush the vines of hopelessness twisting around his heart. He picked up the crystal scepter and held it before him, its brilliant blue light pulsing with each beat of his heart.

"As long as the heart of the king beats in this scepter, I will defend and protect Elysiel."

In reply, Cakrin only smiled his sad smile and said, "Of course you will."

But he did not say if Perthin would prevail.

As his form began to fade and shred apart in the breeze, Cakrin added, "Go to Kael, in Ethryn. And do not be so forlorn, Perthin. Endings are merely beginnings."

Perthin stood there shaking his head, his blood racing through his limbs, every nerve tingling. *Beginnings of what? How can there be a beginning if all is lost?* He listened for a moment to the voices and thrumming of all life in his kingdom, from worm to bird to human, letting the prodigious wave of sound engulf and bury him and his ponderous grief. Then, he shut it all out, his mind emptying like a great river into a beckoning sea.

He picked up from the ground the soft leather case he kept his scepter in and slung it across his shoulder, then looked down at his magic boots, sucked in a breath, and steeled himself. "Take me to Ethryn, to King Kael, Keeper of the sacred site."

In a whisk of wind, Perthin was swept away, his scepter in hand but his heart left behind.

Kael of Ethryn pushed aside the tent curtain and strode out into the blustery afternoon, leaving his military commanders to further plan their offensive attack. He walked along the cliff's edge and stared down at the fields north of the site, the encampments thick with men, horses, and camels, and more were pouring steadily in through the eastern pass from nearby lands.

With autumn came the tempestuous hot winds, which blew gritty sand into mouths and eyes, and Kael pulled his tunic up to partially protect his face from abrasion. He imagined men and beast suffered below while waiting for the command to set off in pursuit of their enemy. He was grateful for their alliances but feared what lay ahead. He had heard rumors of a powerful and frightening man conscripting fighters as he traveled north, forming an army of great number. Some had even said there were those among them that could not be of this world, so frightening was their appearance. Kael had no doubt they spoke of Ezbon. But what was his plan? To return and attack Ethryn? So he could rule as king? If so, Kael planned to be ready to engage him before he could march upon his cherished city.

The Great River glistened in the distance, a reminder of the promise and power of heaven. But the glorious moment of the gushing of water from the earth's rupture had been overshadowed by those foul creatures winging overhead. Their presence gave Kael little time to revel in the joy of hope and restoration the sacred site offered. Seeing the gryphons had unleashed his former terror, from when he'd been a slave building the great tower, and yet he reminded himself of his divine deliverance from Raban and the giants of old. Not even Sha'kath or his foul beasts had been able to stop heaven's plan.

And with divine assistance, he would locate Ezbon, his vizier, and find a way to destroy the gryphons.

After endless hours of puzzling, he could only conclude one thing—that Ezbon *was* Sha'kath. How it was possible, he could not fathom. But he himself had lived a lifetime thousands of years in the past, and it had not been a dream.

Kael fingered the necklace at his throat—the pendant of the star within a star that had been given to him at his appointment as Keeper that night so long ago. He had received it in a vision during his foray into the past, and yet when he'd awoken from his twilight sleep in his bed, here in Ethryn six thousand years later, the necklace was still clasped around his throat. It served as a heady reminder. He would never forget. He had been shown the location of the sacred site and excavated it from under tons of sand. Then, in fulfillment of prophecy, water erupted from the ground to relieve Ethryn of the insidious drought that had nearly destroyed his kingdom.

Surely heaven would not allow Sha'kath to destroy Ethryn— not now, after having just saved it.

How Kael would fight such power as Sha'kath wielded, he did not know. All he had were horses and men, and weapons of metal and wood. Sha'kath had powerful magic. He had once nearly swayed the entire world to his will. Kael had seen up close the way he could bend minds and control men's very thoughts and would never forget that day when all had gathered under his captive spell to watch his sacrifice on the altar at the apex of the tower.

But he had to believe heaven had greater power. He had seen that power streak from above and scatter the wicked. All those in defiance of heaven—bragging of their lofty tower and with giants at their command—had fled for their lives, their languages confused. And when the messengers had come to Kael's village and told him to flee with his family, heaven had rained fire and sulfur upon the evil ones that remained behind, leaving nothing but smoldering ash behind.

He would be a fool to doubt heaven's power. But he didn't want to second-guess heaven's will. Yet all he could do at this point was prepare for war, much to his dismay. It should be a time of celebration over Ethryn's restoration. But sadly, such festivities would have to wait.

Attendants came rushing toward him as he neared his horse, but he politely waved them away and took the reins in hand. He had taken to riding rather than be carried in his litter, as he had formerly done as king of Ethryn. All those years he had spent in the past, helping Ethryn prosper into a burgeoning city, he had ridden a horse. Even at the end of his life, he had ridden alongside the messengers as they accompanied him that one last time to the tower, which by then had been buried under sand.

Kael sighed heavily. How strange it was to have memories of an entire lifetime lived. To have a powerful gift of healing in his hands—hands that had healed countless injuries and illnesses. He remembered every person, every moment from his "former life." He had married, had children, grandchildren. His life in the past often seemed more real to him than the one he was living now.

The joy and sadness of a life lived and lost sat heavy on his heart every waking moment. But it also gave him strength and perspective. He knew which things were precious and which pursuits were futile. What was worth fighting for and even dying for. And he was ready to submit to heaven's will, whatever the cost.

Kael led his horse awhile on foot, sensing a ribbon of cool wind mingling with the hot. Evening smeared pink behind the far mountains, and his stomach growled. He would eat a simple supper this night, knowing the men readying for war did not get to enjoy a finely prepared meal such as Kael could indulge in at the palace. He would have stayed in his tent if he hadn't arranged to meet with Avad, his new chief archivist. He hoped Avad had been able to uncover more scrolls telling of the one called Sha'kath, and the seven sacred sites. He yearned to know if there were other Keepers like himself, and what heaven had shown them. Kael feared what

Sha'kath would do if he found other sacred sites like the one in Ethryn. If only he could seek counsel of these other Keepers—

A strange rush of wind suddenly enveloped him, forcing him to steady his feet. His horse reared up and squealed, and Kael clenched his eyes against the whirl of sand thrown into his face and tightened his grip on the reins. His heart pounded as he feared he was being drawn into one of his visions, then realized those belonged to another man in another time. Yet, this was no ordinary desert zephyr; it smacked of magic.

When Kael opened his eyes, he saw a form bent over a few feet before him, with a hand clung to Kael's tunic sleeve. Kael pulled back and readied in a stance to defend himself from attack, but when he met the man's searching gaze, he relaxed and curiosity overtook him. Kael let loose his horse, and the beast trotted some feet away, finally calming down.

Kael, however, was greatly agitated.

"How . . . where . . . ?" Kael looked around at the bleak desert landscape. The man in simple long tunic and soft cotton pants sporting an unabashed grin had clearly appeared out of thin air. Another messenger from heaven? Kael thought not, for this one chuckled and righted himself before he toppled over. Kael watched curiously as the man got to his feet and brushed sand from his clothes. And then he spotted a strange staff in his hand that pulsed with a blue light.

"I haven't done that for many, many years," the man said, and Kael couldn't help but notice the blend of authority, purpose, and humility in his voice. Although this man seemed younger than himself, he wore the wisdom of many years on his face and in his deportment.

"Pardon my lack of manners. My name is Perthin." The stranger glanced around, his face drawn and questioning. "Where am I? What is this land called? Are you Kael of Ethryn?"

Kael felt blood drain from his face. Surely heaven must have sent another messenger to him. But who was this man? Clearly he was human, not otherworldly.

"I am," he answered with a slight bow. "And you are just outside the city of Ethryn, in the desert to the north."

Before Kael could form his questions, Perthin spoke in an urgent tone, but with great respect. "Your Highness, we have much to discuss. My kingdom, Elysiel, is in danger, and I suspect yours is as well. Is there someplace we can talk at length without disruption—and without a mouthful of sand?"

Kael nodded and walked over to his horse, who had found bits of scrub grass to eat. How odd that this man should seek him out. His pulse quickened with hope. Perhaps this human messenger knew how to stop Sha'kath. He would eagerly hear what this man had to say.

He picked up the reins and gestured to the saddle. "If you are weary, you can ride, and I can walk alongside you. My palace is not far."

"I would be pleased to walk alongside you, King Kael. Tell me—you are Keeper of a sacred site. Would . . . would you show it to me?"

Kael, still astonished by this man's sudden presence and the knowledge he held, rubbed his eyes and shrugged. "If you are hungry, perhaps you would join me for supper. Then after we eat, I will take you to the site."

"That would please me greatly." Perthin fell into step beside Kael, and they walked a few moments in silence as their feet kicked up sand. Kael held his questions at bay, hoping Perthin would explain himself.

"I apologize for startling you." Perthin chuckled. "I can only imagine how strange and upsetting this all is. But I was sent here to find you."

Kael studied his visitor's face and still couldn't get over the sense this man was old beyond his years. He carried himself with a confidence and humility Kael had rarely seen. In many ways he did remind him of the heavenly messengers he'd met with in the past, with their serene expressions, so calm in the face of danger. Then it struck him as he suddenly remembered Avad telling him about a once-hidden land called Elysiel he had happened upon in a scroll when researching the sacred sites.

"Elysiel . . . You are a king as well. And . . . a Keeper." The realization of these facts struck Kael with a slap of understanding. "Elysiel is home to one of the seven sites."

Perthin halted and turned to look into Kael's eyes. "So there are seven." His gaze dropped to Kael's throat, and his eyes widened. "Your chain!" Perthin's hand moved to his own throat. "It is like mine. Where did you get it?"

Kael stepped back, sifting through the confusion in his mind. "Why, heaven gave this to me, when I was appointed Keeper of the sacred site. Were you not given yours as well?"

Perthin shook his head and continued walking, looking at the ground thoughtfully. "The daughters of the former king gifted me this pendant. I did not know it carried any significance. I have worn it for hun—" He stopped again and met Kael's eyes. "What do you know of the other sites—their locations and Keepers?"

It was Kael's turn to shake his head. "Only that there are seven. I was told that the sites are the seven eyes of the Lord in the earth. Through researching many scrolls we have in our great library, I have learned of four, but not how to find them. I do not know if there are other Keepers at these sites, but if you have come to me, I have hope there are others. And that maybe they will hold the key to stopping the Destroyer—"

"Sha'kath," Perthin said quietly.

Kael jerked his head toward the king of Elysiel. "Yes. What do you know of him? Have you seen him or his army?"

Perthin glanced skyward and pursed his lips. "I have only been warned of him, that he poses a threat to us all . . ." Perthin grew quiet, and his face clouded over as if pained. "And I saw his gryphons fly over my kingdom. I was told they are the harbingers of doom." His voice dropped to a whisper. "That the end of all things has come."

Kael's heart clenched. Perthin's words sank like a stone in his gut. "Who told you this?"

Perthin let out a sigh. "That will take some explaining."

"And that staff you carry—it . . . almost seems alive."

"That, too, will take some explaining," Perthin said. He nodded at the structures now visible on the horizon in the dim glow of dusk. "Your palace?"

"Yes," Kael said with some relief. A great weariness seeped into his bones, and he realized it was dread. If this king with his magic had been told the end was upon them, what could he do? What could anyone do? Was defeat inevitable? Could it truly be heaven's will that Ethryn—and perhaps the world at large—be destroyed by the Destroyer? The thought greatly pained him, and his breath grew shallow.

He laid a hand on Perthin's arm. "What you tell me distresses me terribly. What hope is there then? Should we do nothing but wait for Sha'kath to attack? I cannot imagine giving up all I cherish and protect without a fight. I know this Sha'kath and what he can do. But I watched heaven thwart him once before, and I will not believe it is heaven's plan to let this destroyer succeed."

Perthin gave Kael a reassuring smile. "No, Your Highness. I do not believe heaven wants us to roll over and submit to such evil. You may perhaps be right about the Keepers, that we should try to find them. But I was told only one held the key to this dilemma. And that was why I sought you out."

"Me? The key? How would I be the key?"

Perthin spoke as if reciting. "The first and the last. The beginning and the end." He shrugged. "Do you know what that might mean?"

Kael's jaw dropped. "Perhaps . . . well, I was the first Keeper chosen, of the first site established in the world. That much I know. How I might be the last . . . or the beginning and end is a mystery . . ." Kael's mind reeled with all these puzzling thoughts. He had been told on more than one occasion in his "former life" that he was a symbol of things to come. But it was never explained to him just what those ominous words meant. Once he learned of the other sites, he assumed it referred only to his role as Keeper. But now he wasn't so sure. How could he be the last Keeper if he was also the first? How could the beginning also be the end?

And here, standing beside him, was another Keeper, who protected another sacred site—and a king of a faraway kingdom he knew nothing about. A king who could magically transport himself across vast distances in a flash of time.

The sand dunes flattened into dirt road, then cobblestones as they entered the outskirts of Ethryn. Faces turned in curiosity as they walked, the citizens bowing respectfully as Kael passed by them, Perthin at his side. Kael gestured to the east wing of the palace. "Come, let's eat. And please—just address me as Kael. Or would you prefer I call you 'Your Highness' as well? We are more kin than kings to each other."

"True, but I would call you my friend. For we are certainly friends before all else. We both live to do heaven's bidding, whatever the cost."

Kael's heart warmed at Perthin's sage words. "Yes, well said."

Before they reached the arched entryway leading inside, two guards came rushing over and opened the tall ornate doors for them. Perthin followed Kael down the long hallway and into the spacious dining room, where servants bowed and hushed upon their approach. Curious looks peeked out from under lowered heads at the unexpected guest in foreign garb. But Kael noted Perthin was clearly accustomed to such deference and respect, and moved with noble bearing. He wondered what this kingdom of Elysiel was like and how Perthin ruled his people. He hoped they would have plenty of time to share their stories.

Kael had never met the king of any other land—let alone a Keeper appointed by heaven. He could imagine no more honored guest to grace the walls of his palace than this enigmatic king of Elysiel.

When they had been seated, Kael looked more closely at the staff Perthin had laid gently on the large table. It seemed ancient and was beautifully carved, the dark wood resonating a dark oiled sheen. The pulsing light in the handle of the staff beat just like a heart. The magnificence awed him. As much as he wanted to know more about this puzzling object, they had more important things to discuss.

Kael spoke in a quiet tone so none of the servants pouring their wine and laying out platters of food could hear him. "Just how did you arrive in Ethryn? Do you use magic—a spell of some sort?" The idea of magic unsettled him, reminding him of the way Sha'kath had uttered spells and controlled both men and giants. The memory of the sand gushing up out of the ground at Sha'kath's command replayed in his head. Sand that came from Ethryn, so that the slaves could make bricks with which to construct the mighty tower. He shook the memory away, his palms sweaty. He didn't like to dwell on his years as a slave.

Perthin merely looked down at his feet. "King Cakrin—the king of Elysiel before me—gave me these boots when I was a mere boy. I had to travel far to fight a monstrous creature that threatened my village, so I was given these boots to take me there. After that . . . incident was over, I put them in a closet and forgot about them. Until I learned of Sha'kath and his gryphons." He tipped his head, and his eyes took on a playful look. "Very exciting for a young boy who had never been outside his small fishing village of Tolpuddle. I just tell the boots where I want to go, and . . . *whoosh* . . . they take me there."

Kael shook his head in wonder. "Why would the king of Elysiel call upon a boy in a small village and ask him to fight such a foe?"

Perthin waved his hand and smiled. Servants dished food onto his plate as he said, "That's another long story, but I hope we will have time to exchange many such stories. I am sure you must have some wonderful tales of your own."

Kael smiled and sipped his wine. The aroma of the roasted meat and grilled vegetables made his mouth water. "I imagine my tales will be as astonishing as yours. I sometimes hardly believe them. Come, let's eat, and then I will take you to the site."

As they ate in silence, Kael mulled over all the things they'd spoken of. Surely heaven had a plan, for God had sent this great king to him, no doubt to aid him in the fight against Sha'kath. But Perthin's presence also drove home the awareness that this fight was not just about Ethryn. It involved all of mankind. Kael could only guess that Sha'kath planned to finish what he had started all those millennia ago—to conquer and control the entire world.

Kael chewed thoughtfully, the delicious flavors from his meal turning bland in his mouth. *The end of all things*, Perthin had said. *You are the key, the first and last, the beginning and the end.* Kael let out a shaky sigh as he set down his fork, suddenly not at all hungry.

He didn't like the idea that Perthin had been told the king of Ethryn would be the last . . . and the end.

THREE

WALKING ON tiptoe, Meris entered the small dusty room and closed the door behind her with a soft click. Two tiny dirt-encrusted windows near the ceiling filtered in diffused light, and the dust motes swirled in the air as she walked and stirred them from their long slumber. Clearly no one had entered this room in years. And it seemed much older than the rest of her cottage, as if built hundreds of years ago. The heavy rough-carved wood beams were dark and splintered from age, laced with gossamer cobwebs. She didn't dare summon the fireflies, worried they might somehow alert her family to her presence in this room, so she strained in the scant light to see all the many things around her.

Three of the walls had numerous shelves made from thick boards, upon which were stacked all sorts of items. Jars of many sizes, colors, and shapes lined one shelf. Other shelves had strange rolled-up objects tied with strips of leather. The air was thick and stuffy with no circulation, and dust coated everything. She stood surveying the room, then she saw something strange. The rolled-up objects shifted on the shelves.

Meris jumped back and grabbed the doorknob, ready to bolt, but then she listened and watched. Some of the rolls began to glow with a pale light—different shades of yellow and blue and brown.

Some slid from one end of a shelf to the other. Another dropped off the shelf and fell to the floor. Then everything grew quiet and still as dust floated around the room and drifted to the packed-dirt floor like soft mist.

Her heart thumping loudly in her chest, Meris reached down and picked up the object, then set it on a small table that sat in the corner under one of the windows. She drew in a breath and carefully untied the leather string that was wrapped around what appeared to be brittle animal hide, but the leather crumbled at her touch, and the rolled-up hide unfurled and loosened.

With great care, Meris opened the thin sheet of hide and laid it on the table, then pinned down its corners with jars she took from the shelf. The hide was painted with inks that she figured must have been bright colors long ago but had faded over time. There were strange shapes accompanied by black ink squiggles laid out in rows. The squiggles made no sense at all, but the colorful shapes looked like creatures of some sort. However, they were nothing like those in her world.

She ran a finger over a group of silver oval shapes, but the moment she did, they came to life on the hide. Meris gasped and jerked back, but she couldn't wrench her gaze away. Fascinated, she watched as the background behind the shapes turned emerald-blue and undulated like the great sea that stretched out forever from its shores. Then the silver things began to wiggle around in the blue "water." They dove and rose to the surface, then jumped in the air and splashed down again. They had little wings attached to the sides of their bodies that waved back and forth, and something like a wing atop their backs. Their tails made Meris smile, for they were short and looked like little bows that wiggled as they moved. Then, the shapes stopped moving and their color faded, and the "water" turned back to the dull pale shade of animal hide.

Meris shook her head in astonishment. Where had this magical skin come from, and who had drawn this? She grabbed another roll from the shelf and laid it out similarly. This one puzzled her even more, showing the dome arching above the forest a dark indigo color that became pierced with tiny white spots that shone as brightly as diamonds. As they twinkled in multitude, a huge shining butter-colored ball appeared at the bottom of one side of the hide, then rose up into the dome, splashing light across the woods below, then traversed the dome to the other side and sank out of view.

Then the dark dome turned a light shade of blue—how strange! And what was even stranger was the march of fluffy gray objects—like sheep wool—that gathered and darkened in the dome. A tiny cracking sound came from the hide, followed by a streak of blinding light and a deep rumble that shook the table. Meris jumped back, fearful as water poured from the gray masses in the dome, falling in thousands of tiny drops to the trees and fields below. The hide was even wet to her touch. Flowers sprang up in the fields, but ones she had never seen before, and much to her surprise, the small room in which she stood became filled with a sweet floral scent that rivaled the juiciest fruit. Her hands trembled in excitement as she stared, riveted, at the scene before her.

Meris watched as this scenario stilled to quiet and the colors faded. She noted more black scribbling along the bottom of the hide and wondered what they were meant to signify. But unlike the rest of the hide, these scribblings did not come to life. Just what were these hides? Were they someone's imaginative paintings somehow infused with magic? Her sisters would probably claim the fairies had made them, but that was silly.

The more important questions were, why was this room kept locked, and why were she and her sisters not allowed to enter? What secret was this room harboring? She couldn't make sense of these images on the animal skins. Did they tell a story when put together? Something that had to be kept secret for some reason?

She remembered then why she had come inside. Maybe there was something in here that would explain the dome and why the light was fading. She frowned thinking of the images she had just watched, with the dome so dark and filled with sparkling lights. Is that how the dome used to look long ago? What were those sparkles? And that huge creamy ball that arced across it? Maybe nothing, nothing at all. Just drawings from someone's imagination, more than likely. But why would these scrolls be kept secret?

She knew she shouldn't stay in the room much longer. Her father would be finished chopping wood anytime now. And her mother might be looking for her at this very moment. But she had to know. Something had led her to this room, and something—or someone—had opened this door for her. So she very well couldn't leave until she discovered its secrets.

She opened one hide after another and witnessed many odd creatures run and leap across the face of the skins. One showed gigantic mountains, bigger than any in her land, and topped with globs of white. When she touched the mountain peaks, they were freezing cold, and her finger nearly stuck to the hide. What a strange thing this was—this cold white stuff. Her hills had nothing like it.

She couldn't believe all these fantastical things were just someone's imagination. Was it possible they had all been part of her world at one time long ago? Had the world changed so much? Did the dome used to be dark blue and filled with sparkles? She frowned and let out a sigh. If so, what did it matter? She could see nothing that could help her understand why the dome light was fading. Would it become dark again, and if so, what did that portend for her land?

There were two more hides to look at, but she heard faint footsteps somewhere in the house and froze. If she was caught in here, she would be severely punished. She just couldn't be discovered. Was her father able to open this door? Judging by the heavy layer of dust on everything, and not seeing any trace of footprints other than her own, she doubted her father had ever been in here—whether by choice or on principle. But she certainly risked her own hide getting tanned if she tried to remain in here and later sneak out without being seen. She was expected to attend tonight's council meeting with her family, and if she didn't show up for dinner, they would probably start searching for her. But maybe that would give her the chance to sneak out and run behind the cottage. She could then just "show up" after a day in the woods.

Meris sat for a while and listened as the sound of footsteps receded. She let out a long-held breath. The thought of waiting hours in this cramped, dusty space began to make her feel claustrophobic. Disappointment soured her mood. She had really hoped to find something important. Just what was so secret about the things in this room?

She went over to the shelves and started opening jars, but they were all empty, or else had bits of crumbs at the bottom. She found other inexplicable objects that looked like stones and fossilized rock and lumpy pieces of shiny gold, but they seemed so unimportant. Had these belonged to some of the Na'tar lords of old? Why keep them secret? Did they contain some special magic? She wished there was someone she could question, but she certainly couldn't ask her father.

Meris let out a frustrated sigh and listened again. The house had fallen quiet again. She decided to make her move and opened the latch and peeked out. Nothing. No sound. As an afterthought, she grabbed the last two rolled-up hides and stuffed them under her shirt. Who would notice them missing? If her father got suspicious and entered the forbidden room, he'd easily be able to tell someone had been inside. Her fingerprints and footprints were everywhere, imprinted in the dust. But there was nothing she could do about that.

As quiet as a deer, she slipped out and hurried through her father's den, holding her breath as blood pounded her ears. She took a quick glance down the hall, then rushed through the back door and into the woods behind her cottage. It was only after she stopped to catch her breath and glanced back that she realized she couldn't see the room she had been in. How many thousands of times had she played outside her home? There was no small room attached to the den. That door she had accessed from inside had been there her whole life, but if there was no room extending from the house, just where was it? And where had she been when inside? This was even more perplexing than the strange pictures she had seen.

But she had little time to ponder this mystery. In only a few hours she'd have to wash up for dinner.

The woods were quiet. She stood among the firth trees and listened for her father's chopping sounds, but there were none. Fireflies gathered about her head, brushing her cheek with soft wind. Maybe her father was working on the garden fence; over breakfast he'd mentioned his plan to do that. She couldn't see the gardens from where she stood. And her mother and Abrella were probably still inside fussing with Abrella's wedding gown.

Regardless, she couldn't take the chance of being caught with these rolls of hide, and she wondered what they would show and if they would come to life outside the secret room. Was the room responsible for the magic? Or was magic woven into these pictures?

She skipped over to the dell, where the deer lifted their lazy heads from their grassy bed. They liked to snooze in the afternoons, and with this cooler weather found warmth in cuddling close. She went over and petted all nine of them on their heads, and they nuzzled against her palm and then went back to sleep. As she sat down beside them, she stared up at the dome. It was definitely darker than it had ever been, and as she stared she saw the coloring flicker erratically. The sight made her throat tighten. A brisk wind kicked up, and she wished she had gone and fetched her sweater.

Then, for a brief second, the sky went utterly dark.

She gasped and rubbed her eyes. Had that really happened? The deer hadn't noticed, but the fireflies playing in the field nearby were clearly agitated. They sped around, their tiny wings flitting frantically, and they seemed to be careening into branches and bushes. Some fell to the ground and shook with terror. She stood up and watched, aghast. She'd never seen them behave so distressed.

Something was very wrong. Meris shivered, more from fright than cold. She wanted to run back to her father and bury herself in the strength of his warm arms, but first she needed to look at these rolled-up hides she'd hidden under her shirt. She would have to think of a secret cache for them, for she certainly couldn't try to sneak them back into her cottage.

After finding a tree stump nearby, she spread out the first animal skin and touched the faded surface. More black scribblings appeared, and the entire piece turned emerald-blue. Small waves began to fill the sheet, and sprays of water tickled her cheeks as she leaned in closer. Then a strip of brown filled in the bottom of the image. Meris recognized the shoreline that ran along the edge of the great sea and the rocky outcroppings that rose up out of the water. She and her family sometimes picnicked there in the warm months.

She wondered why this piece of hide showed a place she knew. Her sea contained none of those silvery shapes with the wings on the sides and back; it was an endless shimmering world of water that no one had ever ventured across. She and her sisters had spent many long, luxurious days playing in the shallows and making houses out of sand. All the children of Me'arah loved to splash in the cool, refreshing water.

Meris had often wondered if the sea ever ended. Was there a far shore? No one knew because no one had ever tried to cross the great sea. It was forbidden. Even the idea of venturing out on its waters sent a flare of panic to her gut.

She frowned, trying to remember what she had been told about the sea all her life. She supposed it was a silly thought, for how could one cross a great sea? No one could swim that far, and you couldn't ride on a deer's back. Although deer were strong swimmers, they could never carry a person, nor would they allow it. Even when they frolicked in the water, they never ventured far from shore. When she was small she used to imagine there was another kingdom on the other side of the sea, and standing on the shore would be a little girl just like her, wondering the same thing.

She ran her finger along the painted shore on the hide, and as she did so, another shape began to form. She watched, intrigued, as this object, floating far off on the sea, grew larger as it neared. It looked to be made of wood planking, and bobbed on the water but did not sink. Then she made out figures sitting inside it, their chests and heads visible but too unformed to be recognizable. But they were people—eight, she counted. Seven men, one woman.

Meris watched as this floating object slid up onto the shore. Then the people got out and stood at the water's edge. As soon as the last one stepped out, the object that had ferried them across the sea vanished.

How odd, Meris thought, her body tingling with excitement. What if this had really happened? What if there truly was a land across the sea, a place where other people lived? How she wished she could find out, but if anyone would know, it would be her father. He was the most learned in the history of Me'arah, yet, if strangers had at one time arrived on their shores, wouldn't everyone know this? Wouldn't the people in her kingdom want to cross the great sea to meet them and see how they lived?

She let out another frustrated sigh. Either this was just a fanciful depiction or else someone had come long ago. And maybe they hadn't been friendly, and that's why the Me'arans were forbidden to cross the sea, if it could be done.

Yet, she sensed there was some truth in this image that had played out on the hide. There had to be—otherwise why would her father forbid anyone to enter the room? What terrible secrets did it hold?

Meris knew her father would never withhold anything important from his family, but he was also the appointed Na'tar, and with that came responsibilities. No doubt one of those included protecting the secrets behind the door she had opened. She thought of her father's recent distress over the dome light and realized he surely knew more than he was letting on. What other secrets was he keeping from his people?

Meris rolled up the hide and unrolled the other one she had taken. But the instant she laid this one out, a severe pain coursed through her hands. She jerked back and felt instantly sick to her stomach. The colors on the hide darkened and swirled in a chaotic dance, and Meris smelled smoke and heard heartrending screeches and cries, as if dozens of people were in pain.

What was happening? She covered her ears and squeezed her eyes shut, but it was as if she were there, among the frightened and injured people. But where was *there*? She envisioned herself breathless, running, watching the skies with dread, as bolts of light shot to the ground and explosions of rock and rubble flew into the air and struck those around her. And then the most terrifying sound met her ears—a piercing scream that shot terror into her heart.

She opened her eyes enough to see something streak across the top of the animal hide—something dark, massive, with huge flapping wings and a strange long tail. She trembled and cowered beside the tree stump, and the fireflies darted away, nowhere to be seen.

Meris shook all over as she sucked in shallow breaths, telling herself to calm down, that this was just a drawing. But she could not squelch the terror paralyzing her until the flying creature winged away and disappeared from the hide. Then, her eyes riveted, she watched as dozens of people ran past others that had fallen, and she knew those were their friends and mothers and brothers and children that lay dead across the rock-littered landscape.

The odor of burnt flesh and trees filled her nostrils and made her gag. She wrapped her arms around her queasy stomach and prayed this vision would end. Who would imagine such horror? Had this happened long ago?

She could not bear to watch any longer and reached to roll up the hide. But as she touched the edges of the skin, the smells and smoke cleared, and the great throng of people ran over to the base of a sand-encrusted mountain. A great crack rent the rock open, and the people hurried inside. Within moments, they had all disappeared inside the rock, which closed shut behind them, leaving no trace there had ever been an opening. The world fell silent although Meris's heart beat like a loud drum.

She waited to see what would happen next, her hands still shaking and her stomach doing flips. But the image grew still, leaving a disturbing sense of unease in Meris's heart. With the acrid smell still lingering her nostrils, she threw down the sheet of hide, the presentiment of danger growing in the back of her mind. She glanced at the flickering pink dome overhead and knew something terrible was going to happen. She didn't know what, but she knew it as surely as she knew where she had to go.

Without thinking, she took off running. To the sea.

FOUR

THE MOMENT Ta'sus entered his cottage, he knew something was wrong. He set the armful of firewood down by the stone hearth and walked into the kitchen, where he found his wife and Abrella preparing the evening meal.

Drayna turned from the sink with bubble-covered hands and frowned at his expression. "What's wrong?" she asked.

Abrella stopped chopping carrots and looked at him as well. "Father?"

He stood in silence, listening. But the silence was thick and oppressive, nearly screaming at him. He fought the urge to throw his hands over his ears. It wouldn't be advisable to alarm his family when he didn't know exactly what was troubling him. But he sensed the magic, and it was emanating from somewhere in his home.

"Let me wash up," he said with a forced smile. "And then we can eat." Then he cocked his head. "Where's Meris?" Just saying her name sent a tingle down his spine. A flash of an image seared his mind, and although he couldn't make out the blurry form, he knew it was Meris, and she was terrified. His throat tightened, and he forced a swallow.

Drayna dried her hands on a towel and nodded toward the door. "Out in the dell. With her deer. Her woodpipe isn't on her dresser."

When Ta'sus didn't reply, she added, "She knows to be back in time for dinner. And that we have council tonight."

Ta'sus only nodded, the rumblings of worry growing in his gut.

He left them and made for his den, aware of fireflies gathering behind him. Meris's friends. Why weren't they with her now? He let the comforting picture wash over him—of Meris playing her pipe with the darting lights winging about her head. She had no idea they were of his conjuring, made to watch over her and keep her safe. He never worried about Abrella or Sapha. But Meris . . . She had unbridled power, more than he'd ever seen among his people. He knew it was the Na'tar line. Of all Me'arah, his family carried the highest concentration of magic. But no one in his lineage had ever displayed the abilities Meris did.

He often watched her in secret, out of concern, for he so loved her—impetuousness and all. He smiled. He had been like that as a boy, he recalled. Too curious for his own good. She was more like him than his other children, and he felt closer to her than he did to his sons, who were pragmatic and accomplished but showed little signs of the power of the Na'tar line. He had been told that long ago all of Me'arah had been steeped in magic, but that over time the magic had waned.

He knew this to be true. In two hundred years he had seen the way magic seeped out of his kingdom, like dye leeched from cloth. Now, the world around him seemed almost drab and lifeless compared to the vibrancy and wonder that used to spring up around him. With a touch of a hand, most Me'arans had been able alter shape and color, hurry the growth of crops, and make a rosebud burst into bloom. So little of that magic remained. But as much as that filled him with a measure of sadness, he accepted it as the way of the world. Time changed people and place. That was the way of life.

But this agitation he now felt—the heavy foreboding it paired with—was something he rarely experienced. He entered his den and looked around. Then he heard footsteps in the hall, and his heartbeat quickened.

"Meris?"

"No, Father. It's just me. I just got back from playing with Nella." Sapha stopped at the doorway and pursed her lips. "Is everything all right?"

Ta'sus grunted. The rest of his family may not have much magical ability, but they never failed to detect his mood, no matter how carefully he hid it.

"Did you see Meris while you were out?"

Sapha shook her head, but not one hair loosened from the perfectly coifed bun she had atop her head. He wondered how his two youngest daughters could be so different. Sapha always dressed up in pretty clothes and shoes, meticulous about her hair and appearance. Whereas Meris never gave herself a glance in a mirror or paid any mind to her attire or grooming. She was like a wild deer, the way she roamed the woods and explored in the dells, delighting in nature. Yes, she was every bit like he'd been as a boy.

"Do you want me to go fetch her? I'm sure she's in the dell, where she always is."

"Yes, but hurry back. We have council tonight."

Sapha nodded and left. Ta'sus listened to the slap of the back door closing, then once more scanned the room. His eyes caught on the door in the back of the room, and his pulse quickened. With his sight, he could see someone had touched it. A shimmer radiated out from the knob. But who would do such a thing?

He approached the door, staring hard at the wood grains, trying to see behind it. But as always, the door was a barrier to what lay beyond, and the past. He had never opened the door, nor seen what was inside.

When he had been appointed Na'tar more than a hundred years ago, his ailing father had told him little. That the room beyond held the secrets of Me'arah's past, and the artifacts belonged to the first Na'tar called Garog. Why they had to be kept hidden, he was never told. But he was warned never to go inside. And when he grew old, he was to choose one of his sons to be Na'tar in his place, and must instruct him similarly.

If the room was never to be opened, why protect it and keep it secret, drenched in magic? Who was it to be kept safe *from*? What could possibly be inside that could harm his kingdom? And if there was something harmful in there, why had it been preserved and guarded all these centuries? He couldn't imagine there would be someone alive today in his kingdom who would purposely endanger Me'arah. He frowned. Maybe not purposely. Maybe there was something inside that could destroy his kingdom accidentally. Something that had great power to cause harm. Something magical.

Ta'sus's stomach clenched as he thought of Meris. Had she somehow gotten inside? With a trembling hand, he closed his hand around the doorknob. Nausea soured his mouth and he grew light-headed, but he tried to turn the knob anyway.

Nothing happened.

A wave of sickness engulfed him, warning him against his will. But no matter how hard he tried, he could not get the handle to budge or the door to open. He knew it would never open for him.

But he knew just as surely it had been opened, and recently. And he knew Meris was the only one with enough magic to do so.

But why? Why would she break his strict edict, knowing she would be severely punished? What could have possibly compelled her?

He suddenly knew why. She'd had no choice.

On rare occasions the magic in his blood would compel him beyond reason to do something he didn't want to do. Give him strange insights or understandings of things he somehow knew were true, despite all outward appearances. That was why the Na'tar had always been the lords of the land—because they could divine truth from lies. See beneath the outer appearance and spoken word to the core or essence of every situation. That gift had kept the peace for untold years, and secured the respect and, yes, fear of the people.

Ta'sus found himself pacing. He needed to wash up and eat, then get to the council meeting. Tonight would be a most important night. For the leaders of the kingdom could no longer pretend all was well. It was time to discuss openly the fears the lords and councilors had discussed at length, with much worry and anguish, behind closed doors. The people deserved to know. What they could do about it was another issue altogether. None of the brightest minds in the kingdom had any idea of how to stop the dome light from failing. And if it failed . . .

Ta'sus strode over to the alcove off his den and, with a nod, water flowed down the smooth rock wall and filled the shallow pool that came as high as his knees. With another nod, the water flow dwindled to a trickle. Ta'sus tried to push aside all his worries as he scrubbed grime from his skin and face, the cool water hardly refreshing him. He dressed, setting aside his robes to take to the meeting, and was greeted in the kitchen by savory smells of roast lamb and steamed vegetables. One glance told him Meris had not yet returned.

Just as Drayna was about to set the platter of food on the table, the front door flew open. Ta'sus spun around to see a troubled look on Sapha's face as she breathlessly forced out her words.

"I . . . I didn't find Meris. She's nowhere in the dell." She sucked in a deep breath, and Ta'sus waited anxiously, along with Drayna and Abrella, to hear what would follow, for Sapha's eyes held fear.

"Well, that's odd," Drayna said. "Where else would she be?"

Then Ta'sus's eyes dropped to Sapha's hands. She held something cylindrical. A piece of hide, perhaps? Loosely rolled up.

"Where did you get that? What is it?" he asked her. But as soon as the words left his mouth, he already knew the answer. Meris had gotten it out of the secret room. The locked room no one could enter. The object she held was drenched in magic. His limbs started shaking.

Sapha held it out to him, and the fear clawed so fiercely in his heart, he was afraid to touch it. He told her, "Just . . . set it down on the shelf over there—"

"But, Father," Sapha said, "what is it?"

As he fumbled with an answer, he caught Drayna's concerned look upon him.

Then, without warning, a loud noise like shattering pots erupted from the sky. The room was thrust into darkness. Then all grew still.

Ta'sus could hardly see his hands in front of him. His girls gasped. A brisk wind blew through the open kitchen window, and he heard the pottery clatter and the silverware rattle on the table.

In the dark, he reached for his family and drew them close. Sapha's tears wet his shirt, and Drayna stroked his back, her attempt to ease his distress. But he knew nothing would help. The dome had flickered on occasion, and had been dimming steadily over the last few months, but it had never gone out before.

They stood there huddled in the dark, utterly silent except for their loud, troubled breathing.

Abrella whimpered. "Father, what's happening?"

He found her head and stroked her hair, his hope failing. "I wish I knew."

Meris ran and ran. She tried to force the images of the people dying and screaming from her head, but they chased after her, nipping at her heels, along with the terrifying creature flying in the sky. Was she going mad? She knew these were only pictures in her head, but they felt more like real memories, things she had lived through. Why oh why had she gone into that room? And why would anyone keep such a horrible thing as that piece of hide?

She pushed hard up the last ridge until, cresting the top, she could see the azure sea stretched out before her. But the sight gave her no joy, only a strange agitation. She headed downslope toward the beach she and her family frequented—the one the other sheet of hide depicted. Maybe there was something there she was meant to find. What if that thing was there somewhere, hidden—that box those people had used to cross the sea? She didn't know why she was being so drawn to the sea. She only knew she had to go.

Suddenly a loud noise shattered the air. Meris threw her hands over her ears at the deafening sound, then stumbled as darkness clouded her sight. She fell to the dirt and rubbed her eyes, thinking she had begun to faint. Then she realized the sky had gone dark— but not becoming the deep blue she'd seen on the hide, with the little pinpricks of light shining through. Instead, when she looked up, she saw nothing. Utter darkness.

Her throat constricted as the sweat cooled on her skin. Despair gripped her heart. Was this the end? The end of her world, her life?

Then, after a few unbearable minutes, the dome lightened. Slowly it turned pink again, but the light seemed to flicker erratically, the way a candle flame might gutter in a burst of wind. She knew her family would be worried sick over her, wondering where she went. But she couldn't think about that now. She had to get down to the water's edge. Had to . . .

Something was there. Something was calling her . . .

Meris pushed through the heavy brush, following a narrow deer track, ignoring the cuts and slaps from the branches as she hurried down to the beach. As her feet hit the cool sand, she caught her breath and pushed her hair out of her face. A cold wind buffeted her ears, and her face grew numb. But she ignored the cold and stared ahead.

The water before her shimmered like a pink blanket, the light wind ruffling up small waves and tossing spindrift into the air. The sight of the sea calmed her, although she didn't know why. Maybe because it was always there, the one constant in her world, never changing. The face of the town changed year after year, and even the woods changed from season to season, but the sea . . .

Meris suddenly sensed something that caused her to turn her head to the left. There at the water's edge, where the copse of firth trees wandered onto the beach, stood a lone figure. From where Meris crouched, she couldn't make out a face. The person was bent over and seemed frail. She couldn't imagine why someone else would be here, this late in the afternoon, with the frightening events of the day and the chill wind kicking up sand.

It seemed as if the person was gesturing her to come over, so she sprinted down the shoreline and found it was an old woman wrapped in a heavy green shawl watching her as she approached. She didn't recognize the woman at all. Did she live somewhere nearby? As far as Meris knew, no one lived near the sea. She'd never seen a cottage anywhere along the shore. But this woman seemed incapable of traveling far, bent over as if it took great effort to stand. How did she get here? And why was she here?

The woman raised her head as Meris approached, and two glassy green eyes locked on to hers. The woman's eyes resembled milky marbles, but somehow Meris could see into them to a hidden light that resembled that of her fireflies. Leathery skin warped her face, and heavy wrinkles crinkled her eyes and spread outward from the sides of her mouth.

Meris stuttered, chasing after questions that fled before her. Her thoughts hung suspended in the air between them.

"Wh-who are you?" She didn't mean to sound rude, but her words stabbed the biting air, like tiny knives. Her teeth chattered uncontrollably.

The woman merely pursed her lips and held out a gnarled hand. Even bent over, she was half a head taller than Meris, with long silver braids of hair waterfalling over her shoulder and down her back, then disappearing under the woolen shawl. Her clothes seemed as washed-out as her eyes, as if she had tumbled in water for centuries and finally rolled unnoticed onto the sandy beach.

With hesitation, Meris took hold of the woman's hand, which was soft, like goose down, and as cool as the day. The bones in her hands seemed brittle, but the woman's grip was firm.

Meris chanced looking at the woman's eyes again, but they were closed in concentration. Meris waited awkwardly, shivering, her feet stuffed under sand seeking warmth. When her hand started to tingle, the woman released it and said, "My name is Shamara. Come. I'll make us some tea."

"Come where?" Meris asked, trudging after Shamara, whose long, steady strides toward the trees surprised her. But Shamara said nothing.

Not more than twenty feet into the copse of firth stood a thatched cottage, with a simple plank door and two round windows like eyes that faced the sea.

Meris stopped and bit her lip. Plenty of times she had walked through this patch of trees along the water's edge. Sometimes she and Sapha had played hide-go-seek here. She turned and looked back at the shoreline. There were no other trees crowding the water's edge. She was sure she knew this place—but there had never been a cottage, and this one certainly had not been built overnight. Her mind flitted back to the strange room back at her cottage. A room that couldn't be detected from outside.

"I don't understand," she said to the woman's back as the door opened and a warm aroma of something baked and sweet rushed to entice her inside.

Shamara turned briefly to Meris and smiled—a sad smile, Meris thought. "Please sit." Shamara gestured to a well-worn stuffed chair by a unlit hearth. But the small room was warmed by the heavy iron kitchen stove, into which her hostess stuffed a few small branches, setting off a burst of crackling as the wood caught flame. All the furnishings in the room were ancient and threadbare, and aside from bits of driftwood and feathers and pieces of shell, the walls and shelves were bare. A pale brown loop rug adorned the dull wood floor. As Meris sat, the woman busied herself with a tray and teapot, and before Meris could ask another question, a tea service sat on the low table before her, and steam rose from what smelled like spicenut scones.

Shamara took a seat in a rickety wooden chair opposite her and pointed at the teapot. "Please help yourself. You are chilled. And worried. But I've brought you here to ex—"

"Brought me here?" Meris dropped the hand that was reaching for a scone.

"Meris . . ."

"How do you know my name?"

Shamara tilted her head, the way the woodland birds often did, and kindness oozed from her. "My dear girl, I've known you all your life."

"But I've never met you—or seen you before—"

"No. But I know everyone here in Me'arah. All those who are here and who came before you—all the way back to the first to arrive."

Meris sucked in a breath, willing her limbs to stop shaking. "What do you mean—arrive?" The image of the box full of people traversing the sea floated across her mind. "Did our people come from across the sea? But . . . you would have to be thousands of years old, if you knew the first . . . that's impossible!"

Shamara nodded, her face unperturbed, and leaned forward to pour two cups of tea. Meris took the cup from her and sipped the minty brew. Her stomach rumbled, reminding her that her family was about to eat dinner and must be terribly worried about her. She set the cup down and stood.

"I really have to go. My family will be upset that I'm not home yet."

Shamara laid her hand on Meris's arm. "The future of Me'arah rests upon you, dear girl. You are the only one who can help. They will just have to worry."

A wave of dizziness washed over Meris. She fumbled back into her chair. Shamara handed her a scone.

"Eat some of this. It will revive you a bit. You've had quite a day."

Meris narrowed her eyes at this woman, who would surely be crazy if she did not seem to speak with uncanny knowledge. Her head ached as she nibbled on the pastry, which she had to admit was delectable. She was starving.

She pinned Shamara with her gaze. "What is across the sea?"

The old woman sat back in her chair and laid her hands in her lap, keeping her unblinking eyes upon Meris. "Secrets."

"Secrets? What secrets?"

"All in good time, Meris. But first we have other, more important things to discuss." The old woman's voice sounded tired, weak, thin. The warmth of the room dulled Meris's thoughts. The sound of ravens cackling outside punctuated the quiet that seeped into the room.

Meris choked down another bite of scone. Was this woman a lunatic? Some sort of seer? Surely she couldn't be as old as she claimed. And why would she think Meris was so important to Me'arah's future?

The dome.

She leaned close to Shamara. "Why is the dome failing?"

"Ah," Shamara said, nodding. She picked up her cup of tea and sipped thoughtfully. Then she said, "Because I am."

Meris frowned. "You are what?"

"Failing."

"I don't understand."

"Then, my dear girl, just let me explain and listen. And it will all make sense by the time I finish. Although, we may be here a very long time."

Meris fidgeted. "I really must go. Can't this explanation wait until tomorrow—?"

"It's called a gryphon."

Meris nearly dropped the cup as the image of the fearsome flying creature burst into her head and shattered her composure.

Shamara closed her eyes. "Yes, that one."

Suddenly the terror that had sent Meris's feet running to the sea swept over her and engulfed her. Shamara again took her hand,

and instantly the waves of fear lessened until they were gentle ripples against the walls of her pounding heart.

"Wh-what is it? Is it real?"

"Oh, very much so. A horrible thing fashioned by a very evil, powerful being."

"But not here. Not in Me'arah."

"No." Shamara gently released Meris's hand. Meris loosed a tight breath.

"But it is the reason we are here."

"I don't un—"

"I know." She smiled at Meris as if she had endless patience. "Will you stay and let me tell you a story? A story about a brave people under attack . . ."

Meris sat, stuck to her chair, as Shamara's voice lured her in. She forgot about hurrying home, about dinner, about the council meeting. Within minutes she even forgot who she was and where they were. As Shamara spoke, their tea grew cold, and the light filtering in through the lidless windows dimmed.

Without missing a beat in the rhythm of the story she told, a rhythm that pounded like a drum in keeping with the blood pulsing through Meris's veins, Shamara lit candles, set fire to the logs stacked in the hearth, and told Meris the tale of Moreb and of the wizard who made a choice in order to save her people.

And Meris finally understood.

FIVE

JUSTYN REINED in his horse at the top of the ridge. This was the fourth time in his life he'd ridden through solid rock to enter the mysterious land of Ethryn, and it still unnerved him. As did riding in general. Although he had long been regent of the School of Magic in the Heights, a part of him still had difficulty accepting magic in the world—especially when it happened to involve him personally. A leftover stubbornness or lack of faith, Antius used to say to him.

He thought fondly of his mentor, twenty years now dead. He missed the old man with his perky nature and engaging personality. The Heights had lost a great scholar and teacher—and Justyn had lost a great friend—when Antius died.

As he looked down upon the city laid out below him, with its round clay houses and glossy tiled roofs blinking under the hot sun, the dazzle of water caught his eye. He'd heard something about the Great River and the end of the drought. He longed to hear the truth about Ethryn's king, Kael, and how he'd found one of the sacred sites buried under sand. So many strange tellings had filtered into the Heights about miracles occurring in Ethryn that Justyn had to come and "uncover" the facts. He laughed at his pun, thinking of the tons of sand the workers must have dug through to find the circle of rock.

But at least one rumor was true—the river that had looked so meager and dried up the last time Justyn had been here was now a wide, expansive body of water coursing through the desert sands, magnificent and impressive. Justyn imagined there was enough water in the river now to sustain three kingdoms. No doubt the Ethrynians were overjoyed that the drought had ended. But was magic the reason? That's what Justyn wanted to know. The restoration of Ethryn would be his final and most important thesis to date; he wanted to crown his retirement with one last impressive treatise. He only hoped the stern king would grant him visitation and tell his story.

Decades ago, after the village of Wentwater had vanished and reappeared, and Teralyn had told him at length about the circle of rock at the bottom of the lake, he spent many years researching what he came to understand were the sacred sites, or *sha'har sha'mayim* in the ancient tongue. From his travels, he gathered stories and fables and songs, collecting bits and pieces as if digging through some ancient ruins for artifacts to formulate a clear picture of the past. From the scrolls he'd studied here in Ethryn, he learned a little more about these sites, that there were seven, constructed by heaven to prevent evil from taking over the world of men.

Aside from the site submerged in the lake—that long ago had stood on a grassy knoll in the heart of his kingdom until the Great Flood buried it underwater—he'd visited two others—the one in Sherbourne that lay partially in ruins, and the one on the Perilous Plain in Rumble. He shuddered recalling that treacherous and frightening journey into that ringed valley full of blood and death. He'd never seen a land so under enchantment as the site in Rumble. But it had been worth seeing, although he'd had nightmares for weeks afterward.

Yet, to date, he really understood little about these sites. He knew there had to be three more, with this one in Ethryn now discovered. He had read about Keepers, who protected the sites. The strange woman of the lake, who had rescued Teralyn as a babe and miraculously raised her for a time in her underwater domain, had been a Keeper. Although, no one but Teralyn had ever seen her—and Antius. Yet, he would never doubt Teralyn's words—never again. Her life had been bound in magic from the time of her birth, and it was by magic she had restored Wentwater. But he had never found any other Keepers, or learned who they might have been. Or if any were alive today. And he didn't really understand who or why anyone believed these sites somehow held evil at bay. There surely was plenty of evil in the world.

As he rode steadily down the winding road into Ethryn, he thought about his first encounter with magic—when the marsh witch had enchanted him and he stood in the stream of time and stitched his brother's name into the fabric, to cast a binding spell on him. To this day he never forgot the strange sense of timelessness that surrounded him as letters and ideas gave birth to words.

He jostled the memory out of his head as his horse's hooves clacked now on the cobblestones of the city, leaving the mounds of sand behind them. The ornate fountains, quiet and dry the last time he'd been here, spewed water into the air, the drops catching the light breeze and cooling his sweat-stained face. He rubbed a hand across his forehead, the weariness pushing away his prolonged anticipation. He'd traveled west and south many weeks to get here, leaving as soon as the news had reached the Heights about the newly discovered site, and both he and his horse were exhausted. He'd never felt comfortable on the back of such animals, and he would have taken a wagon if time had allowed it, but he'd wanted to get to Ethryn as quickly as *humanly* possible. And that meant dealing with these difficult four-legged beasts.

Knowing the city shifted at random, he checked down streets to find the stables, and the inn he enjoyed staying at, and to his delight they were where he'd left them. But that wasn't always the case. Lingering magic from the olden days, when magic was needed to hide the city from invaders, still acted up from time to time. Justyn chuckled. It didn't really matter to him where the inn was, so long as its innkeepers still served those wonderful platters of mutton and cheeses and steaming-hot brown bread. And the beds were still soft and comfortable and loaded with feather-stuffed blankets. Something his old bones appreciated more and more as the years wore on.

After depositing his horse with the stable hands, he slung his bag filled with clean clothes and personal belongings over his shoulder and walked—a bit sore and wobbly—down the street to the next block, where the inn was located. He was happy to see so many people milling about and shopping with smiles on their faces, so different from the gloomy climate oppressing every-one the last time he was here. With visitors from so many distant kingdoms, the shops and inns catered to every taste. Antius used to tease him for being wary of trying new things, urging him to take a chance and try new foods and sample local customs. Justyn had tried, but he always gravitated back to what was familiar and comfortable to him, and the Desert Sands Inn reminded him the most of the taverns of Wentwater. *And, Antius, you aren't here now to chastise me*, he thought with a rueful smile.

Justyn was shown by a young Ethryn girl to his favorite upper corner room that overlooked the street, where he washed up, trimmed his misbehaving beard, and changed clothes, hurrying in anticipation of a hearty well-deserved supper. The sun was just beginning to set over a streaked crimson sky, promising a bright, clear day tomorrow. With his skin scrubbed clean and wearing garments that smelled fresh and lacked a layer of sand and dirt, Justyn felt his weariness lift, and a spring infected his step. He took the stairs two at a time and entered the dining room, which was almost filled to capacity with boisterous, talkative travelers tucking into their meals and tipping back tall glasses of ale. What a contrast to the dour, gloomy mood that had pervaded the few unhappy travelers the last time he'd been here.

His heart filled with joy, thinking of Ethryn's now hopeful future. As often happened, his blood stirred imagining the amazing stories he would no doubt hear. He let his thoughts wander as he filled his stomach with food and drink, and as he stared at the flickering flames in the large stone hearth, his eyes beginning to droop. The warmth of the room made him drowsy, and the thought of sinking into a soft bed after weeks of camping on hard ground lured him to his feet. With a nod to the innkeeper and the few remaining diners at the tables next to him, he lumbered up the creaky stairs to his room and entered.

He pulled his boots off and fell back onto the bed, his arms and legs feeling like heavy logs. Before he could undress and get into his nightshirt, though, he closed his eyes—just to rest for a moment. All that food and drank lay heavy on his stomach, and he had no energy left to rummage through his bag of clothes.

Suddenly, he felt himself falling. He grasped at the edges of the bed, but his arms swung through thick air. No—water. Hot water. He opened his eyes and saw an explosion of bubbles rising around him as he sank down and down into darkness.

He sucked in a breath that wouldn't come. Water stung his eyes, and the heat burned his skin. His hair flowed and ebbed into his eyes as he kicked hard to find the surface of this nightmare.

After an unbearable few moments, with his lungs about to burst, he broke through the water amid roiling waves. Scalding steam encircled him as he scrambled to the shore and clambered out onto a bed of grass, where he realized by the backdrop of mountains sporting cascades of waterfalls that he was at Lake Wentwater.

His exposed skin throbbed pink, and pain seared his flesh even under his clothes. He knew he had to be asleep, but when he tried to wake, he found no way out of his dream. Backing away on his hands and knees from the turbulent water that spit out streams of hot water, his only thought was to get to safety. But when he got to his feet prepared to run, he heard something that stabbed his heart.

A mournful scream of pain rent the air, but it felt as if it cut through Justyn's heart with a sharp sword. It was a siren of death, a woman's death. He knew without a doubt whose voice he was hearing coming up from the deepest chambers of the lake. Something clenched his heart, and he let out a cry.

In his mind's eye he saw dozens of algae-covered rocks toppling in a slow dance of collapse in the murky darkness of water. One by one they fell in silence, and with each silent impact of stone to mud, the ground under his feet shook. The earth trembled along with Justyn as his mouth dropped open and he watched until every giant slab of stone lay prone on the lake's bottom, the silt stirred up and whirling in a dirge over the fallen site.

And in the center of all the mayhem, a flicker—like that of a candle—wavered violently, then sputtered out. Darkness descended over the world as a faint shriek pierced the sky far above. Even though he could barely hear this lone sound as he lay trembling on the hillock near the lakeshore, it chilled his blood, as if his veins had turned to ice. A fear greater than any he'd ever known pumped into his heart like a poison, and he opened his eyes.

With a hand clutched over his heart, Justyn listened to the quiet in the dark. His breath heaved hard in his chest. A loud knock at his door startled him, and he nearly fell off the bed.

"Coming," he croaked, trying to get his bearings in the dark room and locate the door.

When he opened it, the portly innkeeper studied his face, a troubled look on his own.

"Is everythin' all right, sir?" the man asked.

When Justyn failed to answer, the man added, "I was wiping down the counter downstairs when I heard ya'. A blood-curdling scream." His voice formed a question, but Justyn didn't know how to answer. The strange vision he'd had still clung to him, and his skin still burned with heat. He looked down to his trousers and saw nothing unusual. He turned his hands over and they looked old and spotted with age, but that was to be expected.

"Well, you must've had a bad dream," the innkeeper declared, pursing his lips and no doubt hoping there wouldn't be another one forthcoming.

Justyn stood there and nodded. He shared the sentiment.

SIX

JORAN FOLLOWED two lengths behind his father's galloping horse, his own steady-footed mare keeping up with the young, feisty stallion, all the while wondering how long they'd be gone, how Charris was faring in the north with her family, how many wizards would heed his father's call and show up in Sherbourne, how . . .

Zev reined in his mount at the top of a rise in the road and turned to face Joran. In the early evening shadows, Joran made out a frown—directed at him. He slowed his horse and came alongside Zev, trying to see if the north walls of Sherbourne were yet visible, but all he could make out was the strip of dirt bisecting the brushy landscape on either side of the well-trodden road. They must be close. Would King Adin remember him, after all these years? Would they really find help in this gathering of wizards? If a contingent of wizards had failed to stop the Destroyer millennia ago, what made his father think a handful of opposers could stop him now?

"Your worrying is worrisome."

"Sorry," Joran said, knowing even with careful guarding, his father no doubt heard his troubled thoughts. But he had every right to worry. Yet, his father seemed unbothered. Maybe living for centuries made one inured to impending doom and the end of the world.

His father reached over and laid a hand on his wrist. "Joran, heaven has a plan. You have to trust."

Joran scoffed. "Let me see. You tell me the Destroyer has once again come into the world, along with these gryphons—which are no doubt the most terrifying creatures ever to exist—and he intends to, well, destroy everything. And I am not supposed to worry, not even a little?

Zev chuckled and shook his head. "All right. A little worrying is in order."

Joran blew out a breath, listening to the horses' labored breathing as they fidgeted impatiently, perhaps sensing the unease saturating the world. He didn't feel inclined to impose his sour mood upon them and engage them in conversation. Instead he stared off into the weighty shadows falling upon the road ahead. The night around them edged closer, like a predatory animal. He muttered, "It's getting too dark to see."

His words triggered a brief flash of light from his father's palm, which lit up their immediate surroundings and revealed a smirk on his father's face. Zev then shifted the small orb from his hand to the wagon ruts of the road, where it hung like a lantern on an invisible post.

"Better?" Zev asked.

Joran nodded. He didn't want to speak of the tingling, unnerving feeling crawling up his spine, fearful any mention might summon his recent nightmare. It had been hounding him the last hour, as twilight fell. As if someone was watching him—

His father studied his face, shifting in his saddle. Familiar wolf eyes bore into him. "What is it?"

Joran could tell Zev shared his agitation, but why did he not know the source?

Just then, something pricked the back of his neck and he swung around, his arm striking out at the darkness. But then he realized it was the darkness who was his friend.

The Moon's cream-colored scalp peeked up from the horizon and threw Joran's shadow to the ground. He scowled.

His father's question hung in the air. *Not what. Who.*

Joran pointed to the luminary making a grand entrance back into his life after all these many years. How dare she?

"Her."

To Joran's surprise, Zev's eyes widened. The image of Ruyah the wolf howling at the base of the Moon's silvery staircase invaded his mind. Ruyah, sitting stiffly, his head tipped to the sky, blurting out such a ruckus, compelled, enchanted . . .

He hoped his father wasn't going to give a repeat performance.

But how strange, he thought. All these years, and the Moon—his nemesis, who had captured Charris and nearly killed him in the world of his dream—had never returned to terrorize him. The ordinary moon that rose and set, season after season, year after year, was the benign and silent watcher that shone its gentle light upon the world without virulence or madness. He'd come to believe that the Moon he'd encountered on his journey to save his wife had merely been some aberrant figment of his imagination, for when he'd returned home after so many months of traveling, he found he'd never really left. It had to have been a delusion at worst or a magical vision at best.

But this ominous presence rising into the night sky behind him was no illusion. Her presence was nearly suffocating, akin to the sensation of an intruder breathing stealthily on one's neck. The Moon's scant light, now spreading like spilled milk across the sky, lit up his father's face and showed a distress Joran rarely observed.

So much for centuries of time able to subdue the worries of doom and destruction.

Zev bristled in his wolfish manner, his gaze narrowed at the Moon as she lifted herself majestically into the sky and swooped them both up into another dream. If Zev yet had fur, Joran knew it would be ridged erect along his back. A growl that had long slumbered rumbled in his father's throat, a precursor to fangs and sharp nails. But the wolf never manifested—other than a glint in the eye that spoke of protection. It gave Joran little comfort this time.

Joran looked down and saw he was standing on a high rocky promontory that hung over a precipitous chasm, his father beside him. Cold wind whipped in anger, snapping at his face and ears and stinging his cheeks. He felt he had been returned to the end of the world once more. But the Moon's disheveled shack was nowhere to be seen.

Zev huddled close as stars wheeled above in frantic chaos, as the ground creaked and moaned. Joran waited for the inevitable frost to entangle his legs, creep up and embrace his thighs, but to his surprise, none appeared. At least they weren't at the shore of the churning sea, with a sand castle looming precariously over them, he mused. Another dream, another time.

Something moved between rock, backlit by the Moon, who now dangled like an opulent ornament from a tree. Joran stood, unmoving, unblinking, his father alert beside him. But he could feel the tension ease from Zev's body, a hint of his shoulders slumping, a soft breath released.

Joran narrowed his eyes, but by the sounds coming from the jumble of cliffs—the tripping and pebble-kicking and muttering in singsong and swish of fabric—he knew who was coming. Clearly his father did as well, although he wondered how. Ruyah had never met Cielle.

Joran shook his head, pulling his coat tighter around his freezing body and tucking his chin into his chest.

Cielle—who claimed she was the Moon's sister. He recalled Sola's reaction when he told her about Cielle in the house of the Sun. *"The Moon doesn't have a sister."* No, she didn't. She was a raving lunatic. Mad, incomprehensible. Unpredictable. And dangerous. *Don't forget.*

Cielle emerged, wearing the same flowing gown of greens and blues that swirled like water around her body. She waved her hands excitedly, her many silver rings glinting and scattering shafts of light. "Ah, there you are, my sweet pea. My, how long it has been! Why, you look positively the picture of health and vigor."

Joran cringed as Cielle ambled over to him, tripping erratically over her layers of long sheer skirts, still waving her hands emphatically in the air and shaking her head in spasms. Joran backed away from her eager arms that he knew would wrap him in a stranglehold. Even though she was only Cielle, he didn't trust her—not a bit. And the crescent moon she had imprinted on his forehead with her lips still marked him. He didn't want another "token" of her affection.

Joran took a quick glance at his father's bemused face, then glared at Cielle. Her jangling bracelets rang out in dissonance, hurting Joran's ears. But the wolf beside him didn't seem bothered by the noise. He waited, ears pricked, eyes alert.

"What do you want?" Joran asked her, making no effort to mask his ire and suspicion, his cheeks turning to ice from the battering of wind.

"Want?" Her smile twisted into a sour frown, and she fluffed up her unkempt hair. Glowing pearls dropped at her feet like tiny moondrops. "My little pumpkin, what do you think I *want*?" Her sinuous voice rose in pitch as she threw her arms up in the air and continued.

"Those nasty creatures messed up my lovely rock garden! My precious circle, the one I've been watching over for—well, no one really knows, munchkin, do they?" She waved her hand dismissively. "But, regardless. They had no right." She muttered under her breath, Joran only catching a word here and there. However, one word smacked him in the face. *Gryphon.*

Joran looked to Zev for rescue but found none. His father held a serious expression, listening between the words that Joran understood were more than sounds stuck together.

"So, my little buttercup" she said, now in full rant, "what do you plan to do about it?"

She took another big step toward Joran. He would have backed away further, but he was pressed against rock.

"My fine lady," Zev said, holding open palms out to her as if beseeching her. "We mean to stop him—"

At that, Cielle let out a vociferous guffaw, and pearls catapulted through the icy air. "Stop him?" She looked at Zev as if only now just noticing him. "You—you have magic," she declared, then scrunched up her face. "But it won't be enough . . . *wolf.*"

Zev answered evenly. "There are others."

When she only glared at him, he added. "We are on our way to take counsel in Sherbourne. They are waiting for us." He paused, his words acting like a salve on her sour face. "M'lady, you are delaying us."

"Hmmph!" she said, spinning around in such haste, her skirts flew up into Joran's stunned face. She stomped a few feet, then stopped and looked back. Her face flushed with anger.

Joran clamped his mouth shut as the Moon inched higher behind Cielle, now tainted red, splashing dark crimson shadows across the landscape. The chill had either dissipated from the air or he was now too frozen to feel it.

Cielle pinned her eyes on him and said, "Have you forgotten? The Moon sees it all. She marches across the heavens, circling and circling, higher than the gryphons can fly. She sees the armies amassing for battle, ramparts being built, weapons forged, men like tiny little ants, like locusts, spreading hate and evil and cruelty across the land. Oh, and does she care? No, not one bit."

Cielle then bent forward and pointed a long manicured finger at Joran, then waggled it. "But what she *does* care about is anyone ruining her *pretty little rock garden* . . ."

With that, she fell in a heap on the ground with a choking sound, the cold wind whipping her hair, and sobbed her heart out. Between heaves and tears she sighed and mumbled. "Why? Why would they do such a thing? All my pretty rocks, fallen, fallen down. And I have no way to put them right." She shook her head forlornly and wiped her face. Tears frozen into pearls clattered around her tiny glass slippers.

After a few snorts and snuffles, she got to her feet and smoothed out her skirts. With a flair she threw back the hair that had fallen in her face and looked at Joran, whose jaw had dropped.

"My little bumblebee, please . . . You must avenge this travesty." She stood tall, gazing out over the precipice as if seeing something afar, snuffling quietly.

Zev took a step toward her, his face awash in understanding. Joran wished he understood.

"My lady, tell us how."

His words sat heavy in the air, expectant. Only then Joran realized Cielle knew more than she let on.

Zev waited, along with the stars, which had ceased their frenzied dance and shimmered with tiny fire. Joran closed his mouth; his tongue was numb from the cold. His eyelashes, frosted over, stuck together. He hoped Cielle wouldn't take all night to answer.

They might end up as icicles, and then what good would they be to her or anyone?

Finally, she cocked her head to the side, and a smile found its way to her sad but encouraging face. "Find the seventh site. The Moon has searched past the boundaries of the world, but there is no trace of it. But it must be there. The seventh site is the key."

Joran spoke before he realized the words jumped from his mouth. "The key to what?"

Cielle let out a dramatic sigh, came to Joran, and stroked his cheek. Her fingers were strangely warm in the midst of this chilling wasteland.

"My silly wombat—the key to the kingdom." She slapped the side of her head and laughed. "Oh, I am the silly one—I am!"

Joran exchanged puzzled glances with his father, who remained oddly quiet and still. The wolf had submerged. Even with a blood-red Moon rising into the heavens to take her place in rotation.

Cielle gave Zev a sly smile, as if she finally got the meaning of a hilarious joke. "No wonder she couldn't find the seventh site." With raised eyebrows, she gestured to Zev to answer, but he said nothing. Cielle then chortled and slapped her thigh.

"Why, the kingdom is in your midst!"

A blast of wind knocked Joran off his feet, causing him to hit his head backward on something unpleasantly hard. When he rubbed his eyes and looked around, he was on the ground beside his mare, whose soft, warm nostrils were puffing breath onto his face. Two dark-brown eyes looked at him with curiosity as if he'd just fallen out of the sky, but the horse said nothing, merely snorted.

When a loud thump made Joran swivel his head, he wondered if he truly had.

Zev lay on his side, dust billowing around him, and he wiped his face as he made to stand. The young stallion nickered from a few feet away and ambled to Zev's side.

"Well," was all his father said.

Joran waited, but no more words followed. He dusted himself off and mounted his horse. When Zev got up into his saddle, Joran asked, "I told you she was mad."

Zev's expression underscored the understatement.

Joran lifted his heavy head and closed his eyes. The welcome light breeze blew warm, thawing his cheeks. He loosened his coat and took up the reins.

Zev looked up into the night sky. A docile eggshell of a moon hovered above them.

Joran asked as they resumed their trek along the road to Sherbourne, "What did she mean by the seventh site is the key to the kingdom? What kingdom? And how can a kingdom be in our midst?" Joran scowled and clenched his fists tighter around the reins. "I thought I was done with the Moon's riddles."

Without taking his eyes off the road, his father answered evenly, "Apparently not."

SEVEN

WHEN PERTHIN entered the atrium to the Great Scroll Room, he stood and admired the magnificent paintings adorning the archways over the entrance. Majestic snow-frosted mountains, expansive fields of golden wheat and barley, a cozy village nestled among towering trees, cradled by dark forests that crowded up high peaks. He noted there were no depictions of the sea—of any harbor kingdom like Paladya, or his humble seaside village of Tolpuddle. He wondered if the artist had ever seen the sea, and Perthin's musing made him suddenly nostalgic for the home he had left hundreds of years ago. Busy ruling Elysiel, he had little time for travel and adventure. He smirked. Well, he was certainly on one now. Although, he wished it portended something less troubling and fateful.

On this bright and shiny fall morning, with the soft drops of cool water from the marble fountain caressing his skin, it was hard to imagine the danger fomenting just beyond the borders of this land. Last night, King Kael had taken him to see the sacred site under a rising full moon, and when they had ascended the rise north of Ethryn and maneuvered their horses through the cutaways in the sandstone rock formations, Perthin had gasped at the sight.

The pristine light caught the slabs of towering stone and cast a perfect five-pointed star in the center—just as his site in Elysiel did every full moon, ever since the ice cavern had melted and the site became exposed to the heavens above. A glance at Kael showed the awe and peace caught in the king's visage, illuminated by more than just heavenly light. Perthin sensed, then, great divine favor upon this ruler, and after hearing Kael's long and moving tale of his past life at the dawn of history, the story of how the hound of heaven had chased him through the years and appointed him Keeper, Perthin was dumbfounded. This king, so humble, had every right to boast of his position and power, but after telling his story, Kael merely laid a hand on Perthin's arm and said, "I don't know why heaven chose me. I never wanted to be a king or a healer or a Keeper, and I resisted and ran from my destiny." With a chuckle he added, "But we can never outrun destiny, can we?"

So true, Perthin thought then, as he thought now, turning and looking into the cavernous room in front of him, full of thousands of scrolls. Carved white columns marched in even rows down the great hall, supporting an ornately detailed ceiling laced with gold filigree. And rows upon rows of shelves showed innumerable stacks of rolled scrolls. He'd heard Ethryn had the greatest library in the world, but he never envisioned something as spectacular as this. He had never even seen a written scroll when he was living out his youth in Tolpuddle. Yet, all the while he was mending fishing nets and combing the beach for castaway treasures, the greatest treasures of the world were being studied by scholars who came to Ethryn to find answers to their questions. Here, where dozens of archivists studied and cataloged the annals of the world's history.

He wondered, as he stood there watching the dozens of visitors perusing the shelves and poring over scrolls at the many long polished tables, how much he'd find here written about Elysiel. What legends and poems might have seeped out of his hidden kingdom over the centuries to make their way to the Great Scroll Room of Ethryn. Well, if any were to be found anywhere in the world, they would no doubt be here.

Movement caught Perthin's eye. From around a far corner of the scroll room came King Kael, accompanied by an aged man with long gray hair and a trimmed beard. In contrast to the simple garb the king had worn the previous evening, he now donned a violet robe that was wrapped in gold embroidery and fastened at his waist with a crimson silk sash. The man beside him wore a different kind of robe—pale green, with a hood that fell around his shoulders. As for his own clothes, he had brought none with him on his "whirlwind" trip to Ethryn, but Kael had seen to providing him with comfortable, cool attire that bespoke both practicality and luxury, including supple camel-skin boots, although Perthin decided he would keep his magic boots ever close at hand, should the need arise to use them expeditiously. Perthin wondered this morning as he dressed if he shouldn't have left so hastily without thinking to pack a bag of necessities. But he had been so keen to find Kael. He also regretted he had told no one of his departure, although he thoroughly trusted his governors to manage a short time without him.

The two men spoke quietly to each other as they walked in Perthin's direction, intent in their conversation and unnoticing the servants and visitors that bowed respectfully as they passed. Halfway across the room, Kael looked up and caught sight of Perthin and smiled. His eyes sparked with hope and mystery as he came to greet him.

"King Perthin," Kael said, gesturing to the man beside him, "this is Justyn, a regent from the land of Wentwater. They have schools of learning there."

Perthin met Justyn's eyes and saw a deep respect and awe swimming in them. No doubt Kael had informed this man about Elysiel and its king.

"I am honored and humbled to meet you," Justyn said, lowering his head. When he raised his head, he added, "I came here to learn about the sacred site, as word had come to the Heights of Wentwater of this wonderful find."

Kael interjected before Justyn could continue. "Justyn informed me that one of the sites exists in his land—at the bottom of a great lake."

"Another of the sites?" Perthin had heard of the small kingdom of Wentwater but could not recall anything about it. This was good news.

"What do you know about this site? Does it have a Keeper?" Perthin asked.

"Keeper?" Justyn replied. "What is that?"

King Kael glanced around the room. Perthin noticed many faces turned away as the king looked in their direction. "Let's go out into the palace gardens, where we may speak freely."

Perthin followed, noticing a somber pall suddenly upon the two other men. They did not resume speaking until Kael had them seated on polished marble benches under swaying willows at the far end of a long pebbled walkway.

Kael turned to Justyn and pulled down the neckline of his tunic to reveal his neck chain. Justyn's face paled. Both Kael and Perthin raised eyebrows.

"You seem to recognize the king's necklace," Perthin said.

"I do," Justyn answered. "A . . . friend in Wentwater had the identical necklace. Although hers had a pearl in the center instead of a gem."

Perthin pulled his necklace out from under his shirt.

"You have one too!" Justyn said, shaking his head.

Kael nodded. "King Perthin is also a Keeper of a sacred site—one very similar to the one here in Ethryn. We can only assume all the Keepers are given one."

"Does every Keeper have such a necklace?" Justyn asked.

Kael shrugged. "I was appointed as the first Keeper, and my duty was to protect and cherish the site and the appointment, to seek heaven's face and do God's will. To do all in my power to prevent evil from taking hold in my land. Upon my appointment, I was given this to wear."

Justyn grew lost in thought, and silence lay heavy upon them. Perthin listened to the songbirds chortling in the willows above and found the peace and quiet refreshing. How strange to be in another land of which he had no intimate connection. He could hear no one's thoughts, and had no awareness of the life teeming around him. He was just an ordinary man in another king's domain. He smiled. The break from his usual life in Elysiel was welcome, although it gave him a strange sense of disconnection. He would have to rely on his natural senses and acquired wisdom, and there would be no ghosts here to counsel him. He hoped he would make the right decisions. But then, he had Kael to consult with. And a thousand or more scrolls. But did they have time?

"Justyn," Kael said, puncturing the silence, "tell King Perthin of your nightmare."

Justyn's face turned dark and bothered. "I think it was more a vision, and I fear it will come true—if it hasn't already."

Perthin listened as Justyn told his tale, and when he heard him describe the boiling lake and the heartrending scream, a pain stabbed his heart.

Justyn stopped talking and studied Perthin's face. "What do you think? Was it a warning?"

Perthin caught Kael's frowning expression. He said to Justyn, "More than a warning, I fear. The Destroyer means to annihilate all the sites. I was told . . . that the gryphons meant doom. That this is the time of the end—"

Justyn's face turned ashen, matching the dull gray of his beard. "The end of what? Of the entire world?"

"And I'm to be the last of Elysiel's kings," Perthin finished, the words deflating his spirit, as if speaking them confirmed their veracity.

"But is there nothing to be done about it?" Justyn asked, searching first Perthin's face, and then Kael's.

When Kael said nothing—only stared out over the garden's prolific blooms—Perth said quietly, "I was sent to find King Kael. My predecessor told me he is the first and last, the beginning and end. That he holds the key to the gate of heaven . . ."

Justyn turned to Kael. "What does that mean—that you hold the key? If King Perthin is also a Keeper of his site, doesn't he also 'hold the key'? Do you have any understanding of what these words mean?"

Kael shook his head. "There is much I do not understand—but one thing I do know, Justyn of Wentwater . . ."

Perthin noted the stark despair clouding Justyn's face and wondered if his own face showed a similar expression. He did not want to believe Cakrin's pronouncement, did not want to believe he truly was Elysiel's last king. His heart ached at the thought, and his mind jumped to the scepter now lying on his bed in the palace. He pictured the beating heart in the scepter's handle slowly dwindling to a stop, never to beat again, and the image stung his eyes with tears.

Kael continued. "Heaven has brought us together for a reason, and evil will never be tolerated forever. God will not let the wicked go unpunished forever. He is a God of justice and righteousness, and although he has allowed men to follow the paths they've chosen these many centuries, there must be an end, an accounting. Otherwise God would not be righteous and just."

Justyn nodded thoughtfully. He looked to the building before them. "I have come to Ethryn many times over the years, seeking answers—and finding them in the scrolls within those walls. Perhaps not every question can be answered that way. But I believe some can."

Kael's mouth tightened. "My best archivists have been researching for months. They have found little about the sacred sites, other than there are seven. It stands to reason that if the sites are what keep the world from succumbing to evil, then the Destroyer means to destroy them all to remove divine protection from the world. I can only guess our task is to prevent this from happening—if it is possible. Which is why we must find all seven."

Perthin stood and paced, restless and feeling a need to do something. "One in Ethryn. Another in Elysiel, and in Wentwater."

"I visited one in Rumble, just northwest of Ethryn's walls," Justyn added. "And there is one in Sherbourne. But I saw no sign of any Keeper."

"That makes five sites. We are missing two," Kael said, shaking his head.

Perthin turned to Justyn, weighing his words. "The woman of lake—no doubt she is the Keeper. She gave your friend the necklace, although the reason is unclear. Perhaps . . . she knew she was going to die?"

Justyn's face looked seared with pain. "Teralyn was never a Keeper, from what I understand by the experiences you both had.

She was never appointed to guard the site or serve heaven in any capacity. The necklace was given in love and affection, not as a charge of duty. And Teralyn died nearly ten years ago. I do not know what happened to the necklace, although I suspect it would have been given to her oldest daughter."

Perthin shook his head. "I've been thinking maybe we need to rally together all the Keepers. That maybe together—"

Kael interrupted. "Maybe we must work together to find the answers to this riddle—about the key."

"If you are the key," Justyn said, "then maybe the other Keepers are like the five points of the star, with you in the center."

Kael quickly retorted, "If there are even other Keepers left in the world. And by your count, that makes six, not seven."

Perthin's eyebrows narrowed. "You were given the censer, and the priestly robes. Heaven placed you in the center of the circle when power was loosed from above to stem the tide of evil," he said, recalling what Kael had related to him last night as they stood under moonlight in the center of the site. "Perhaps if we gather all the Keepers together at Ethryn's site—the first site—heaven will give a repeat performance."

Kael shrugged. "There is no way to know whether or not that would happen, or if this site holds some special significance. I am troubled by what your predecessor told you—that the end of all things has come. That is the crux of the matter. If there is no way to avoid the coming of the end—whatever that means—no matter what we do, it will fail." Although his words bespoke failure and hopelessness, his tone seemed merely analytical.

"But *you* are at the crux," Justyn said. "You are the first and the last, the beginning and the end. It started with you. It must end with you. Whatever *it* is."

Perthin added, looking at Kael, "And, as you pointed out, we have no idea if there are any other Keepers alive. It is possible all the others are gone from this world."

"Regardless, I think we need to find the last two sites, and see if we can learn of any Keepers still living," Kael said.

"Your Highness," Justyn said to Kael, "I know your archivists have searched the scrolls, but I have made research my life's vocation, and I excel in ancient languages and writing. I ask that you would at least grant me the opportunity to do my own research and see what I can find."

Kael smiled. "Of course, Justyn. I would be grateful for your efforts, since . . . we seem at a loss at this point regarding what else to do. My armies are gearing up for war, and we are establishing blockades and building ramparts on the northern borders of Ethryn. But I fear it is much like throwing tiny pebbles at giants in an attempt to defeat them. I can't see how anything we do can stop Sha'kath the Destroyer."

"But we have to try," Perthin said, resolute.

Kael gave a sad smile. "Yes, we must." He stood and turned to Justyn. "Come. I'll introduce you to Avad, my chief archivist. He will be glad for your help and insights."

Without further speech, they walked somberly back to the palace doors, Perthin's head swimming with all this information. No doubt heaven had seen fit to bring this regent of Wentwater to aid them. Perhaps the scrolls would tell them what they needed to know.

Perthin tried to hold on to that ray of hope, but, like a sunbeam, it only slipped from his hand.

• PART TWO •

"MOMI, YOU didn't tell me the whole story!" Aron shimmied up onto his stool and picked up his spoon. Steam from the cooked grains swirled around his face as Alia scooped out the rest of the cereal from the pot and plopped it into her wooden bowl. A glance out the large window above the sink showed the tip of the giant orange sun riding along the horizon, streaking the sky with a rainbow of pastel shades, and casting enough light for Alia to make out the dense forests in the distance. These twilight days—for months on end—took some getting used to.

The trees here on this planet reminded her of Me'arah—squat, with thick, dark trunks and heavy limbs that looked as if they were burdened with the weight of their shiny scalloped leaves.

The Destroyer had given the people of Moreb little time to gather their seeds and livestock, with his gryphons attacking and the city ignited in flame. But she had insisted they quickly gather what they could, knowing she would have to make do with what they brought with them in haste. Only she knew they would never again return to the surface of their world—which had become a place drenched in evil, and too perilous in which to remain.

Alia sat in the stool opposite Aron, who swung his legs in restless abandon. "I didn't finish the story," she said, nodding at her son to keep eating, "because you fell asleep."

"Did not!" He stuffed a spoonful of cereal into his mouth and chewed thoughtfully. "Well, maybe I did, a little." His eyes brightened. "But, can you tell the rest now?"

Alia gave an exaggerated frown. "Don't you want to go riding on Berra's remoraphant today? Her father mentioned something about taking you to see the caves."

Aron's mouth dropped open. "Oops, I forgot." He slipped off his stool and rushed out of the room, yelling, "Momi, you have to find my crystal headlamp! I bet I'll find the biggest crystal ever."

"Aron, come back and finish your breakfast—"

"Not hungry," came the muffled reply. Alia pictured pajamas flying across the room and Aron digging through his dresser drawers for the appropriate "caving" clothes.

When he ran back into the kitchen, Alia muffled a laugh. "Here, you have your shirt on backward."

He stood, wiggling like a trapped worm, while she set his shirt right and smoothed down his hair. She gave him a once-over and nodded. She was impressed; he'd done a fair job tying his bootlaces. After sifting through the trunk by the door, she pulled out the headlamp and positioned it on his head.

"There, you're ready to go."

Aron's face beamed and his eyes sparkled. The sight of such innocent excitement warmed her heart.

"I bet we'll find a cave as big as Me'arah." He leaned close to her and whispered, his face animated and flushed. "Maybe I'll even find a secret entrance—like the one Shamara made."

She nodded and smiled, then kissed the top of his head. Before she could say another word, he was out the door and off running down the leaf-choked path to Berra's house up on the next ridge.

Her son's words took her back to the day of that battle, so many centuries ago, when she had been called by another name— before all the reborn were given new names.

Shamara. Watchful, protected, guarded by God. Names given by heaven had meaning then, although when she had been assigned to the people of Moreb, she had no idea how much so.

The memories were like faded movies, the colors and sounds subdued. Even the fear and terror of that attack now played in her mind ever so quietly, as from a distance. But as much as the memories had dimmed, she knew she would never forget.

She laid a hand on the smooth stone counter and felt the rough rock of Moreb. When she closed her eyes, she saw the towering sandstone cliffs they had run to, as the gryphons shrieked their hideous cries and as her people ran crying, falling, dying . . .

She shook her head, flinging her thoughts away, as she heard footsteps. The sleepy face of her husband greeted her as he ambled into the kitchen. His hair askew like tossed straw, he asked, "He's gone? Already?"

Alia nodded, and went to pour him his tea. "Off with Berra's family to the caverns."

Glynn looked thoughtful as she slid his mug to him. Even after these many years, she still had flashes of the old man he had long-ago become—the gray beard and eyebrows that had grown bushy. The skin mottled and sagging, the irises of his eyes cloudy and vacant. Those last few years he had gone blind, and—stubborn as always—refused to allow her to help lead him around. She chuckled at the memory—so long forgotten. She had grown old too, she recalled. An old woman who lived in solitude under the thin veil of magic, in a copse of firth trees along the shore of the great sea, both her eyes and heart failing. But that had been centuries after she had buried Garog . . . now called Glynn.

"What?" she asked, studying his face as she sat down on the stool next to him.

"I was just remembering the cavern. Me'arah."

The word hung in the air between them. She supposed she could have come up with a more creative name for the land she had fashioned out of the bowels of the earth, but it *was* a cavern. A place she had carved out with magic, a beautiful land, and she had used every bit of her power to create and maintain it. And the effort had taken its toll.

She lifted a hand and stroked Glynn's hair as he sipped his tea, his thoughts far away, in distance and time. She'd had little time for Garog, or their three daughters, those first years. He'd been so young then, and so needy. He understood the tremendous burden she carried, but—so like humans—sometimes resented her power, and her responsibility. He alone had known what she truly was—not some kindly, sweet fairy that twittered about and visited with children and left them gifts on their front stoops. He'd kept her wizardry a secret. They had no idea that it was her doing, when she led them through the crevice of rock down, down, through dark tunnels, bringing them—bewildered and in awe—to the edge of a great cerulean-blue sea, water as far as the eye could see.

While they boarded the boats she had prepared for them, she curled deep into herself to quickly plan out the stages of creation—the first order of business being the manifestation of light. Using the Book as her pattern and guide, she began—cyclical light forming day and night; plants springing up from the ground, reproducing according to their kind. But her creative power had its limits, and so whatever livestock they carted with them—or animals that wandered in through the portal she constructed—they'd had to make do with.

The large barges were easy to fashion so they'd be sturdy enough to carry such heavy weight, and once they'd served their purpose were dissolved in a whisk of magic. She could not take the chance someone might try to flee back to the surface—and alert the Destroyer of their existence. And over the years many did try to leave, pulled by their longing for things left behind. But she made sure their attempts to cross the sea failed by casting a confounding spell over the water. Those who built their own boats and tried to navigate across only found themselves back on a familiar shore. She then added terror to her spell to further discourage them from leaving. After three generations of attempts, no one ever tried again.

So with a word, a dome spread above them as they rowed their dozens of boats, Garog glancing at her huddled in the bow, a worried frown on his face. She blotted out the voices and cries, the worry over the dead and injured, the doubts railing at her heart. These were her people, and she'd been assigned their protector. Their keeper.

A pang struck her upon knowing she would probably never see Valonis—or any of the other wizards—ever again. She had watched Lorec fall while trying to protect her. Had all the wizards in the world come under attack? Had any survived? Would it ever be safe to return to the surface? Perhaps. But how would she know? She pushed down longing and regret and concentrated. So much to be done. So little time to fashion a world ready to be inhabited. But somehow she managed the rudimentary foundations of what would become Me'arah.

When the boats finally slid onto the sandy beach on the other side of the sea, a pristine, untouched land greeted them. Exhausted, she slumped to the floor of the boat, and Garog lifted her with his strong arms, his eyes shining with love and reassurance. He didn't know she was carrying their first child—not yet. Nor that he would be the first of the line of the Na'tar, or caretakers, of this strange, new world. And through their children, magic would flow and embellish the land, offering the people of Moreb respite and peace and safety from the evil ravaging the real world miles above them.

"You're awfully quiet this morning, my love," Glynn said, searching her eyes for explanation.

She smiled and said, "I was adrift in that boat, the day we escaped."

Glynn nodded, his face soft from sleep. He chuckled. "I remarked at the pink sky—"

"It was all I could manage—"

"I got used to it." He smirked. "We all did." He added, "We had to learn to adjust to a new life. Which is essentially what we do now, every time we venture to a new world."

"But at least I don't have to make these worlds."

He put a warm hand on her cheek and said, "No, you are relieved of that responsibility. Instead, you are free to make me breakfast—"

She playfully smacked his shoulder. "It's your turn today."

"I know," he said, getting to his feet and pulling her to him. He wrapped his arms around her as he had so many countless times on countless worlds. "But I do miss those bogberries. I don't know if I could have survived living all those years in Me'arah without them."

She shrugged and pulled away. "There are plenty of other berries—on this and other worlds. Perhaps one day, on some remote planet in another solar system, we'll find them again. You mustn't give up hope, dear." She gave him a playful wink.

He laughed and got busy in the pantry, looking for ingredients. "Oh, never. Never give up hope. Always need something to hope for, to strive for. It's a human attribute."

"Or a curse. Depending on how you look at it." She raised her eyebrows, challenging him to refute. But he merely chuckled.

"Right now, my love, the only thing I'm striving to do is to cook you a wonderful breakfast. So, what'll you have?"

Alia smiled and sighed. "Surprise me."

EIGHT

IN THE FAINT light of dawn, Joran made out the turrets flanking the northern gates and entry into the city of Sherbourne. He didn't expect any guards to stop and question them. The land had thrived for decades under the peaceful reign of King Adin. In his mind he pictured a young man, only a few years his junior, that day the prince had ridden to Tebron to seek word of a sister he'd left centuries in the past. But the king would now be an old man—such as Joran himself.

Although, Joran hardly looked his age. Being half wizard promised him a long life. How long, he had no idea. But it hurt his heart to think of the many lonely years that lay ahead of him, long after Charris would be dead and buried. Already her bones were weary and her hair gray. If she begrudged him the magic that gave him longevity, she never indicated. And Joran knew she found comfort in the fact their children and grandchildren would benefit from the infusion of magic in their blood. Their three sons, in their forties, hardly looked older than teenagers.

"They're here," Zev announced, pulling his sleepy stallion to a halt.

Damp mist clung to Joran's clothing and hair as he stopped next to his father and looked where he was pointing. Three figures stood off to the side of the road, near the gate, watching them.

"Who are they?" he asked, not seeing anything remarkable about their appearance. The two men were dressed in faded peasant garb and both had short silver beards. One was dark-skinned and tall. The other stood a head shorter, and was heavier and stooped over. The woman was lithe with a long face and pale hair falling in braids over her shoulder. Her gown seemed elegant and not what a lady would wear traveling. But since they carried nothing, Joran wondered where they'd come from.

One thing was certain—they were wizards. Joran had lived enough years with his father to be able to detect the subtle signature of magic that radiated around them. His father had summoned the wizards' help—but only three had come? He chewed his lip and waited for his father's next move. How could they defeat Sha'kath with only a handful of wizards? The bad feeling he'd had after waking from that disturbing dream now grew into a very bad feeling. His hands clammy, he tightened his grip on the reins as the three came over to them.

Zev dismounted and greeted each one with warm embraces and tears pushing out the corners of his eyes. Joran was taken aback by the unexpected show of emotion. The three other wizards shared quiet words with Zev, their affection for him apparent and unabashed.

Zev turned to Joran after a moment. "Joran, I'm pleased for you to meet our new traveling companions."

Joran's weariness from the long ride and disruptive visit from Cielle dissipated upon greeting them. For after getting down from his horse, they all shook his hands and patted his back, looking him approvingly up and down the way a long-lost relative might after years of separation. Their warm gazes made him feel like family, and he supposed that in a way he was. A family of wizards. How many were left in the world? Would they know? Had these wizards married ordinary humans, like his father had. And like he had?

The tall, dark man Zev had introduced as Relgar said, "Do you always have so many questions, Joran?" With a bright laugh he added, "I would expect Zev would have had answered them all for you by now."

"Relgar, don't tease him so soon," Valonis, the captivating female wizard, said, her eyes locking on to his like barbed hooks. "You'll make him regret coming on this . . . quest with us." She said then to Joran, "He means no harm. Just doesn't like it when anyone gets too serious."

"There will be plenty of time to get serious, Valonis." Relgar narrowed his eyes, and the humor fled from his face. "And Hinwor has enough seriousness for us all." He goaded the shorter man with his words, but Hinwor only frowned.

"I'm pleased to meet you, Joran," Hinwor said, his voice deep and sounding as if rocks were rattling in his throat. Joran imagined he must be very old, knowing aging was inevitable for wizards as well as humans. But his own father was centuries old and hardly looked forty.

"I'm eight thousand, six hundred, and twenty-three years old, young man," Hinwor told him, the corners of his frown edging up a little—but not enough to be considered a smile. Maybe this was the closest thing to a smile Joran would see on the wizard's face. "But I've still got a few good years left in me." He punctuated those words with a grunt.

Joran fumbled thinking of something to say to him. Were congratulations in order?

Zev interrupted his thoughts. "We need to mask our power, and soon." The other wizards nodded, but Joran wondered why.

Relgar turned and looked at Joran. "Too much magic in too small a space. The Destroyer will be able to pick us out—like a shiny red apple hanging from a bare-limbed tree in winter."

Zev turned to Valonis. "Will you do the honors?"

She nodded, then lightly took hold of Joran's sleeve and pulled him close to her, wedging him next to Relgar. Zev and Hinwor completed the tight circle. Zev glanced around, as if checking to see if anyone was watching, but the road remained vacant this cool, foggy morning.

When Joran saw they all had their eyes closed, he closed his as well. And then droning words settled over him, which at first were soft and warm like a sheet of silk, but then grew thick and heavy, smothering Joran as if the very words were made of wool. He breathed through his open mouth, fighting panic, and the air quickened and heated.

He felt Valonis take his hand, and the suffocating sensation eased. Then, before his wonder had a chance to settle, the circle broke apart. Joran looked at the faces around him and tried to sense what had changed, but he couldn't make out anything other than a dull feeling in his mind.

Relgar raised his eyebrows at Joran and said, "There, you see." To Zev he said, "Your boy has a good nose for magic. A sensitive one." He nodded vigorously. "Well, perhaps we should rouse the old king from his bed, eh?"

Hinwor frowned at Relgar's frivolity. Joran doubted that was the first—or the last—time the old wizard reacted in such a manner. The worry lines around his eyes and mouth seemed permanently affixed.

"He's already roused," Valonis said, then a concerned look came over her face. She grabbed Joran's arm once again, and a shock of fear coursed through his body.

Joran stiffened. "What is—?"

Zev held his hand up, cutting off Joran's words. The ground began to shake—a gentle vibration that quickly grew into a sporadic shake that jostled Joran from his footing. Valonis's firm grip kept him upright.

Joran looked into his father's eyes and noted the agitation present there. Relgar and Hinwor were already running toward the open gates.

"Hurry, Joran," Zev said, sprinting after the other wizards, and leaving the unconcerned horses to graze amid the tufts of grass alongside the road.

"What's happening? Where are we going?" Joran asked. But no one answered him. Valonis practically pulled him along as she ran, though how she managed such speed in her gown and stylish laced-up boots, he couldn't say.

They ran past farmers and shopkeepers, past vendors selling wares from their carts and their curious customers. The citizens of Sherbourne seemed puzzled by this odd group hurrying up the road toward the palace in the early dawn hours. If the ground was still shaking, Joran couldn't tell while running over the wide rutted dirt thoroughfare that passed rows and rows of cottages. Over the years he'd made trips to Sherbourne and enjoyed the delights of the city. But he'd never run through it at such a fast pace.

By the time they crested the knoll upon which the majestic palace sat, Joran was winded and worried. When they rounded the western walls and entered the orchard, he joined the others, who had stopped and were staring at the sight before them.

A strange black cloud roiled in the sky above the sacred site— or what was left of it. Another dusty gray cloud choked the air.

The wizards beside him were silent, a somber mood settling over them.

Joran's jaw dropped as a light breeze tickled his ears. Underneath the whorls of cloud lay a gigantic mass of stones, all tumbled to the ground and shattered into pieces small enough to carry in his arms. The stone circle that had stood on the knoll for centuries, protecting the bubbling spring in the center, was no more. This was his nightmare come true.

A strangled cry came from his throat and rang out in the still air. The gryphon had been here. Sha'kath . . .

A door in the palace wall flew open, and someone ran out.

An old man dropped to his knees at the sight of the devastation and cradled his head in his hands.

Zev went over to him and put his hand on the man's shoulder, waiting unmoving while the man wept. His heavy sobs shook the air. The other wizards exchanged glances, but Joran could not tell what unspoken message passed between them.

Only when the man raised his head and looked around with misery etched on his face did Joran realize this was King Adin.

Zev said, "Your Majesty, where is Reya?"

Reya? Who is that? Joran wasn't sure what to do, so he stood by the trees in the orchard, keeping silent but alert. Now others had come to the knoll—townspeople and palace guards. All looked on in disbelief at the pile of rubble strewn about the pristine green lawn. Joran shook, every inch of him, as his nightmare replayed in his mind—the stone slabs at the house of the moon falling one by one. The lake boiling, the piteous cry heard across blood-drenched moors, the sacred sites toppling one against another, shaking the ground. His empty stomach soured.

King Adin got to his feet, confusion on his face. "You're . . . Zev." He looked around him, his eyes red and glinting with tears. "I . . . Reya is inside. She's safe."

Joran watched as the other three wizards came and encircled the king.

"Your Majesty," Zev said, "is there someplace we can go where we can speak privately?"

King Adin nodded, wrenching his eyes from the pile of broken rock that had once been the sacred site. "Follow me."

Joran hung back behind the others, but he could hear what they were saying as they ventured down a long high-ceilinged hallway and into a spacious room that looked like a banquet hall. His knees were so weak, he was unsure he could keep up.

"We need to speak with Reya," Zev insisted with a gentle but firm tone. He looked briefly at Joran, his face suppressing worry. Zev clearly knew what he was thinking . . . and remembering.

"She's resting, but . . . I am sure she will want to see you." Adin signaled a servant over. The girl, a housemaid who had been cleaning the shelves, nodded as he instructed her to fetch Reya—whoever that was. Someone who worked for the king?

After more hallways and turns, they arrived in a chamber that appeared to be a library or study. A beautiful large hand-oiled table, with wood from a tree that could come from no place other than Tebron, was the centerpiece of the room. A dozen or so ladder-back chairs bordered the table facing the king's ornate upholstered chair.

King Adin sat and gestured his company to follow suit. His entire countenance seemed drenched in grief and distress. Valonis reached over and took the king's hand, and although a rather forward gesture to make to the king of Sherbourne, it was clear Adin took comfort in it.

She said in a kind tone, "My name is Valonis, Your Majesty. We've come to help. Can you tell us what you saw?"

The king looked at the others seated at the table. His eyebrows raised just enough to imply his surprise. "You are all wizards—like Zev." He studied Joran's face for a moment, then said, "We've met before, haven't we?"

Joran cleared his dusty throat, wishing for a drink of water. "Years ago, Your Majesty. In Tebron . . ."

"The blacksmith—with the fantastic tale. Your wife had been captured by the Moon." He nodded at Joran, his eyes snagging on Joran's forehead. "You still carry her mark."

Mindlessly, Joran rubbed the imprint of the crescent moon that had been branded into his skin more than forty years ago. His legs finally stopped quivering, but his heart still raced.

Adin managed a sad smile. "I don't expect you would be someone I would easily forget. And now you are here." His last words were a question.

"He's my son," Zev said. "Joran."

"Ah," Adin answered, his smile a little freer now. "And you are?" He looked over to Relgar and Hinwor, who proceeded to introduce themselves.

After giving a polite and somewhat formal welcome to his visitors, King Adin let out a sigh, and his shoulders slumped. He let his gaze wander to the window, which faced south and gave an expansive view of his kingdom. Joran wondered if he had chosen this room because it did not look out over the ruins of the site. Joran knew the site had special meaning for the king, but wasn't sure what. Just what part did King Adin play in all this? Clearly, he knew very well what the destruction of the site implied.

"I heard the commotion from my study. The ground shook so hard, it knocked me to the floor." Adin stood and began pacing. "I ran outside and into a thick black cloud that I knew by . . . my sight that it wasn't smoke or something . . . natural."

Adin's words tangled in his throat, and he cleared it to speak once more. He went on to describe how he stood and watched the stones fall, one by one, and break into bits as if a hand from heaven had come down with a hammer to shatter them all.

"The noise was deafening. And worse, a knife stabbed my heart with each crack."

"Did you see anything in the sky other than the cloud?" Hinwor asked, leaning forward and listening to every nuance of every word.

Adin shook his head.

Hinwor added, "A bird. Something flying."

"No," Adin said. "Not that I noticed."

"You'd notice this," Relgar muttered, no doubt to himself, but the king heard him.

"Notice what?" Adin asked him. Then a look of horrified understanding came over him. He lowered his voice. "Not many days back, I had been returning from the abbey—where I buried my mother. Reya had startled at something. I followed her gaze to the sky and searched the drifting clouds. Something dark rode on the evening's updraft, casting a shadow that raced across the road before us, striking me with a terrible sense of dread." He sucked in a breath at the memory. "A faint cry grew louder and louder. Without a doubt, I knew the source of this powerful winged creature racing overhead, and it sent fear through my heart. I asked Reya to name it for me—"

"Gryphon," Zev said evenly. Adin nodded.

"Reya then said she would send for . . . you"—he turned and looked at Joran—"but she did not say you were the son of a wizard." He looked back at Zev with new understanding. "She summoned you, and that's why you are here." He walked back to his chair and collapsed into it. With hands formed as if he was praying, Adin continued. "Now what? What do I tell my son Yasha, who is the king of the land in my stead? Is Sherbourne under attack? Is there anything we can do?"

"Sha'kath means to destroy the protection against evil in the world, which are the seven sites heaven erected long ago. The Keepers were appointed to protect the sites, but I fear they can do little against the Destroyer. Men's hearts have grown weak over the centuries, more readily succumbing to evil influence and sin," Zev said.

"And so, in a sense, help empower evil—allow it room to flourish not only in their hearts but in the actual world," Hinwor added with his customary frown.

Adin scowled. "So if all the sites are destroyed, then does that mean Sha'kath will have the means to . . . rule or whatever he intends to do?"

"He's the destroyer," Hinwor said, somewhat testily. "His intent is to destroy."

Joran wondered why his father didn't mention the dream. In it, Joran had seen at least three of the sites destroyed. He gulped past the rock lodged in his throat. Had this already happened?

Just then the door to the study opened, and an old, frail woman came rushing in, her face distraught. She clutched a robe around her as if she was cold. But Joran knew fear when he saw it.

"Reya," Adin said softly, gesturing her to sit in one of the chairs. "These are the wizards you summoned."

Adin allowed Zev to introduce them all, and Joran could tell right away the king had great affection for this woman.

"She is the Keeper of this site," Adin said, to Joran's surprise. Zev had only briefly mentioned these Keepers to him, and for some reason Joran pictured young, strong warrior types guarding these sites. He nearly snorted thinking about Cielle. She must be one of the Keepers as well. *Some protector. She can't even keep track of her cooking pots.*

Joran asked Reya, "Are there Keepers for every site? Are you . . . immortal?"

Reya let out a small laugh, but her eyes held much pain. "Joran . . . I am glad to meet you. Adin told me the story of how he'd stayed with you in Tebron all those years ago. But to answer your question: there have been numerous Keepers over the centuries. Sometimes more than one at a site at a time. Whatever heaven decreed for the place and time. The Keeper before me contacted me before he died, and appointed me"—she played with a black choker at her throat—"and from that moment on my task was to watch for the one who would break the curse that lay over Sherbourne." She gave Adin a look that beamed with love. "I thought my years of service had ended and I could go to my grave satisfied, but I see now . . ." Her words trailed off, and she looked forlornly at Zev.

Valonis, who had been silent all this time, spoke up. "Reya, there is no need for you to accompany us on this quest. We seek knowledge, but at this point do not know where we must go—"

Joran shook his head, getting everyone's attention. "The Moon—I mean, Cielle—told us to find the seventh site. That it held the key."

Joran looked at his father, perplexed that he'd said nothing at all about their "encounter" with Cielle. Did he mean to keep that bit of information secret for now? Joran didn't see why.

"Who is Cielle?" Relgar asked.

Zev rolled his eyes. Joran answered, "Long story. And, to be honest, she's a lunatic, and perhaps nothing she said will be of use. But, all the same . . ." He looked back at his father, who merely stared out across the room, unblinking. "She told us the seventh site held the key—the key to the kingdom—"

"Which kingdom?" Adin asked. "Sherbourne?"

"Not Sherbourne," Hinwor answered pointedly. "You already 'hold the key' to this kingdom, Your Majesty." His face burrowed deep in thought.

Joran said, "And she said that the kingdom is in your midst."

"My midst? Here?" Adin asked, even more perplexed. Reya shook her head.

"That's a quote from an ancient text," she said. "More literally it is translated from the law'az as 'the kingdom in the midst of you is.'"

Joran cocked his head. "And what does it mean?"

Reya snuffed. "I have no idea. The words were spoken centuries ago by a holy man." She looked around at the other faces, but no one ventured an answer or a hypothesis. "But I have always known there are seven sites. Even though I am familiar with only this one . . . now gone . . ." Her face tightened in pain, and tears fell from her eyes.

The room fell silent, and Joran could almost hear everyone's thoughts grinding like gears.

Zev finally broke the quiet. "One of the seven sites lies at the end of the world, at the house of the Moon. Joran and I have been there, and from all appearances, the site has long been ignored. It has also been destroyed." He rested his eyes on Joran as he spoke. "Joran's brother, Callen, encountered one of the Keepers in Rumble, south of Sherbourne—on the King's Plain, also called the Valley Perilous."

Joran winced, recalling this dreaded place he'd seen with terror in his nightmare. The putrid stench, blood seeping from the ground . . . the piteous squeal of an animal in pain . . .

Had that been the cry of the Keeper suffering in the throes of death? A chill shot down Joran's back.

Joran cleared his throat. "I have no doubt that site, as well, is no longer standing." He saw the questions in the wizards' eyes and sighed. "I watched the sites fall, one by one, in a dream. The one at the house of the Moon, and the one in Rumble. And there is another site, somewhere underwater . . ." Joran blew out a hard breath as he recalled the boiling, burning water scalding him and seeing the stone slabs at the bottom of the lake fall in slow collapse. "And that site was destroyed as well."

Hinwor said, "We must assume, then, that all the sites are gone—or will soon be."

Reya slumped in her chair, her face in agony. "Where, then, can you go? If this woman, Cielle, has told you to find the seventh site, even if you locate it, it may be too late."

Hinwor scowled. "Do we follow the instructions of a raving lunatic?"

Valonis answered, "Do you have a better suggestion?" She frowned at Hinwor, but Joran could tell she was not chastising him.

Joran spoke up. "Cielle said the Moon has been searching the world over for the seventh site and has not found it. If she cannot see it in all her travels, how will we? Is it hidden?"

"How can anything be hidden from the Destroyer?" King Adin asked.

"If it is cloaked in magic, then perhaps a wizard could find it—or many wizards," Reya offered. "Maybe a wizard hid it to protect it."

Hinwor grunted. "It would have to be hidden well, then. Perhaps under tons of rock. A sacred site set up by heaven does not vanish easily—"

Relgar jumped out of his seat and brandished a hand in the air to quiet the others. "No, Hinwor, it doesn't. But . . ." He narrowed his eyes in thought while scratching his beard. His dark skin gleamed in the morning light now filtering in through a side window. "It is also no easy feat to make an entire kingdom vanish. Yet I was witness to such an occurrence—centuries ago." He cast a compassionate look at Valonis, who paled. "During the battle with Sha'kath at Moreb."

Again the room fell thick into silence. Valonis's eyes glinted with tears.

"Where is Moreb?" Adin asked gently.

"Was . . ." Hinwor said, just as softly.

Adin looked back at Relgar. "How could an entire kingdom vanish? Where did it go?"

"I will gladly tell you this story, Your Majesty. But it is a long one."

He waited for a sign to begin his tale, but King Adin stood and said, "Then let us first break the day's fast and eat. I'll have the cooks prepare us a meal and serve us in here, where we won't be bothered."

Reya rose from her chair and grasped the back of it to steady herself. Joran noted sorrow still weighing heavy on her heart.

"I will make the arrangements," she said, then shook her head. "Odd, all the while you were talking," she said to Relgar, "I kept seeing images of deer. Small red deer . . ."

Valonis made a noise like a strangled cry. Relgar shot her a knowing look, then spun to face Reya. "Did you see anything else?"

Reya blew out a tired breath. "No . . . just deer. But I heard a sweet tune playing on the wind. From some kind of musical pipe."

Joran watched Valonis's face, since it was apparent this held some sort of meaning to her.

"What is it?" Zev asked Valonis. She only shook her head, unable to speak.

"Her sister, Shamara, died in that battle," Relgar said, his voice full of tenderness. She was the wizard who protected Moreb—"

"She was their fairy. Often appearing as a deer, mostly to the children . . ." Valonis said with a withering expression. Seeing the puzzled look on Joran's face, she said to him, "Wizards throughout time have often changed shape and size, in order to mingle among those they protect without arousing fear or mistrust. People sometimes called them fairies, which means 'enchanted,' since they often witnessed these protectors using magic on their behalf. There are legends found in all the kingdoms of the world of various 'fairies' that took the shapes of animals or diminutive people, or even winged creatures like moths or fireflies."

Joran nodded in understanding. He'd heard a story or two about fairies while growing up in Tebron. His mother used to tell what she called "fairy tales" at bedtime, although he couldn't recall any particular ones at the moment.

"When Sha'kath attacked Moreb," Relgar said, patting Valonis's hand as he spoke, "I watched the great wizard Lorec fall. Then, while battling the Destroyer's forces, I was temporarily blinded by a bright flash of light. I lay unconscious for some time—how long, I am unsure, but night had fallen by the time I'd awoken, and the world around me was shrouded in a pall of death and destruction."

Joran looked at the faces intently listening to Relgar's story. Relgar continued as King Adin stood beside Reya, his arm now draped around her shoulders.

"The kingdom of Moreb lay in ruins among the dead. But"— he cast a quick glance at Valonis—"there were few dead compared to the number who had lived in Moreb at the time. I assumed they had been captured and taken prisoner. Although, long searches turned up nothing."

"Did you find Shamara's body among the dead?" Adin asked, glancing at the other wizards' faces, who Joran could tell already knew the details of this story.

"No," Relgar answered. "We assumed she had been captured."

Valonis began to cry, although she held up her head and made no attempt to stem the trickle of tears spilling down her cheeks.

"But what if she hadn't been captured?" Reya asked gently, turning to Hinwor. "What if she went into hiding? What if she used her magic to hide her kingdom?"

Hinwor scoffed. "Hmph, it would take a lot of magic to hide an entire kingdom."

"She was one of the most powerful wizards in this world," Valonis countered, her face lit up by the idea.

Zev nodded. Joran asked, "But where can you hide a kingdom—in plain sight—for untold years? You said the Destroyer can detect strong magic"—he looked at Relgar—"so wouldn't he have detected such an emanation of power?"

"Which brings us back to what Cielle told us," Zev said. "That the seventh site is nowhere to be found on the face of the world. The Moon, will all her power, cannot find it. But she claims it exists."

"So, are you implying that Shamara's possibly hidden kingdom is somehow connected to this missing site?" Joran asked.

"I don't know," Zev answered. "But perhaps it would be a good assumption to start with. Since we're not aware of any other 'disappearing' kingdoms."

"I've been back to the ruins of Moreb many times," Valonis said. "And I've never detected any magic there."

"But were you looking for a people in hiding?" Hinwor asked. "If you assumed your sister and her people had been killed or captured, you may not have picked up any subtle signatures of magic nearby."

Valonis nodded. Joran could see a spark of hope lighting her face.

"If there is a chance she might still be alive . . ." Valonis said. "We need to go to Moreb."

"It's far," Hinwor said with a frown. "And we certainly can't risk using magic to transport ourselves there."

"We'll have to travel by ordinary means," Zev said, "which will take weeks." He looked at Valonis and nodded. "But I agree, we need to go to Moreb and see for ourselves if there is some trace of magic there." He then turned to Reya. "I do not believe this vision of deer is random. It was Shamara's chosen shape. She felt a kinship to their nature."

King Adin straightened and held out his arms. "Then, it sounds as if a plan is forming. One that will require full stomachs to execute. I will go with Reya to have a word with the kitchen to prepare a hearty breakfast and to pack stores for your journey. And then I'll summon the stable master to ready the sturdiest horses. Whatever you need, speak the word, and it will be provided for you."

"Thank you, Your Majesty," Zev said, as the others around the table dipped their heads in gratitude. "Although we could conjure up all we need, from this moment on we must not use magic for any purpose. We can't risk the Destroyer noticing us—not with his gryphons lose over the world. We must appear as ordinary travelers, with no urgency about us."

Joran looked in the faces of those around him. They were in agreement with his father.

Adin gave a nod and left with Reya, and the wizards remained seating at the table, deep in thought.

Joran smirked. He was about to go on yet another long adventure. Thoughts of Charris drifted into his mind. She would find his note upon her return home and learn he was gone. He hated to leave without seeing her one last time and saying good-bye. There was no telling what would happen or if—heaven forbid—he might not ever return to her welcoming arms.

After traveling to the four ends of the earth to rescue her from the Moon, he'd sworn he'd never venture far from Tebron ever again. But at least he was with his father this time as well—who would always be his wolf, Ruyah. His father had kept him safe from the perils they'd encountered years ago. He had to believe he could still keep him safe.

Keep us all safe, Joran added. But what would happen if they encountered Sha'kath? Would they have to fight him? What if his gryphons spotted them and attacked—?

"You worrying is worrisome," his father said to him with a sad smile.

Joran attempted to smile back, but he couldn't help feeling this adventure would hold just as much danger, or more, than his last.

"I know," he said, sinking down into his chair.

NINE

FTER THE dome turned dark pink, signaling night-time, an hour before the council meeting was to be called into session, Ta'sus paced in the anteroom to the council chambers, the palpable agitation and fear of the citizens of his land surging against his heart like giant waves. But what gnawed at his composure even more was Meris's disappearance. For he knew without a doubt that magic was responsible. This was not a case of his daughter losing track of time.

He could not tell Drayna the thoughts that unsettled him, for she would only overreact. The situation called for remaining calm and level-headed. The rolled-up scroll Sapha had found in the dell confirmed Ta'sus's great fear—that Meris had somehow gotten into the secret room, and had discovered something that frightened her, causing her to flee. He'd longed to look at the piece of old hide, to know just what was on such an arcane treasure, but he didn't dare—not yet. There was no telling the consequences of looking upon a relic drenched in magic. And not without knowing what its power had wrought on Meris. Oh, where was she? His gut soured in worry.

"Lord Na'tar."

Ta'sus spun in his robes at the summons. He nodded at Elward, the senior councilor of Me'arah and his closest friend, who gestured him into the small chamber with a concerned look on his face. Ta'sus had never been good at keeping secrets from Elward. Although, tonight he planned on withholding nothing from the group of seven men and women who sat around the table, ready for him to address them before the meeting. The candles lit on the sideboard illuminated their faces and cast hard shadows behind them, and the smoke rising from the wicks made the room stuffy and warm.

Ta'sus let out a long breath and chose to stand instead of sit. He drummed the top of the empty chair with his fingertips as he gathered his thoughts. Where to begin? Should he tell them about the secret room? About the scroll? His daughter's disappearance? Were all or any of these things connected to the dome's failing light? How could he know? The mysteries of magic were the purview of the Na'tar lords alone. Yet, if he didn't explain what he knew about the magic that infused and sustained this world, how could these wise ones offer advice? Keeping them in the dark was as good as condemning them—and all of Me'arah—to darkness. Yet, he knew so little. The story that had been told to him by his dying father had been brief and lacking. There'd been no time for questions, yet Ta'sus sensed that even if his father had been well enough to answer them, he would have declined.

He gripped the top of the chair harder in frustration. He could hear voices outside—the people of Me'arah gathering in the hall, waiting for an encouraging word. He studied the faces of the councilors, which confirmed they looked to him for a solution to the dome's failing light. But he had no solution. He would offer them no hope tonight, no advice other than to prepare for the worst.

Yet, why had Meris gone into the secret room? Why *now*? Ta'sus held on to a tiny filament of hope that the answer to their crisis lay in that room—and in Meris, the only one who had the ability to enter it. Who had *ever* entered it, from what Ta'sus understood. How did the door know to open to her? The realization that his daughter might hold the key to saving Me'arah made him even more anxious to find her. Was she in danger?

His feet trembled with the need to rush out and search for her. What good would it do to address the council—or the crowds eager for a word of assurance? He could give none of them such assurance. Not until he found Meris.

He sucked in a long breath and blew it out, letting his eyes fall upon the councilors waiting for him to begin. "My fellows, I regret—"

Footsteps pounded in the hallway, and before he could continue, the door flew open behind him, ushering in a waft of cool air. Ta'sus turned to see who would dare intrude on their private meeting. No one in Me'arah would show such blatant disregard—

"Father."

Ta'sus's jaw dropped, and his heart throbbed in relief.

"Meris!" He took in his daughter's shining face, which displayed an expression he hadn't expected to see upon finding her. His eyes then shifted to the old, frail woman at his daughter's side.

Meris's arm was linked with hers—this tall woman with long silver hair in braids and dull, watery green eyes. She wore a green shawl and faded threadbare gown that fell to her unshod feet. As hard as he tried, Ta'sus could not place her face, and he was sure he would have met such a woman. She must be nearly as old as he. And the set of her mouth showed she presumed as much authority.

As inappropriate as it was for his daughter to enter unbidden into the council chamber, Ta'sus noted more astonishment than ire on the faces of his fellows. They said nothing, deferring to him to properly respond to this intrusion, but Ta'sus cared little at this moment for rules. He threw his arms around his daughter, with tears pushing out the corners of his eyes, careful not to knock down the woman by Meris's side.

"Oh, Meris. I was so worried—"

"I know, Father. But I'm all right. Everything will be all right."

He pulled back, puzzled, studying her eyes and startled at the strange confidence in her voice. His little girl sounded so grown-up.

He stroked Meris's hair as he turned to the woman beside her, wondering why she was here. He bowed his head in greeting to her. "My lady, I am Ta'sus, the Lord Na'tar of Me'arah."

To his surprise, she cackled with warmth and affection, then took his hands in her cool bony ones. "I know you, Ta'sus." She nodded, her smile revealing old yellowed teeth. She narrowed her eyes and gazed at him with a playful sparkle in her countenance. "I used to watch you play when a little boy. You loved to climb those trees behind your cottage and throw seed balls down on your sisters." She chuckled, lost in some memory.

Ta'sus gasped. She couldn't possibly have known him all those years ago. She couldn't be that old—

"Older," she said, now looking curiously at the others in the room, who were leaning forward, fascinated by this strange old woman. Elward let out a noise that sounded like he found her claim ridiculous, but he covered his mouth with his hand when Ta'sus glared at him. Ta'sus felt his mind tickled in a way that confirmed magic.

"I know you all," she said without malice or condescension. Rather, her face expressed such compassion and affection, Ta'sus didn't know what to think. Who was she?

"Her name is Shamara," Meris told him, answering his unspoken question.

He looked into the woman's captivating eyes, noticing a fiery spark of life in them, in contrast to her withering body and the wan pallor of her wrinkled skin. The name meant nothing to him.

Meris once more took the woman's arm, and Ta'sus marveled at the tenderness his daughter showed this stranger. For surely Meris had only just met her—that was evident.

"Father, councilors," she said, "I apologize for barging in on your meeting, but our world is failing, and the dome's light will soon dim to darkness—as you all well know. So Shamara has come here to tell you why, and what must be done to save Me'arah."

Dagul, one of the youngest councilors, held out his hands, palms up. "But how do you know how to save our world?" he asked, nearly breathless. Ta'sus waited along with his fellows for her answer, his every nerve tingling as if awash with magic.

Shamara smiled and gave a little shrug. "Because I created it."

TEN

LONG, TEDIOUS weeks passed, with the scenery shifting from woodland to prairie to desert as they traveled south and east. But unlike his previous epic journey to the houses of the Moon and Sun, and the cave of the South Wind, Joran never felt as if in a dream. Instead time dragged on, one uneventful moment after another. Although, Zev was often wont to remind him how grateful he should be for the uneventfulness of their days. That was the point, wasn't it—to keep undetected from the Destroyer and his gryphons? They'd seen no sign of their nemesis or his winged creatures, and the whole world seemed unaware of the danger it was in. And sometimes Joran even forgot, until reminded by the wizards through the gripping, terrifying stories they told in hushed voices under the star-studded nights while they camped.

King Adin had graciously provided their three wizard companions fine steeds to ride, as well as pack horses. Joran and his father had fetched their own mounts outside the north gate of Sherbourne after they'd met with King Adin that fateful morning. Their two horses hadn't ventured far—not with all the tall grass theirs for the chomping.

They chose not to take a wagon, as they had little in the way of provisions to carry, and wagons often suffered broken wheels or axles.

Joran would have enjoyed an occasional nap in the flat bed of a wagon over the unaccommodating back of a horse, on a hard leather saddle, but he knew better than to complain. All passing them on the roads traversing towns and open country saw only a simple, weary group of five, with nothing indicating the true nature of the travelers. *If they only knew the combined power of these "ordinary folk," they would faint in astonishment,* Joran thought as they passed a simple farmer prodding a fat hog to the local marketplace they'd just passed through.

Joran had witnessed only some of Ruyah's great power over the years, as his father was not one to flaunt his wizardry or use his ability except when no other option sufficed. He had taught Joran much, but since Joran had a human mother, his powers paled in comparison to his father's. He couldn't change his shape and could barely manipulate natural elements like fire and water. Mindspeaking with animals seemed his strongest gift.

But Joran had never aspired to great power. He'd accomplished in his life what he'd wanted—which was to live quietly in his forest village of Tebron with his beloved Charris, raising their children and working as a blacksmith. When Zev had returned one day with Joran's mother, Rhianne, shortly after the magical adventure he and the wolf had been on, he had been overjoyed to finally meet her. And although she and Zev lived high up in the crags of the Sawtooth ridge behind his cottage, his mother spent much of her time with him and his family, helping raise and teach her grandchildren. Having such a close, loving family was all he wanted and needed. And he remained close to his "stepbrothers"—never sure what exactly to call Callen, Maylon, and Felas. Yes, he was truly blessed with so much.

And because of that, he never felt a need to explore or use his magical abilities, and his father never pressured him—although he insisted he learn and hone skills just in case he was ever in danger. He now wished he had practiced those skills a little more, reluctant to rely on this consort of wizards to always be around to watch his back. Which he hoped wouldn't prove necessary.

On this fog-drenched morning, he rode up alongside his father, whose vigilant gaze kept watching the skies for signs of trouble, even though they'd seen nothing but an occasional threatening rain cloud.

"How much further?" he asked, looking at the row of jagged mountain peaks he could barely make out ahead of them to the south. Just this morning Relgar had told them they only had one more pass to climb, and then they would arrive in the region that had once been Moreb. Joran was more than eager to get to their destination, but then what? What if they found nothing? This trek seemed pointless, and now more than ever Joran wished he was back home with Charris, looking out at the towering trees of Tebron and smelling the moist, cloying scent of the woods. The air here was dry and acrid, and although past the scorching days of summer and a pleasant temperature, there was little to look at. Hills, open plains for miles, a few cottages sprinkled here and there next to pockets of water.

"Only a few more hours," his father answered, his eyes on the horizon. "And then we will crest the mountain. From there we will be able to look down upon the expansive valley where Moreb once sat."

His father appeared distant and undesiring of conversation, so Joran rode up to Valonis, curious to hear more about this once-great kingdom that had vanished without a trace. She had spoken little about it, as even the mention of her sister, Shamara, choked words in her throat. Joran could see now, as he came trotting up to her on her horse, that she was deep in thought, with a glaze of expectation and worry over her features.

"Hello, Joran," she said in her usual friendly greeting. Even though he was considered an old man in his village, he knew that to her he was like a mere child. He had no idea how old she was—none of the wizards other than Hinwor volunteered their ages—but he could understand how he might seem naïve and inexperienced. She always seemed to speak to him in the tone of a kindly old grandmother, yet always patient while amused by his responses to her questions.

She gestured him to come up alongside her. Joran glanced at Hinwor and Relgar, in heated discussion a few paces ahead. Joran frowned, wondering what they were arguing about.

"It's an old debate," Valonis told him, shaking her head and smiling. "One they pick up every time they are reunited, and pick apart."

Joran questioned her with his eyes but said nothing. Did he really want to get in the middle of some centuries-old argument?

"They have been postulating about Sha'kath's whereabouts over the last five centuries. Although many continued to worship him and his god, Cho'sek, in one form or another, no one had seen or heard of him until recently. Or, at least his gryphons have been seen—attesting to his mysterious reappearance."

"Can we be certain it's Sha'kath who is sending the gryphons out to destroy the sites? Couldn't someone else have . . . found those creatures and tamed them, or something?" Joran knew his suggestion was asinine, but he knew nearly nothing about this feared Destroyer. His father had told him little—that he and many other wizards had fought against him in battle after battle, at the dawn of civilization, when humans first came upon the earth and evil tried to make inroads into human society. He knew Sha'kath had some great power, and had influenced the minds of kings and used them as pawns to gain control of their kingdoms. That this Destroyer wanted nothing less than to bring all humanity under his control. Yet, somehow he had been stopped.

"And Moreb was the last kingdom he attacked," Valonis said. Joran no longer startled when the wizards completed his thoughts. He could not mindspeak with them the way he could with animals, but he did feel a bit at a disadvantage that they could hear everything he thought. *At least they are polite enough to engage me in conversation, with their voices, from time to time.*

They rode side by side across a lonely, open prairie as the fog began to dissipate and the summer sun's rays radiated warmth into the air. Like a mirage, the mountains wavered in the distance, appearing much closer than they actually were. It seemed to be taking forever to get to them. Valonis continued.

"Through dogged persistence, Sha'kath had managed to quell the power of wizards in all but this one kingdom. Some had been killed; others had been forced to go into hiding or flee. As you heard us mention, Shamara was one of the most powerful wizards assigned to watch over a kingdom of humans, and Moreb had lived in harmony and peace without a king for centuries. Unlike many kingdoms, this one was a simple agrarian land populated by those who cherished nature and honor. Shamara's noble spirit had drawn those with good hearts to her, to live under her protection, although they had no idea she was a wizard or that she had any influence on them or their kingdom. She often appeared to them as a deer—mostly to the young impressionable children whom she helped mold by her subtle and sweet manner to become upstanding and honorable adults. This was her way—to appeal to hearts, and instill a love for all that is good and precious, and to abhor all that is evil and hurtful."

Valonis grew quiet, and Joran turned his gaze to the ever-receding mountains, letting the plodding rhythm of his weary horse lull him into a stupor. By late afternoon, they had finally reached the base of the mountains and began climbing. Relgar led them along a deer track that twisted around jutting rock but provided an unbroken path to the summit. The mountains were nowhere near as tall as the Sawtooths backing the forest of Tebron though, and by the time evening neared, they gathered atop the ridge and looked down at the desolate plain below.

From where they sat on their horses, all Joran could see was a flat dry land, with no water source in sight, ringed by steep mountains all around, forming a long oblong valley.

"This was once a fertile region," Relgar said in a solemn tone. "Under Shamara's blessing and nurturing, it was a sight to behold. No other land thrived so heartily with such abundance." He shook his head sadly. "The lakes and streams have all dried up or soaked into the parched earth."

Joran's father craned his neck, staring out with keen wolf eyes. "I see no sign of any habitation. Almost as if the ground were cursed, like in Antolae."

"Or like the site near Rumble," Joran uttered barely audibly. He recalled Callen's description of the blood oozing from the ground, and the haunting sounds of battle and screams that lingered on the air as if trapped in time. Just recalling the small bit he had seen in his nightmare made him tremble anew.

Hinwor gave a grunt. "I'll set up camp." He scanned the evening sky, undisturbed by wind or cloud. "The horses need to be fed." He dismounted and led his horse to an area sheltered in part by a rock overhang.

Ever practical Hinwor, Joran mused with a chuckle.

He slid off his horse and stretched. His limbs didn't ache as much as they did at first from the long days of riding, but his spirit was tired from the journey. He sensed heightened emotion from the wizards, now that they'd arrived. Had they expected to see something, or detect magic, from up on the mountain? He stole a glance at Valonis, who sat unmoving on her horse, staring down at the valley below. No doubt she was lost in her memories of her sister, and wondering what her fate had been.

Joran could little imagine the loss and pain she felt, harboring such feelings for centuries. He had lost Charris for a time, but only for a few months—if it had truly happened at all. Even to this day, he couldn't say with certainty if what he had experienced in his journey to rescue his wife had actually been real and not a dream. Yet, the pain he suffered as he worried over her fate had been unbearable. He wished he could say something comforting to Valonis but knew anything would sound trite. Instead, he offered his hand and helped her down from her horse.

"Thank you, Joran," she said, smoothing out her simple gown. Even in such peasant's clothing it was hard to hide her regal beauty.

"My lady," he said, tipping his head in respect to her. In some ways she reminded Joran of Sola, the Sun's mother, with whom he had spent innumerable days in the house of the Sun.

Relgar and Zev came over to them, on foot and leading their horses. They stopped in front of Valonis, then removed the saddles and bridles and laid them on the ground covered with scrubby vegetation. The horses set upon the meager clumps, eating heartily. Joran did the same with his horse, knowing they wouldn't wander far and didn't need hobbling. There really was no better, more appealing place for them to graze.

Zev's face showed empathy. "Maybe once we are down in the valley, in the morning . . ."

"I'm sure if there is any sign of magic, any hint that Shamara found a way to hide her kingdom, we will find it," Relgar added, giving Valonis a quick smile of reassurance.

Joran heard a sound behind him and turned. Hinwor was chopping up old gnarled branches he'd found on the ground, preparing to make a fire. "We should go help him with dinner."

The others nodded, although Valonis seemed to struggle with wrenching her gaze from the valley.

As they walked to the clearing where Hinwor had set down his saddlebags full of food and cooking pots, Joran asked, "Why didn't we ask Reya to come? If there is a sacred site hidden somewhere, wouldn't she be . . . somehow connected? I mean, I would think she would be able to sense the rocks—more so than any of us. I saw some of the sites in my dream, but not once on this whole journey have I had another dream like that one." His stomach grumbled, reminding him how hungry he was. And his hunger was beginning to make him irritable.

"We could use a Keeper . . . or two," Relgar said, nodding. "They are powerfully linked to the sites, as Joran noted."

"But we don't have any Keepers with us now," Zev said, "and I didn't feel it right to ask Reya to take this long journey with us. She is only human, and old, and it would be wrong to subject her to whatever danger we may face."

"But it's perfectly fine to subject me to it, and I'm half human," Joran said a little too grumpily. Sometimes he wondered whether wizards had the same kind of appetites as humans. They ate plenty and often enough, but he noted that they could just as easily go without for days and not care. He recalled that on their epic journey Ruyah had caught rabbits and pheasants for him and made a big show of his catches but hardly ate a bite.

He said, "I think I'll go help Hinwor prepare the food."

"And I think I'll summon a Keeper to come help us with our search," Zev said, his brows narrowed in thought.

Joran stopped abruptly and spun back around. Valonis and Relgar were looking at Zev with curious expressions.

"And where do you hope to find a Keeper?" Relgar asked.

"And how will you summon one without using magic?" Valonis added in a whisper, as if Sha'kath were loitering around the bend and listening to their discussion.

"Oh, just a tiny bit of magic won't be noticed at all," he said, spinning a hand in the air and producing a fat pigeon sitting in his open palm. Before the others could protest—if they had a mind to—his father stroked the docile bird and set it cooing.

"Joran, pull out your paper, pen, and ink. I need to write a message."

Relgar grunted. "Well, why not use magic to conjure up a note, while you're at it?" Joran could tell he was not pleased with Zev's little magic trick. What next? Pull a rabbit out of a wizard's hat?

Zev scowled at Relgar, but Joran could tell he meant nothing by it. "Paper and ink I have. A bird, I had not."

"And how are you planning to get the bird to do your bidding? Which is . . . what, by the way?" Relgar retorted. Valonis merely smiled at their banter and shook her head.

Joran went and fetched the supplies from the pack still tied to his saddle strings. He heard his father answer, "Joran will tell it where to go. He's the best mindspeaker here, when it comes to animals."

Joran came back and handed his father the supplies. "And where do you want me to tell this . . . well-fed bird to fly to? I hope it's not all that far. Couldn't you have conjured up a hawk or a falcon? Something more . . . practical for long distance?"

His father huffed. "This is a carrier pigeon. In some places, they are used to carry messages for hundreds of miles." He patted the bird quite lovingly on its crown, making it coo louder. Joran shook his head, wondering what had gotten into his wolf to make him downright domestic. In his former incarnation, he'd have that bird gripped tightly between his powerful jaws.

Joran shook his head. "I still think she's a bit too fat to make a long journey." He met the bird's eyes. *Sorry, no offense intended.* The bird merely huffed and looked away. Joran huffed also. Birds were not the easiest creatures to communicate with, having flighty minds and little patience. The thought brought little Bryp's face to mind. Even with her flightiness, she and other birds had saved both his and his father's life. Although she had died long ago, her progeny still flitted around his barn and cottage, retelling the tales of their adventurous and brave ancestor.

He looked back at his father. "So where should I send her?"

Valonis and Relgar turned to Zev, awaiting his answer. Zev cleared his throat and set the pen, ink, and paper on a somewhat flat rock in preparation to writing his note.

He straightened and smiled. "To Ethryn and King Kael—Keeper of the first and most ancient of all the sites."

Ethryn? Joran recalled stories of his forbears' land Callen had shared with him. Kael had been a mere boy—heir to the throne—when his brother had visited the desert city decades ago. Joran had no idea there was a sacred site there, or that Kael could also be a Keeper.

"You think he'll come?" Valonis asked.

"Ethryn is leagues west," Relgar added. "What if it takes him weeks to get here?"

"If we don't find any evidence of a hidden kingdom or a sacred site, then we wait. What else have we to do?"

The two wizards nodded. Joran only frowned. More waiting. It wasn't that he was in a hurry to face the Destroyer, not at all. But he hated waiting. And, unlike his father, he disliked mysteries. Ruyah had once told him that the riddles of God were more satisfying than the solutions of man. The wolf loved a good riddle, and this one surrounding Moreb's fate must be the best yet, Joran gathered by the look on his father's face. Much to Joran's dismay, Zev looked positively excited.

ELEVEN

ERIS FELT uncomfortable in the small council chambers, as she had never been inside, and only those who committed serious infractions of their laws ever stepped foot in the room in order to face judgment. But as she stood next to her father, she noted the eyes of all seven of the councilors were keenly observing Shamara—and no doubt sensing the ripples of power, however weak, that emanated from the old wizard. She sensed her father stiffen with amazement as this unexpected visitor spoke to them in her simple, easy manner—as if she were a common citizen of the kingdom and not the creator of their world and sustainer of all their lives.

Meris's mind spun with all the shocking things Shamara had told her in the small lakeside cottage. *A cottage draped in magic and hidden from all.* To think that one person had imagined up this entire world, and not only envisioned it but brought every bit of it into existence. But what flabbergasted her even more was Shamara's declaration of a world—an entire world—somewhere above them. How was it possible there were layers of worlds? If anyone else had told her their ancestors had once lived miles above the dome and had journeyed through rock down into the heart of the earth to this place, Meris would have scoffed. But when Shamara told her how she led the people of the land of Moreb underground and given them a new kingdom in which to dwell, Meris knew in the deepest part of her being that Shamara spoke truth.

Now, it is all up to me, Meris thought with some discomfort. Shamara had assured her that she would teach her everything she needed to know in order to revitalize the dome and help sustain the land so Me'arah could again thrive for centuries. Then, someday in the future, Meris would pass the mantle of responsibility on to her successor—whoever that might be.

Meris let out a long breath, feeling frustration well up. Why wouldn't Shamara answer her questions about the land above them? She only said that a dangerous situation had forced them to flee, and Meris knew she was talking about what was illustrated on the piece of animal hide. But that had been centuries ago. Surely that threat was long gone. Why couldn't they return, then, to the land of their ancestors? Why stay here in Me'arah at all?

As much as she loved her kingdom and its beauty, just knowing there was something beyond the great sea made her fidget with restlessness. Surely if everyone knew what she knew, they'd want to leave—at least to see what the land above was like. But Shamara had sworn Meris to secrecy, insisting that no one in Me'arah could know the truth. That it would foment a great unease and curiosity that could be dangerous. Dangerous to the peace of their kingdom. It would be Meris's task to develop and hone her magic so that she could bring stability and order to the elements Shamara created, as Shamara's power waned and eventually faded to nothing. Meris made a sour face. Here she was being asked to bring light to her world, while all the while keeping everyone in the dark.

When Meris asked how long all this training would take, Shamara couldn't say. But she made it clear there was no one else who could take her place. The thought of wielding such power both frightened and excited Meris. *But why not leave?* The question kept eating at her as Shamara spoke to the councilors.

The men and women in the room were enraptured by Shamara's words. Meris wondered how the wizard would explain to these wise ones just how Me'arah began, for surely they would ask.

"At the time Me'arah was formed, I was married to a man named Garog. He took on the role of the first Lord Na'tar"—she nodded at Ta'sus—"in order to establish some sort of hierarchy of accountability. When we crossed the great sea and arrived in this place, it was barren and uninhabitable."

"Excuse me . . ." One of the women councilors, whom Meris did not know by name, seemed flustered. "What are we to call you? Great Wizard?" She shook her head in humility, no doubt overwhelmed by Shamara's presence.

Shamara smiled and waved a feeble hand in the air. "Oh heavens, no. Please just call me Shamara. We are family, and friends. There is no need to differentiate one from another here."

The woman nodded in gratitude, as did the others seated around the table. The councilor continued. "Thank you, Shamara. But I use your name with the greatest respect and admiration. And gratitude." She looked around at the faces of her peers. "For how can we even begin to express our gratitude for what you have done for us, for all of Me'arah, all these centuries?"

"I did what had to be done." Shamara turned to Meris and said, "And young Meris here will continue in my stead. I will be teaching her all she needs to know to sustain our kingdom. No doubt you will give her your support and make sure all in Me'arah understand the importance of her health and safety. She has the strongest of magic in her blood, but she is only human."

Shamara let the words and their implied emphasis linger on the air. For it was clear that Shamara was anything but human; the magic Meris sensed in her was not just great but different. A wizard, truly? What did that mean? Were there other wizards above?

Already Meris was thinking in those terms—above, below. She would never think of her beloved land ever again the same way. Now this kingdom that once seemed expansive and free felt a bit small and restrictive. She had always thought the dome was endless open sky, but now she understood it was an illusion fashioned from magic. A light hiding tons of rock beyond it. How would she ever look up at the sky now and feel anything other than trapped in this underground cavern?

Her father's friend Elward then spoke. "This is all so very confusing . . . Shamara. Why was this kingdom created, and where did all the people come from?"

Shamara glanced at the faces—all showed the same puzzled expression as Elward displayed. "We once lived across the great sea." A few of the councilors gasped at this idea but no one said a word. "But conditions demanded we leave and start anew. That is all I can tell you." She added in a firm tone that quenched any further questions, "There is no going back. No ancient home to return to." She eyed each one in the room, and Meris trembled, aware of the tinge of magic in her words. Words backed by powerful persuasion and spoken to quell any further curiosity.

Was this the kind of magic Meris had within her—the ability to shape others' thoughts? The idea unnerved her, and made her wonder if all in her kingdom were bespelled. She understood the truth in Shamara's warning to her, when they talked in the cottage by the sea—the need to keep secret the truth of the world above. But she couldn't help thinking it wasn't right to withhold the truth, that everyone should be allowed to choose if they wanted to stay in this hidden kingdom or join the world on the surface. Their true home and land. *This . . . life is an illusion,* she realized. *Like a bedtime story told to put a child to sleep. We are all asleep . . .*

Shamara continued. "We have lived here, in peace, for thousands of years. We have a rich, abundant life here in Me'arah. You all have homes, families, food to eat, and the dome's warmth to nurture and comfort you. You are very blessed."

Meris watched as those around her nodded in understanding and agreement, but she could tell a spark had been lit behind the councilors' eyes. Would they be content to obey Shamara and never give in to their yearning to cross the sea? Even despite the trepidation they might feel upon trying?

Meris's father took her hand and gave it a squeeze. He said, "We will do everything we can to help Meris take on her new role and support her. Just tell us what we are to do." He spoke for the rest, but it was clear to Meris all were in agreement. But what choice did they have? None.

Shamara cleared her throat. "My dear friends, there is nothing, really, for you to do. Other than keep all this secret. No one need know the truth, for soon they will see the dome bright again, and all restored to their natural cycles."

"But is that fair—to keep an entire kingdom ignorant of the truth?" one of the younger councilors asked. The older man beside him nodded and made a noise of agreement.

"The truth is not always helpful to living a happy life," Shamara answered. "You have lived many years without knowing the truth, as had your parents and their parents before them. Did this lack of knowledge deprive them in any way?"

"No, but—"

"How will it help the people of Me'arah to know their ancestors had long ago come from a hostile land and settled here? If anything, it might cause a seed of curiosity to grow into an obsession"—she cast a quick reproving glance at Meris—"and give them a longing for something that they can never have—"

"When you say 'hostile,' what do you mean?" Elward asked, now fidgeting in his chair. Meris noticed her father, too, seemed uneasy, as if questions were roiling in his mind. "Are there other kingdoms, other *people*, across the sea? If so, why wouldn't we want to reach out to them now? Perhaps we can . . . trade goods, exchange knowledge. Why, surely by now, those who had been a threat are long gone—"

"There is no going back, and no one left across the sea." Shamara's tone was firm, intent on discouraging any further discussion of that matter. Meris noted how crestfallen the councilors looked. The thought of other kingdoms was enticing, for now they all knew there was land on some far shore of the great water that edged their kingdom. But how far away? Who could say? Yet, Meris believed that Shamara was right. And if all in the kingdom knew this truth, no doubt some would find a way to construct a conveyance—like the one she saw on the scroll—that could ply the waters, to satisfy their curiosity. And what would they find? Nothing, according to Shamara. She had told her that the way through the rock was sealed and hidden, preventing anyone from ever finding the passage she had carved out that led to the surface, many miles overhead. They were truly trapped.

Back in the cottage by the sea, Shamara had explained that the scrolls Meris discovered—scrolls Shamara herself had drawn—told the story of her people's exodus from the land above to their arrival in Me'arah. Shamara had built the small room Meris had entered, which had been draped in magic and kept secret all this time—until the one to succeed the wizard would open it. That was how Shamara knew who Meris was, for the magic in the room and saturated in the scrolls had merged with Meris's own, urging her to find Shamara at the edge of the sea.

Shamara had destroyed those boxlike crafts that had brought them across the sea, and ever since then, no one had made an attempt to venture out on the water. Meris thought about the scroll that showed a dark-blue sky filled with prickles of bright lights, and the one with the strange water creatures that swam and leaped across the piece of hide. Then she closed her eyes and pictured the towering, jagged mountains bathed in lavender light, with a cap of white topping each peak. The thin chill air she'd breathed in as she gazed at the sight invigorated her, but at the same time set off a niggling yearning to see such a vista with her own eyes. Frustration welled up once more, and she felt suddenly stifled in the small, smoky room, listening to the councilors ask more questions that Shamara chose not to answer.

"Why was Meris chosen, and why now?" her father asked Shamara. The question made Meris swivel her head around to hear the answer.

"As you are aware, Ta'sus, being of the line of the Na'tar means magic runs more strongly in your blood than in anyone else's. You are a direct descendent of my line, and although all in Me'arah have some amount of magic in their blood, through the centuries the Na'tar purposely married those most closely related, those showing the most magical abilities—to ensure that one day, when my power dimmed, someone would have enough magic within them to take over my role as sustainer of the kingdom. The Na'tar, at first, were told about me and the purpose of their line. But as centuries passed, they had forgotten why they kept to such traditions of marriage." She looked away, remembering. "They had forgotten me." She suddenly turned to stare at Meris's father. "Which was my intention."

"But this is such a weighty responsibility for a child," Ta'sus said, again squeezing Meris's hand. "Is there no one else who could take her place?"

Her affection for her father swelled, knowing how much he loved and worried over her. And he had asked the one question Meris had been afraid to ask. For how could she turn down this appointment? And she could tell by her father's face that he already knew the answer. He himself had more magic in him than anyone else in the land—that is why he had lived such a long life and was still hale and strong. He would know if any had more power than he. But had he known her potential? Even she had no idea she was so special—until Shamara had told her.

Meris thought her own abilities were a little unusual, but to be the most powerful person in all of Me'arah? That was hard to believe. And surely her magic was meager compared to Shamara's. It seemed impossible that Meris could do the things that would need doing to keep their kingdom from destruction. Yet, Shamara appeared to be confident Meris could do just that. *But at what cost?* she thought, echoing her father's concern. *How will this change my life? Will I have to hide in some cottage, cut off from everyone else?* Suddenly this burden that had been thrust upon her felt unbearable.

As if her father could read her thoughts, he slipped his big, comforting arm around her shoulders. She knew that whatever was required of her, her father would be at her side to help, and that eased her panic a bit. Still, it irked her, in a way, that no one had asked her what she wanted to do—if she wanted to accept this burden. It was not a choice but a command, and although she felt both honored and amazed, a part of her fought resentment. She imagined herself sitting in some cottage, all alone, for hundreds—maybe thousands—of years. Everyone she knew and loved long dead . . .

Suddenly her throat closed up, and she couldn't breathe. She craned her neck and sucked in air, shaking her head in distress. Her father grabbed her by both shoulders and made her look at him.

"Just breathe, Meris. That's right. In, out . . ."

Finally her airway opened, and the rock in her throat shrank to an uncomfortable pebble. Her father's eyes searched hers. He then turned to Shamara.

"I think Meris has had a very . . . traumatic day. I'd like to take her home and put her to bed." When Shamara smiled, he turned to Elward. "You can officiate the town meeting tonight. I'm sure Shamara will tell you what to say to ease the concerns of the citizens."

Elward nodded. Meris looked at the faces of the concerned councilors as she tried to keep her breath calm and even, but images of the gryphon came into her head, making her skin crawl. She couldn't get out of the small chamber fast enough. She hurried to the door and threw it open, her father following after her. The day's events weighed on her heart as she rushed into the cool night, the subdued pink light of the dome overhead doing nothing to soothe her agitation as her uneasy father, with his arm entwined with hers, led her down the cobbled road toward home.

TWELVE

KING KAEL stood on the bank of the Great River at summer's end, staring out across the sparkling water in the warm afternoon, the sight of such abundance warming his heart. Perthin had wanted to see this mighty river that was the lifeblood of Ethryn, and so at first light that morning, they had ridden out together.

With the king of Elysiel at his side, they watched in contented silence as the many fishing barges floated peacefully down the flowing channel, drawing in nets overflowing with spangling fish, the captains exchanging friendly banter among themselves and their crews. He thought it a strange thing how life went on, with people needing to eat and sleep and provide for their families, all the while a threat and prophecy hung like a sword over their heads. All of Ethryn knew of the war preparations, and had been told about Ezbon—their vizier—and his treachery. But Kael had kept from his people the heart of the truth, sparing them the fear it would strike into their hearts. Only he, of all Ethryn, knew who Ezbon truly was—Sha'kath, the Destroyer, heaven's and man's greatest enemy, whose origins were from the beginning of time.

He lifted his eyes, unable to stop himself from scanning the skies for the gryphons. Although, he believed he would sense them before he would see them. Their evil nature—if one could call it nature in such bewitched fabrications—was palpable. Were they destructible? How could anyone know, or make sense of creatures that had been transformed into sand for millennia—and then revived? Surely they weren't really alive, were they? Well, alive or no, Kael had seen them kill men by gripping them with their fierce talons and dropping them from the heights of heaven to their deaths. Kael could hardly forget the screams of his fellow slaves as they fell . . .

"Kael," Perthin said, dismantling his concentration. Kael realized every muscle in his body was tense. He let out a breath and unknotted.

Perthin nodded toward the south. "Here is Justyn. Your chief archivist must have told him where to find us."

Kael nodded and watched Justyn gallop up on a horse. The sight brought a grin to his face. It was clear the old scholar hadn't ridden much in his life, although Kael knew Justyn had journeyed in this manner from Wentwater to Ethryn. And by the expression on Justyn's face, it was also clear he didn't much enjoy the experience.

When Justyn pulled hard on the reins, his mount slid to a stop in front of the two kings, nearly running them over. Perthin took a step back and laughed. Kael reached for the reins and calmed the horse—who seemed a bit flustered by the rider upon its back.

Justyn swung down from the horse onto shaky legs. "I don't . . . like moving that fast on a horse," he offered in apology, taking in huge gulps of air. "But I . . . wanted to tell you what I found . . . and it couldn't wait."

Kael laid a hand on Justyn's heaving shoulders, and the scholar's breathing instantly slowed down. Justyn looked over at Kael and said, "What . . . what did you do to me? My heart was racing so hard, and I just couldn't get my breath—"

Kael was aware of Perthin's gaze upon him. "I have a gift." He felt like shrugging, but knew it was nothing to treat insignificantly. The gift of healing he'd been given was of inestimable value, but he'd helped so many people over the years that it was mostly second nature to him and nothing he wanted to discuss. Not when Justyn had something important to tell them.

"Come, let's sit over on the bench and you can tell us of your findings," Kael suggested, gesturing to the stone bench perched on a high spot along the marshy bank. He first led the scholar's horse over to the tree that he had tied the other two horses to. With alacrity, the animal started cropping the tufts of tall grass along with his companions.

Justyn had shared a few minor discoveries with them in the last few weeks, but nothing that helped them learn more about the other sites or the Keepers. They still only knew of five, and had no way to know if any of the Keepers were alive—or if that mattered at all. Kael had spent his days visiting his commanders, learning that none had seen or heard any sign of Ezbon or his gryphons, which troubled Kael greatly. The waiting and silence perturbed him. And Perthin had spent his time visiting the city, displaying much more patience than Kael could seem to muster. But then, Perthin was more than three hundred years old, and Kael imagined he had a different sense of time passing than others. Maybe all this waiting seemed like a brief moment in time to the king of Elysiel.

When they were all seated, Perthin said to Justyn, "What has you so excited?"

"I found some references—obscure ones—but they tickled something in the back of my mind, and on a hunch I cross-referenced them. Well . . . to get to the point, I found an old faded scroll yesterday that had the number seven in it repeatedly, but nothing about sacred sites or rings of rocks. But since seven is the number of heavenly completion and the number of the sites, I worked on deciphering it awhile—with the help of your chief archivist, Avad. A wonderful young man, I must say, and full of much knowledge for his years! And he introduced me to his betrothed—who was the one who actually helped me figure out the expression I couldn't quite make sense of. The scroll is written in the law'az—the ancient language of my city—which no longer exists, and there is little to nothing written in it. But we were able to find a key that helped—"

"Justyn, you are circling the point," Kael pointed out, amused at Justyn's enthusiasm. "What did you learn?"

Justyn looked at Kael, then Perthin. "Have you ever heard of the expression 'the seven eyes of the Lord in the earth'?"

Kael felt blood leave his face. Those were the words the messenger said to him when he'd been appointed Keeper of the site—thousands of years ago. Kael had never uttered these words to anyone in either of his lives. Yet, someone had heard them. Another Keeper? Had a Keeper penned that scroll?

"I have heard it," Kael answered, feeling strangely anxious. "Did you or Avad determine how old the scroll was?"

"Old," Justyn answered. "Perhaps thousands of years old. Do you know what the eyes are referring to?" he asked Kael.

Kael glanced at Perthin, who was listening with rapt attention. "The eyes are the sacred sites. I never thought to look for mention of them using those words . . ."

"Who spoke them to you?" Justyn asked, his eyes burning with curiosity.

Kael shook his head. "It's . . . not important. But tell me, Justyn of Wentwater, why does this discovery excite you? What more did the scroll reveal about these seven eyes of the Lord in the earth?"

Justyn played with his beard as he spoke. "There was mention of judgment against the wicked. Something about living stones, whatever that could possibly mean. And then we recovered a partial passage about a kingdom not made by human hands." He questioned Kael with his eyes and waited.

"I don't know what any of that means," Kael offered, then looked at Perthin.

"The sites—or seven eyes in the world—were not made by human hands," Perthin said, "so one might assume this is speaking of a kingdom set up by heaven, in the manner of the sites."

"But what kingdom, where?" Justyn asked. "There is no evidence of any kingdom in the world that was erected by heaven itself. And then there was a line about the key to the kingdom. In the ancient law'az the line literally reads 'the kingdom in the midst of you is,' but knowing what little I do about the structure of the law'az—and that is very little, granted—I believe it would be more accurately translated as 'the kingdom is within you.'"

Kael scrunched his face. "That makes no sense. How can a kingdom be inside you?"

Perthin answered, "Perhaps the writer was using the expression metaphorically or figuratively."

"That was my thought," Justyn said, "As if saying 'heaven rules inside your heart.' The phrase is prefaced by something like 'Don't look to the east or to the west for the kingdom, as if it were far away, for the kingdom is within you.'"

"Which does sound figurative," Perthin said, nodding. "Don't look outside yourself for peace or direction; look inside. But how would this help us in any way?"

"I do not know," Justyn said, "But what might help us is the line that follows the bit about the seven eyes of the Lord in the earth."

Something in the sky caught Kael's attention and snagged his breath. But it wasn't a gryphon; only a small bird winging on the updraft toward them. Relief tumbled through him. He watched it flap its wings in a hurried approach as Justyn continued.

"It said, 'The key to the seventh is hidden from sight.' And I doubt it meant a literal key."

"But that could be just as figurative," Perthin replied. "For if heaven abides in your heart, the key could be something like your attitude."

"Then why say 'the seventh'? That sounds as if the writer was speaking of one particular kingdom—the seventh kingdom," Justyn argued.

"That exists in one's heart," Perthin said, then looked at Kael.

"Or somewhere inside oneself," Kael added, distracted by the bird that was now flying in circles overhead. It appeared to be an ordinary water bird of some sort, but not one Kael recognized. His companions hardly gave it a glance, but there was something odd about it.

"But I don't see how the kingdom in one's heart has anything to do with the seventh site on earth, which has to be a literal site, like all the others. Seven eyes of the Lord *in the earth*," Justyn said.

Perthin looked at Kael. "I was told quite clearly that *you* hold the key to the gate of heaven. Could it mean the seventh site? Are we talking about the same key?"

Kael grunted. "The key to that site is hidden. I'm not hidden, am I?" This discussion was going in circles, just like the bird.

But then the object of his distraction dove, headed straight for Kael's head.

"Look out!" Justyn shouted, pushing Kael to the side as the bird flew to the ground and landed on its feet between them.

After getting over his shock at being attacked by what looked like a docile fat dove, Kael leaned down to examine it. The bird pecked at the grains of sand, perhaps hoping to find something edible. He shook his head, puzzled.

"What do you make of that?" Perthin asked at Kael's side.

"It's a carrier pigeon," Justyn said. "They were used in the Heights ages ago but were thought to have gone extinct. Curious . . ." He bent down and touched one of the bird's legs. "Hello, what's this?"

Kael watched as Justyn fiddled with something attached to the leg.

"Ah," Justyn said, standing back up. The bird looked up at them as if wondering what to do next. Justyn unrolled what looked like a piece of parchment, and Kael's eyes widened in surprise at the size of it once fully opened.

Perthin chuckled and shook his head. "That's a neat trick."

When Justyn unrolled the tiny piece of parchment, it was a full foot long and wide. He looked at it briefly, shook his head, and handed the missive to Kael. "It's for you." He shrugged and then made a face when Kael showed his surprise. "Well, who else would it be addressed to, being sent to Ethryn? You are the king, after all." Perthin laughed even harder at Justyn's serious assessment.

As surprising as this was, Kael had seen many things much more surprising in recent weeks. He read the message, which was written in his language—also not surprising—and learned it had been sent by a wizard named Zev, who required his assistance in a place that had once been called Moreb.

He looked at Justyn. "Have you ever heard of a land called Moreb?"

Justyn thought for a moment, then shook his head, the action quickly followed by a wary frown. "Does this mean we have another long, tedious search in the Great Scroll Room ahead of us?" He let out a tired breath. "May I read that, sire?"

Kael handed him the parchment and waited while Justyn perused it carefully.

"Wizards!" Justyn said. "Are there truly still wizards in the world? I had read of their battles of long ago. Legends and fables—"

"Apparently they exist," Kael said, knowing there were numerous scrolls in the Great Scroll Room that spoke of the noble deeds wizards of old had done. But he also did not know any still remained to this day. "I would very much like to meet these wizards. If they are fighting the same evil we are—"

Perthin asked Kael, "Who is the letter from, and what does it say?"

"A wizard named Zev. A small contingent of wizards need a Keeper to help them in this place called Moreb."

"Help them do what?" Perthin asked.

"It doesn't say," Kael answered. "But we don't have time for this, do we? With war on our steps. I have never encountered any wizards in my life—unless Sha'kath could be considered one."

Justyn looked up from his reading. "There are records of wizards dating back to the beginning of the world."

"Are they good or bad?" Kael asked. "And why would one need a Keeper? For that matter, how did this Zev know I was a Keeper?"

"He probably heard about the discovery of the site, and the speech you gave there," Perthin said.

Justyn looked first at Kael, then Perthin. "You are both Keepers of your sites. Perhaps this wizard is looking for one of the sites and thinks you can help. Can Keepers find other sites?"

"Not that I'm aware of," Perthin offered. "And without knowing who this Zev is, we can't know what his intentions are. He may mean you harm, Kael."

Kael nodded. "He asked me to come to Moreb as quickly as possible. But he did not say where it was."

Justyn's shoulders sagged. "So, it's back to the scroll room. Maybe we can learn something about the wizards and Zev—and Moreb. Then we can decide what to do," he said. "Although that could take much time, and the urgency in the letter was apparent."

"Yet, we have no idea where Moreb is, so until we do, we cannot do a thing," Kael answered. "And what if this place is thousands of leagues from here?" He blew out a frustrated breath. "Why did this Zev not explain more?"

Perthin grinned and held out his hands. "Ah, but we don't need to waste all that time researching. We can go to Moreb in no time at all. And then we can see just what these wizards are up to. If it's a trap and we've walked into danger, we can just walk away," he said, chuckling. "Or rather, *fly* away."

Kael's eyes widened. Perthin's boots! He'd forgotten about those.

"What?" Justyn asked. "What on earth are you saying?"

"A brilliant idea, Perthin," Kael said, although he wasn't keen on being whisked away in a flash of magic. He saw the way Perthin had looked when he materialized in Ethryn. But he had recovered soon enough. "But can you take others with you?"

"I suppose we will find out," Perthin replied.

"All right," Kael said, "but maybe we should first pack some things we might need for this journey." He recalled the day he fled from the tower, with no food or water. Yet, heaven had provided for him and the men he had delivered. Still, no sense being hasty and rushing off without supplies. Who knew how long they would be in that land? And surely this Zev did not expect a neat trick of rapid transportation via magical boots.

"I agree," said the king of Elysiel with a smile on his face.

"I don't understand," Justyn said wearily, shaking his head.

Kael laid a hand on the old scholar's shoulder. "I'll explain, my friend, as we ride back to the palace."

"I don't know if I'm up to a grueling and long journey," Justyn mumbled, walking toward the horses, a frown on his face.

Kael could understand Justyn's reluctance. If the short ride from the palace to the river had agitated him so much, Kael imagined a long trek across the world—or wherever Moreb was—would be the death of him.

Perthin patted Justyn on the back. "Oh, do not worry, Justyn. The trip to Moreb will be short and . . . brisk."

"Brisk?" Justyn's frown deepened. "How do you know?"

Perthin gave him an encouraging smile. "Trust me."

Justyn took the reins to his horse and sighed. "Why should I come? The wizard asked for you," he said to Kael.

Kael walked over to the bird, which just remained standing in the same spot, almost as if it were a statue. He picked it up, surprised it didn't protest, but when he started toward the horses the thing disappeared in a puff of air, leaving him with empty hands.

"Well!" Kael said, staring at his palms.

He turned to Justyn, whose mouth hung open.

Kael shrugged. "I had planned to send back a reply. But I suppose we will just have to show up unannounced."

He gathered up the reins to his horse and mounted. He looked down at Justyn. "You're a scholar, a seeker of knowledge. You still have one more adventure left in you, don't you? Besides, we might need a scholar along to make sense of . . . something we find."

"And hopefully one day, when this is all over, we will need a historian to record the events at the end . . . of all that will end," Perthin added, sounding melancholy.

Perthin mounted alongside Kael. The two kings sat patiently while Justyn struggled to get his foot into the stirrup. When he finally swung up onto the back of his horse, Perthin said to him, "You are the head of the School of Magic. I would think you would want to meet a wizard or two." He added, "And you really won't want to miss the journey to Moreb."

As Justyn sat uneasily on his mount, he gulped, then mumbled, "I can't wait."

THIRTEEN

JORAN RUBBED the grit from his eyes, and as he struggled to sit up, he noticed he was stiff and bruised. Too bad they couldn't use magic. A nice feather mattress on the cold, hard ground would have made his sleep a lot more restful throughout the night. He racked his brain for a moment, counting up the days since they'd left Sherbourne. Twenty-seven. Way too many nights to have slept on dirt. His bones were starting to creak with every movement.

A cool breeze rose up from the valley below and whistled through the rocks around him. The desolation of this place sent a shudder through his limbs. How bleak and lonely. Joran had a hard time envisioning the fertile, lush valley that was once Moreb.

He looked over at the ledge he'd stood upon the previous night and spotted Zev speaking quietly with Valonis. After slipping on his heavy wool sweater, he ambled over to Hinwor, who had a crackling fire going, and was stirring something in the great iron pot he'd brought on the trip. No doubt porridge—what they'd been eating every morning.

A little magic would be nice around breakfast time as well. Just the thought of some conjured bogberry muffins and fresh chicken eggs sputtering in hot butter made his mouth water. The thought of waiting days—or even weeks—in the hope that the king of Ethryn might show up made Joran irritable. His thoughts drifted to Charris, and he wallowed in his missing her, wishing for her warm arms and smile, her body against his to dispel the dawn's chill. He thought of the way her smile twisted just so in her sleep, with the covers bunched around her throat. So many years they'd been together now, and with their sons now grown and living their lives with their families, it was just him and Charris once more in their humble forest cottage, their abode draped with the many paintings and throws and pillowcases Charris had made over the years to add such a colorful and homey touch. He felt out of place in more ways than one in this desolate place, and even more unsure that he could be of any use on this quest.

He plopped down on a large boulder near the fire and warmed his hands. The penetrating heat felt delightful. He said a polite good morning to Hinwor, who merely nodded and concentrated on stirring the pot.

The old wizard never spoke much in the morning, and Joran had learned quickly—by way of a severe look—not to try to engage him in conversation when he was preparing breakfast. The wizard made a somewhat religious ritual out of the whole procedure, but Joran didn't mind so long as he got fed. His job was to wash dishes, but he was used to that chore. Charris had appointed him dishwasher decades ago when they married. That was something he excelled at, although his contribution to this party was trivial. He helped with chores as much as he could, but was at a loss to see why he was on this trip with such company as this. If Sha'kath attacked, he'd be no help. And he had no idea how to solve the riddle of the missing kingdom. He was terrible at solving riddles, as his father well knew. But he was great at getting into trouble, and the last thing he wanted on this trip was for Ruyah to come to his rescue, baring teeth and claws in an effort to save his life.

As Joran mulled over his uselessness, Relgar came and sat beside him, rubbing the chill out of his hands.

"How are you today, young man?" Relgar asked, his deep-brown eyes peering into his.

It was hard for Joran to think of himself as a young man at sixty-three, but he was feeling more and more ignorant and unlearned by the day, being around such ancients. How odd time must seem to them, he thought. If the years sped by quickly now, at Joran's age, did time practically vanish as the centuries—and millennia—passed? What would it feel like to live for eternity? After a million years, would one even notice the passing of a day? Or would it all merge into a blur?

"Your father was right—you are plagued by questions. How do you ever sleep?" Relgar let out a little chuckle, then patted Joran on the knee. "Are you up to a hike? After breakfast we should search the valley for signs of . . . well, anything that might tell us what really happened to Moreb. Although, I can't imagine after all this time, Shamara—or any descendants from Moreb—could be alive anywhere."

"Do you really think there is a connection between the hidden seventh site and Moreb?" Joran asked him, his stomach grumbling at the sight of Hinwor pouring porridge into bowls.

Relgar shrugged and rubbed his neatly trimmed silver beard. Morning light tangled in his short curly hair on his head. "Zev told me about your encounters with the Moon. A fascinating tale. I've never met anyone who has actually spoken to her. Zev tells me she is quite . . . unhinged."

Joran blurted out a laugh, remembering the way her front door to her shack at the end of the world hung precariously on its hinges. "Yes, that's the perfect word for her. She truly is a lunatic."

"Yet, Zev believes within the madness of her words lies truth."

Joran watched as Hinwor approached with two large steaming bowls in his hands. "She was very adamant that we find the seventh site. That it's the key to the kingdom, and is hidden beyond sight." He took one of the bowls from Hinwor; each had a spoon plopped in the porridge. "Thank you, Hinwor," he said with as much gratitude as he could. Their "cook" merely nodded and returned to stirring his pot, no doubt making sure its contents didn't get lumpy or overcooked while he waited for Zev and Valonis to return. There seemed something wrong with a powerful wizard reduced to stirring porridge when the world needed saving.

"The kingdom is in your midst." Joran said, thoughtful. "She can't be speaking of the same thing as the site. The seventh site has to be a real place, like the other six sites. I wonder—did she mean by finding the seventh site, we would find a key that would lead us to some special kingdom? To this hidden kingdom? Or if we find the hidden kingdom, it will lead us to the seventh site? And if we find it, what then? How will it help us stop the Destroyer? This is just too confusing to me." Joran grunted. "But Cielle is always confusing, and full of riddles. I'm sure she knows the answers. We should have traveled to her house instead—and throttled her a bit."

Now it was Relgar's turn to snort in laughter. "Joran, you are the only one I know who has ever been to her house at the end of the world. One cannot just . . . journey there and show up on her doorstep. It can only be visited by way of dreaming."

"How well I know," Joran said, the image of Cielle prancing about her messy kitchen fixed in his mind. He looked down at his bowl of gummy, bland porridge. He could sure use some of the Moon's soup right now, though. He'd never tasted anything so delicious or so magical. As he slurped down his porridge, he tried to remember the explosion of tastes that came with each mouthful of clear broth—nuts, fruit, spices. Cielle may be a lunatic but she was a marvelous cook.

"I don't know why the Moon cast her eye on me. She kidnapped my wife and trapped her in a sand castle above the sea. Charris and I nearly died escaping her. And I had to kill . . ."

He closed his eyes as the pain of the awful moment rushed back to him. Even though it all had ended happily, even after more than forty years Joran still felt the stab of anguish anew. He knew Ruyah was alive and would always live as his father, but for three days the wolf had lain dead at his feet, and Joran's grief had been consuming.

He turned his head and watched his father walking with Valonis toward the fire, their heads close, their conversation low and personal. Joran's heart swelled with love thinking of the ways Ruyah had protected and saved him. Had sacrificed for him. Would he have the courage himself to give his life without hesitation, if the moment called for it? He thought so, although he hoped very much that such a test would pass him by. *If there is a kingdom somewhere that lies hidden from the forces of evil, I would like to live there.*

But then he reminded himself that not every goodhearted person in the world could go into hiding. Hiding didn't take care of the problem of evil; it only ignored it. And evil, without the sacrifices of those with honor and morality, would run rampant and devour the world. *If we can't ever eliminate evil, then we need a new world, one in which evil is not welcome.*

"Relgar," Joran said, turning back to face him, "if heaven set up seven sites on earth to prevent evil from infiltrating and overtaking the world of men, then why would it be so easy to destroy the sites? Why would heaven allow it?"

A sad smile rose up on Relgar's face. "We aren't promised answers when we come into the world, Joran. We are only given hope. Hope that all is not hopeless, and that heaven has a plan." He added, "It is fine to ask questions, but to expect answers will only leave you frustrated and grumpy. Hope is the anchor for our souls. Grasp it and do not let go."

Joran nodded. He remembered that Noomahh, the South Wind, had told him this, although at the time he had not wanted to hear it. Yet, heaven had not only rescued him but also helped him save Charris and reunited him with his true parents. What appeared to be a hopeless situation turned out to be a rich blessing. He knew he should never doubt, but the problem of evil was a complicated one.

Joran sat mulling over these disturbing questions, Relgar quiet at his side. *Probably getting tired of hearing my mind churn over and over*, Joran thought. He watched the other three wizards eat their breakfast in silence, and when they were done, they came over to Joran and Relgar.

"We found a navigable path leading down into the valley. We should camp on the valley floor. There is vegetation for the horses, and maybe we can locate water," Zev said.

"We have to find water soon—if we are not going to use magic to procure it," Hinwor said, looking around uneasily.

"What is it?" Valonis asked, smoothing out her long hair over her shoulder and studying Hinwor's face. She looked entirely rested and unruffled. Joran wondered how she'd managed sleeping comfortably on such hard ground.

The breeze that had been steadily blowing fell into a strange calm. Joran shot his gaze over to his father, but Zev's face showed no concern.

"Magic . . ." Hinwor said, sniffing the air.

Joran threw a questioning glance at Relgar, who shrugged. "He has a nose for magic. But I don't sense anything."

The horses, still tied to their high line, pawed the ground. Joran spoke to them.

Do you sense anything coming?

The horses' heads jerked toward Joran, looking up from the ground they were digging up. One mindspoke him, but he wasn't sure which horse it was from this distance.

Coming? No. When do we get breakfast? We're hungry.

Soon.

Joran stood, spurred by the hunger in the horse's "voice." He started to head over to untie them, but his father stopped him with his hand.

"I feel it now," Zev said, checking the sky with narrowed eyes.

Maybe looking for that pigeon, Joran thought. Zev gave Joran a chastising expression.

"What?" Joran said. *Your pigeon was formed from magic.*

His father mindspoke back—something he almost never did. *It's larger than a pigeon.*

Larger? Joran wondered how a wizard could tell the size of something magical that hadn't appeared yet. At least, he assumed something was about to appear. He couldn't sense a thing. So much for his gift at being able to detect magic.

He stood and waited, watching the wizards' faces. They were all alert, listening, unmoving, but showed no worry. It surely couldn't be one of those gryphons.

Valonis suddenly stepped to the side. A brisk wind gathered, and then Joran sensed it—a powerful surge that made his head dizzy. He pressed on his eyes with the palms of his hands, and dirt and grit spun in the air and pelted him. He heard the horses whinny and felt their agitation.

Zev's hand gripped Joran's forearm, holding him firmly in place. Maybe his father was worried he would run and accidently fall off the cliff. But Joran had no interest in running off. He knew the safest place to be if something awful materialized was in among a group of wizards. If they couldn't protect him, nothing could. Still, the waves of magic unnerved him—despite the fact he was somewhat of a wizard himself. Although he hardly ever thought of himself that way.

Without warning, a loud noise made Joran open his eyes. He realized they were shouts and groans, all coming from a few feet in front of where he stood. Once the cloud of dust settled, Joran made out three shapes, hunched over and tumbling on the ground. He quickly moved back when Zev released his grip. His father's eyes had opened wide in surprise, and not a whole lot of things ever surprised him.

When the shapes straightened, Joran saw they were three men. Two appeared well along in age, but the third had a timeless quality to him, and in his hand he held some sort of staff. Was this one a wizard? Had more wizards somehow heard his father's call and found them here in this desolate land? But the more pressing question was, how in the world did they get here—and find them in this place? Would this display of magic alert the Destroyer?

Joran stood to the side as his father and Relgar reached out to help their visitors, who seemed unsteady on their feet.

"Thank you, my friend," one said to Relgar, who had a grip on the man's arm. This one, dressed in simple, ordinary garb like the others, had the bronze skin and features Joran had seen in many in his village of Tebron. But his shaved head made Joran think of Ethryn. Could this be the Keeper of the site—the man his father had summoned?

The younger man adjusted quicker to the sudden arrival, and looked around with a gleam of curiosity in his face. He smiled, his excitement evident. The third man held his head as Zev steadied him. He had a trim silver beard and long gray hair that flew about his face from the wind, which had now eased into a soft tickle of wind. He seemed thoroughly rattled by their journey.

The bronzed man nodded thanks to Zev, then cleared his throat. "Which of you is Zev?"

Joran looked at the amused faces of the wizards as the three men questioned the group with their eyes.

Zev said, "I am." He chuckled. "I take it my pigeon reached you?"

"Yes," the younger man said, reaching his hand out in friendship to Zev. "We came as quickly as we could."

Hinwor snorted, shaking his head from side to side, a wide grin on his face. Joran had never seen the old wizard with such an unabashed smile. "A lot quicker than expected." He looked the man over, his eyes resting on his feet. "Neat trick, that. Who gave you those boots?"

Boots? Joran wondered. What did his boots have to do with their strange and sudden arrival?

The man's eyebrows lifted. "The former king of Elysiel. My predecessor."

Relgar took a step forward and tipped his head respectfully at him. "Then you are not the king of Ethryn—but . . . you are a Keeper—and the king of your land."

"Yes. My name is Perthin." He gestured to the bald-headed man standing next to Relgar. "My esteemed companion is King Kael." Perthin then nodded at the third man, who was brushing off his clothing and mumbling incoherently. "And we brought with us a learned scholar from Wentwater—Justyn, regent and historian from the Heights."

"Two Keepers, two kings, Zev," Valonis said, entirely pleased. "We are honored by your presence, and thank you for coming to our aid."

The man called Justyn turned and looked in each wizard's face. "You are all . . . wizards?"

Zev nodded. Justyn's face lit up with amazement. "I've never known a wizard. And until yesterday never knew any existed. This is . . . quite humbling."

"We are pleased you all came. We can use your assistance," Relgar said, then proceeded to introduce the others. Joran caught a glimpse of Valonis's face, which shone with joy. He hoped she wasn't holding too tightly on to that hope Relgar talked about. Dashed hopes were more disheartening than not hoping at all.

When the introductions had all been made, King Kael asked in his curious accent, "So what do you need a Keeper for? Is there a sacred site nearby?"

Hinwor said, "That's what we are hoping to discover. We are looking for the seventh site. We believe it's hidden, and that it may perhaps have something to do with the ancient kingdom of Moreb."

The faces of all three of the visitors paled. The morning settled around them into quiet as the wizards waited with intrigued expressions. It was clear to Joran these visitors knew something important about the seventh site.

King Kael found his voice. "We, too, have been searching for the seven sites—in the scrolls at Ethryn."

"I was told to seek out the king of Ethryn." King Perthin looked at each of his listeners, one by one, his manner and speech belying his apparent youth. Joran could only conclude this king was much older than he looked. Perthin continued. "And was told that Kael was the first and last, the beginning and end. And that he holds the key to the gate of heaven."

Joran about choked on the king's words, and noted all the wizards looked as shocked as he felt. This could not be coincidental—that King Kael had come to them. But what did those words mean? This one man held the key? Just what did he know about this seventh kingdom, if anything?

Relgar spoke excitedly. "Well, it's evident heaven has brought us all together in this fight against Sha'kath." He let his words sit in the air and studied the kings' faces. "I see you know who Sha'kath is. That is interesting . . ."

King Kael frowned as if plagued with painful memories. "Unfortunately I know him well. I knew him at the dawn of history—a great and powerful wizard who helped build the tower."

"Tower?" Valonis asked, gulping. "How . . . could you have known him so long ago? You are human." Joran shared her surprise. This was a tale he wanted to hear.

The king gave her a shrug. "It's a long story—"

"And we have a long trek down into the valley, and the horses are hungry," Hinwor said, his usually stern eyes sparking with curiosity. "We will hear your story as we make our way down to the valley—where the great kingdom of Moreb once thrived."

The horses! Joran didn't mean to be rude, but he needed to feed their animals. He rushed over to the saddlebags lying on the ground and pulled out their bag of feed, which would have to do until grass was found for them to graze on. He tuned out the grumblings of the horses as he fed them, one ear listening to the conversation behind him.

King Kael spoke. "We will tell you all we know. I hope you can shed some light on this mysterious kingdom and enlighten us with what you've learned about the seven gates of heaven. And maybe explain what the ancient dead king of Elysiel meant when he called me 'the first and the last.'"

Relgar sucked in a breath. "A dead king spoke to you? This tale is getting more interesting by the minute."

"Then let's pack up and head out," Hinwor said, flitting his hands about. "The sooner we do so, the sooner we can hear the whole astonishing tale."

Joran turned and looked at Hinwor, who scurried about faster than Joran imagined possible. He laughed. The other wizards watched Hinwor too, with puzzled expressions. Clearly this was a rare event—seeing Hinwor excited about something.

But Joran understood his excitement. He, too, couldn't wait to hear what two kings and a scholar had to tell them about the sites and Sha'kath. And what of this tale of the king of Ethryn's having lived centuries in the past? Could it be true? How could a mere human accomplish such a feat?

Energized, he hurried to ready the horses for travel as the others quickly broke up camp and packed all their things in the saddlebags. Within minutes they were ready. But would they find anything once they arrived in the valley?

Joran could hardly think. What esteemed company indeed. Five wizards, two kings—who were also Keepers of sacred sites— and a noted scholar from Wentwater. If between them they couldn't find any trace of ancient Moreb or Shamara, then surely no one could.

FOURTEEN

KING PERTHIN paced on a rock ledge at the southern edge of the valley. Evening cast a radiant hue of gold across the horizon, and the air was deathly still. Off a short distance away, their horses pulled at clumps of grass next to the small spring of fresh water they had found. The stark beauty of this place moved him. He wasn't certain why he was racked with such a lonely, empty feeling, but he assumed it was caused by the absence of awareness. He had only been away from Elysiel a few short weeks, but this disconnect with his land created an unpleasant restlessness.

For three hundred years he'd felt, heard, and seen every breath and flutter of every living thing—plant, animal, human—within the borders of his kingdom. Not a second passed without him being linked to millions that lived under and above the ground, and flew in the skies. His kingdom lived in him and comforted and filled him. Being separated from Elysiel was like having a missing limb.

He looked at the staff in his hand and watched the heart beating steadily in the handle. *More like a missing heart.*

Perthin pushed aside the encroaching unease and watched the others in his party search the ground and rocks for signs of magic. They had all shared what they knew about the sites, and yet, they were no closer to understanding the many riddles plaguing them.

They now were informed of six sites—Perthin had listened with rapt attention when Joran told his tale about visiting the house of the Moon and the site at the base of the stairs below her shack. What a strange place to set up a gate of heaven. But maybe in an odd way it made sense. If the sites were the seven eyes of the Lord in the earth, who better to view the entire world, night after night, than the Moon?

What distressed Perthin the most was the abiding sense that his own sacred site—the place he had been appointed to protect and cherish—was surely destined to be destroyed. If it wasn't already. He had no way of knowing whether Sha'kath had attacked yet, but since the gryphon had flown overhead—the precursor to destruction of a site—it was only a matter of time.

Ever since the ghost of King Cakrin had told him an inevitable end was coming, Perthin refused to believe it. He had to hope this was one future that could be changed. The crystal slabs had never shown him this or any such vision—not at any time in the last three hundred years. Yet, he'd be a fool to discount what the previous king of Elysiel said. The ghosts of past kings never lied or misled with their words. *But maybe his words were symbolic, not literal.* Perthin clutched a small spark of hope that his site—and his kingdom—would endure.

But why should his site be miraculously preserved when Sherbourne's had not been spared?

Zev told them about their visit to the prominent city to the west and how the site there had been destroyed only moments before their arrival. Joran had shared how Cielle decried the destruction of her site at the end of the world. Justyn had been given a vision showing the site at Wentwater destroyed. And in Joran's dream, the site at Rumble was annihilated. That left only Ethryn and Elysiel, of the six known sites . . .

Perthin did nothing to hold back the tears spilling down his cheeks. Yet, as much as he mourned for his kingdom, he couldn't help but see clearly the peaceful visage of King Cakrin as he told him, "Do not be so forlorn, Perthin. Endings are merely beginnings."

"The time of the end . . . the fullness of time . . . everything comes to an end."

Perthin would be the last king of Elysiel. Did that mean Elysiel itself would be destroyed, or did it mean something else? As he wiped his wet cheeks, he mulled over and over Cakrin's words.

He stood unmoving as night tinted the sky to a deep blue. In the failing light, the others gave up their search and gathered on the ledge where Perthin stood, speaking in hushed tones. But Perthin didn't detect any sense of defeat. Yet, the valley before them was enormous. How many days or weeks would it take to scour the region for traces of magic?

Behind him, the rock walls of the valley towered, etched with deep crevices drenched in thick shadows. The group shared a companionable silence for a moment, then Relgar spoke.

"Every time I come here, it's the same." He looked out across the long stretch of barren, dusty land—a patchwork of grassy plots. "I can see Moreb in all her beauty. The rivers, the meadows splattered with colorful wildflowers, the herds of deer grazing . . ." He released a long breath and looked at Valonis.

Perthin saw the pain in her face. She had told him about Shamara, her sister, who had been lost—or somehow vanished—during the great battle with Sha'kath. Perthin didn't need to hear her thoughts to know exactly how she felt. He had lost so many he'd loved over the long years. In some ways he felt a kinship to these wizards, who also suffered the anguish of seeing those they cared for live much shorter lives than they.

Relgar continued. "When Shamara left, she took all her magic with her. And not only that—her blessing upon the land. Without her, this place reverted to its natural state." He turned and gave Valonis an apologetic look. "I'm sorry, Valonis. I can't sense her presence anywhere. Nor can I find any signs at all indicating anyone survived Sha'kath's attack, other than those who stumbled out of the valley on their own weary legs that day."

Valonis looked in each face. *Looking for hope*, Perthin noted.

Zev laid a hand gently on her arm. "We've only been looking one day. Maybe tomorrow, or the next day—"

Joran made a noise in his throat, causing all to turn to look at him. In the darkening night, Perthin could not see his expression, as he stood a few feet behind Zev.

King Kael, beside him, pursed his lips and said, "Do not be discouraged, Joran. If there is a sacred site, heaven will reveal it. Just as he revealed the site in Ethryn to me—"

"That's not the matter," Joran said, somewhat testily. He walked to the lip of the rock ledge and looked up at the sky.

The others said nothing. All Perthin could hear were the horses snuffling as they cropped the patches of grass and their occasional soft snorts.

Joran stood as a dark silhouette against the even darker sky, unmoving, stiff. Zev came alongside him, but neither spoke. Then Joran spun about, and Perthin noted his face was full of alarm. His eyes flitted around him, searching for something.

"What is it?" Hinwor asked him, taking one of Joran's arms in his grip.

"You don't hear her?" Joran asked, first questioning Hinwor, then looking into the others' faces.

Only Zev seemed to know what Joran was talking about. "Cielle." He made a noise like a snort. "She's singing."

"And I wish she wouldn't," Joran said, with a sour expression. "Her voice is grating."

The others looked around.

"You mean the Moon?" Justyn asked. "Or . . . the woman who tends the Moon's house?"

Relgar turned to him. Now all were standing on the edge of the rock platform, staring out across the valley. He said, "Same person. The Moon and Cielle."

"But how can that be?" Justyn asked, then shook his head. "Never mind. I'm sure I wouldn't understand even if you tried to explain it to me."

"Where is she?" Valonis asked, her tone merely curious. However, Perthin could not miss Joran's agitation. And Hinwor's touch was doing little to calm him.

Joran looked into the faces beside his. "So you don't hear her?" he asked. He turned to his father. "But you do."

Zev nodded. "Maybe because I was with you the last time."

Joran shook his head in apparent frustration. "What does she want with me now? Will I never be rid of her? And why isn't she showing herself?"

"She is," Valonis said, pointing to an outcropping of rock fifty feet in front of them. "There."

The breath Joran exhaled was loud enough for Perthin to hear from where he stood. All eyes lit upon the figure coming out of the shadows. Kael came and stood beside him, his arms crossed over his chest.

What a curious, perplexing creature! Perthin thought, watching this lithe and lean woman dance about on her toes, swirling and flinging her long silver hair. Bracelets jangled on her wrists as she floated toward them. Perthin looked in her heavily painted face, astonished by her sudden appearance. How could this be the

Moon? Another thought struck him. *And she's a Keeper of a site.* Was that why she'd shown up—to help find the missing gate of heaven?

"What do you want, Cielle?" Joran asked as the "woman" sidled up to him, smiling, and tickled his chin. He jumped back from her touch, and Perthin saw Relgar chuckle. If any of the others knew Cielle, they didn't show it. Other than Zev, who—to Perthin's surprise—nodded in polite acknowledgment to her.

"My silly potato! You know why I'm here." Her singsong tone turned mean in a fraction of time. "To help you stop the Destroyer who destroyed my beautiful rock garden! And to show you the way to go—to find the seventh site."

Perthin was a bit surprised at Joran's critical expression. Wasn't that what they all wanted to know—where the seventh site was hidden?

Joran rubbed his eyes in weariness. "You told me it was hidden. That the Moon had searched the face of the world and could find no trace of it."

Cielle threw back her head and laughed, sounding like a stuck pig. Perthin winced, as did his companions. The old scholar put his hands over his ears.

"But now," Cielle drawled, "my honeycomb! With all these wizards . . . and all this magic . . ." She shot each wizard a knowing glance, as if she shared a joke with them. "Well, the Moon was curious and wanted to see what her little snickerdoodle was up to with all these *very important people* . . ." She poked her finger into his chest to emphasize those last three words.

"The point?" Joran asked, a bit snippy. Perthin could hardly believe he was hearing this conversation. And he wondered why no one else was talking to her. He caught a hint of amusement on Zev's face.

Cielle blew out a breath and glared at Joran, placing her hands on her hips. "I told you before, back when you visited me all those ages ago. And why haven't you come back? It's lonely at the end of the world, and it would be nice to have some company from time to time. Do you know how absolutely unexciting it is to cook for oneself. Why, it's hardly—"

"Dear Cielle," Zev said gently, causing the woman to shut her mouth and study his face. "What did you tell Joran about the Moon when he visited with you?"

"Oh. That the Moon is forgetful. And do you know what she forgot? No?" She looked around at her captive audience. "No? Huh. Well, let me see . . . oh, yes. She is forgetful, and it's hard to remember all the millions of events in history that she witnesses day after day after tedious day . . ." She sighed with bluster and turned to Joran.

"So, my little bumblebee—here's the thing. As soon as she saw you all up there"—she pointed up the rock face to the place they'd camped the previous night—"she remembered!"

Silence fell around them as they waited for more.

"Remembered what?" Joran finally asked in a long exhale.

Cielle leaned close and lowered her voice so Perthin could barely hear. "The awful battle." Cielle looked far across the valley, shaking her head. Perthin saw tears dribble out of her eyes. "All that screaming and death. Oh my! And all those poor, sweet people, running hither and thither, with nowhere to go, no way to escape . . . those beastly creatures flying overhead." Cielle shuddered, causing all her jewelry on her wrists and the silver earrings on her ears to jangle loudly.

Perthin caught a glance of Valonis's expectant face. She alone ignored the histrionics of their visitor and seemed to be listening for the meaning behind all the clutter.

"I remember the battle all too well," Relgar offered. "I was there."

Cielle swiveled in his direction and said, "Of course you were, dear boy." She spun just as quickly to face Valonis. "And your *sister* was there too." She tightened her mouth and leaned in to Valonis. "And you *lost* her."

Valonis drew back, eyes wide, as if Cielle had struck her face. Perthin sucked in a breath. How could this woman be so rude?

"But now you'll find her!" Cielle said, clapping her hands in delight and ignoring—or perhaps failing to notice—the effect her slight had on her listeners. She turned to Joran. "Isn't that right, my little pumpernickel?"

"What do you mean?" Joran asked without hesitation.

Cielle put her hands on her hips and scowled at him. The dark bowl of night overhead was now sprinkled with stars, and the air was turning chilly. Perthin wrapped his arms around his chest, waiting for Cielle's answer. *Maybe she goes round and round in circles because that's what the Moon does endlessly, without ceasing.* He hoped she would circle back to her point—if she even had one. What a strange creature!

"Listen, muffin. For an old human you are pretty dense. Well, part human. Part dense." She threw her hands up in the air and, to Perthin's surprise, stormed off back toward the rocks she'd come out of. "But you'll figure it out soon enough," she added before she slipped into a crack in the rock and disappeared.

No one moved. Zev finally spoke. "Well."

Hinwor looked at him. "Well? That's all you have to say?"

Zev shrugged and Hinwor grunted. "Why did she bother to come? She didn't tell us anything."

"Maybe she wants to help," Justyn said, staring at the place where she vanished. "Where did she go? And how did she get here?"

Relgar patted Justyn's arm rather patronly. "Best not ask such questions. They will only give you a headache."

Hinwor brushed his hands together and cleared his throat. "We must set up camp. It's getting too dark to see."

"But the moon should be out shortly—" Relgar said.

Perthin saw Joran bristle. Another scowl came over his face. "She's here now. Making one of her grand appearances." His voice was laced with cynicism.

All turned to look at the eastern sky, where a piece of the moon lifted up from behind the towering rock wall of the valley and oozed light over its edge. Perthin startled at the color of the orb—blood red.

"What does it mean?" Justyn asked, fear streaking his face.

"She's angry," Zev answered. "Which could be a good thing . . . or a bad thing."

"The Moon's anger can be destructive. Cielle told me how, when the Moon gets mad, the tides rise into giant waves and destroy shorelines and cities, and she rocks the earth with temblors," Joran said nervously. He kept his eyes on the bulging shape rising higher in the sky.

Perthin walked over and stood next to him. "If she's angry at Sha'kath, I don't think she will hurt us." *What is she really up to?*

"Not on purpose," Joran replied. "But you've noticed she's a little scatterbrained. She may do something foolish and forget we're in the way. We must look like tiny ants crawling over the dirt to her. What's one ant, more or less?"

"She seems to be fond of you," Zev said with something of a mischievous smile, then added quickly, "in her own quirky way."

Joran rolled his eyes.

Hinwor grumbled something, then marched off to where they'd put all their belongings. Joran had told him earlier that

Hinwor had a thing about punctuality. He seemed irritated that Cielle's visit threw off his schedule; it was past dinnertime.

Perthin wondered why they showed little excitement over Cielle's words. She told them she would show them where the hidden site was. But, he supposed, they did not believe her.

Kael went over to Joran and laid a hand on his shoulder. "Come. Let's tend to the horses, put them on a high line. Best they're not left to wander at night—not with . . . that." He nodded at the moon, which cast its crimson light across the valley floor, like spilled blood. Although, the horses didn't seem a bit perturbed by the strange goings-on.

Just then the light radiating from the moon shifted in hue, from red to yellow to blinding white moonlight. Perthin squinted at the sudden change, and Kael threw a hand over his eyes. Joran merely studied the moon with narrowed eyes as it lifted even higher above the rocks.

"Look!" Zev said, pointing across the valley to a spot perhaps a half league away. "Do you see?"

Perthin tried to make out what Zev was pointing at, but the glaring light occluded his sight. Kael said to him. "It's like the light that shot out from heaven into the sacred site—when I was appointed Keeper all those centuries ago." His voice sounded wistful to Perthin. Justyn came over and huddled close to them.

"What does it mean?" he whispered.

"I don't know," Kael answered, "but this is ethereal light, not anything of this world."

"Light from heaven?" Justyn asked.

Kael said nothing. He stood, unmoving. Perthin watched as Zev swung himself up onto his horse's bare back and without a word rode off to the place he'd indicated.

"I see it now," Kael said. "A shaft of light hitting the rock, in just one place."

The other wizards hurried to their horses. Perthin noted that Hinwor made haste to run after Zev, abandoning his dinner preparations.

Joran called over to Perthin and his two companions. "Set up camp. We'll be back shortly."

Justyn looked at Kael, then Perthin. "I'd really like to see what's there."

"Then let's go," Perthin said. He winked at Kael. He couldn't help but feel a bit amused at ruffling the old scholar a bit. But the boots he wore were a gift not to be ignored. He now wondered why he'd never thought to use them over the centuries, to visit other places and meet other Keepers. Which made him realize he could ask the boots to take him to wherever the remaining Keepers happened to be at the moment—whichever ones were still alive. He would propose this suggestion to the wizards at the right opportunity. But for now, it was just possible this lunatic may have directed them to their prize—the hidden seventh gate of heaven.

"Oh no," Justyn said, looking down at Perthin's magical boots. "I think I'll walk."

Kael laughed. "Come on, old man. It will take you too long. Just hold on to Perthin's shirt. Like last time."

Justyn blew out a long breath. "All right . . ."

He grabbed fast to Perthin's right arm, while Kael grasped the other.

Perthin chuckled at the look on Justyn's face and said, "Take us over to that shaft of light," and pointed at the illuminated rock.

Perthin squeezed tight his eyes, and when he opened them, they were standing before a large cut in the western rock wall of the valley, where light streamed in like milk—revealing a partial cave. The dizziness subsided almost instantly—perhaps due to the short distance they traveled. Justyn, although clenching his teeth, seemed none the worse for wear. Kael merely smoothed out his clothes and wiped dirt from his curious eyes.

By the time they'd dusted themselves off and the whirling wind abated, Zev rode up on his horse, his face showing surprise.

When he slid off his mount, he looked at Perthin and said, "Hmm, I supposed I could have asked you to bring me here and spared the horse the trouble." He peeked into the small cave that was tucked away from view. "What do we have here?" Bathed in bright light, the four entered as the other wizards rode up to Zev's horse and dismounted.

"There's nothing here," Justyn said, feeling the uneven sandy rock walls with his hand.

Zev walked around the six-foot-deep enclosure and shook his head. "No, I sense something . . . faint but . . ."

Relgar hurried in and stopped short when he'd run out of room. "What did you find?" he asked Zev, noticing the look on his face. Only a shaft of cold moonlight filtered in now, and when the rest squeezed inside, Perthin could hardly see a thing. The air became stuffy with so many breathing in such a small space.

"Why did the Moon shine her light on this cave?" Joran said, running a hand through his hair, which had gotten tangled from the ride over. "It's just rock. Do you see any markings on the walls?" he asked his father.

Zev shook his head.

Valonis spoke up. "She was here." Her voice sounded taut, and Perthin looked at her and saw her skin flush with color. She put her hand on one wall, then pressed her cheek against the rock. "I feel her. She's alive."

"What?" Justyn said. "In the rock?" He looked at Perthin and Kael. Perthin shrugged.

"Do you mean Shamara? Your sister?" Kael asked.

"Give her room," Relgar said.

Hinwor inched his way out of the cave. "I'll wait outside." That freed up a little more space, allowing Valonis to move down the wall. She kept her cheek against the wall and closed her eyes.

"I don't understand . . . but I feel her magic. It's very close, very strong." She opened her eyes and looked at Zev. "We need to get through the rock."

Zev's eyebrows lifted.

"But this is a mountain," Joran said. "Solid rock. Do you mean to create a tunnel leagues long to come out some other side?"

Valonis slid her hand slowly around the wall in one place, then squatted and drew her hand down to the ground. Her face paled.

"Not some other side, Joran," she said. "Down."

"Down?" he asked, his face wan.

Valonis nodded. She looked at Zev, then at Relgar. The two wizards nodded back at her.

Perthin held his breath as Valonis shut her eyes and laid both hands on the ground. As she squatted there, she muttered words Perthin could not decipher; they were in a language he had never heard before.

Within a moment a rumble started, shaking the walls of the cave. Perthin felt the magic vibrate, pinging off the rock and increasing in frequency and volume. A roar of noise built to a deafening cacophony. Valonis's face tightened under the strain of effort, and her whole body trembled.

"It's . . . the spell is strong . . . too strong . . . there has to be a weak spot . . . somewhere . . ." She then gritted her teeth and let out a growl.

Perthin pushed back against the wall of the cave as rocks flew through the air and crashed down on them from the ceiling. But no one ran out. They braced themselves and protected their heads with their arms as the cave broke apart.

Perthin heard Hinwor's voice. "What in blazes is going on in there!"

But by the time he pushed his way into what was left of the cave, Valonis tossed her hair over her shoulder and straightened up. The shaking stopped, and the last bits of grit floated lightly to the cave floor.

When the dust cleared, Perthin gasped, along with the others.

The cave was no more. The entire side of the mountain was demolished. The open maw of night overhead was void of stars. Only the moon hung above, bright red and simmering, and Perthin sensed something emanating from it—something that felt like fury.

And at their feet lay a staircase of gray rock—leading far down into the heart of the earth. A dark passageway that had no doubt been hidden and unused for centuries.

• PART THREE •

A LL RIGHT, if you stop wiggling, I'll begin."

Alia waited for Aron to get his covers just right, which he did every night. The sheet had to lay smoothly at his chin, and all his stuffed animals had to be righted and staring ahead, as if listening. Big Pig and Puppy had to flank him on either side, glassy-eyed sentinels of his dreams. Alia wondered if he told them stories in the dark. She thought he might; he loved stories that much.

She thought of a life long ago that equated darkness with uncertainty, night with fear. A world steeped in darkness and one she worried had long disappeared while her people lived pro-tected but naive underground. For Aron, the dark night contained nothing frightful. No monsters hiding under beds or in closets.

No evil riding on the wind seeking to squelch all that is good and holy. Now light and darkness were equals—two sides of one coin, like day and night. No longer could anyone hide despicable deeds under the cloak of darkness, for the light that heaven brought to shine upon creation banished all shadows and burned without ceasing. A light of goodness, purity, and truth. A light that healed and consoled and mended broken hearts.

"Okay, Momi. I'm ready!"

Aron's bright face made her smile.

"Let's see . . . where did I leave off last night? Oh yes, where Shamara brings the boats to shore and the people step foot in their new land—"

Aron scowled. "You already told that part—two nights ago."

Alia nodded and pursed her lips. "That's right. I did. Silly Momi. Well, I think I'm at the part where she appoints Nehum, her grandson, as Na'tar?"

"Yes, that part. And the part about the *secret room*!"

"And the cottage she built on the shore of the great sea—"

"Just tell the story, Momi," Aron urged with a yawn. He rubbed his eyes and settled back into his pillow.

"All right." She drew in a breath and looked at the crystals sparking moonbeams into rainbows that splashed color on the walls. The air was thick with the fragrance of amani flowers blooming just below the open window. The curtains huffed in the light breeze seeping into the bedroom. She shook her head. Sometimes the saturation of peace astonished her, as it did now.

Alia spoke in a soft tone, knowing Aron would hardly last more than ten minutes.

"So many years passed. Year after year after year. Shamara raised her three daughters, and all in the kingdom of Me'arah prospered. The last attempt to cross the sea had been more than two hundred years ago, and the people lost their yearning to leave, to return to what they'd left behind. Like a soporific, the spell Shamara cast upon them all made them forgetful, and although it took nearly a millennium, forget they did.

"Shamara buried Garog only fifty years after entering the cavern, for he was merely human. But her daughters, with their strong 'fairy' blood, lived very long lives. They married men of Me'arah, and magic passed through their blood to their children, and their children's children. But as Shamara decreed, Garog had been appointed the Lord Na'tar, and it fell upon the male descendents to take up that mantle and officiate over the affairs of the kingdom."

"Why didn't Shamara let women do that?" Aron asked, his eyes closed and his head sunk deep into his pillow.

Alia's eyebrows raised at his unexpected question. She chuckled. "Garog felt a bit useless, seeing Shamara create and sustain the world around them. He needed a job, an important one. Men are like that," she added, tickling Aron under the chin. "When you grow up, you'll want a job too. Some important work to keep you busy."

"No I won't." His eyes opened, and he glared at her. "I just want to play. And explore."

"You do now. But later, when you're older, you'll tire of playing all the time. There is a time for every work under heaven. A time to work and a time to play. Humans were created to enjoy the work of their hands."

Aron only hmphed and closed his eyes again. "So, go on."

"All right," Alia said, smoothing down his blankets. "When Shamara's first grandson, Nehum, came of age, she watched from the dais as the robe was draped around his shoulders. He, just like everyone else, did not wonder about the past or remember a time when their ancestors lived above Me'arah. Nehum knew nothing of Shamara's magic, nor that she kept the world alive moment by moment. Like everyone else, he thought the stories of a people brought down through rock into a hidden cavern below the world was merely a bedtime story, a fairy tale. Over the centuries stories were told of fairies that lived among humans, that protected and guided them, that taught them wisdom and prudence. Fairies that sometimes appeared small with wings, or took the shape of deer or other woodland creatures. But Nehum, like everyone else, thought they were only made-up stories—"

"So imagine his surprise!" Aron recited, knowing exactly the words Alia meant to say next. She chuckled and wondered why he wasn't asleep yet, so entwined in the tale.

"Yes, imagine his surprise when Shamara took him aside, and in the evening, under the dim pink light shining from the dome, led him to the secret room in her cottage—the cottage she'd been living all these centuries, long after Garog had died and her daughters had married and started families of their own.

"'You are the Lord Na'tar now, Nehum,' she told him. 'And you will govern Me'arah for many years. I know you will be a wise and kind servant of your people.' Nehum was very fond of his quirky grandmother, who loved to paint pictures on bleached animal hides. He, of all the grandchildren, had spent hours painting with her by the shore of the great sea, and Shamara had taught him how to make soft paintbrushes from the cattails that grew along the banks of the ponds.

"'I've never seen this door, Grandmother,' he told her, a puzzled look on his face. 'Has it always been here?'

"Shamara told him, 'Yes. Always. But it is draped in magic.'

"'Magic! What do you mean?' he said. For no one in Me'arah remembered the magic. No one alive then had been alive when she created their world. Although magic was now infused in every fiber of every living thing in Me'arah, the people of her kingdom could not see it. For they didn't know how to tell the difference between what was magical and what was not."

Aron sat up, a weary expression on his face. "Momi, I don't understand."

Alia frowned. "Don't understand what?"

"About magic. I mean, isn't everything magical? The sunrise, the stars that appear in the sky and then vanish, the flowers that pop up from the ground."

"Why, of course, Aron. But people don't see life that way. They take it for granted."

"What is *granted*?"

Alia paused, thinking how to put it. "Granted means they don't *see* anymore. See with the eyes of a child. Like with your eyes—with wonderment." She sighed. "Everything in the world is truly magical. Life is magical. But the people of Me'arah forgot."

"People here forget too," Aron said quietly.

"People everywhere," Alia added. "But we must never forget."

Aron nodded and let out a long breath. "So, can you finish that part of the story? About the room?"

"Yes. So Shamara muttered the magic words and opened the door to the small room. And when they stepped inside, she showed him all the pictures she had painted and explained the story of how Sha'kath had attacked the people of Moreb, and how they had fled through rock and journeyed down into the heart of the earth. How she was a wizard and that she had created a safe haven for them all—"

"And he didn't believe her. Not until she *proved* it to him."

"That's right. Although she knew in her heart of hearts that he doubted. He thought the magic scrolls were neat tricks, clever conjuring—nothing more. After she told him and showed him everything, he laughed and decided she was short a few pebbles. It was then that Shamara knew she had to seal the door—"

"And it could never be opened again—not until the right time," Aron said under his breath, sleep pulling him under its wing.

"Shamara gave the cottage to Nehum and walked to the edge of the sea. A loneliness came over her then . . ." She looked over at Aron when she heard his breathing deepen. He had finally fallen asleep.

As she stroked his hair, she said to the night, "She was so very lonely. Yes, she had her daughters and grandchildren and great-grandchildren. And she had all her people, the people of Me'arah. But she missed Garog. And keeping a secret was a weighty burden."

She gave her sleeping son a tender kiss on his forehead. "But not as weighty as the burden of disbelief."

Alia stood and looked out the window at the three moons hanging in the sky like tree ornaments.

All those centuries, she had pushed aside her curiosity, knowing it was foolish to hope. Then, after showing Nehum the room and the scrolls depicting the real world above, she was gripped by a painful yearning to leave. It was not that she was tired of sustaining her kingdom with her magic; she knew she could continue for many more centuries without faltering. She knew that one day the door in that cottage would open for the one who would take over her task before she finally succumbed. She did not resent her commitment to her people.

But if she meant to keep on this way for thousands of years more, she needed to know if she was doing the right thing—forcing her people to live a lie. A safe and lovely lie, but a lie nonetheless. She could justify keeping them ignorant if there remained a threat in the world above. But what if it was now safe? What if her people could return to the surface and live in the world the way they were meant to live? Wouldn't that be heaven's will? Was keeping the truth from them now a kindness or a travesty?

Something terrible was happening in her soul—she had begun to doubt. And it was a horrible burden.

There was only one way to find out the truth, but she resisted with all her will. Eventually the burden pressed its suffocating weight upon her until she could bear it no longer. Resolved, she would cross the great sea and take the path she had carved out of rock back to the surface. She would do what she swore she would never do. But then she would know.

FIFTEEN

JUSTYN TOOK up the rear, listening behind him for any strange noises. What he paid the most attention to was the sound of rocks falling, trying to ignore his worry that an avalanche would trap them. Zev had insisted on using a bit of magic—although the other wizards tried to persuade him against it. Although why they did so after Valonis's outburst of power, he didn't get. Zev didn't want the entrance to the cavern to be detectable by their enemy, and they had no means of hauling large boulders to close it up. So with a quick spell, the way in—which must also be the way out, Justyn surmised—was shut. The moonlight that had been spilling down the stairs was suddenly blocked, and they had brought few supplies with them. He couldn't help feeling like a trapped rat.

Although Justyn felt they were acting too impulsively, he said nothing as they followed the rock stairs down into the cool heart of the earth. Zev had conjured up torches for them all to carry, and assured the group that the horses would be safe in their absence. Although, Justyn wondered how he could manage protecting them from under the ground. But Zev was a wizard, and Justyn had to concede that he still knew very little about wizards.

He shook his head, thinking of all the courses he had taught in the school of magic. His studies of the unraveling of Wentwater had taken up a good part of his life—the years he spent unraveling that mystery! And then he had journeyed to Ethryn to meet the king and see the miracle of the sacred site, thinking it would be the most astonishing experience of his life—and his last chance to see the evidence of magic in the world. Never had he expected this—magical boots that transported him across the face of the earth in mere seconds. Nor that he'd eat and chat with wizards who were thousands of years old. He shook his head. And who would ever believe him if he told the tale of the Moon and Cielle? No one, that's who.

As he trudged carefully down the uneven steps, he knew his retirement would have to be delayed—if he ever did return safely to the Heights. How would he find the time in the few remaining years of his life to record all this? His mind mulled through the new courses he would have to plan—courses on the history and abilities of wizards, the tales of Sha'kath the Destroyer. And what about Elysiel and King Perthin's heritage and the crystal scepter? Oh, there was just too much to research and write about and too little time. For the first time in a long while, he cursed his mortality and felt a restless stirring in his soul—a fervent desire to live past his assigned years.

Justyn felt his old bones creak as they continued their descent, aware of both the shortness of his breath and of his life. The only other person on this journey who was a mere human was Kael. But he too had lived longer than any mortal alive—if one could count the entire life he had lived in the past. When Justyn had heard his story, he thought it more a dream than reality. But it wasn't. Kael had truly lived an entire life six thousand years ago. Who knew how many of the citizens of Ethryn today were his descendents?

This strange thought stuck in his head for hours while they descended into the earth, his limbs growing cold and achy by the time Zev held up his arm and brought them to a halt. Exhaustion rattling him told him he'd missed an entire night's sleep.

"This is a good place to rest," Zev said, choosing a flat-topped boulder to sit upon. His son sat beside him, looking as weary as Justyn felt.

They must have walked miles, although Justyn, having lost all sense of time, could not begin to guess how far.

"We've only walked two miles," Relgar said to him as he approached. "But in this damp and cold, and taking care not to trip, it does feel much farther." He laid a hand on Justyn's shoulder, then handed him a water skin. "Here, drink. You look flushed."

"Thank you, Relgar." Justyn sipped, all the while noticing how fresh and perky Relgar seemed, which made Justyn curse once more his frail humanity. The wizard then handed him something dark and chewy to eat. Justyn wasn't sure what it was, but it did refresh his energy and stopped the rumbling in his empty stomach. He sat down on the hard ledge of rock, and Relgar joined him.

They had stopped in a small cavern that allowed them to gather together—a nice change from the narrow pathway they'd traversed although a chill dampness penetrated into his old bones and made them ache. The others milled about, talking quietly among themselves, but Valonis kept a hand on the rock wall, glancing from time to time at the next set of steps that picked up at the other side of the cave.

"The walls appear to be naturally formed." Hinwor came over and sat beside Justyn, then took a long drink from his own water skin. Justyn was glad that Hinwor, at least, had thought to bring a large pack of food and water. Although, Justyn didn't doubt these wizards could conjure up whatever they needed. They all seemed piqued with excitement. Was he the only one worrying?

"I imagine you didn't anticipate finding yourself on such an adventure, Justyn of Wentwater."

"No, hardly. But what do you think we will find . . . down wherever it is we are heading?"

Relgar drew in a breath and looked over at Valonis. "She says the further down we go, the stronger she senses Shamara's magic."

"Does that mean her sister is alive down there? Alive after thousands of years, living under the ground? How is that possible?"

Relgar shrugged. "It's possible, but unlikely. She would have to use magic to sustain her life every moment—to provide food, water, air . . . and surely she didn't escape down here alone; she would never have abandoned her people to save her own life. The expenditure of that amount of magic, day after day, would take a toll on her life and health. But Shamara would not have hesitated to do whatever it took to take her people to safety, away from Sha'kath."

"Perhaps this is only a tunnel leading to another exit. Maybe it comes out leagues from here, and provided an escape route that way."

Relgar shook his head. "Then why did she carve a path downward? That makes little sense. If she meant to take them to another land on the surface of the earth, she would have gone straight through the mountain. And there would have been some trace of her existence on the surface of the world. No, she burrowed deep, like an animal in winter seeking to hide from the harsh elements and remain undetected."

"Long winter . . ." Justyn muttered.

Hinwor, who had been quietly listening all this time, said, "I'm concerned for her." He tipped his head at Valonis. "She holds too much hope in her heart."

Relgar smiled, but it seemed a sad smile to Justyn. "If we let go of our grasp on hope, it will fly away and leave us in despair."

"But what if she finds her sister has been dead long years, and what she is sensing is but a residue of her power still locked in the earth?" Hinwor asked.

Justyn noted Hinwor's face tended toward a perpetual frown, but now, close up, he saw that the old wizard was only thinking. His fondness for Valonis was evident.

Relgar stood and ran his fingers through his beard. "Then her questions will be laid to rest. I imagine we'll have the answer to that soon enough. The path cannot go on forever."

"Maybe it's bespelled," Justyn offered, a sinking feeling overtaking him. "Maybe we only think we're going down, and we're actually going in circles."

Hinwor snorted, but his eyes were amused. "A wizard might create such a spell to confound her enemies, that is true. But even a wizard as powerful as Shamara would not be able to fool Zev. He has a wolf's nose for that kind of trickery."

Relgar chuckled. "He's known to have pulled off some canny tricks in his early years, in the wizard wars of old."

Hinwor brightened, and a big smile came up on his face. "Do you recall that time he diverted the enemy with that hoot owl gimmick?"

Relgar now laughed—a big belly laugh. "It is hard to find anything to laugh about regarding those dark days. But yes, that was a moment to cherish."

Zev then stood and announced, "Let's continue." He turned to Valonis and gestured her ahead with his hand. He then looked directly at Justyn and said, "Not much further now. We are almost there."

But where is there? Justyn wondered.

He didn't have long to wonder. For after only trekking a few minutes, the tunnel grew brighter, and light streamed in from the path ahead. The walls grew farther and farther apart until they opened up completely and ushered the group into open air—fresh air, swollen with moisture, that Justyn sucked in deeply.

Those ahead came to a sudden stop, and Justyn heard the quiet gasps of astonishment.

"Well, I never imagined . . ." Hinwor uttered in front of him.

Justyn pushed between Hinwor and Relgar to see the vista ahead, but what met his eyes completely befuddled him.

Before him, a sea of emerald-green water stretched out to the horizon, illuminated in ripples of pastel colors. Above, an expansive dome of pink light shone down upon the waters, casting a strange hue over the faces around him, giving an eerie sense of teetering between dawn and dusk. The pebbly ground at his feet ended not more than ten feet on all sides, with water everywhere. He strained to see across this vast ocean but could make out nothing.

"This is it?" Justyn said, searching the faces of the kings he had traveled with. They seemed as perplexed as he. "There is nothing here but water. Surely Shamara isn't . . . living under the water?"

Relgar laughed. "No, not likely."

"Well then, is the water an illusion? Where did it all come from?" Joran asked, kneeling down and putting his hand in the sea, then flinging water drops from his fingertips.

"It's real enough," Zev said, looking around. "But it did not come here naturally. This sea was made with magic."

"What do you mean?" King Kael said.

"Shamara created it," Valonis declared, studying the sea as if seeing something in it. But Justyn could see nothing—no sign of plant or fish life. It was like a giant ceramic bowl filled with water.

"Now what?" Joran asked, straightening up. "There is nowhere to go. Unless you want to have a swim." He looked at his father with a wry expression.

"That, young wizard, would be a very tiring swim," Valonis said, her eyes sparkling as if set on fire.

"What do you mean?" he answered.

"It means she knows where Shamara is," Relgar said, watching Valonis's face.

"Where?" Justyn asked. No one was making sense. If the water was real and not an illusion, just where could Shamara be?

"Across the sea, dear scholar," Valonis said. And with a wave of her hand, she called out in a language Justyn had never heard before. The air wobbled, followed by a shimmering blast. Justyn shielded his eyes, and a hard wind pushed against him. Sand sprinkled his cheeks.

When he pushed the hair from his eyes, he saw before him a large wooden boat—more like a box—bobbing in the water a few feet from shore. Just the right size to carry their party of eight.

Without hesitation, the wizards began clambering into the boat, followed by the kings of Elysiel and Ethryn. Relgar leaned out with his legs braced on the boat's floor and offered Justyn a steady hand.

As Justyn grunted and swung his leg up over the side of the boat, he asked, "But what's across the sea? On the other side?" *If there is an "other side."*

Relgar gave him a hearty pat on the back, gesturing Justyn to sit on one of the wide benches that spanned the width of the boat. "That, dear old scholar, we will soon discover."

SIXTEEN

IN THE COOL misty morning, Meris drew in a deep breath and held it, clenching her eyes and concentrating, but her thoughts wouldn't cooperate.

"Relax, Meris," Shamara said, resting a bony hand on her shoulder. "Relax . . ."

Meris knew she had to clear her mind and attune her magical energy to the dome above her. She'd had little success until yesterday, when she'd felt a tingling work down her arms and out her fingertips. And in that moment she actually saw the color in the dome brighten. Just a tiny bit, but even that encouraged Shamara, who clapped her hands in delight and urged Meris to try again. But the effort was exhausting, and by the end of each day her body trembled and her head ached.

For hours every day this week Shamara had taken her up to the top of the hill that rose behind the sea cottage. There, Meris would gaze out over the sea, seeing nothing beyond the far horizon, wondering how long it would take a vessel to journey to the cavern Shamara had brought her people through. While Shamara readily answered the other pressing questions Meris had, this was one subject she would not discuss. "Later," Shamara said. Later she would explain the magic of the sea and the spell cast over it.

Now Meris understood that it wasn't just superstition that prevented the people of Me'arah from trying to cross the sea. There had been many attempts in the early years, Shamara explained. But a dread fell over them only a few feet from shore, causing imprecise fears to well up in their hearts, like dark shapes emerging from the watery depths. Followed by fear came disorientation, so that upon rowing out farther and father, the one attempting to flee would end up turning back and find himself back on shore, puzzled.

Meris would have to keep this spell in place, Shamara had explained as they hiked up the hill this morning. But how would she be able to do all this? Sustain an entire kingdom?

"Perhaps you should rest a bit, my dear girl," Shamara said, shaking Meris out of her musings. "Your mind is too full of questions and doubts." The old woman gazed deeply into Meris's eyes, her milky green orbs unsettling Meris. She seemed to be able to hear every thought and feel every emotion Meris felt. Nothing could be kept secret from Shamara—not even Meris's discomfort over that fact.

Shamara chuckled. "It's a choice, Meris. One I don't often indulge in. Wizards have always been able to mindread and mindspeak—particularly to each other and to animals. But we respect privacy, and don't intrude unless necessary. Only someone evil, like Sha'kath, would use such power to control and manipulate."

Shamara clutched at her waist and grimaced. Meris knew the old wizard was trying to hide some constant pain she suffered. But it was evident to Meris her mentor was dying. Did all wizards live for thousands of years? If so, how long did it take for them to die? Would Shamara linger on in pain for decades and eventually expire? Meris wanted to ask how much time they had together, and how long it would take for her to learn all she needed in order to take Shamara's place, but she thought it would be inconsiderate.

Meris sighed, sadness pinging her heart. The more she got to know Shamara, the more affection and awe she felt for her. What a tremendous burden and sacrifice she made for the people she loved. How would Meris ever measure up to that?

Meris thought back to what Shamara had told her of this destroyer and shivered at the memory of the scroll she had looked at. Her father had sensed the saturation of evil in the scroll, which was now back in the secret room. Meris had learned how Sapha had found it in the dell and brought it back to the house, but her father refused to touch it.

When they'd returned from the council meeting that night, he showed her the shelf it lay on, then instructed her to put it back where she found it. He stood at a distance and watched her turn the knob on the door and enter the magical room. After she came out and closed the door, they didn't speak of it further.

But the look of fear on his face had unsettled her.

She turned to Shamara, who was sitting on a pillow on the soft grass beside her. "Do you think he's still . . . alive? Up there, in the real world?"

Meris studied the pink dome above her. Shamara told her that once her magic was strengthened and focused, she'd be able to see beyond the dome to the rock behind it. But she saw nothing but pink light now.

"There's no telling. Thousands of years have passed. There may be nothing alive left on the surface of the earth."

"You can't sense anything? Your magic is so great, it created an entire world! Can't you use it to somehow see what it up there?"

Shamara pursed her lips. "I dare not. Using magic to probe the world could be detected by Sha'kath."

"But why would he still be looking for you or the people of Moreb after all this time? Surely, even if he is still alive, he would have forgotten about you. Moved on to other . . . evil deeds. What harm would it cause to venture to the surface—"

"No." Shamara's tone was sharp, and the word pierced Meris's heart. "You must put that thought out of your mind. You do not understand the danger, the risk. It may be safe, yes. And maybe there is a world to return to, one thriving and peaceful, one no longer under attack by the Destroyer and his minions. But I cannot take the chance." She snagged Meris's gaze and held her there, like a captured pheasant. "And, my dear girl, you mustn't take the chance. There is too much at stake."

Meris blew out a frustrated breath. Her head pounded—from the effort to link her magic to the dome and from the growing aggravation in her gut. "I don't understand. What is at a stake but a small kingdom of people, living peaceably, intending no harm? Why would a powerful being like Sha'kath care at all for such a kingdom?"

"My dear girl, because any kingdom that is not under his rule he will crush. All those long years ago, he set out to kill all the wizards. There were . . . many wars, dark wars. And many wizards died. I watched one of my dearest friends fall in the battle in Moreb. I left my sister behind . . . and I don't know if she is still alive . . ."

Meris turned at the sound of Shamara's faltering voice. She could tell the old woman—wizard—was choking back tears. Meris fell quiet and closed her eyes, feeling bad for stirring up such troubling emotions in her teacher. But she just didn't understand. Why should her kingdom, her people, remain hidden underground while all the other people of the world might be enjoying the real world created for them? Was it heaven's will to have them hide for thousands of years or to face their challenges—like everyone else?

She glanced over at Shamara, who sat wiping her eyes and looking out over the sea. *Or was it merely Shamara's will?*

Meris stood, noticing how stiff she felt. She had been spending so many hours each day sitting, concentrating. She longed to run with her deer and forget about all this magic and lessons and responsibility.

"Go, then," Shamara said, her voice flat. "Come back tomorrow and we will continue. You've worked hard, my dear girl. I know this is not easy for you." Shamara pushed her long silver braids back behind her shoulders. "Be you must beware of one thing."

Meris looked down at Shamara, who sat unmoving and still gazed out over the sea. Water rippled pink under the dome—empty water coated in magic. "What is that?"

"Doubt." She swallowed. "And there is nothing more ruinous than doubt. Be on guard."

Meris opened her mouth to protest but found nothing to say. Surely Shamara knew her thoughts—whether she heard them in Meris's mind or read them on her face.

She sighed and bid her teacher good-bye, the fall day warming ever so slightly. Fireflies came from all directions, flitting about her ears and tickling her with their tiny wings. She couldn't help but smile at their antics to cheer her up.

As she trekked down the hill, she wondered why such heavy sadness lay on her heart. Shouldn't she be happy? For months now, all in Me'arah—herself included—had grown fearful over the failing light, and hope had guttered. But now there was every reason to rejoice. And Meris was to be that hope for her world. She should feel happy, honored, relieved.

So why did she feel so miserable?

When she got to the bottom of the grassy swale, she started toward the path that would lead to the dell, but suddenly stopped. She turned and stared out over the sea, and a strange foreboding gripped her. What was it? Was her imagination toying with her? Or was she just exhausted? All this serious effort to draw magic from her blood made her skin tingle and heightened her senses. Shamara had told her that summoning her magic would alter her. That she would feel power begin to course through her veins, and in time would learn how to control the flow of magic and channel it with her intent. But she had felt only an inkling of magic in her lessons with Shamara.

But this sensation . . . This was something potent and close by.

She closed her eyes and let herself be drawn toward this magical niggling. Like hearing a whisper caught on a breeze, she chased down the flitter of magic in her mind, and her limbs began to shake. Whatever the source, it had something to do with the sea. Something *across* the sea.

Her heart pounding, Meris walked to the edge of the water, straining to see what lay beyond her vision. The horizon line lay flat on the water, as sharp as a knife's edge. Now, not a ripple marred the surface of the sea. And yet . . .

Meris squinted. The air took on a strange quality, as if thickening like pudding. Subtle shifts of color caught her eye—in the distance. And the water wavered in a blur. She rubbed her eyes, but the disturbance only grew worse, until she had trouble seeing even a few feet in front of her. The fireflies that had been circling her head flew off in a sudden fret. But Meris could not be concerned with what that might mean.

She held her head with her hands as a dull throb beat against her temples. What was happening to her? Was all this effort to summon magic from her blood creating hallucinations? She had never seen anything like this in her life.

And then, the wavering stopped. She looked back across the water and now saw distinct colors and shapes. Her mouth dropped open.

For not all that far away—no, hardly a stone's throw from shore—something was emerging, as if from nowhere. A large box bobbed on the water. And there were people in it. Exactly what was painted on the scroll in the secret room. She clutched her throat.

Meris scurried behind a pile of broken boulders that had long ago tumbled down the cliff to the shore. A stab of fear shot through her. The scroll she'd seen—it wasn't a picture of the past; it depicted the future. This moment, this place. Were these people bad? Had they come from the surface? She gulped, now gripped so tightly by fear she could hardly breathe.

Had Sha'kath sent them here? To find the remnants of Moreb? And why would they arrive now? Did they somehow know Shamara was dying and that Me'arah was vulnerable and indefensible? All these centuries her people had lived in peace, hidden away. How had they been discovered? What if it was her fault? What if by enhancing her magic the Destroyer had somehow sensed her down here? Was her magic truly that powerful?

Meris sank to the ground, peeking between boulders as the vessel came closer, on a direct course to this very beach. Toward *her*.

She held her breath as the vessel, propelled along by a half dozen large wooden paddles held in the hands of its passengers, slid quietly up onto the sandy beach. From where she hid, she watched as those aboard stepped out. She was too far to make out faces, but she could tell at least one was a woman—the one in a pale green gown. Their clothing was odd—nothing like what her people wore. But they appeared human—of ordinary stature—and did not carry any weapons. In fact, Meris sensed their emotions, even from here. And she could not detect any malicious intent. Quite the contrary. Their delight and surprise was surpassed only by their good will.

They mean no harm, Meris realized, much to her relief. But she dared not let them see her. Not until she could suss out their intention.

Just then a few heads turned in her direction. She ducked down and held her breath, then chided herself. They could hardly hear her breathing from this distance. But how had they found this place? How had they crossed the sea? Shamara made it clear the water was enchanted. But maybe only to those in Me'arah. Yet their vessel had materialized out of nothing. Were they wizards, like Shamara? Meris longed to probe them, to send out her magic to them to see what she would uncover. But she knew that was too risky. What if these were powerful mages that could mask their intent? What if they were only pretending to be peaceful?

If only Shamara was here with her. Meris needed to find her, tell her, about these visitors. But, then, how could Shamara not know of their arrival? Surely she would have sensed the moment they appeared on the great sea. But if these travelers meant harm, would Shamara be able to defend herself? Protect Me'arah? In her condition, Meris thought it unlikely.

The questions kept pummeling Meris as she squatted behind the rocks. She waited until the party of eight set off on the wide trail that led to the center of town, and once she was sure they were long gone, she ran to their vessel.

Breathless, she placed a hand on the wooden siding of the box that had conveyed them to her kingdom. The instant her hand touched the surface, she let out a gasp and pulled her hand back.

She had never in her life felt a surge of magic so intense, so concentrated. It was as if the box were constructed of magic itself and had no real substance in the world. How could that be? She peered over the edge into the box, but only the paddles lay on the bottom—nothing else. Why had these visitors brought nothing with them? Was the surface so close to the sea that they didn't need supplies? Did they know what they would find upon arriving?

Meris touched the box again, this time allowing her hand to rest on it. Magic surged through her limbs like heat from a hearth. And like such warmth, the sensation tingled through her body, filling her with an irrepressible joy.

She closed her eyes and sank into the luxurious feeling, drawing strength and peace from the surge of magic. Without thinking, she climbed into the vessel and stood with her hands gripping each side. Magic flowed in waves in through her hands—so much stronger and vibrant than the magic Shamara had shared with her—as if her teacher's magic was depleted and old and this was young magic. Or the combined magic of many powerful wizards.

In her mind's eye, she merged with the box, and there it disappeared and only existed in her imagination. She touched it with her mind, then shaped it until it became her legs and arms, her sight. With closed eyes, she found the heart of the enchantment and drew it to her will. So simple, so simple, she mused, astonished. As effortless as breathing.

Suddenly she was moving. She opened her eyes and found she was far from shore, standing in the box and looking back at the beach and the copse of trees. Amazement washed over her, but she had no time to study the land this far out at sea. She sucked in a breath as the air thickened once more around her, then engulfed her in a whirl of blues and greens moving so quickly she squeezed her eyes to keep from falling.

When she opened them, she was beached on a rocky shore, and her land—the land now across the sea—was nowhere in sight. She swallowed and pushed down her sudden panic. Where was she? Still underground? She clambered out of the box with shaky legs and looked around. She had no doubt this place was drenched in magic. Water surrounded her on all sides, as if she were in a small room. But it was now evident to her where the travelers had come from. Footprints on the patches of sand amid the rocks showed their steps leading to the water's edge from the mountain of rock before her. A crevice revealed a narrow path leading inside, and when Meris peeked into the dark space, her mouth dropped open.

A flight of stone steps led upward into more rock. Rock that Shamara had led the people of Moreb through thousands of years ago. Rock that fashioned the backdrop to the dome covering Me'arah.

Rock that led to the surface.

Had Shamara lied to her? The thought sent a shudder of discomfort through her gut. Shamara had said that the passage had been sealed and there was no way back to the surface; they were trapped down here. Yet, here were steps. But maybe, Meris suddenly realized, she would find them end at a wall of rock once she got to the end of the staircase. It was possible Shamara was telling her the truth. She hated to think otherwise, for, that would mean maybe other things Shamara had told her were falsehoods. Then what would she do?

Then another thought came to her: What if Shamara truly thought the way up through the rock was sealed—but these visitors had opened it? The strength of their magic, from what Meris sensed in the boat, was undeniably powerful. But why had they come, and what did they want? She hoped her instincts were right and they meant no harm.

As much as her feet wanted to turn back and hear what they had to say, Meris couldn't dare ruin this chance to see the true world above her. Even if she could just peek out, for a second, then hurry back—that would satisfy her curiosity. Maybe she would be able to sense whether the world boded ill or not. Would she be able to tell in such a brief glance? She hoped so. Surely if the world was drenched in evil, she would be able to tell, wouldn't she? She could then return to her kingdom, content to remain below and undetected, and keep her secret land safe for many years to come—without regret. She owed it to her people to know the truth, in order to be the kind of wizard they needed.

Meris trembled and laid a hand on the side of the mountain. True to her suspicion, this was no enchantment; the rock was real. She could sense its density, its solid structure. It was her land, her world, that was an illusion, she mused. A wizard's fabrication.

But not this. This was a piece of the actual world above. The world that was created ages ago, designed for humans to inhabit. The world she and her people were from and were meant to be a part of.

As wonderful as the box had felt under her hands, moving to her will, this rock felt even more wonderful. For it spoke to her heart and soul. To her origins that cried out in her blood. She felt as if she had been wandering lost her whole life, looking for her true home. She knew now she had found it.

Without a glance back to the box or the sea or the magnificent kingdom that lay on the other side of the wall of illusion, she slipped in through the crevice of rock and started climbing the steps, her heart pounding in joy.

SEVENTEEN

KAEL TOOK in the magnificent world as he walked a few paces behind the rest of the group. The landscape spread around them was vibrant, and although many of the plants were similar to ones he had seen, the colors were different, indescribable, everything tinged with pink. How could there be new colors in the world? The air smelled delightfully fresh, and a crisp wind tickled his back. The trees along the water's edge and the trail they were now following had silver bark, bare of leaves, indicating, perhaps, that this world experienced the seasons much like on the surface of the real world.

When they'd stepped out of the boat onto the shore, Valonis had explained that Shamara was indeed alive—of that there was no doubt—and had created this entire world. Not only created it but sustained it—all by herself.

What power she must have, Kael thought, looking up at the strange pink sky, which gave an appearance of endless heaven above. An illusion that would fool anyone that didn't know an entire mountain range sat above it. Kael had seen heaven's mighty arm that night he was appointed the first Keeper thousands of years in the past. And he knew power personally when he burned down the gates surrounding the great tower with his rage and intent. But this was a different kind of power. A sustaining one, which held the shape of a world second after second, century after century, without wavering. How was that possible?

Perthin slowed and joined Kael. "Astonishing," Perthin said. "If Shamara brought perhaps a hundred people with her into this place all those years ago, how many people must live here now? Thousands? Tens of thousands?"

Kael shrugged, casting a glance across the rolling hills they climbed. "Imagine living life down here, not knowing the truth. Do they grow food? Spin wool and weave cloth?"

"I imagine we'll know soon enough. Valonis says there is a dense population not a league ahead." He stopped and turned to look back. Kael stopped to see what Perthin was looking at.

Back behind them, the glassy water reflected the soft pink of the sky. Perthin grew thoughtful as the rest of their group passed in through a grove of trees and out of sight. He made a small noise like a chuckle.

"What are you thinking?" Kael asked.

Perthin pursed his lips. "Perhaps we are just like these people of Moreb. Day after day, they live their lives, completely unaware there exists another world above them. Just out of reach, as if separated by a thin veil."

"A veil of magic."

"Yes. But think, Kael. We live on the face of the world, under a dome of heaven. But it could be an illusion. Don't you ever stop and ponder how the heavens stretch out endlessly, without boundaries. How perplexing that is! What if—like this place—there is something above the heavens, just beyond the veil. A whole other world above us we know nothing about because we can't see it, aren't meant to see it." He turned and looked at Kael, probing his eyes. "What if our time here on this earth is like . . . living in this cavern? And everything is illusion, not real at all?"

Kael smiled and patted Perthin on his shoulder. "My, you're waxing quite poetic. Do you do that often when in Elysiel?" Kael had tried to imagine how Perthin could be aware of every living thing at once—and not become completely muddled by all the thoughts and voices of millions of creatures and people. He gave up trying; the effort made his head swim. "And let's say you are right, and there is some other 'land' above our very real sky. That world could be an illusion as well, encapsuled inside another dome, and on and on it goes," Kael said wryly.

Perthin grew even more thoughtful. "I feel so different . . . away from my kingdom. I've left Elysiel before, taken short trips to other lands. The experience is unsettling, for I'm driven by a need to stay connected to all that lives there." He looked down at his hand holding the scepter that glowed with its faint blue light. "But the separation is also good for me. It reminds me that I'm only human, and that I've been given this power and gift of ruling by heaven's grace. I'm more keenly aware of my *self*, my individuality, and that's something I never truly feel when inside the borders of my land. One the one hand I'm terribly worried what might happen while I'm away, and I fight off feelings of guilt for abandoning Elysiel at a time when she most needs me. And then I remind myself that King Cakrin told me to find you, and that we have something we—all of us—must do together, to stop the Destroyer." He added with a solemn expression, "If that is what we are meant to do. Cakrin did not tell me in so many words."

Kael let Perthin's words fade as they continued to stare out at the magical sea they had come across.

"It looks like it goes on forever, doesn't it?" Perthin said, nodding at the water. "But we came through a veil only a short distance away and there was the shore." He looked at Kael. "An illusion. Just like the sky." He tipped his head and looked up.

"Maybe you're right," Kael said, touching Perthin's sleeve and bringing his attention back. "Maybe this life is the illusion and there is something *real* on the other side of the veil, just above the dome of heaven. I suppose we will all one day find out. But is it something to concern ourselves with now, in this time, in this world? I think not. I think we are meant to live our lives to the full, believing in the realness of our time and place, for all we have is now, the present. The past has passed, and the future will never come so long as we wait for it."

Perthin smiled. "Now who's waxing poetic?" He patted Kael's arm and gestured to the woods ahead. "They've gone on without us. We should catch up."

Kael nodded as they started walking again. "Not like we wouldn't be able to find them. They're trapped in an underground cavern, same as we are. And I imagine the only way out is the way we came in."

Perthin gave Kael a conceding smile, then marched into the grove of silver trees, and Kael followed.

Ta'sus, the Lord Na'tar of Me'arah, paced outside the assembly hall under the silver leaves of the quaking firth trees as the cool mist of morning dissipated and a warmth from the dome overhead radiated down on his stiff shoulders. Drayna had dragged him to the marketplace to help with the weekly shopping as dawn dusted the sky, hoping to shake him out of his mood, but he felt too many eyes upon him with their looks of gratitude, and many came rushing over to him, thanking him for the hope they now felt, as if he were responsible.

Elward, in the town meeting that had followed the night Shamara had appeared in the council chambers, had vaguely indicated the problem of the dome's light had been solved—without giving any details, as per Shamara's instructions. Not knowing whom to thank, the townspeople credited the councilors, no doubt thinking they had pooled their wisdom together and miraculously came up with a solution. Shamara had practically vanished as if she'd never come to them, and life went on, with none the wiser—none, that is, except the seven council members who were still reeling from the truth—that their ancestors had journeyed from a kingdom across the great sea once upon a time.

After a half-dozen people had come over and pumped his hand and gushed with gratitude as he shopped with his wife at the fruit stand, he needed a reprieve. He told Drayna he wanted to take a walk to clear his head, and she waved him off upon seeing Elward's wife down the lane. His musings had led his feet unconsciously back to the assembly hall—the place where all his pressing questions had sprouted that night. Sprouted into a tangle of weeds.

He'd hardly been sleeping these past nights—how could he have expected to, after meeting the wizard, Shamara, and hearing her story of how she created this world? His world. He didn't doubt her story, for she proved her claim of longevity and gave evidence of her power in a startling display by snuffing out the dome's light with a simple utterance—which gave him and the other councilors in the chamber a deathly fright. And just as easily, with a word, she turned the light back on. As simply as turning the knob on a lantern. Those who had grumbled in disbelief earlier had been silenced and humbled. And whatever tendril of doubt he himself had had was crushed by her demonstration.

But her vague explanations of the origins of this world and how and why she created it in the first place did not sit well with him. Her words kept rattling in his head. *"There is no going back. No one is left."*

He fought the urge to find the wizard and ask her more questions—questions that were burning in his heart—but he dared not. Dutifully he sent Meris off to learn from Shamara each morning, so that his daughter could soon take over sustaining their world. And as much as Meris reassured him she wanted this responsibility, he saw in her eyes the fear and worry that simmered there. Maybe in time, he tried to reassure himself, as she came more fully into her power and gained mastery over it, she would feel confident and fulfilled. But a part of him wished—yes, he had to admit it—that he'd rather someone else and not his own precious daughter had been the one entrusted with this grave duty.

He turned abruptly at the sound of someone calling him.

"Ah, there you are, Ta'sus," Elward said, giving his old friend a tired smile. When he came up to him, he added, "I hear your daughter's lessons are going well." He glanced up at the sky and cocked his head. "The dome is shining brighter—can you tell?"

Ta'sus nodded, forcing a smile, but Elward knew him well; he furrowed his brows at him. "Come now, friend. You mustn't worry. The wizard has been caring for our land all these centuries—a labor of love with no personal reward in it. Surely she will treat Meris with kindness. I would think your daughter would find this all very exciting."

"She does," Ta'sus conceded, thinking of Meris detailing her training at the dinner table last night. Instead of feeling like the odd one in the family, Meris now had the rapt attention of her mother and sisters, although Ta'sus suspected Abrella felt a little overshadowed by Meris's important role. They hardly spoke of her upcoming wedding, which until recent events had been practically all they spoke about in his home. Ta'sus was glad to see Meris wasn't getting a swelled head from her appointment or her burgeoning magical abilities, but time would tell if, after the newness and thrill wore off, the power would go to her head.

That was another worry on his heart. He hoped he had raised her well—enough so that she had the wisdom and humility to keep things in perspective. To see that magic was more a burden and a charge than a privilege or badge of superiority. Well, he would have to see to it she did. He had carefully nurtured her all these years, to prepare her to be able to handle the magic she hardly knew she had.

He shook his head and swallowed past the lump in his throat. Now, though, he no longer would have that oversight. Shamara was her teacher, and would teach Meris things way beyond the scope of his abilities or understanding. And that saddened him a bit. Would Meris someday live alone in that cottage by the sea, without a husband or family? Would she become lonely in a need to isolate herself, the way Shamara did all these centuries? Ta'sus let out a long breath as he envisioned her hundreds of years from now—old, lonely, her family and all those she loved long dead and gone. Spending each day using her magic to sustain a world of thousands that depended on her in order to live, every minute without fail. For if Meris failed, all would die.

Why couldn't the burden be shared among all those with magic in their blood? Why only Meris? Who would sustain her while she sustained all? It just didn't seem fair. Those were more questions he wanted to ask of the wizard. For some reason, he didn't wholly trust Shamara. She didn't even try to hide the fact she was concealing vital information from them. Information she believed they didn't need to know. He always mistrusted those who weren't forthcoming with their knowledge. Did she know something about the lands across the great sea that she didn't want them to find out? *Is she lying to us?* That thought he quickly chastised himself for, but it came creeping back. *What if there are people still living across the sea and for some reason she doesn't want us to know they are there?*

Ta'sus grunted. Usually when someone hid a fact, it was to maintain advantage over others. The ancient saying "knowledge is power" came to his mind. So long as Shamara had knowledge they didn't, she would hold the power. And one person wielding all the power over a people could hardly be for the best. Ta'sus sighed. But Elward was right—she'd been caring for the people of Me'arah for centuries, and they had prospered. How could he complain or doubt her intentions?

"Come, Ta'sus," Elward said, taking his arm and leading him to the edge of the copse of trees. "You are too tangled in your thoughts. Let's go to my home, and I'll make you lunch. I'm sure our wives will be hours shopping in the marketplace and won't miss us a bit."

Ta'sus gave Elward a warm smile. Just like him to try to distract him from his worries. And he knew just the right way—lunch. "Thank you, dear friend, I—"

Ta'sus stopped and gripped Elward's hand on his arm. His friend searched his face, and then looked across the open field, to the path that led down the hillside to the beach, where Ta'sus was staring, his jaw slack.

"What is it, Ta'sus?" Elward, of all people, knew of Ta'sus's keen senses. But he had no idea what Ta'sus was feeling in this moment.

A rush of dizziness overtook Ta'sus as the magic assaulted him. What its source was, he could not say, but he'd never felt anything like this in his life. Certainly nothing like this from Meris or even Shamara. Magic as thick as honey coating him in suffocating surges, as if radiating from the ground. No, from the sea. Every pore in his skin tingled; every hair on his arms and neck stood on end. His pulse pounded in his ears like a loud drum.

Time seemed to slow to a crawl as he became sharply aware of every little sound—bees buzzing among the clover at his feet, wind soughing through the firth leaves and creating a patina of tinkling chimes, fireflies' wings fluttering in a frenzy in the air above him. His tongue grew thick in his mouth as words fled.

And then, from out of the brush at the top of the trail, figures emerged. Seven men and one woman, in strange garb, entirely unlike the woolen clothing the people of Me'arah wore.

"What . . . ?" Elward mumbled, stiffening beside Ta'sus.

Whether his friend sensed the magic in some way, Ta'sus didn't know. But one thing he did know—not all of these people were human. Some exuded magic from the very core of their being, and the magic in his blood cried out in recognition. The two in front—the woman in the long green gown and the short man with a trim silver beard walking beside her—had to be wizards. Ta'sus had sensed the ageless quality of magic in Shamara, which made her different from everyone he'd known. He now knew that all in Me'arah, except her, had human blood in their veins—some more than others. But these visitors . . .

Ta'sus could only do one thing. He fell to his knees and put his hands on the ground. Not in an act of worship but in unspeakable astonishment. His whole body shook as Elward trembled beside him in fear, dropping the ground in like fashion, cowering. Why had they come? And where had they had come from?

Realization swept over him like a windstorm, clearing any trace of doubt from him mind.

He knew the answer, for there could only be one answer—from across the great sea.

EIGHTEEN

JORAN STOPPED abruptly when his father raised a hand, signaling him to go no further. Up ahead were the outskirts of a village, simple one-story dwellings made of rough-hewn logs and branches, with thatched roofs. A narrow dirt lane wended down the other side of the hill they were cresting, but Zev blocked his view.

"Why are we stopping—?" Joran's eyes widened when he came alongside his father. Standing—or rather, kneeling with bowed heads—in the road were two men. Human enough, from what Joran could tell, but . . . there was something unusual. He smirked when he realized what he was sensing.

Magic. He'd already felt the trappings of magic in this land—not just while on the boat Valonis fabricated but from the land itself, the moment his feet had touched sand. Yet, at this moment he felt a tingling much more specific than the general ambiance of magic—that sustaining oscillation present all around him. And it was coming from one of the men.

As the others in their group slowed and gathered next to Joran, Zev—fronting their group—spoke to the men prostrating themselves.

"Please, arise. We bring peaceful tidings, and mean no harm."

The two men straightened and got to their feet, and the one with the thick auburn beard and bright green eyes stared unabashedly at the group now facing him. The old man with thinning gray hair next to him seemed struck speechless, his mouth open. Joran wondered if they understood their speech. How could they, if they had been underground for millennia? No doubt one of these old wizards would be familiar enough with their speech to be able to interpret or translate their language.

It must be apparent they were strangers to this land. Perhaps all the inhabitants knew every one of their neighbors and so any new face would be a shock. Or maybe it was their clothing. Who was to say? He wondered just how many people lived down here, under tons of rock hidden behind a pink sky. How odd. How very odd, the thought of living underground and yet having no idea there were other lands, other people, a day's walk from them. His hidden knowledge of this fact unnerved him as he looked upon the two men.

The bearded man cleared his throat. "My friends, welcome." Although he spoke with a strong and unusual accent, Joran found he had no trouble understanding the man's speech. Then he realized the wizards, all of them, were somehow making this communication possible. Joran was not thinking in his native language at all—and he hardly even noticed. Did these men sense something odd here as well? If they did, Joran couldn't tell.

The bearded man held out his arms in a gesture of invitation. "Forgive us for our . . . shock. We in Me'arah have never had visitors to our land."

Me'arah? I wonder what that word means. The man's creased brow relaxed, and he gave a respectful bow.

Surely Zev could sense the magic emanating from this man, couldn't he? Joran turned to catch a glimpse of his father as the others in their party stood in polite silence, allowing Zev to engage this man. Joran saw the questions swimming in the man's eyes—eyes that reminded him much of his father's. It struck Joran then—this man was also a wizard, and was much older than he seemed. Older even than King Perthin, whose life was extended only by the scepter he held in his hand and the covenant to Elysiel that came with his position.

The other man then stepped forward and said, "Where have you journeyed from? Did you traverse the great sea?" His voice was filled with astonishment, but Joran understood their awe. Imagine thinking you and your neighbors were alone in all the world—then have strangers wander in of no accord, seemingly out of thin air. *Which is much like what we did.*

"We did," Zev answered plainly, but did not elaborate. "We have come to inquire . . ." Joran turned to his father and saw him thinking, no doubt wondering how to word their purpose. But Valonis took the opportunity to speak.

"I sense much magic here"—she took a small step toward the men and tipped her head toward the older man—"especially from you. Are you . . . a leader of this realm?"

"I am. My name is Ta'sus, and I am the Lord Na'tar, appointed as the keeper of the land."

Valonis's eyebrows rose inquisitively at that.

Joran pursed his lips. *Keeper? Could the seventh site truly be hidden here, in this underground kingdom?* He turned and looked back at King Kael and King Perthin, who stood off to the side, watching this meeting of worlds. He wondered what thoughts were mulling in their heads right now.

"This is Elward—one of seven councilors entrusted with governing Me'arah."

Joran noticed a strange look exchanged between the two men, one that gave Joran the impression Ta'sus was upset about something.

"Me'arah," Valonis said thoughtfully, nodding at the name. "What does that name mean—do you know?"

Joran puzzled at her question and tone of voice. For clearly she knew exactly what it meant—he could tell by her reaction to the word when Ta'sus spoke it. It was as if she was testing him for some reason.

"I do not, dear lady." He drew in a deep breath as the warmth of the day seeped into Joran's shoulders. Did this place have seasons? Day and night? Did Shamara create everything down here—plants, animals, birds, insects—?

Zev shot Joran a look that told him he'd have all his answers shortly. He didn't need to mindspeak his amusement over Joran's lapse into a litany of questions.

"But may I please ask—why have you come? I sense . . . much power from you." Ta'sus glanced around at the party of eight facing him. "All of you." He narrowed his eyes a bit and took a step closer to Valonis, so that he now stood just a mere foot from her as he studied her face. "But you," he said, pursing his lips and pausing to think. "Your magic . . . *feels* like the magic here. As if you have some . . . kinship to this place."

Valonis's face streaked with surprise. "You are aware of your power? Of the magic around you?"

The one called Elward spoke. "All in Me'arah have this . . . magic of which you speak, to some degree. The Lord Na'tar and his line have the most. That is why their lineage was chosen to govern, for they have more insight and longevity than any others."

Ah, of course, Joran thought. If Shamara had children, her magic would have infiltrated all her progeny over generations. By now, everyone in this land would have some wizard magic in their blood. *As if Shamara is the mother of them all.*

"Chosen by whom, may I ask?" Valonis said in a quiet, wavering voice. Joran knew how important their answer was to her.

The two men exchanged a quick look, as if they were unsure if they should reply.

The Lord Ta'sus exhaled a long breath and his face softened. "The one who made this kingdom . . . and who sustains it even now with her power."

Valonis gasped and faltered. Relgar rushed to her side and supported her by her elbow. Joran had never seen her so stunned.

"So, it's true!" Hinwor exclaimed, coming forward. The two men of Me'arah exchanged more puzzled glances.

Elward said, "What is true? You heard about our land?"

Relgar, holding on to Valonis's arm to steady her, said, "We had . . . a suspicion you were here. That is why we came. To seek out this one, this wizard—"

"Shamara," Valonis stated plainly, opening her eyes and directing her gaze upon Ta'sus for confirmation.

"Yes," he said, and this time his mouth dropped open. "But how did you know . . . ?" His voice trailed off as his eyes widened in some understanding. "You are . . . her sister?"

"Why, how could you know this?" Valonis asked, studying him as if he were some fascinating specimen she had discovered.

Ta'sus shook his head and shrugged his shoulders. "I just know." He chuckled. "How did you know you would find her here?"

She sighed and smiled. "I just knew." She laid her hand on his arm, and his eyes shone.

"I must hear more. Everything," he said. "Please, come with us. Come inside, and we will get you some food and drink. No doubt you've traveled far."

Joran shook his head in amazement. *What will he think when he hears the truth? Or will the wizards choose not to tell him? How much does this man know about the world above—anything at all?* Joran tried to envision the reaction of hundreds—or perhaps thousands—of people when they learned about the real world above. Would they all rush to the surface?

He frowned. Of course they would. And they would radiate all this magic for the Destroyer to sense. Which would lead him . . . where? Here? Was the seventh site hidden here? The Moon had told him the seventh site held the key to the kingdom, and that it was hidden, yet in their midst—whatever that meant. The last thing the wizards would want is the news of this kingdom set loose upon the world. No, he imagined they would not tell this lord or the inhabitants of Me'arah the truth. At least, not until they had spoken with Shamara. Who apparently was still alive and powerful. And who, more than likely, had not told the inhabitants of her land anything about the truth of their kingdom—perhaps out of fear of Sha'kath. But their ancestors had known where they came from. Had time erased this fact gradually over the generations? Or had Shamara something to do with them forgetting? Joran's frown deepened. Now he had even more questions than ever.

Ta'sus gestured the group to follow him along the path leading to the closest structure, which sported a wide door leading inside.

Valonis hesitated as if reluctant to proceed. "Do you know where Shamara is? Would you take us to her once we've answered your questions?"

Ta'sus smiled. "To be truthful, I do not know just where she is at the moment. But my daughter Meris is with her, for Shamara is training her to . . . be her replacement, in due time." His smile then drooped. "Your sister . . . much of her vitality has been spent on her unselfish devotion to her people. It has taken its toll upon her health."

Valonis grew still, then walked over to Ta'sus and took his arm. "You feel much gratitude toward her, Lord Ta'sus."

"We all do. We owe our lives to her. She's carried a weighty burden for many centuries." He turned thoughtful and looked in the direction of the sea. "But now, Meris will be the one . . ."

Joran noticed the man's eyes glisten with tears, and sensed some great sadness in him.

"Some nice, cool water would be refreshing," Relgar offered jovially, shaking both Valonis and the lord of Me'arah out of their somber mood.

"Come, friends," Elward said, walking over to the wooden door and opening it. "We have plenty of stores inside—fruit, meats, vegetables, bread. They may be different from what you are used to, but will no doubt refresh you. And after you've eaten and rested, we will see about finding Shamara for you." The group began heading inside, Zev and Ta'sus leading the way.

"There's no need for that, good man," a quavering voice called out from the copse of trees they had just come through.

Joran swiveled his head and watched as a hunched old woman in a dark-brown shawl hobbled toward them.

Who is that? Joran searched the faces of the wizards and saw them looking at their new arrival in curiosity. But then a wave of magic washed over him, as strong as the waves that had pounded and eroded the cliffs in his dreams. And the magic was coming from this humble figure that took one painful step after another.

He didn't need his father to tell him whom he was looking at, for despite the deeply etched lines on the woman's face and her emaciated body, the resemblance to her sister was evident.

Valonis let out a cry so poignant and joyful, Joran's heart ached in resonance. The wizard who had never given up hope over the centuries ran and threw herself into the arms of the old woman, whose tears streamed down her cheeks from her milky green eyes. The other wizards gathered around her in a tearful reunion as Joran joined Perthin, Kael, and Justyn alongside the men of Me'arah. Joran had never seen such emotional display among wizards before. But then, it wasn't every day one witnessed the greatest reunion in the history of the world. Or the greatest discovery, at that.

They had found Shamara—and the descendants of the kingdom she had hurried to safety under tons of rock thousands of years ago. The people of Moreb.

The hidden kingdom.

NINETEEN

MERIS LOST track of time as she climbed the uneven and crumbling rock stairs that led upward. Although, time itself seemed to be transforming as she ascended. She sensed a shift deep inside her body, some awakening—or maybe it was her own cyclic rhythm now adjusting to some other natural meter. Like shifting from a slow waltz to a spry jig. She thought about the scroll she had examined, the way the colors changed in the sky above, from dark to light to dark, with those pinpricks of light and the creamy illuminated ball arcing from one side to the other. A wholly different world awaited her, and the reminder made her ignore her hot, throbbing feet. She wished she'd worn better shoes. But she hadn't known she would be climbing through miles of rock when she'd dressed in her soft slippers this morning.

Would these stairs never end? She slowed when she arrived at a wider, flatter place, then sat down with a plop, weary and thirsty. She chided herself for her haste. She'd brought nothing with her— no water, no food, no warm shawl. At least the temperature in the rock was cool and comfortable. But what would she find upon reaching the surface?

Well, she promised herself just a quick peek and then she'd return home. Although, she knew such a short look could hardly tell her what she needed to know about the world above. Would she sense that evil presence—Sha'kath, Shamara had called him—if he was still there? Surely he could not have eyes still upon Moreb after all these years. Was the world so small that he could keep watch on all its inhabitants? Shamara had not told her, and Meris couldn't even begin to imagine.

It took a citizen of Me'arah six days of walking to span the length and breadth of their kingdom. Twenty-two days to walk the entire perimeter, which met with towering cliffs none could climb or traverse. She'd heard people speculate over the years about what lay beyond the cliffs—and some had even tried to climb them but failed to crest them. Some postulated there might be fertile land beyond the perimeter that they could till and plant, although they lacked a pressing need to try harder to find such a place, with plenty enough arable land in Me'arah to grow the food needed to feed all who lived there. Meris understood now that Shamara had carved the kingdom entirely out of rock, like scooping out the fruit of a melon. There was nothing to be discovered on "the other side." A perfect illusion.

Her pulse pounded in her ears as she sat and rested. Even the air now felt different, thinner. Her body seemed lighter, and she drew in deep breaths that made her head spin. If the air had a taste, she would say its flavor was more bitter, more acrid, than the air in Me'arah. Dusty and dry. The great sea and all the creeks wending through her kingdom always kept the air moist year-round.

Thoughts of her family invaded her mind, sending a twinge of guilt to her gut. She knew they would have discovered her missing by now. She could only imagine what her father was thinking. Did Shamara know where she was right now? Meris assumed Shamara was aware of every little corner of the kingdom. Yet, Meris was outside the kingdom, wasn't she? However, all anyone needed to do was look for the vessel that had brought those visitors to Me'arah to learn it was missing and easily conclude who had taken it. With their magic, perhaps they could make another such vessel and come after her. The thought made her jump to her feet to continue her trek. The last thing she wanted was her father, accompanied by a contingent of wizards, searching for her. Maybe she'd be back before they realized she'd left.

Breathing quick, shallow breaths in the thin air, Meris ignored her spinning head and kept placing one foot in front of the other, barely seeing ahead of her in the dark passage that took her up, up, up, winding through tunnels she often had to stoop through. After an interminable amount of time, she turned a corner and found herself in something like a small enclosed chamber. Small rocks and debris lay littered all over the rocky ground, and she felt along the walls with her hands, wishing her fireflies were with her so she could see the space she was in. But even without light she could tell she'd come to a dead end. The only opening, at least from what she could feel with her hands, was the one she'd come through into this chamber. For all she knew, there could be some opening higher up. Another tunnel—or an exit to the surface of the world.

Maybe somehow she could conjure some light. Shamara hadn't taught her how to do anything like that, and she wondered if her ability would enable her to do so. She'd only been shown how to draw upon the magic in her blood to connect with the material world Shamara had constructed and sustained. Yet, if Meris truly had more magic in her blood than anyone else in the entire kingdom, including her father, surely she could do something as simple as make light appear. How hard could it be?

Meris felt around to find a somewhat smooth spot on the ground, then brushed away the piles of pebbles and sat. With her eyes closed and her legs crossed, she willed the magic down from the top of her head and into her arms. It took some time, but soon her arms were tingling with power, from her shoulders all the way to her fingertips. But now what?

Shamara had told her to pour her intent into the dome, willing it to brighten. It had taken some time to get the feel of how to move the power from her hands and heart to the dome above, for it was like trying to reach out and grab something in a dream. But she had begun to use her will to affect the world around her. She hoped she could do the same here, for she needed to see her surroundings to be able to find some way out. She frowned. Or maybe the wizards had sealed the passage and only they could reopen it.

Well, she would find out as soon as she could see this place she was in.

She squeezed her eyes tight, then willed herself to relax, reminding herself that she could not force the magic through her body. It was more like coaxing or summoning, like opening a spigot and letting water flow through a pipe rather than squeezing it through a tight channel. She drew in a long deep breath, then exhaled slowly through her nose, imagining particles of light dancing upon the specks of dust swirling in the air around her.

A faint tremor tickled her skin, and a vibration in her feet and hands alerted her that her magic was stirring. Like some slumbering beast awakening in its den, it stretched and surfaced, causing her fingers to feel on fire—hot but not burning.

Suddenly her whole body washed hot. Her eyes flew open to the sight of a bright cavern of shimmering rock, lit up as if a lantern spit out light from every direction. The air itself seemed alive and charged with energy, the way her fireflies often flitted about, especially when fearful.

But despite her amazement at the ease of accomplishing her objective, her heart sank. With careful consideration, she examined every inch of the walls and ceiling, only to find no tunnel, no passage, nothing that led any further. Nothing that would show her the world she so longed to see.

Her great longing turned sour, quickly changing to grief and disappointment. She could try to use her magic to blast her way through the rock, but she had no idea just how far she was from the surface. She could very well be crushed by tons of rock in the attempt. And although it was clear to her that some magic was in place here sealing the exit—or entrance, depending on one's perspective—she had no idea how to work with magic that wasn't her doing. She was all too new at this.

She slumped back down to the ground disheartened. So close and yet so far! Would she ever find a way to the real world? Was she—and everyone else in Me'arah—trapped? Surely those wizards didn't intend to spend the rest of their lives underground. They would leave Me'arah sometime. If she had been better prepared she might have been able to wait for them here, or perhaps find a way to hide and then secretly follow them out. But how silly was that idea? Wizards that powerful would not be easy to hide from. She would just have to ask that they take her with them, when they left. Or at least show her how to get out—just so she could satisfy her curiosity and see the real world. Would they?

Her head swam with these thoughts, all coated with the weight of her failure and disappointment. As much as she needed to hurry home before she was missed, exhaustion bore down on her. Tears filled her eyes, and she brushed them away. The thought of clambering back down all those stairs, then taking the boat back to the shore of her home, seemed daunting. Just a little nap would help. She was tired, so tired.

She bunched up the lightweight shawl she had wrapped around her shoulders, fashioning it into a pillow, then curled up on her side and closed her eyes. Sleep overtook her in a few blinks of her eyes.

TWENTY

KAEL STOOD with Justyn and Perthin, full of amazement, watching the wizards in animated discussion. Zev had asked Ta'sus and Elward if they wouldn't mind excusing themselves for a while, until the wizards had time to confer with Shamara. The two men of Me'arah went inside the building and promised to wait until summoned back out. Kael knew there were things about to be said that Zev did not want the men to hear—at least not until all could be discussed. How shocked the men seemed to have visitors, but if they learned the truth of who they were and where they'd come from, would they faint dead away?

Kael looked over at Shamara, who stood hunched over, hanging on to Relgar's arm for support. To think that this old, feeble, unassuming woman was a wizard powerful enough to single-handedly create this magnificent world around him . . . well, it was hard to fathom. Even though he himself had seen wonders beyond belief, this magic far exceeded anything he'd experienced in either of his lives. Heaven truly favored this kingdom by seeing that it remained preserved and flourishing over six centuries. Could it be because it housed the seventh site?

What gave him pause even more was the understanding that Shamara had fled with her people underground close to the time he had lived in the past, when the tower was being built. From what he could gather from the bits of history Relgar had shared with him, shortly before he'd been conscripted to build the tower, Sha'kath had gone on a rampage to annihilate the thriving kingdoms that would not cooperate with him.

And from what Kael recalled, the rulers of the six remaining dynasties had joined with Sha'kath in his mission to defy heaven, but then, when the languages had been confused, they fled in terror, each back to their respective land. Over the years, as Ethryn grew and prospered, as Kael lived out his past life from youth to old age, he had wondered at Sha'kath's silence. When he questioned visitors from faraway lands—their communication greatly hindered by the language differences—he gathered none had seen the powerful mage or his gryphons. It was as if, when the tower was buried, Sha'kath had been buried as well.

Still, only one conclusion made sense—that somehow Sha'kath had been reborn or taken over his vizier, Ezbon, but how that was possible, Kael couldn't begin to guess. The gryphons had transformed from stone to flesh when their sandy tomb was excavated. Witnesses testified to that fearsome event, and Kael had later seen the corners of the great tower where the creatures had broken free from their long slumber. The gryphons were Sha'kath's fabrication, so the Destroyer was somehow tied in with the buried tower.

Kael studied the wizards' faces. They had existed from the dawn of time, from before the tower had been built. Before the earliest civilizations of man. How strange time must seem to them. Here they were discussing the events of Moreb's attack as if it had been but yesterday. Kael let out a long breath of air. Maybe to them it was only yesterday—much the way it felt to him. For it had only been a few weeks ago that he'd awakened from his twilight sleep.

When he had stood at the top of the dunes under the hot desert sun as a dying old man and put the gemstone in the altar and the scroll in the stone chest. Only weeks . . .

Zev turned and gestured him and his companions over to his side.

"Shamara, may I present King Kael of Ethryn. And this is King Perthin of Elysiel, and Justyn, regent of Wentwater."

Shamara nodded in greeting and grasped each of their hands, one after the other. When she took Kael's hand, he was surprised by how warm her papery skin felt, and how strong her grip. Although her eyes had the milky glaze of old age, she looked deep into his soul as if shuffling through all his memories and knowledge. The sensation unnerved him, but he stood respectfully and waited for her to speak.

"Kael of Ethryn." A smile rose to her face, crinkling her cheeks. She turned to Valonis, shaking her head. "I didn't know . . . all these kingdoms . . . there is so much I don't understand, so much that happened after I went underground . . ."

Valonis wrapped her arm around her sister, whose tears streamed down her face. Shamara walked over to Relgar and stroked his cheek. Relgar wiped his eyes and smoothed out Shamara's long silver hair that lay in braids down her back. She told him, "I thought you'd died that day. I saw you struck down, but I couldn't . . . couldn't help you. I had to get my people to safety." She looked at Zev. "I thought the Destroyer had killed you all, that you were all gone . . . lost to me."

Relgar pulled her close as she wept. "Now, now. We are here and safe. You did the right thing, what you had to. Do not berate your choice."

Valonis stood close by, a grieved look on her face. Hinwor took her arm in silent support. Kael wondered what Valonis was thinking.

All these years, her sister had been alive but hidden. All these years Shamara assumed the world above had been destroyed and was unsafe and uninhabitable. Only a mile or so of rock had kept them apart from each other, but it may as well been an entire universe.

Why had Valonis not ever sensed Shamara those times she had come to the ruins of Moreb looking for any trace of her?

Zev came alongside Kael and said, "Perhaps heaven meant to keep this kingdom undetected all this time, until now. There is a purpose to everything under heaven, Kael."

Kael nodded, not surprised the wizard could read his thoughts; they were probably clear just by the look on his face. What Zev stated, Kael knew to be true—without a doubt. It did seem divinely timed for them to find this hidden kingdom now—when the world faced its greatest threat.

"We have much to discuss, Shamara," Relgar said. "The Destroyer disappeared for many centuries, but he has somehow returned, and we must do all we can to stop him."

"This is why we have come," Valonis said, taking Shamara's hands and leading her to sit at a wood-plank bench situated under some trees.

"You seek my help? After all this time?" Shamara held out her hands. "I'm old and drained. What help could I possibly give you against Sha'kath? Do you expect me to leave this land and my people and fight in another battle?" She gave a weak chuckle at the thought.

Zev went over to her and knelt before her. "Of course not, dear friend. But we are seeking something you might have knowledge about . . ." He glanced over at Joran, then waved him to come over. Joran complied, but his face showed his confusion.

"This is my son, Joran," Zev said. "Look at his dreams, Shamara. That will explain our quest without wasting precious time."

Joran gave Zev another confused look, but turned to Shamara as she stood and took his hands, then closed her eyes. Zev nodded at him, and Joran shrugged. *Why Joran, and why his dreams?*

Kael watched, along with all the others in their company, but minutes went by without Shamara so much as blinking. Joran stood, fidgety, but kept his eyes closed until she released him.

A wash of understanding brightened Shamara's eyes when they opened. She turned to Zev, and her mouth dropped open. "Oh my, oh my," she said over and over, looking at her visitors as if seeing them for the first time.

"Seven sites, set up by heaven to protect the world from evil. But . . . they have all been destroyed? All but one?"

Hinwor spoke. "We are not sure how many have been destroyed. Four, most likely. We do not know of Elysiel's or Ethryn's fate, at this moment."

Shamara turned and looked at Perthin, then Kael. She hobbled over to him and reached for his neck. As she fingered his necklace, she said. "You are a Keeper of the site. A *ra'wah ten'uah*—keeper of the promise. I can see these gates of heaven . . ." She closed her eyes, then opened them again. "You are the first, and the last. The beginning and the end."

Kael sucked in a gasp. "Do you know what that means?"

Shamara shook her head apologetically. She looked at Valonis and the other wizards. "You are seeking the seventh site, the one hidden, the one in your midst." She swiveled to Joran, her face scrunched in question. "The Moon told you that?"

When Joran nodded—the gesture accompanied by a roll of his eyes—Shamara rubbed her forehead and sighed. She touched Kael's necklace again and said to him, "I know nothing about this seventh site. We have no *sha'har* here in Me'arah. Heaven did not appoint me, or anyone else in this kingdom, to be a Keeper—or give a token such as this. I fear you have come to me in vain." Her face then brightened. "But I am glad of it. Glad to know there is still a world above, that people have lived all these centuries without the threat of the Destroyer—"

"But evil has still ruled the world, and creation has groaned in pain all this time, waiting for deliverance from heaven," Kael said.

Joran frowned. "And you have told your people nothing about the real world? They know nothing about their past?" When Shamara shook her head, Joran blew out a breath.

"You were wise to create this refuge for your people, Shamara," Zev said in a reassuring tone. "While humans have thrived, they have also suffered much. You have spared them that. You should not regret your decision. You have given them centuries of peace and prosperity."

Shamara studied Zev's face, putting a hand on his cheek. "You have always been able to see my heart, dear Zev. Are my regrets and doubts so obvious?"

Zev refrained from answering.

Hinwor spoke up. "What now?" He looked questioningly at Zev. "If there is no seventh site here, what about all that talk of the 'key to the kingdom'? Were those words just the ravings of a lunatic moon?"

"She wasn't the only one to speak of that, Hinwor," Perthin said. "The ghost of my predecessor, King Cakrin, said similarly." He turned to Kael. "He told me King Kael held the key to the kingdom."

"But what does that have to do with Me'arah?" Shamara asked.

Hinwor sighed. "We were hoping you would know."

Silence fell about the group. Then Valonis said quietly to Shamara. "What will you do now?" She tipped her head back and looked up at the pink dome above. "Will you stay here?" She let a pause linger between them. "Will you tell them the truth—let them leave, if they choose? And what of you? Will you come with us?" Her eyes showed the hope and longing she felt. How could Valonis bear to leave Shamara now that she'd found her?

A cry caught in Shamara's throat, and her eyes glistened with tears. "How could I leave? And do you not think I have struggled with those questions every day of my life? If I tell them about the world above, and they leave and are put in danger, I would never be able to live with that—"

Shamara broke into sobs. Valonis drew her in, wrapping her arms around her and laying her head against Shamara's.

When she stopped enough to draw in a breath and wipe her eyes, Hinwor came close and said evenly, "They may be your people, but they are not young children. If you clearly present the truth and the dangers, they should be the ones to decide their own fate."

"Are you saying I have been cruel to them—?"

Hinwor stepped back. "Oh course not. You did what you thought best. But now circumstances have changed." He nodded toward the building behind her. "Your people know we are here. There is no hiding our arrival. Our appearance shatters the illusion that they are alone in the world. Their curiosity will be roused, and nothing you can say will quench that."

"How will you answer them then?" Valonis asked softly.

Shamara's face turned hard, and after a long moment of thought she said, "I will tell them the truth." She turned to Zev. "Will you speak to the assembly, and explain it all to them? I don't have the heart . . ."

She closed her mouth as if her words had shriveled on her tongue.

"Of course I will," he told her.

Shamara turned to Valonis. "As for what I will do . . . I . . ." She sucked in a breath and held it a long while before letting the air seep out. "I went to the surface once, many hundreds of years ago. I swore . . . I would never again. I will stay here, train Meris— if she continues to be willing—and assist her until I can no longer go on . . . That is, unless *everyone* chooses to leave. Then, I suppose, there would be no more need for Me'arah." Her expression turned melancholy.

Zev looked at her solemnly. "Shamara, you need not be bound to this task any longer. It is no difficult matter for us"—he gestured to the other wizards listening intently—"to infuse enough magic into your kingdom to sustain it for many generations. You no longer need Meris to take on your burden—should it prove necessary to keep this refuge thriving." His face softened with urging. "You can return with us, take your place once again in the natural world."

"You may be surprised," Relgar added. "Once your people learn how dangerous the world above is, some may cling to this haven you've created for them. But, Zev, can we now assure them they will remain safe? Our entrance through the rock has been sealed with magic, keeping your secret safe. But if we open it, and these people leave—"

"We must carefully consider this," Valonis said. "We cannot not risk Sha'kath discovering this world, or us. Or the magic contained herein."

Hinwor raised a hand. "Those are logistics that can be figured out later. We have greater concerns right now."

Zev nodded. "Hinwor is right. We came because of the threat to the sacred sites. It seems we have no way to prevent them all from being destroyed. But we've been told that the seventh site is the key. And that Kael has some part to play in that."

"And you thought the seventh site was here, in Me'arah," Shamara said evenly.

"We were told it was hidden. The Moon could not see it anywhere on the face of the earth," Joran added. "It stood to reason—"

"But she also said it was in your midst," Justyn said, speaking suddenly after being thoughtfully quiet all this time. "Or, that is it within you. Which makes no sense, since all seven sites are said to have been made by heaven as eyes upon the earth. We should be looking for a real site, like the others."

Joran rubbed his face, clearly weary of this circling around these same points of confusion. "Does this mean, then, that we have to look for another hidden kingdom? How many could there be? And how in the world could we find them?"

"Reya had a vision of the red deer," Valonis said, which made Shamara's eyebrows rise. "I was sure she meant Moreb."

"And perhaps she did," Zev said. "It could be that although the seventh site isn't here, in this hidden kingdom, we were meant to come here."

"To find Shamara?" Valonis asked.

Zev merely shrugged.

Justyn said, "Is it possible it truly is here, and she just doesn't know it? Or that something else is here that we need?"

"I don't see how," Shamara answered pointedly. "Everything that is here, I made. Or we brought down here from the surface." She smiled wryly. "There is nothing *hidden* in this hidden kingdom."

"Other than the truth," Justyn blurted, then flushed with regret at his words.

Shamara looked at him with sadness. "Do you think to judge me, Justyn of Wentwater? I wonder, what would you have done in my place?"

"My apologies, m'lady. I imagine I would have done the same." He straightened and tugged nervously on his beard. "However, I agree with Hinwor, though. Our arrival has cracked the wall of their naiveté and ignorance. The glaring light of truth is going to brighten with every whisper."

"Well said, Justyn," Hinwor remarked. "What now?"

The group grew quiet. Shamara then began walking to the nearby building. "We tell them," she said.

TWENTY-ONE

MERIS AWOKE to pain streaking from her legs to her neck. She stretched her sore limbs and stood. How long she'd been asleep on the hard rocky ground, she had no idea. Her stomach growled in hunger, and her mouth was gummy and dry. Before a yawn escaped her mouth, she chided herself for her stupidity.

She pushed matted hair from her face and was struck with the image of her father searching for her, sick with worry. With a long glance around her at the still-illuminated room, she sighed. What good was all her magic now? She should have waited until she'd learned more about wielding magic from Shamara before running off looking for a way to the surface. She was stuck in a cave of rock, with no choice but to hang her head and return home. To a tongue-lashing, no doubt. But, she knew she deserved it. Abrella was right, often chastising Meris for her thoughtless, reckless, unthinking behavior. *Will I ever learn?*

Then another thought came to her—maybe she wasn't running *to* something as much as she was running *away* from something. The truth sank into her empty, complaining stomach and sat there like a hard rock. When she'd stood alongside Shamara in the council chambers and listened to her father voice concern over the tremendous mantle of responsibility about to be draped across his daughter's shoulders, she'd felt that weight descend on her and press her down. Ever since, she'd been trying to ignore it, push it aside, but now it faced her head-on.

She didn't want to be a powerful wizard. She didn't want to be the one everyone relied on to keep Me'arah going day after day. Why her? Didn't she have a choice? She didn't want to end up alone, spending every moment of her life channeling power into the dome and the crops and whatever else she would have to sustain. She just wanted to live a normal life, like everyone else. Play music on her pipe, run with the deer, maybe learn a skill, like weaving on a loom or woodworking. There was so much she longed to do, but now—if she went back—she would never have the chance to do any of it. All of Me'arah would look to her and rely on her and make demands on her.

If I go back . . .

Meris clenched her mouth and blew air out her nose. With every passing moment, she felt more convinced of the wrong-ness of the deception Shamara had perpetrated. What right did she have—creator or no—to withhold the truth from her people? Shouldn't the choice to stay or leave the hidden land be up to each individual? It was one thing for a parent to make decisions of great import for a young child, one who did not have the wisdom or years to do so for herself. But the people of Me'arah were mostly adults, with free will, able to decide the course of their lives. *But Shamara had taken that right away.*

The seeds of anger and outrage she had squelch had now grown into a full-fledged weed garden of doubt and disagreement, and the tendrils tangled her heart in confusion. She thought about all the years that her people had lived in ignorance, under rock, completely deprived of the beauty and bounty of the real world they had been given as an inheritance. It was as if Shamara had taken them all into captivity, depriving them of their rightful place in the world. And why? All because of fear. *Her* fear.

Meris understood Shamara wanting to provide a place of refuge and safety from a clear and present danger—this evil Destroyer named Sha'kath. But just as a small child can't hide under his bed from monsters forever, Shamara, like any good parent, should have taken them back home once enough time had passed. Surely not everyone in the entire world had been destroyed by this enemy. Surely there were other lands the people of Me'arah could have scattered to, in order to begin anew and settle and raise families— the visitors' appearance attested to that. Surely—Shamara should have let the people decide, not have kept them in the dark. *Or should I say, in a cavern lit by a pink sky?*

Meris looked down and realized she had been pacing the small chamber, walking in circles. She stopped and rested a hand on the wall and closed her eyes. Just as in the vessel she had crossed the water in, the wall of rock resonated with magic—the magic of the visitors. It was their magic that had sealed the entrance to the steps down to Me'arah.

Wizard magic. The same kind of magic Meris had running through her blood.

She thought back to the moment in her cottage when she had summoned that bolt of lace. How she'd only had to concentrate and will it to come to her. *Command* it to come. Shamara had taught her how to envision the magic moving through her body, but the way Meris had done it was the same. It was a matter of intent, nothing else. She just needed to picture the desired result and then will it to happen. Only her doubt stood in her way to success.

Meris opened her eyes and looked at the wall, then looked through it, in her mind's eye. She pictured a gaping hole in the rock, leading to open air—to that dark sky she'd seen on the animal hide, a sky pricked with white lights. She pushed away the imposing image of that creature—*gryphon*—that had terrified her, telling herself such a creature could no longer be out there, waiting. Instead, she saw those towering hills capped with white frosting, and drew in the crisp, cool air that drifted from their peaks, letting it saturate her body while willing the magic into her limbs.

The small chamber began to thrum, softly at first and hardly noticeable. But soon Meris had to find sure purchase for her feet to keep from being thrown to the ground. The shaking didn't scare her, though, for she knew she was its source. Then she understood what she had to do.

Like drawing moisture into a cloth, she set her attention on the magic around her, which permeated every bit of rock and dust and particle of air. She could now see past the illumination to something deeper, more potent, more essential that coated everything around her, like invisible icing.

This was the spell the kept the world outside from finding the steps leading down to her kingdom. A spell the wizards had cast. A spell Meris now saw so clearly, it almost made her chuckle. A spell she now knew she could break.

Perthin studied the old wizard's face as she stepped back from her intimate embrace with her sister. He'd kept a polite distance, alongside Justyn and Kael, during the tearful reunion of these long-separated loved ones. The sisters spoke affectionately in hushed voices, and the joy radiating from Valonis was palpable, filling the pink-tinged air. The land seemed charged with joy amid the tears flowing freely.

Zev had gone inside to fetch Ta'sus and Elward, and Perthin wondered how they would react upon hearing the truth about their kingdom. Would chaos ensue once everyone knew? How would Shamara feel if all her people rushed to the surface, eager to leave the beautiful kingdom she'd made for them? Would any remain?

Perthin thought about the girl, Meris, that she mentioned. Ta'sus had said his daughter was training to take over her task of sustaining this world. Would the girl even need to, now? It seemed a sad day, to him. Another possible ending. Me'arah, no doubt, was the oldest kingdom in existence. It would be a shame to close its "doors" and make it all vanish with a spoken word. Perthin could not begin to imagine the effort and time it had taken Shamara to fashion this place, let alone keep it alive and thriving every second.

He, perhaps of all those here, knew the scope of life within a kingdom—from tiny insect to foraging beast to plant to human. Millions of living things interconnected, a web that supported itself, but was so delicate that one harsh stroke could rip it. He never had to sustain all the life in his kingdom, but he was aware of its fragility and preciousness, the first and last breath of every living thing. The ephemeral quality of existence that plagued all. Kingdoms came and went. People lived and died. The longer he lived, the more time seemed to speed up. The quicker his friends and family members grew up and aged and passed before his eyes. Was this truly all there was to life? Was there nothing more?

Perthin sighed, feeling the longing to return to Elysiel tugging on his heart. He looked down at the scepter in his hand—this scepter he'd been wielding for three centuries now, its heart always beating steadily, faithfully. As faithfully as the sun arcing each day across the sky, and the moon rising in the east. As faithfully as the seasons rotating through the years, never ending, never slowing. The world seemed like clockwork. And now—was it meant to wind down? Would everything truly come to a full stop? An end?

He heard again Cakrin's words in his head. *"Endings are merely beginnings."*

Perthin looked up at a noise—Shamara had audibly gasped. Her visage darkened, and her eyes searched beyond the gathered group in the direction of the sea. Perthin noted her agitation.

"What is it?" Valonis asked, gripping Shamara's elbow and looking off in the same direction.

Shamara turned and looked at her. "Do you not sense it?" She pinched her lips together. "No, I suppose you would not."

Zev studied her. "What has happened? Is someone coming?"

Perthin noticed Shamara's expression growing even more distraught. "Not coming. *Leaving.*"

Before anyone could question her further, she pushed past Valonis and Zev and made her way over to Ta'sus, who stood beside Elward next to the doors to the building they'd been about to enter. Perthin glanced at the wizards, who seemed as puzzled as he. Why would someone leaving be upsetting to Shamara? Leaving where? To where? At least no one was sensing the Destroyer. Wasn't that what mattered most—that Zev had successfully sealed the entrance to the path through the rock and the magic had not alerted Sha'kath?

Ta'sus hesitated no more than a second upon seeing Shamara's face.

"Where is my daughter, Meris?" He frowned at Shamara's look of surprise. "It doesn't take magic to be able to tell something's happened to her. But"—his brows narrowed and he closed his eyes—"she's not in danger. I would know. I would sense her fear—"

"No," Shamara answered, "not in danger. *Yet.*"

Ta'sus stiffened. "What are you saying? She is about to head into danger? From what source?"

Shamara let loose a sigh and laid a hand on the Lord Na'tar's wrist. "It's time," she said evenly.

Ta'sus stepped back with a scowl. "Time for what?" He eyed her, awaiting an answer.

The old wizard's shoulders slumped, and her face softened. "There are things I must show you, Ta'sus of Me'arah. Things of the past. In order to prepare you for your future."

Perthin, standing in silence in the warmth of the day, understood. This lord of Me'arah knew nothing of the truth of his existence, that he lived in a kingdom under the true world. But perhaps they needed his help to find the seventh site, and so he needed to understand why. Shamara had said Meris was leaving, about to face danger . . .

The blood drained from Perthin's face. Ta'sus's daughter had left. She was trying to get to the surface.

He looked at the wizards and saw they had come to the same conclusion. If Meris somehow escaped from the protective magic of this kingdom, it would not be just she who faced danger. This entire kingdom would be at risk. No wonder Shamara was distraught.

Zev went to her side. "Does he not know the history of Moreb?"

Ta'sus scrunched his face. "Moreb. What is Moreb?"

Perthin heard Hinwor mutter, "Apparently not." Relgar elbowed Hinwor.

Valonis shook her head and told Shamara with assurance, "Zev sealed the way. She cannot get out."

Ta'sus spun to her, his face reddening. "Out? Out where? There is no *out*." He rubbed a hand over his eyes, then faced Shamara again. "Where is Meris?" he asked again, this time in a weary, hopeless tone.

Shamara stood lost in thought. The group waited.

"She must have taken our boat," Joran whispered, and Zev hushed him.

Ta'sus, nearly frantic, spun to face Joran, "What is a boat? What are you hiding from me?"

Perthin caught Hinwor rolling his eyes as if thinking, *This is a tale Shamara had no intention of telling this man.*

But tell she must, Perthin gathered.

"Lord Ta'sus," Shamara said after a long minute of decision, "we must go to your cottage. There are things you need to see."

Ta'sus gulped. "The secret room?"

Shamara nodded.

A secret room? Perthin had the niggling sense that things were soon going to get turbulent in this underground kingdom. Had their arrival caused this trouble? He hoped not. But he couldn't hold back the ripples of worry emanating from his own heart as he replayed the ghost's warnings about the end of all things. Would it end here, in Me'arah? Was the seventh site hidden under all this rock, and was Sha'kath going to find it? In their effort to find the hidden kingdom and stop Sha'kath, had they inadvertently led him to it?

An urgent need to flee seized him. He had to return to Elysiel. How could he have left his kingdom unprotected?

Ta'sus asked, "Is there something there, in that room, that will help Meris, protect her?"

Shamara shook her head. "There is an ancient saying: 'Knowledge saves the life of the one wielding it.' But there is another saying: 'With knowledge comes pain.'"

She said nothing further.

Perthin fought to stem the rising distress in his heart. *No truer words than those.* Knowing some end was approaching was knowledge he wished he hadn't been given. If there was nothing he—or any human or even wizard—could do to prevent the inevitable, what good was it to be told about it? Why did Cakrin tell him to seek out Kael if there was no hope? Why tell him Kael held the key to the kingdom?

He felt like a hapless soldier who had been sent empty-handed into a great battle against thousands of well-trained warriors with sharp swords. Such a soldier would fare just as well hiding beneath his bed. Although he might still be killed, what purpose would his foolish valor serve him? None at all. He would still be dead. And if he did not have the means to protect those he loved, they would die also.

Well, even if he could do nothing to stop the end of the world, he would rather be in his rightful place, back in Elysiel, with his people. He'd been gone too long; his heart yearned for home. How could he help these wizards fight the Destroyer anyway? He had none of their powers. His only magical power lay in his connection to the land—and with the object that rested in his hand. Although the scepter only served Elysiel—no other place.

He glanced at the heart beating in steady rhythm in the handle of the scepter, the reminder of his solemn oath and charge. His fingers gripped the staff tighter as the wizards strode toward him and Kael and Justyn.

He stood aside as they walked at a fast clip along a trail wending up a ridge, Ta'sus leading the way, with Elward and Shamara right behind him. Valonis hurried to join Shamara at her side, while the other wizards spoke in hushed voices as they trekked. Perthin waited with Kael, and then, with a nod, followed after them. They walked up and down hills and dales for most of an hour, and Perthin was surprised that Shamara, who seemed hardly able to move at such a fast pace, kept up.

"Where are we going?" Justyn asked, hurrying to join Perthin and Kael. Perthin stopped and waited while the old scholar caught up to them, laboring to catch his breath. Kael stopped a few feet ahead, a wry smile on his face.

"It's not fair," Justyn panted out as he wiped his brow. "You are all older than I . . . ." He bent over with his hands on his hips until his breath caught up with his body. Kael put a calming hand on Justyn's shoulder—as he'd done once before—and the man's breathing slowed. Justyn narrowed his eyes.

"I wish I knew how you did that," he told Kael, relief filling his face.

The king of Ethryn chuckled. "I wish I did as well. It's a gift. One I'm happy to extend to you anytime, my friend."

Justyn grunted. "Can you give me a young body?" At Kael's smirk, Justyn said, "I didn't think so." He gestured to the rest of their group descending into a wooded dell. "Well, I'm probably the youngest in our odd contingent, but I'm the only one out of breath."

"Perhaps you need to spend less time studying books at a desk and more time walking the Heights of Wentwater," Perthin said good-naturedly. Justyn only glared in response.

"As to where we are going," Kael said, "it appears we've arrived." He nodded at the small cottage tucked in the grove of silver-leafed trees that the wizards and their escorts—Ta'sus and Elward—had stopped at. They followed the leaf-blanketed path and met up with the rest of the group.

A handsome woman with long dark braids came out of the house. She quickly took in the party standing at her doorstep and gasped loud enough for Perthin to hear at the back of the gathering.

"Ta'sus, wh-who are these people?"

The lord took his wife's hands in his. "They are . . . visitors."

The woman looked shocked. Perthin could only imagine the reaction when the entire kingdom learned of their arrival.

"Visitors? What do you mean?" She trembled on wobbly knees. Her husband wrapped a supporting arm around her shoulders.

"They have come from a land across the great sea—"

"Oh my!" She clutched a hand to her heart. Ta'sus helped her sit on a bench beside the cottage door. "How . . . how can that be?" She sucked in short, frantic breaths as her face paled even more.

Kael went over and knelt beside her. "If I may?" he asked Ta'sus, gesturing to the wife's hands. Ta'sus nodded with inquisitive eyes.

Kael took her hands in his and immediately the color returned to her cheeks. She gave Karl a questioning look as her breathing slowed and she visibly relaxed.

"Wha-what did you do to me?"

He must get that a lot, Perthin thought with a smile.

"Drayna, these good folk are here on an urgent matter. I must show this kind woman something inside our house." He nodded at Shamara, who gave Drayna a sweet smile. Shamara came up to her and laid a hand on the woman's cheek.

"Have we met?" Drayna asked her, looking at her quizzically.

"Oh, perhaps, in the marketplace."

Drayna nodded, but her eyes showed her bewilderment. She grew calm and quiet as she returned in a daze into the house.

Ta'sus gave Shamara a knowing look, then nodded at her to enter the cottage. She turned and held up her hand.

"We won't be long." Then she and Ta'sus entered through the open door.

Perthin heard Joran grunt and say, "Long to her. Could mean days we'll be waiting." He turned to Zev. "She must have been watching us—when we landed on the shore."

Zev nodded. Perthin suddenly realized he meant Ta'sus's daughter, not Shamara.

"She took the boat," Joran added. Zev nodded.

"And you don't think she can get past your spell, find a way to the surface?"

Zev shook his head. "Only another wizard could detect and break that spell. And if it's undetectable by Sha'kath, surely a young girl would not be able to perceive it."

Joran made a face that showed his doubt. "But she is going to walk right into your magic when she gets to the top of the steps. And if she has been chosen by Shamara to take her place, you may be underestimating her ability. She will sense the spell."

Zev's face twitched.

"Shouldn't we go after her and stop her? What will happen if she breaks through? If she has that much magic in her blood, the Destroyer might notice. Surely Shamara has not taught her how to mask her power; she didn't need to learn that here, did she?"

Relgar, who had been standing a few yards away, listening, threw up his hands. "I see what you mean about Joran and his questions—"

"But they are important questions, no?" Kael asked.

Valonis fretted and shook her head. "We need to talk further with Shamara and about what is happening above in the world. She has no idea what danger she is in—or her people."

Hinwor added, "Danger we are all in."

The man Elward came from out of shadows. Perthin had forgotten about him. His face was seared with worry, and he clenched his hands at his sides.

"Please, would you kindly tell me what this is all about, why you have come? I fear something terrible is about to happen."

As Zev turned to say something to him, Perthin felt a horrific pain stab his chest.

He clutched at his shirt and dropped to his knees. Blood raced in a fury through his veins, and his throat closed as tight as a vise. He sucked at air that would not enter his mouth. The crystal scepter slipped from his grasp to the forest floor.

With his arms flailing, a rush of explosive sound filled his ears. He clenched tight his eyes as black spots pelted his vision like inky raindrops.

"He-help me . . ." he eked out on a thin wisp of breath.

Arms grabbed his arms and led him somewhere. He felt his back pressed up against a wall, but he could not open his eyes. More pain avalanched, striking his chest as hard as any boulder.

Finally, he caught snatches of air and pulled them hard into his lungs. His body suddenly felt as heavy as a sack of rocks, with every muscle aching as if he'd been trampled by a dozen horses. Every ounce of strength seeped from his body, leaving him a limp shell of a man. His heart struggled weakly to beat in his chest, one feeble pulse after another.

He forced one eye open enough to see Kael holding his left arm and Justyn his right, fearful looks of concern on their faces.

"Can't you do something, Kael?" Perthin heard Justyn say in a frantic tone.

Perthin's head whirled in pounding pain. The beating did not let up even though he felt hands laid upon him and heard Kael muttering something unintelligible.

"I don't understand," Kael said. To Perthin, it sounded as if the king's voice was miles away, underwater. "I can't help him."

"What are they doing in that house?" he heard someone else say, although the haze of pain prevented Perthin from identifying who spoke.

Another said, "Nothing that would hurt Perthin like this." Zev's voice.

Perthin moaned as his body throbbed. His limbs seemed to be disintegrating, one tiny bit at a time. And his heart felt broken.

Broken . . .

He forced his heavy eyelids open but couldn't move his head. He pushed stubborn words out of his mouth. Kael came close, almost touching Perthin's face with his own, to hear him. Perthin felt the king's warm breath on his cheek.

"What? What are you saying?" Kael kept asking him.

"Need . . . need . . ." He strained to lift one hand. He watched Kael's eyes widen.

"His scepter—bring it!"

Perthin gave one nod, then his head dropped from the exertion of trying to speak. Never in his life had he felt such pain, such weakness.

There had to be some reason for his suffering. Was no one else affected? Why him?

As soon as the scepter was placed into his open, waiting hand, he knew the answer.

It struck his heart with one final slashing blow, shattering it into pieces.

He didn't even need to open his eyes to see it. He could feel it through the dead, cold wood of the staff in his hand. The heart in the handle had stopped beating. The heart of King Lantas, the first king and Keeper of Elysiel, his beautiful kingdom. The heart that promised to beat for every Keeper, from the first to the last, until the end of all things.

"You are the last king of Elysiel."

Cakrin's words drifted over him and sank into his old bones in silence as his breath grew shallow.

In his mind's eye, Perthin saw them fall. One by one, the massive stone slabs tipping and crashing to the ground, two gryphons circling overhead under a hot, angry sun.

The sacred site of Elysiel—destroyed. The heart of his kingdom—crushed.

With a last gasp, Perthin clutched the scepter to his chest, pressing the stilled heart in its handle up against his own. And, as if in synchronous response, his own heart gave a last beat, then beat no more.

TWENTY-TWO

TA'SUS SUCKED in a breath as the old woman—*the wizard*, he corrected himself—reached for the doorknob. He'd stared at that door innumerable times over hundreds of years, ever curious why it was there and why it was locked. He knew now it housed secrets to Me'arah's past and guessed that Shamara had been the one to build this room and bespell it. But why create such a room in a cottage in the woods? If she had something valuable to hide, why not hide it in her own house?

"Because, Lord Ta'sus," Shamara said, halting with her hand on the knob and turning to look at him with affectionate eyes, "this used to be my house." She added a smile, no doubt intended to reassure him in some way, but it did nothing to dispel the growing sense of doom in his heart. He wanted her to hurry, to explain why Meris might be in danger, but the haste she'd showed in their hurry to arrive here was now erased from her features.

She sighed wistfully. "Long ago, I lived here with Garog, my husband—the first Na'tar." She looked around the room as if trying to conjure memories that had taken place within its four walls. "We raised our daughters here, and then . . . the years drifted by, and I watched my husband and children grow old and die. Oh, many years elapsed, but, well . . ." She straightened and set her jaw. "It was time to move out. I gave the cottage to my grandson,

Nehum, and appointed him the new Na'tar. I showed him everything in this room—what I am about to show you—but he scoffed
at the remnants of the past and called me a doddering fool, albeit
with his touch of affection."

Shamara shook her head sadly, although her eyes still held her
smile. "He didn't believe in magic—neither the magic I showed
him in this room nor the magic surging through his blood. Magic
radiated everywhere in Me'arah, but by then, few noticed. The
people underground had no idea how much magic existed in their
everyday world—"

"Wait!" Ta'sus said, his mind halting to grasp the word that
snagged in his ears. "You said *underground*. What are you talking
about? And please, what does this have to do with Meris and why
she is in danger?"

Shamara gripped the knob firmly and turned it. "Everything,
my lord Ta'sus."

The door swung open, and Ta'sus's eyes widened in astonishment. A shaft of light set afire the dust motes that had been stirred
up from her action and now danced on the air, teasing him to
enter. He'd repressed his curiosity all these years, but now it held
him in a tenacious grip. His heart pounded in anticipation.

Shamara stepped inside the room and gestured him to follow.
"Allow me to tell you the history of a land called Moreb . . ."

Justyn wiped the tears off his cheeks as he cradled the body of the
last king of Elysiel in his arms. The others had gathered around in
shocked silence. He looked up scornfully at Kael.

"Why couldn't you save him? You have the power." He shot a
look of disdain over at the powerful wizards, who stood and stared.
"Or you . . . wizards. Surely you could have done something—"

Justyn's throat choked closed, clogged with more tears. He dared glance at the glassy-eyed gaze of horror frozen on Perthin's face.

Kael laid a hand on Justyn's shoulder, and studied the scepter lying nearby. "His scepter stopped beating." Justyn looked in his face and saw Kael's eyebrows furrow.

"Sha'kath," Hinwor said in a scowl. "The king was linked at heart with his kingdom, his sacred site."

Valonis put a hand over her own heart and gasped. "Elysiel's site must have been destroyed." She looked down with great sadness at the dead king's lifeless body.

Kael said, "I never would have asked him to come with me to Moreb had I known he would die if his site was destroyed."

"I don't think Perthin would have come either, had he known. But he didn't know," Zev consoled. "Yet, his ancestor told him to seek you out," he told Kael. "I don't believe there was anything Perthin could have done to prevent this had he stayed in Elysiel."

Justyn wiped more tears and stood, his emotions a jumble of anger and grief. "We don't know that. Perhaps he would have found some way to prevent the site's destruction."

Relgar walked over and put an arm around Justyn. His face showed great sadness and commiseration. "None of the other Keepers—from what we can tell by Joran's dream and the Moon's declaration—had been able to prevent their sites from the gryphons' attacks. Why think Perthin would be able to do what the Moon could not?"

Justyn only nodded, a rock lodged in his throat, preventing him from saying more.

"And if Joran's dream portends truth, then the site at Ethryn is the only one left standing—of the six we know of," Zev said, looking pointedly at Kael, who seemed agitated and ready to run.

"The first and the last . . ." Justyn muttered bitterly, then shot a look at Kael. "Your site was the first built—and maybe is the last to be destroyed."

Kael's face paled. Justyn knew he had just voiced the very fear that Kael was imagining.

The king of Ethryn let loose a long shaky breath. "Perhaps then it is inevitable. And there is nothing at all we—any of us—can do to stop the Destroyer." He knelt next to Perthin's body and tears began streaking down his face. In a quiet voice he said, "I am sorry, friend, that you are gone. I only knew you a short time, but you found a place in my heart, and there you will remain forever."

A somber silence spread among their group, leaving only the clinking of silver leaves in the trees surrounding them, stirred up by the breeze wafting through the dell.

Elward come over to Justyn from behind the group of wizards. "We can give him a burial place of honor here in Me'arah—"

"No," Justyn said, sounding a bit too harsh to his own ears. He softened his tone. "No, he must be returned to his people, his land."

Elward shook his head. "But, wherever that is, it must be a long journey?" He glanced from face to face for confirmation.

"We can neither afford the time nor the risk to take him—" Hinwor began, then stopped speaking when he looked at Elward. Justyn knew what he was thinking. It was not his place to explain about the real world above this hidden kingdom.

Justyn set his face and looked at Hinwor. The truth would come out regardless. What did it matter now? Justyn would do the right thing, and he didn't care what anyone else thought. The king of Elysiel must be laid to rest in his own land.

He swallowed and said, "I will return him to his people. I alone. I am not needed here on . . . this quest. I am merely human."

The weight of his years pushed him down to his knees as an unmerciful sadness suffocated him. His arms pinged with pain as he reached for Perthin's boots and began to unlace them.

"What are you doing?" Joran asked.

"He's taking the king's boots off," Hinwor said, as if scolding him for asking.

"But why?"

Justyn's feeble, shaking fingers struggled with the knots.

"Here," Kael said, kindness oozing from his voice, "let me help you, Justyn."

Justyn looked into Kael's pained face, and he knew they shared the same understanding. Kael said quietly, "I would go with you, but I must see this through—for Perthin. I can do no good going to Elysiel with you. I don't know what you will find there," he said in a grunt as he pulled first one boot, then the other, off Perthin's feet, "but it's an honorable thing you are doing, Justyn of Wentwater."

Justyn felt all eyes upon him as he slipped off his own shoes and tugged on the king's soft leather boots. Thankfully they were a tad big, and he laced them up as best he could.

"I don't understand," Elward said, shooting Justyn a puzzled look.

The wizards stood in respectful silence until Justyn said, "What should I do? I can't carry him." Would this even work? Would the boots be able to pass the magical barrier erected at the surface? Did they only work on Perthin's feet?

"Sit," Valonis said gently, taking Justyn's arm and helping him to sit beside Perthin. "Just cradle him in your arms." She gave him a tender smile and stroked his cheek. Justyn's breath hitched in his chest. Despite his anger, he felt his affection for these honorable wizards bloom.

"You are a brave man, Justyn, and it has been an honor," she said. The other wizards nodded.

Zev rested a hand on top of Justyn's head. "Go, and tell the people of Elysiel what Perthin told you. Who knows what you will find when you get there. The people now have no king or Keeper. They will be afraid and need answers."

"The answers I give them will not inspire comfort or hope," Justyn said bitterly. "It appears there is no hope left in the world—not if the sites have all been destroyed." He tipped his face up to look at Kael. "Do you not want to return to Ethryn, to stop Sha'kath? To save your sacred site? Or do you feel it too—the hopelessness of our quest?"

Kael swallowed. "If it truly is heaven's will that all the sites are to be destroyed, then who am I to try to prevent it from happening?"

Justyn scoffed. "Isn't that why we came here—to try to find the seventh site and stop the Destroyer?"

Kael sighed. "I don't know anymore." He looked at the other faces around them, then back at the face of the dead king of Elysiel. "I just don't know . . ."

Zev turned to Kael. "You are the first and the last, and hold the key to the kingdom. We don't yet know what that means, but one thing I know, King Kael of Ethryn: everything heaven does is for a reason. There is a purpose for everything under heaven. Heaven set up the seven sacred sites to prevent evil from gaining a stronghold over the world, and now heaven is allowing evil to conquer. Perthin said his predecessor, King Cakrin, told him 'endings are merely beginnings.' I suppose we will just have to wait to see what this 'ending' portends. And what beginning is to follow."

Kael only nodded and looked forlorn. Justyn reached over and pulled Perthin close, so that the dead king's head rested in his lap. Justyn closed Perthin's eyelids over the empty, glassy eyes and looked up at Kael.

"I don't think we will meet again, King Kael, but it was a great honor to know you and hear of all your tales. Thank you for taking me along on this amazing adventure." He looked at the others encircling him, who showed tenderness in their expressions. Here he was, among the last wizards in the world, part of their company. He felt truly awed and humbled. What human had ever had such an honor? His throat choked with gratitude for the kindness they'd shown him.

"If I ever make it back to Wentwater, I will have enough to write about to fill a dozen heavy tomes for the School of Magic." He frowned. "Although, I doubt anyone would believe a word of it. Kingdoms hidden underground for centuries? Wizards with the power to create worlds? Magic boots that can transport someone across leagues in an instant? They will think I'm daft—if they don't already think it."

He forced a chuckle, but it pained his chest to utter it, and Kael met him with his own forced smile. As much as he tried to make light of how he felt, a horrible sense of doom prevailed over his heart. He didn't even know if these boots would work for him, but he had to try. And would they take him back to Wentwater once he completed his task of burying Perthin in the tomb of the kings in Elysiel? He had no idea. But Justyn supposed he would soon find out.

"Good-bye, Justyn," Kael said, patting him for good measure on his shoulder. He stepped back and nodded. "And heaven be with you."

"And you too, Your Highness," Justyn said respectfully, tears blurring his vision. He sucked in a deep breath, gave his companions one last glance, and said to the boots on his feet, "Take us to Elysiel, to the sacred site."

A whoosh of bone-snapping cold air enveloped Justyn and spun him in such a tizzy that he squeezed his eyes shut and clenched his teeth. He lost all sense of time as he tumbled through space and as bile rose up his throat. Every bone in his body ached as if beset with a great chill, and he lost feeling in his feet and hands. A roar assaulted his ears, and he longed to press his hands over them to snuff out the sound, but he didn't dare release his hold on the king.

By the time the whirling and rushing of air subsided, his jaw pained him and his teeth chattered uncontrollably. He peeked an eye open, looking down, and saw he still held on to Perthin's body, then let out a sigh of relief.

He then raised his head and strained to look out through the deep gloom engulfing him. The air had a foul smell and hung wet and heavy around his face. Was it nighttime? He couldn't tell. It seemed more an eerie twilight between day and night, between worlds. He strained to listen, but the roar of wind still echoed in his head, making it impossible to hear anything at all. Could this be Elysiel, or had something gone wrong?

But then his eyes adjusted to the scant light, and when they did, he wished he'd never opened them. He wished he hadn't thought to come here. For where he lay with the dead king in his arms, a huge pile of rubble surrounded him. Huge pieces of shattered rock lying in piles, like the bodies of slain men, the dust from the debris swirling in the air. The ground at his feet lay covered in frost, and icicles hung from the few remaining slabs that made up what once was the sacred site.

He thought back to the nightmare he'd had when he arrived in Ethryn—which felt like years ago—of the rocks at the bottom of Lake Wentwater toppling over in slow motion, and the despairing scream he'd heart that rent his heart.

The pain and fear of his nightmare revisited him, and a scream tried to rise up in his chest and force its way out of his mouth. But Justyn clamped his mouth shut and looked around him, hoping to see someone, some sign of life, even animal or bird. But a heavy desolation hung in the air, and now that the roar in his ears had faded, he heard nothing, just dead silence draping the land.

Surely this was not Elysiel, was it? The beautiful land King Perthin had described—verdant and prolific with life? Where was everyone? Why was it so quiet?

He did not try to hold back his grief and sorrow; the tears streamed down his chilled cheeks and nearly froze on his chin. His breath came out in white frosty puffs. His heart beat weakly in his chest, and then sped up in a start when he heard a shriek pierce the silence like a sharp knife.

Terror rushed through every vein in his body, and he shook so hard he almost fainted. A frantic scan of the dark roiling clouds above him showed nothing but ominous shadows, but he was certain the sound came from above him, although it rippled out across the land beyond the site. Justyn cowered, hugging the king's body tight against his chest and moaning as the terrifying cries struck him again and again with the pain of a sword thrust.

A sudden downpour of snow pelted him, turning to hard hailstones, and Justyn did his best to tuck his head down into his flimsy shirt that provided neither protection nor warmth. The icy pebbles stung his scalp and scattered on the ground around him. His old heart ached as it beat with fury in his chest.

Now knowing the futility of his intent to return Perthin to his land and see him buried properly, Justyn yelled at the boots: "Take us to Wentwater, to the Heights, to my cottage!"

Nothing happened. Between teeth chatters, Justyn yelled again: "Take us to Ethryn, to the palace!"

Again, nothing happened. Justyn tried to stop shaking, but could not. Ice gobbled up the ground around his feet. His teeth kept rattling in his head so hard he thought they would drop out. Now his tears froze on his cheeks before they made it to his chin. His arms and hands were so numb, he could not lift them to wipe his face. He was cold, so cold . . . he drifted off to sleep . . .

Then, strange apparitions appeared before him. Ghostly shapes that tore apart and came together in the whipping wind that cut his skin and burned his ears. He saw faces of men and knew he must be delirious. Gray smoky arms reached out to him, fingers wiggling as if they wanted something from him. The sight struck terror in him.

"What, what do you want? Go away, go away!"

Justyn swung at the air, trying to dispel the shapes descending upon him, but they came closer, tighter, thicker, and soon the gray mass engulfed him.

Justyn, in a panic, tried to get up, but he could not move—not even a finger. His body would no longer respond to his wishes, as if it were lifeless.

Then, through his muddled confusion, he felt an encompassing warmth, as if these shapes had fashioned themselves into a wool blanket that had been heated by a crackling fire. Justyn took in two deep breaths and shuddered as his feet tingled and feeling returned. He felt nearly weightless, floating, unencumbered and free.

He dared look out into the gray mass, and what he saw further confused him. The faces were still there, looking upon him curiously, but the one closest, only inches from him and whose body hovered a foot in the air, had none other than Perthin's visage.

Justyn startled and stumbled to his feet. The silence was even thicker now, as if this blanket was muffling out all the sounds in the world. He swatted his hand at the apparition, and it dissipated.

I must have lost my mind. What is wrong with me?

A voice spoke to him—sounding just like Perthin.

"You are dead, like me," it said.

"Dead . . ." Justyn repeated in a whisper. He put a hand over his own heart and, to his, shock, felt nothing. He pressed harder. His heart was not beating. He caught a glimpse of the shadowy shape that was now to his right, and he turned his head to look at it. Eyes cast downward directed his gaze to the hard ice-encrusted ground. There, lying prone, with his arms wrapped around the king's body, was his own body—lifeless, gray, frozen.

Dead.

His eyes darted back to find the one who had spoken such nonsense to him. He must be hallucinating. Or ill, or under some enchantment.

"Come," the voice said to him, the shape rematerializing now undisputedly into the form and beckoning face of King Perthin of Elysiel. "Come with me, my friend."

"Come? Come where?" Justyn looked back at the two bodies lying on the ground and shook his head. *I don't understand. What is happening?*

"I have something to show you, Justyn of Wentwater," the ghostly form said, and Justyn perceived, to his puzzlement, a slight smile rising on the blur of the face looking lovingly at him.

"What is it?" Justyn asked on a wisp of breath, a strange excitement welling up inside him.

"The seventh site."

• PART FOUR •

W ELL, LOOK who is all snuggled tight in bed and ready for more of the story," Alia said.

"I am!" Aron answered, wiggling so hard, he knocked Big Pig to the floor. "Whoops!" He leaned over the side of the bed and pulled his stuffy to his chest. Aron draped his arms over the pig's head. "This is my favorite part of the story, Momi."

"I know. But I can't tell the rest of it all in one night."

Aron nodded solemnly. Alia smoothed out his unruly hair and glanced up as Glynn came to stand under the curved archway framing the entrance to the room. Aron's eyes lit up upon seeing his father.

"Dadi, where were you all day?"

Alia smiled watching Glynn come over and plop on the bed next to Aron. He tickled his son and ruffled the hair Alia had just tamed. She chuckled as Aron erupted in giggles.

"You know I was on a survey team, exploring the southern territory."

"Did you find any neat stuff?"

"Yep. But I'll tell you all about it at breakfast."

Alia nodded in the direction of the kitchen. "There's food for you, in the thermador, if you're hungry—"

"Momi made s'ketti and smashed 'tato pie!"

"Yum," Glynn said to Aron. "I'm surprised you left any for me."

"Silly Dadi! Momi is smart. She knows to make a *lot!*"

Glynn laughed and tickled Aron some more. Alia watched her son squirm, trying to get out from under Glynn's determined hands.

"Well, it's late. Shouldn't you be getting some sleep?" he asked Aron.

Aron looked shocked. "Momi hasn't told me my story yet." He narrowed his eyes. "We're at the part where Meris sneaks off and tries to get out of Me'arah."

Glynn paused, then nodded. He gave Alia a questioning glance that she well understood. He turned back to Aron, extricating himself from the avalanche of stuffed animals and getting to his feet. "That is an exciting story, and Momi is the best storyteller in six galaxies."

"More!" Aron said. "In all the universe!"

"I see." Glynn brushed pink pig fuzz from his shirt. "I'm going to take a shower and have something to eat." He leaned over the bed and gave Aron a big kiss on his cheek. Aron gleamed.

"Night, Dadi."

"Sleep tight, little bug."

Glynn gave Alia a soft kiss on the top of her head. Only she could hear the words he then whispered to her.

"You don't tell him everything, do you? Won't he get nightmares?"

"No secrets!" Aron said, eyeballing his father.

"I thought you didn't want to hear mushy stuff," Glynn said to him.

Aron only crossed his arms and hmphed.

Alia gave Glynn a kiss on his cheek and whispered back. "Of course not. He's too young to hear what really happened."

"I don't know if he'll ever be old enough to hear it. It took years for you to tell me the truth."

Alia caught the concern and love merging in his eyes. She remembered how she felt after she returned from the surface of the world. How could she forget? Its malaise stuck to her like a sticky film she could not wash away—not until the last age sputtered out and the new age was ushered in. It was a madness that had coerced her to sneak away and take the steps up through the rock, those many centuries after she had led her people to safety and created the hidden kingdom. Even though the memories were old enough to petrify, Alia knew she would never forget the horrible despair she felt upon reopening the crevice in the cliff and stumbling out onto the dusty plain that had once been her verdant kingdom—a kingdom full of prodigious, vibrant life.

Under a sweltering sun, in dry, dizzying heat, she had stopped a few feet away from the towering sandstone walls that used to enclose Moreb. The land that had once been thick grassy meadows, lush dells and rolling hills, sparkling rivers with thunderous waterfalls had shriveled up like abandoned fruit at the base of a neglected tree.

It was not just the arid, severe landscape that shocked her heart. As far as she could sense, there was nothing alive for leagues around. No animals, no birds, not even insects. As if the Destroyer had sucked the life out of both land and beast and left a withered shell.

She took fearful steps, suddenly feeling vulnerable and exposed, adrift in a foreign sea, with no safe shore in sight.

For the first time in years, she knew terror. She had forgotten the way it could slither up and suffocate her, snuffing out hope and reason and faith. The empty land mirrored her desolate spirit, which had become its own wasteland. There was too much space, too much nothingness, no end to the despair that spread like the spilled blood of her people all those centuries ago.

She fell to her knees remembering. The images and sounds assailed her. Screams of pain and death. The stench of dust and blood. Her hands touching cold skin, seeing glassy, unfocused eyes. Her people, dead. She had been helpless to save them, to prevent the attack, to stop the Destroyer.

She lifted her eyes and saw Lorec struck by a minion of the Destroyer. He collapsed as the gryphons circled, circled. Shamara put her hands over her ears, but the shrieks pierced through them. She fought the urge to run to Lorec, her dear friend, then saw a flash of light from the corner of her eye. Relgar, with his staff raised in defiance to the whirlwind whipping at his clothes, threw his other hand over his eyes and tumbled onto his face.

Her cry strangled in her throat. She was the last wizard standing. Her kingdom's last hope. A gryphon dove, and a dozen people fell dead. Her people. The people she had been appointed to watch over and care for and protect.

She shook her head, her grief battling with her guilt. The sense of failure and betrayal pulled her under, and she drowned as the screams rippled like sea waves over her cowering body.

With the last bit of her resolve, she lifted her gaze and let her eyes light on the bodies strewn across the gay meadows dotted with wildflowers. The pristine creeks babbled in a soft murmur under the dissonance of attack, a stark incongruity amid the carnage of battle. With one last brief look, she took in the smoldering forests of newly budding trees, the burning cottages that used to be shoals of warmth and family affection. Of safety from the dark and frightening elements loose in the world. She let her gaze drift to the razed storehouses, to the panicked livestock stampeding across the fields, then to the hordes of her people huddled against the cliffs, the heads upturned and eyes wide in fear as the gryphons rose on an updraft, preparing for another attack, armed with magic and evil intent. They would not stop until every last human was dead.

Shamara shook herself from her self-pitying stupor and ran to those left, those still alive.

"Come," she yelled, waving for them to follow her. Their eyes lit with hope. She saw how they trusted her still. Even now . . . Her heart clenched in pain. How could she have let them down like this? She should have known Sha'kath was coming. She'd heard of other lands, other attacks. Her naïve belief that he would overlook Moreb had been her error—one her people were paying the price for.

As she ran, she summoned all the magic she could muster from the dregs of her soul. Her despair fueled her power, and under her urgings it grew to a conflagration she could hardly contain. With nowhere to run to, no safe haven in sight, she knew she had to fashion a refuge out of what magic she had left.

Shamara let the memories play out as she stood under the hot, merciless sun in what was once her kingdom. Its too-bright eye bore down on her in judgment as if condemning her anew. She stared across the vast barren land and listened to the quiet.

But even the quiet held condemnation. Even after all these centuries.

Sha'kath was long gone. The threat lingered only in her memories. She could sense nothing—neither good nor evil—in the wasteland and the lands behind the ring of cliffs that had once sheltered Moreb.

Was there a living world somewhere out there, beyond her powers to sense? Were there humans still alive on the face of the earth? What she would give to know the truth . . .

But she could not take that chance, any chance. Her carelessness had cost hundreds their lives, and those who had perished had no inkling that their demise was her fault, all her fault. They had lived their peaceful, secure lives in happy ignorance, unaware of the wizard who watched over them, the fairy that guarded their land and played with their children in the form of a small red deer.

She could never again be so rash and careless as to jeopardize her people. She had failed them once; she could not do so ever again. They depended on her for their every breath.

That day, when she had ushered them to safety in through the crevice of rock and down into the bowels of the earth, she had made a vow. She would keep that vow, even if it meant she had to lie to those she loved more than life itself.

Even if she had to lie to herself.

It was not safe to return to the surface. It would never be safe. She could never take that chance nor allow anyone in her kingdom to do so. She would return underground, to Me'arah—the kingdom she created—and spend the rest of her life caring for her people. And keeping them in the dark. But it was a necessary darkness, she told herself as she allowed one last look before turning back.

As she trudged down the stone steps, deeper into darkness, she used her magic to once again close up the entrance behind

her. The rumble of rock met her ears and echoed against the narrow tunnel she descended, until a thick silence settled around her
like dust. It was the dust of disintegrated hope, of dashed dreams,
of stark truth . . .

"Momi, you're crying."

Alia, startled, turned to Aron. His eyes showed fear. She had
never cried in front of him. For, why would she ever? She had no
reason to cry now, not on this world, not in this new life. Even
tears of joy were a rare occurrence, for joy now held no tinge
of bitterness or disappointment or regret. Joy in this new age
didn't call for tears. So she knew Aron was perplexed and a little
afraid.

Alia quickly wiped her eyes and summoned a smile to her
face. She stroked Aron's hair, thinking what she could say to him,
how she could even begin to explain.

"Do you have an owie, Momi?"

Alia chuckled. "Yes, I suppose I do. But it's healing. Just like all
owies."

"Oh," he breathed out. "I thought maybe you were scared—
about the story. The scary part."

"Me? Scared?" She feigned shock at such a thought, her eyes
wide.

Aron laughed. "Silly Momi! Stories aren't *really* scary. They're
just *stories*. Not real." He wrapped his small, warm arms around
her waist, and Alia felt warmth rush into her chest. Healing
warmth. *Children have no idea what healing power they have.*

"Scary stories are good," he told her.

Alia cocked her head. "They are? Why?"

Aron yawned. Clearly she wasn't going to get very far in her
storytelling tonight. "Because when the story is over, you know it's
all pretend, and it makes you happy that it's not real."

"I see. You have a good point there."

Aron gleamed, then threw himself down against his pillow and pulled the blanket up to his chin. The Ganari crystals sliced rainbow light across the bed and Aron's sleepy face. The three moons hung in the sky outside the big picture window, softening everything in the room, even Alia's unease. The memories had shaken her. She drew in a deep breath, let it out. *We are safe, we are safe. Forever safe.*

She had muttered those words upon returning to the shore of the great sea after her risky foray to the surface. No one had noticed she had left, or returned. She never told a soul in Me'arah what she had done or seen. Not until the day Meris had opened the door to the secret room and Shamara had summoned her. Then she told the truth to the one person she felt must know.

What a great mistake that had been.

TWENTY-THREE

JORAN PRESSED his head into his hands as he sat on the bench outside Ta'sus's cottage. He felt Zev's firm hand rest on his shoulder, but he did not care to look up and see his father's calm face. Not even when he heard the squeak of the cottage door open and Shamara utter questions, answered by the wizards' somber replies, did he raise his head.

His heart felt as heavy as iron, and he could not get Perthin's death out of his thoughts. Even as Zev gently urged him to stand, telling him they must leave, he saw only the dead king's expression of pain and shock, which was now imprinted in Joran's own mind.

He swiveled his head upward and looked at Zev, noticing the others already hurrying back up the trail they'd come down. Hushed whispers drifted to his ears, and Valonis stopped and looked back at Joran, full of compassion, her eyes urging him to follow.

He grunted. What choice did he have? He could hardly stay here in this hidden kingdom, hide and pretend the real world did not exist. No, this would not provide any safe haven for him or anyone, any longer.

His mind shifted to thoughts of Charris, his cozy cottage nestled in among the towering trees, the gentle mist that fell in the mornings and evenings, the setting sun streaking colors over the Sawtooth Mountains encircling his village of Tebron. A wave of homesickness struck him hard, and he regretted he had no magic boots to transport him in an instant back into his wife's loving arms, back to a place of solitude and safety. He would bury his head in his life and dreams, in ignorance and naiveté, if he could. Pretend the evil in the world did not exist, could not touch him and those he loved, could not invade and poison everything he loved dearly in the world. So what if it was a coward's position to take—embracing denial of the truth, the painful truth, that the world indeed was somehow coming to an end? He would rather die in a false peace, unknowing of the evil that ravaged the lands abroad, intent on destroying everything heaven created, the legacy given to humankind—now being wrested away.

Why? Why would heaven will this to happen? It made no sense. No sense at all.

"Joran, come," his father said, gesturing with his arm. "It's time."

Mindlessly, Joran rose to his feet and let them step forward on their own accord. Zev walked beside him, silent for a time. And then he spoke.

"No questions? Your mind is in turmoil."

Joran snuffed. "My questions are foolish, for there are no answers."

Zev smiled as their boots crunched the carpet of leaves choking the winding path leading up through the copse of silver-leafed trees. The pink light lent a soft glow to the woodland, and Joran sensed the magic all around him, sinking into him, stirring him.

He looked around and listened to the quiet chattering of birds and watched them flitting from tree to tree. He suddenly remembered little Bryp, the bird who'd joined him on his journey to save

Charris from the Moon—and all the beautiful birds he saw in the cave of the South Wind. All these magical places—would they soon be gone as well? What would happen to the South Wind, and the Moon, and Sola?

A sideways glance showed his father holding back a smile. Well, there were his questions, if Zev wanted them. Joran grunted and picked up his pace.

"Where are we going?" he asked his father. "Is Shamara going to tell her people the truth about their kingdom? And what does the name Me'arah mean, anyway?"

"To answer your questions succinctly: to the surface, not at this time, and cave or cavern."

Joran worked to piece the answers to each of his questions. "Wait, we are leaving this place, now? To go back to the surface? Why? Has Shamara learned something about the seventh site?"

"It seems the Lord Na'tar's daughter has . . . escaped Me'arah. And we must find her before Sha'kath does. Before the Destroyer discovers this kingdom."

Joran stopped. "What? How is that possible? You sealed the entrance with a spell—you. Do you—does Shamara—think a mere girl could break through your spell?"

"Can and has," Zev answered evenly. "Perhaps she did not want to take Shamara's place here. Ta'sus seemed concerned by this burden of responsibility thrust upon his daughter."

"I understand entirely. That is a tremendous weight on such small shoulders."

"Yet, Shamara had no qualms over choosing her—"

"Maybe she had no other choice. No one with as much power as she. But still—"

"It's a moot point, now. Now we must find her, and quickly, or who is to say what might befall this place and its people."

"But isn't it too late? Won't all these people now know there is a 'land across the sea'? For the first time in forever, there are strangers among them, clearly from another land."

"Shamara will cloud their minds," Zev said, as if he approved of such behavior. He swung his face to look at Joran. "What? This is no time for summary judgment, Joran. Some stopgap measure must be taken to prevent hysteria or hasty flight. And neither Shamara nor our contingent has time for lengthy explanations or engaging in a discussion of the merits or detriments of telling the people of this kingdom the truth, which would entail divulging the entire story of their past, and that would take up precious time we can little afford."

"All right," Joran said, putting up his hands in defense. "No need to get all huffy and highbrow. How hard do you think it will be to find her? She can't have gone far, right? And with all these wizards among us, surely we will be able to locate her."

Zev hmphed and sped up. Joran finally saw the others almost to the top of the ridge where the assembly hall sat. "We cannot risk using any magic to locate Meris. And I can do nothing to help mask her magical signature from here. Perhaps when we reach the surface."

"But how can you put a dampening spell on her if you can't find her?"

Zev merely shook his head. They joined the others waiting at the top of the hill. Joran glanced back through the woods, seeing Perthin's warm and kind face in his mind, then recalling the way he was stricken with pain and fear, clutching the scepter, and died, right before their eyes. His heart ached anew.

"Justyn will lay him to rest, Joran." Zev met his eyes, and Joran saw the compassion swimming in it. His irritation at his father melted. Sometimes it was hard for Joran to even begin to imagine what it must be like for his father to have lived these many centuries and to have fought the battles against evil, and seen such cruelty and pain humankind has suffered for so long. Joran smirked. Maybe the end of the world was a good thing after all. No more suffering and pain. No more evil running rampant, cruel men inflicting their tyranny over innocents. The world was groaning in pain, longing for relief, to be put out of its misery. Would it not be a mercy to do so?

The weariness of these last days pushed down on Joran's shoulders. He marched in silence behind the others, with Shamara and Ta'sus in the lead. Joran noted the looks of surprise on the lord's face, and Elward's as well, as their group passed villagers on the path, who nodded at Ta'sus but clearly did not see his companions. Another spell of deception Shamara had cast on her people. *For their own good, for now,* Joran told himself, knowing his father was probably right. But he couldn't shake off the feeling that all this deception would merit a price. And maybe Meris's flight was only the first coin to be paid. Just what would it cost the people of Me'arah—of Moreb—in the end? Their lives?

Meris, her eyes squeezed shut against the explosion of dust, coughed hard into her hand and drew in her breath as shallowly as she could, to keep from choking on the grit. When she felt and smelled the air had cleared, she took a deeper breath, noticing heat pounding the top of her head and making her skin tingle.

What a strange sensation. And the air tasted different than in Me'arah. It slipped in a thin stream down her throat, which was now more scratchy and drier than before. Her heart pounding, she ventured to open her eyes, then shut them tightly, wincing in pain.

The light was so bright! She had expected the cool of night, the black canopy overhead pricked with white holes, some strange light shimmering behind that colorless sky.

With a hand shading her eyes, she peeked at her surroundings. It took a moment for her vision to adjust. Still squinting from the harsh glare, she made out walls of rock, and an open field—dry, with little vegetation. A strange and intriguing landscape met her eyes, but its barrenness gave her a sinking feeling in her gut. Was this the real world, what lay above her beautiful kingdom?

She tipped her head back and sought out the source of the great heat and blazing light and only saw a glimpse of the orb straight overhead before she cried out in pain and threw her hands over her eyes. Why did the sight of that light cause such pain? A black circle swam in her closed eyes, and when she looked again, it was pasted over everything she saw, as if burned into her vision. Her pulse quickened and her palms grew sweaty. Perspiration dripped down her face and neck. Had she destroyed her eyes by looking at that orb? In the animal skin she'd watched, that bright orb traversed the sky, but it had not been as bright as this.

Oh, what was this harsh world? This cruel light? Is this what humans had to deal with each day? This was nothing like the soft pink glow of her sky—a sky Shamara had created, no doubt to be soothing and comforting. So much better than this merciless light. Already she could feel her shoulders burning as if on fire. She had to find shelter.

She craned her neck to see across the vast open field, the land-scape unwelcoming and desolate. As the black imprint faded from her vision—much to her relief—she now could make out small shrubs and boulders scattered about. Nothing living. No water or trees. She had never seen anything like it in Me'arah. Her kingdom was alive, vibrant, breathing and prolific. This place—this was . . . death. Emptiness. Wasteland.

This couldn't be all of the world, could it? Had that Destroyer done this? She thought of the beautiful scenes she'd seen on the scrolls—the majestic mountains capped with white frosting, the creatures in an azure sea leaping and frolicking in the water. Herds of sleek, graceful animals grazing in prairies of verdant grass growing to their shoulders.

A longing to see such sights grew in her heart and caused her to moan with despair. Were her people the only ones left in the whole world? How could they be? These wizards had found her kingdom. Surely there were others alive somewhere. But where? And how far away. She wished she had prodded Shamara to tell her about the world above—how big it was and what was beyond this rock-ringed valley she stood in. She wished she knew where to find those animals and mountains, for they surely weren't anywhere near here.

Sweat poured down her face as the hot sky grilled her. She spotted a large rock overhang off to her left, barely visible through the strange wavering waves rising up from the scorching ground, and ran toward it. The heat sapped her strength, and she found it difficult to suck in enough air. Her skin was dry and now throbbed as if seared. She looked at her arms and they were tinged red, as if she'd stuck them into a fire. How could humans stand to live in such a world?

She choked down her desire to run back down the rock stairs to her home, and into her father's arms. That would be cowardly. And besides, it meant returning to all that was expected of her. As much as she loved Me'arah and her family, she owed it to herself and her people to know the truth. Was the world completely uninhabitable? Was it void of life? Or was there beauty beyond this walled enclave? She couldn't go back now—not until she knew for sure. She had to explore, even if for just a day or two. See how far she could get. Once she had some food and water, and perhaps a hat to shade her head, she would fare well. And if that animal skin accurately described this world, that hot orb in the sky at some point would move and finally disappear—at least for some period of time—and the heat would no doubt lessen, making traveling easier. But how long would it take for the orb to traverse the sky? She had no sense of time here.

In Me'arah, the dome dimmed in the evening and brightened midday. In winter the light was fainter, and days were shorter than evenings. But who knew how things worked in the real world? For all Meris knew, this heat would last for days and days before bringing on that cool, dark period—before that luminescent orb cast a soft glow across the landscape. It was as if one orb chased after the other—bright then dull, bright then dull. A cycle of sorts, like the seasons in Me'arah. Were there seasons here too?

Her thoughts exhausted her. She needed water. It was time to stop pondering and second-guessing what was out there, beyond her vision.

She plopped down under the rock ledge, grateful for the shade, although the heat engulfed her on all sides, from rock and dirt ground. She pushed past her weariness and thirst and dizziness and concentrated. *Water, I must have water.*

She closed her eyes, aware of the utter absence of any magic in the world around her. Such a contrast to her world, which was drenched in magic—she now realized that. This world was dead and lifeless in more than just appearance. Its spirit was dead as well. Nothing animated it. The rocks and dirt and grass were lifeless and had nothing Meris could draw from. Like trying to suck water from an empty pouch.

Well, she would have to draw magic from herself then. She knew it was in there; she had to try. For if she failed, she would have no recourse but to return home, never to know the truth.

Her stomach growled, and her scratchy throat made it hard for her to swallow. Once more she chided herself for not bringing food and water. *But why could I not use magic to conjure some up? If I could create that light in the cave, and shatter the wizards' spell and open the entrance, why not use magic to provide all I need to explore this land?* Then another curious thought came to her. *Why can't I use magic to re-create the world on those scrolls?*

With a deep breath, she began. She turned her attention inward, to the source of her power, which seemed so weak and puny. But she knew its potential—Shamara had told her she held tremendous power within her. She just had to learn to wield it. She'd done it with the light, and then when she broke open the rock walls to the sealed entrance. She could do this. She could do anything she set her heart on. *Just envision it, and it will manifest.*

She still found it hard to believe that within her own body lay so much power. Power she had hardly known was there. Power to do amazing, miraculous things. She was a wizard, in her own right. If she could sustain worlds, she could create them too, couldn't she? Her only limitation was herself, her doubt. She knew this now.

She squeezed her eyes shut and called on that power, then felt it course through her limbs and radiate out into the air around her. The sweltering, stifling air now seemed charged with magic, like a shimmering robe enwrapping her. She concentrated harder, pushing the waves of magic outward, making her circle of power bigger, stronger, pulsating in waves now like the waves of the great sea, a disturbance that began to ripple out across the barren land. She pictured the dry, desolate valley erupting with tall grasses and wildflowers. She envisioned the rocky cliffs stretching and growing and rising into the sky, capped with frosting. She sent out blasts of magic and saw in her mind's eyes creeks and rivers and water-falls, and trees springing up along the banks filled with ripe, plump fruit. The world in her mind came alive, the way the scrolls had, as if she re-created those paintings in her head.

Power surged from her arms as she held them out and threw back her head and laughed. Without opening her eyes, she knew what she had done. A cool breeze tickled her cheeks and ears, and the sound of water running over rocks set her heart laughing. She understood now. All this land needed was magic. A wizard to imbue every particle with magic, in order for it to live and flourish. This was the role of wizards in the world, she surmised. To create and sustain life. To be caretakers and nurturers. This is what Shamara had asked her to do, needed her to do, and now Meris understood that this was her destiny, her purpose.

But not to sustain a make-believe hidden land, a land secreted away in fear. No, her purpose was here, in the real world. To restore Moreb, the land of her ancestors.

She opened her eyes and looked around. She was startled—not at what she saw but why she ever doubted. It was now so clear, what she was meant to do. Shamara had saved her kingdom all those centuries ago—saved them from a dire threat. And now it was Meris's turn to save her kingdom again—from the deception and imprisonment thrust upon them.

As she gazed upon the prodigious valley full of greenery and grazing animals and rivers of life, a smile broke out on her face. Now she could return to the hidden kingdom and free her people. Tell them the truth about the real world. Escort them out to the place they were meant to live. Once Shamara saw what Meris had done, no doubt she would be relieved and grateful. She could rest from all her hard work, and take delight in seeing her people and kingdom reestablished in the world. It would be Meris's gift to the old wizard.

She rushed over to the closest creek and dunked her hot, dusty head in the cold refreshing water. After a taking a long quenching drink, she tipped her head back and chuckled. Her chuckle turned into a laugh, and she jumped up and danced and danced in the tickly grass, her joy soaring to the heavens.

And then, she froze and raised her eyes skyward. A shiver ran across her neck, and a cold hand of fear clenched her throat tightly. She felt more than saw it—a dark, foreboding shadow that blotted out the bright orb overhead—that cast a chilling shadow across the valley, a shadow that raced over trees and flowers and grasses blowing in the soothing breeze she had summoned.

And when that shadow fell upon her and raced over her heart, she felt as if a herd of deer had trampled her and crushed her, and Meris, stricken with terror, fell to the ground, clutching her chest and crying out in agony.

TWENTY-FOUR

I DON'T UNDERSTAND," Ta'sus said, exchanging fearful glances with his most trusted friend Elward as they approached the calm waters of the great sea. He imagined the councilor was just as flabbergasted as he was; Ta'sus could make no sense of all the strange happenings that had befallen him this day. Elward merely shook his head spasmodically from side to side. He hadn't said a word after Ta'sus tried to explain to him that Me'arah was actually underground, that an entire world existed above them. How could it be possible?

But at the moment he couldn't allow himself to think of that and all it portended. All he wanted was to find Meris, but the old wizard's words made no sense, none at all.

"Why are we here, at the shore of the sea?" He looked at Shamara for an answer, but she only turned to the wizard called Zev and spoke to him.

"I am too weary, old friend. Would you . . . ?" She gestured at the water, and Zev nodded.

Elward came alongside Ta'sus, fear searing his eyes. In a whisper, he said, "Did you see that, back there? The villagers—they noticed nothing. As if the wizards were invisible. Someone will have to tell them the truth—tell them . . . all this . . ."

Ta'sus merely shrugged, his mind spinning with confusion and his heart heavy with fear. The story Shamara had told him about his kingdom, and about the world above, was too fantastic to be true. Yet, why would she lie to him? She told him Meris had fled to the surface, to the land above, but how? Was there a hidden path? He shuddered thinking about the animal skin she had shown him—of the frightening creatures streaking across the sky, attacking and killing those trying to run to safety. *My people, my land*, he thought, the idea of such a heritage still incomprehensible. Was this the danger Meris was rushing headlong into? Shamara had refused to say, but her eyes could not hide the answer.

He pushed the rising anger down, telling himself to trust Shamara. But back in that secret room, he knew she was not telling him everything. No doubt whatever trouble Meris had gotten into was his daughter's own doing, not the wizard's fault. Yet, Ta'sus couldn't help the thought niggling at his mind—that Shamara must have said or done something to frighten Meris and send her running. But running where? And why would a contingent of powerful wizards be so concerned?

Ta'sus looked out at the smooth glassy surface of the emerald sea, the waters so peaceful and undisturbed—a contrast to the emotions raging in his heart. He tapped his foot impatiently and looked in the faces of the others. He wondered what happened to the other two men that had been with them. They were nowhere to be seen. When he and Shamara had emerged from his cottage, the faces of Shamara's friends showed they were distraught and grieving, yet they told him nothing. Only conferred privately with Shamara, their thoughts shielded from his meager magical ability. Something terrible had happened to those men, and they were gone. Had harsh words been exchanged? A fight or disagreement?

He grunted. He'd thought he was gifted with so much magical power and longevity, but he was a worm compared to these visitors. Was the world above filled with wizards of great ability? Were they at war with each other? If Meris had ventured out into such a dangerous evil world, what hope did they have to find her and bring her back to Me'arah?

Elward gasped and yanked on Ta'sus's sleeve. Ta'sus swiveled around and looked where his friend pointed. On the sandy beach lay a strange object. Some sort of giant box made of wood. Where had that come from? Before he could open his mouth to speak, two of the male visitors pushed the thing along the sand and into the water. And then, to his astonishment, the group of wizards climbed into the box and gestured for Ta'sus and Elward to join them. Although, Shamara waited, standing on the sand and resting a hand on the box and looking back at him.

Elward stepped back. "No," he said, shaking his head briskly. "I won't go in that." He studied Ta'sus's face, fear etched on his own. "They are going to take that . . . thing across the great sea."

The thought made Ta'sus tremble, and a terrible feeling gripped his gut and wrenched it. He finally found his voice. He said to Zev, whose gaze seemed the most empathetic, "Is that . . . where Meris went?" His feet refused to move.

Shamara said to the wizards, "They are under an illusion; they cannot fathom crossing the sea. Just the thought makes them tremendously anxious."

Hinwor frowned. "We need to make haste. Are you sure it is wise to take him with us?"

"We may need his help in convincing Meris to return," she answered. She then walked over to Ta'sus on unsteady legs.

"Lord Na'tar," she said as she came over to him and grasped his hands. Her expression was kindly but her tone firm. Her eyes bore into his. "You needn't be afraid of the sea any longer."

She closed her eyes, and Ta'sus startled at the stirring in his body. A surge of magic raced from his fingers to his chest, and from there caused his body to shiver. Something dislodged in his heart, and the anxious feeling laced with fear melted away.

"How did you—?" He shook his head as Elward stared at him curiously. "You did this—to our people." It wasn't a question, and Ta'sus fought a tingling of outrage. "Why? Why make us afraid of the sea?"

Shamara took his hand and led him to the box. Elward kept back, watching in silence.

"I believe, Lord Na'tar, you will understand once we cross to the other side."

"What side? There is nothing but water—"

"There is nothing but illusion, dear Ta'sus." She looked lovingly into his face, and his anger dissipated. "You know now this is all an illusion, this entire kingdom. Yet, an illusion that has kept all in Me'arah safe for more than five thousand years."

Ta'sus gasped. "Five thou— How can that be? Are you"—he turned to look at the wizards watching this exchange from the box that bobbed gently on top of the water—"and the others are truly that old?"

Shamara nodded and with Zev's help climbed into the box. Ta'sus hesitated.

All these years the old woman had lived in this kingdom she had fashioned under rock. It was hard enough imagining such power of creation, but the idea that an entire world existed outside their land—*above* the tons of rock overhead, was how she described it—was even harder to accept. He longed to ask the wizards what that world was like now, if the scrolls Shamara had shown him in the secret room truly depicted the world they live in. If those horrible flying creatures still roamed the skies.

But they seemed reluctant to speak, as if a weight heavier than rock lay on all their hearts. Something terrible had happened; he could tell. Even when they first arrived Ta'sus felt it. They came for a reason, and they needed Shamara, and now Meris was gone. Had the wizards brought the danger Shamara feared? The danger Meris was now facing? Oh, why had they come?

Ta'sus threw a look to Elward. They had been friends so long, he knew Elward would understand his unspoken intent. Elward would have to make some excuse to Drayna, to explain why Ta'sus and Meris were gone. He would make sure she did not worry. With a nod that was anything but agreeable, Elward turned and began the trek up the trail back to the village.

Crossing the sea. To where? Shamara said Meris had gone to the world above. Ta'sus could not sense her anywhere, and this distressed him. How long would it take to get to the other side? He could see nothing—no shoreline or land in the distance. No one ever had. It seemed as if the sea went on forever.

"Illusion." Shamara's voice spoke to his mind. But the sea was real; the water was wet and cool.

He was wasting precious time. His heart ached thinking that Meris might be hurt or frightened. Maybe this was all his fault. Why had he let Shamara take her? She was too young, and the responsibility thrust upon her was too burdensome. He'd allowed his concern for his kingdom to outweigh his concern for his own daughter. He had let her down.

With a heavy heart, he climbed into the box and sat on the floor as it rocked erratically. He pressed his palms flat to steady himself and took a deep breath. Even though his anxiousness about traversing the sea had fled, he didn't like the idea of floating on water, although he'd seen birds do it without effort. He knew the wizard's spell would not allow them to sink, but still—it was unsettling.

And then they moved. Ta'sus peered over the back of the box and watched the shoreline recede, and after a few minutes, he could barely see the beach. He looked back and saw water surrounding him. It gave him an odd sensation of loneliness. He tried to picture Meris in another box—the one the wizards said she took to get to the world above. How had she known where to go? He gritted his teeth so hard his jaw ached. He should have never let her out of his sight—not after the evening Shamara announced she would train Meris to take her place. His frustration and worry simmered.

The wizards were silent. Ta'sus blew out a breath, willing his heart to stop racing, his mind to stop chasing questions. He would get his answers soon enough, and perhaps then he would not want the answers presented to him. But there was no bliss in ignorance . . . or in waiting.

Then, as sudden as a summer squall, the air grew thick and heavy—heavier than water. The colors of the sky and the sea swirled around him, pink and green and brown blurring his vision and making him lightheaded. He tipped and banged into Relgar, who grasped his arm and steadied him. And then, the bottom of the box scraped against something rough, like rock, and Ta'sus spun his head around and saw they had landed on a rocky beach flanked by small sandstone cliffs. And set in the cliff was a narrow cut revealing a path through the hillside.

Now he understood what Shamara meant by illusion. They had not gone all that far, and surely, if this place was as close as it seemed to the shoreline they'd departed from, he would have seen these cliffs from the edge of the great sea. It was as if they had passed through a giant mirror that reflected back only water and air, hiding what lay behind it. If his people had known this was here, no doubt they would have built similar boxes to cross the sea and explore the other side. But Shamara could not allow anyone to know about the world above, and so she created this glamor to hide the truth.

Ta'sus shook his head. The way out of the hidden kingdom had always been a stone's throw away. Right there, under their noses. Why had he never sensed it? For that matter, why had he never thought there might be more—more world, more life, more to existence than what he knew and saw and experienced? But why would anyone suspect an unseen world beyond that one they experienced from day to day? How would anyone know of such a thing unless it was told or shown to them?

Ta'sus kept his thoughts to himself as he followed the others out of the box and along a trail that led through the crevice in the rock and into the cool overhang of the cliff. Zev uttered quiet words, and a round ball of glowing light hovered over his open palm. Ta'sus made out an uneven rocky path leading upward, and as he followed the others, in places he had to duck or turn sideways to fit through. The wizards' hushed conversations were too quiet to make out, but he noticed their growing agitation as they ascended higher and higher, and as the air became thin and dusty, the motes stirred up and shimmering in the scant light.

All the while, Ta'sus thought of Meris and where she might be and what they would find when they came to the end of the path. There was no longer room for any doubt about Shamara's claim that his kingdom was hidden under rock, deep in the bowels of the world. For they were now far above his home, far above the dome that lit up his world. It all lay underneath him. The thought made him dizzy with amazement.

The wizards then stopped. When Ta'sus caught up and calmed his ragged breathing, he saw stunned looks on their faces. His limbs shook as he took a few cautious steps forward. Cold air wafted across his face, and he shivered. He'd expected to see a dark sky, like the one he'd been shown on that skin in the secret room. But what met his widened eyes as he pushed his way through to Shamara's side was an altogether unexpected vista.

A verdant valley, longer and wider than anything in Me'arah, stretched out to a far horizon. The colors, lit up by a blinding bright light in the sky, were unlike any he'd ever seen. He squinted at the harsh light, which cast the world into such brilliance it took his breath away.

His gaze slipped across sparkling fields thick with spectacular flowers and swaying trees he'd never seen before, across waves of tall grasses populated with herds of graceful creatures that grazed and lifted their heads in curiosity at their presence. Water babbled in streams and roared over waterfalls cascading down towering cliffs. The warm air felt drenched in moisture, infused with the fragrance of sweet flowers and warm grass, filling his nostrils as the aroma carried on a playful wind. It was as if he'd stepped out of one world and entered another wholly new one.

He turned to Shamara, and saw tears running down her face. His heart clenched at the sight. Why was she crying?

"Where is Meris?" Ta'sus demanded, pushing aside his awe and disbelief.

He spun around and looked at Zev, who had his head tilted back. He was scanning the skies.

Joran asked him, "What is it? What's wrong?"

Hinwor looked at Joran, then said to Shamara, "This place was a barren desert. Nothing but dirt and weeds."

Valonis took Shamara's arm. "You're trembling."

Shamara dropped her head. "He's taken her." She shot daggers with her eyes at her sister. "You should never have come." Ta'sus's heart lurched at the tone in her voice. *Taken her? Is she speaking of Meris?* She added, "After all this time, why would he still be out here, waiting . . . ?"

Zev hurried to her side. "She did this—she used her magic to re-create Moreb."

"And Sha'kath found her," Joran said, his eyes wide.

Ta'sus felt a stab of pain in his chest. "No!"

Zev steadied him with his arms. "Lord Ta'sus." His voice was tender, but Ta'sus's anger burned. He spun to face Shamara.

"It's your fault! How could you have let her leave? Where is she? How will we find her?" And then he narrowed his eyes and asked Zev, "Why does he want her?"

Zev let out a breath and shook his head. "He is looking for the seventh site. He knows it's hidden."

"Seventh site? What sites?"

"He thinks if he can destroy all seven of the sites heaven set up in the world, he will be able to rule mankind. He has destroyed at least five"—he cast a glance at Kael for some reason—"perhaps six." Ta'sus noted Kael's pained expression but did not know what this meant to him. What in heaven was the wizard talking about?

Relgar nodded. "He thinks Meris will lead him to the seventh site. He sensed her magic."

Ta'sus could barely speak. "Wh-what will he do to her?"

The silence that followed was answer enough. He dropped to his knees and wept. *Oh, Meris, my sweet daughter . . .*

Shamara looked at her sister. "What do I do, Valonis? Can I not, with your help, seal the entrance and keep my people safe? Must I bring them out to face the Destroyer once more?"

Ta'sus trembled at her words.

Hinwor spoke sternly to Shamara. "Your decision has been made for you." He nodded back toward the rocks they'd come through. "He now knows of Me'arah. Your people are not safe anymore. And we cannot protect them, not now. His gryphons will return, and they will finish what they started all those many years ago."

Ta'sus wiped his eyes and face and felt an unexpected compassion in his heart. Shamara looked nothing like the powerful wizard she was. She appeared broken and frail. Defeated. Yet, building beneath his compassion was his outrage.

The soft murmuring of the nearby brook sounded like bitter laughter to Ta'sus's ears. Birds chattered in the massive overhanging boughs of the nearby trees, but their lively banter only hurt his ears. How ironic that such beauty surrounded them in this moment.

"If you could manage to get your people to Ethryn, my kingdom," Kael said to Shamara, "they would be welcome. And they would have a home." His face was weighed down in worry. "If Ethryn is still standing. For all we know, the site may lay in ruins, along with all the others. My people may be under attack . . ."

"We should head to Ethryn," Zev said. "You are the first and the last, and you hold the key to the kingdom. Whatever is to transpire will probably take place there."

"What does that mean?" Ta'sus asked, his throat tight and aching, not willing to go anywhere except after Meris. But how will he find her? He must. This Destroyer must have a fortress somewhere.

"Please," he begged, searching the eyes of those around him, "can you not use your magic to find my daughter? Is he so much more powerful than all of you?"

The wizards exchanged looks. Zev told him, "If we remove the spell shielding our power, he will sense us—and come after us, no doubt."

Joran snorted. "Not a good idea."

"But," Relgar said, "there is a chance that by pooling our power we can defeat him. Kill his gryphons—"

"They are not alive," Kael said. "They are some kind of fabrication of Sha'kath's mind and power. You will have to destroy him to destroy them."

Shamara nodded but studied Kael curiously. "You are right, Kael of Ethryn, but how do you know this?"

"I . . . lived for a time under Sha'kath's rule. And have experienced the terror of his creatures."

Shamara's eyes widened. "I hope one day to hear your tale, Kael. But we have no time to waste." She turned to Ta'sus. "It would be better if you returned to Me'arah with me. To tell our people what has transpired. To help them prepare to . . . leave the hidden kingdom and journey with King Kael to Ethryn."

"Do you really think the Destroyer will allow you safe passage? What if Ethryn is already destroyed?" Joran asked in all sincerity. Everyone fell silent.

"What other choice is there?" Valonis replied to him. "We cannot leave them underground, where they could be trapped or buried alive. And we cannot leave them here in Moreb, waiting for Sha'kath to return. With our protection, they may have a chance to resettle in Ethryn."

"How far away is it?" Shamara asked.

"Far," Hinwor said. "But if we are no longer concerned about hiding our power, it will be an easy feat to transport them without delay." He looked in the other wizards' faces for confirmation.

"Wait," Ta'sus said, his impatience getting the better of him. He looked at Relgar. "I can't just leave . . . can't leave Meris . . ." He hid his face in his hands and wept.

"Lord Na'tar," Valonis said with a comforting hand on his shoulder, "tend to you wife and daughters. We won't abandon Meris, but we must first save your people. Once they are safely in Ethryn, we will see what we can do to bring her back to you."

Ta'sus wiped his eyes and looked into the wizard's compassionate face and nodded.

Zev gestured back the way they came. "Hurry." The wizards turned and went back through the rubble of rock, but Ta'sus lingered. Shamara hobbled up to his side.

"Meris did all this," she said, sweeping her arm out to take in the sublime beauty displayed before him. "She has come into her power, and it is great."

"But not great enough to withstand this Destroyer," Ta'sus added bitterly.

Shamara fell silent. After a moment she said, "Come, Ta'sus. We need your calm and voice of reason. Your people need you."

He clenched his jaw. "My daughter needs me."

After a last lingering look at the bright, beautiful world spread out before him—his precious daughter's handiwork—he turned and made his way back down the dusty rock trail, back to the illusion that had been his home for hundreds of years. An illusion now shattered by the painful light of truth.

TWENTY-FIVE

HER HEAD throbbing in stabbing pain, Meris forced her eyes open, trying to make out the space she'd been thrown into. It hurt to move, so she shifted her numb legs on the cold rock floor and felt with her bruised and blood-encrusted hands to find the wall to brace against.

Her memory was hazy, but as she pushed herself to stand and grabbed the side of her head as dizziness assailed her, she began piecing together the last hours. Terror sought to pull her under again, to the place of deceptively safe dreams, of imagining her father's large warm arms ensconcing her. Tears threatened, but she sucked them back down her throat and steeled her emotions. An attempt to summon magic from her limbs proved futile; whatever the Destroyer's men had done to her made her powerless and weak.

Her heart wrenched thinking of the beautiful land she had created by her will. A land for the people of Me'arah. But that was not to be. Her spirits sank even deeper, into a deep well of despair, thinking how foolish she'd been to run off. To abandon her family and not heed Shamara's warning to stay below in the hidden kingdom. There was a bitter side to truth, Meris realized. Maybe it was better to live in peaceful ignorance. Maybe Shamara was right.

And now? Had Meris endangered everyone she loved? The thought made her shrivel with shame. Her dream to explore the world above—this world—was a fanciful wish, a selfish one that she'd indulged in without thinking, without heeding the warning given her.

Her thoughts shifted to her captor. What could he want with her, and why hadn't he killed her? Did he want her magic? If so, how could he take it? Her heart pounded in protest. She would die; she knew it was inevitable. Holding on to any hope that she would be allowed to leave was foolish. But she would rather die that allow this Sha'kath any advantage.

She looked around the small stone chamber, barely visible from the shaft of light seeping in from a narrow slit in the wall. She went over and pressed her eyes against it and peered out but could see nothing but harsh light erasing her surroundings. The pain in her shoulders reminded her of the tight grip that creature used to transport her across the landscape, but in her fright she'd kept her eyes squeezed shut, the wind whipping grit against her face as she screamed and screamed, her cries still echoing in her ears now as she slumped back to the hard floor and let the tears stream.

Oh, Father, what have I done? I'm so sorry, so sorry . . .

A creak made her look up. The door opened. Meris's heart pounded so hard it hurt her chest. A burly man in dark leather garb stomped over to her and grabbed her arm, yanking her to her feet.

Meris cried out in pain and tried to pull away.

"The master wants you." As if she were a sack of feathers, he dragged her out the chamber and down a long hallway of more gray stone, not allowing her to get her footing. Her soft-soled shoes scraped along the rock, shooting pain into her feet. She had no choice but to grit her teeth and bear the pain. The sound of their steps blended with harsh voices bouncing off the walls as Meris resigned herself to her fate.

I will try to be brave, but I don't know how. A trembling sigh escaped her mouth when her captor push open a heavy door of hewn wood and tossed her into the room he'd brought her to. On her hands and knees, with every inch of her body screaming in pain, she raised her head.

Sitting on a towering stone chair across the room was a man dressed in rich robes of purple and black. She startled at the sight, for she had expected some horrific beast to be her nemesis. But this was merely an ordinary man with a silver beard and long gray hair pulled back behind his head. His careworn face was etched with deep wrinkles. The man was shorter than her own father. Was this the great Sha'kath, the Destroyer? How could he be a mere man?

She glanced at the rows of mean-faced guards standing stiffly on both sides of their master, bearing weapons of metal in their tight grips. She would do well not to doubt this ruler's authority or power. Shamara had told her how Sha'kath had destroyed kingdoms with the gryphons he had created. How he had turned the hearts of kings to do his bidding. How, she could not begin to fathom, but she would not doubt Shamara any longer. This was a man to be greatly feared. But why would heaven allow any man such cruel power?

"Approach," he demanded, his stare like the thrust of a sword into her gut. She doubled over, stunned at the force of his gaze and the command in his voice. Magic of immeasurable power crushed her body and spirit.

Pressing her legs to move, she hobbled inch by inch toward him, her head hung and her heart in her throat. If only she could use her magic, somehow, in some way. Even if only to stop her heart and prevent this Destroyer from interrogating her. She did not doubt his power now. Magic oozed from him, rippling over her in waves. More magic than she ever imagined possible—and all coming from a mere man.

Yet . . . she sensed other things as well. Some strangled cry whispering from an anguished soul. Her curiosity dampened her terror as she listened with her heart and heard more. Who was crying out to her? It was as if someone was inside Sha'kath, some tormented man. She cringed at the thought that such evil might be inhabiting the body of a mere mortal and creating horrible torment.

Her gaze was pulled to the Destroyer's cold, cruel eyes. He glared at her, his mind working. Yet, behind the hard visage Meris saw someone looking out. It did not take magic to see the war battling within this man's soul. But what did that matter—to her and her fate?

She fell before his feet.

"Who are you?" he demanded in a strange accent, his words sounding foreign, yet she understood them. "And where are you from?"

She knew it was no use trying to lie. A compulsion gripped her, and she could do nothing but speak truth, although every muscle in her body trembled in defiance.

"I am Meris, from Me'arah."

"Me'arah? Where is that place?" Although his tone was even, Meris sensed the anger and impatience in his words. His *need*.

"It is a kingdom underground."

"Underground?" He jumped to his feet and scowled at her. "And how long has this kingdom existed?"

"I-I cannot say exactly. But it was created thousands of years ago."

"Thousands . . ." He bore down on her and she cringed. His magic was like a heavy rock pressing on her body. "Who? Who created your kingdom?"

Meris tried to keep the word from escaping her throat, but she could not prevent its escape. "Shamara."

His visage darkened as if a storm had rushed into the room. His face contorted in anger. "Shamara." He paced back and forth in front of her. She kept her head down and shook from head to toe. The Destroyer remembered the wizard.

"So, the wizard of Moreb did find a way." He stopped and glared at her. "And this kingdom . . . underground. Is there a large ring of rock, a sacred site, in your land?"

An odd question, but she feared what he would do if she did not give him the answer he sought. "I don't understand. I know of no ring of rock or any sacred site."

Without warning, he grabbed Meris by the throat and hefted her up in the air. She choked out a cry as her airway was crushed and she struggled to breathe.

"Think! The site must be there. I must see it!"

He dangled her mercilessly for a moment, and Meris felt the creepy fingers of his mind probing hers. She gagged and bile gathered in her throat. Then, when her life seeped from her body, he dropped her back to the ground, and she grabbed her reeling head with both hands. She screamed in pain as his mind probed hers. For an excruciating minute she again felt him in her head, rummaging through her thoughts as if he were slicing her up with a knife.

"No! Please, no more!"

He kicked her in the side, and she curled into a ball moaning. She heard him say, "Take her away. She knows nothing. That wizard must have hidden the site. If she could hide an entire kingdom, she could hide the seventh site as well. This one is of no more use to me, magic or no."

Strong arms lifted and dragged her out of the room and back down the hallway. Meris faded in and out of consciousness, her head about to explode and her throat throbbing from where he'd choked her. They threw her to the cold floor of her cell and slammed the door. As the bolt was drawn across the door, she wept, knowing what awaited her kingdom. All those she loved were doomed. And it was all her fault.

Kael waited off to the side of the dais that stood under the pale pink dome of sky. The Lord Na'tar had summoned the entire kingdom by striking a large hanging iron bell. The peals rang out across the land, and when the hundreds of men, women, and children came running, they looked aghast at the strangers in the midst, all lined up on the tile platform that elevated them all at one end of the marketplace.

Kael looked over the crowd in awe of what Shamara had done here. Not just of the physical world she had formed out of rock and magic but the peaceful and prosperous society she had nurtured and guided for thousands of years. It stood as a sharp reminder of humans' lack of ability to rule others selflessly and without corruption. How many nations in all of the history of the world could boast of such harmony? There had never been even one uprising or rebellion. But then, none in Me'arah knew that a wizard had been ruling their land, as well as sustaining it. None knew, either, that they had been placed under enchantment to forget their past and shudder at the thought of leaving.

Which made Kael ponder heavily many ethical questions as he watched the murmuring spread and grow through the crush of people eager—no, anxious—to hear what Ta'sus, their lord and protector, had to tell them of these curious strangers they now saw in their midst. He was a ruler too. In fact, he had ruled over two Ethryns separated by thousands of years. And rulers were pressed to determine what kind of rule they would wield—one of honesty and transparency, or one of tyranny or manipulation. The age-old

question came to the forefront of his thoughts: Did the end justify the means? And just what were the rights and responsibilities entrusted to one who ruled, who held lives in his hand? Did
Shamara have the right to hide the truth from her people? To use
magic to manipulate their minds, albeit for what she felt was their
own good? Was it wisdom or arrogance—or perhaps irrational
fear—that led her to decide to make the choices she had?

How would her people react when they learned the truth? And
now learned they must flee immediately, leaving everything they'd
built and the land they loved behind, never to return? Yet, this is
what the people of Moreb had done five thousand years ago in
order to find safety from Sha'kath. And he had once fled from the
Destroyer as well. So he, more than anyone in the world, knew
why she had done what she did. Yet . . . it did not sit well—not
at all—that she kept the truth from her people and used magic to
make generations forget their past and the knowledge of the true
world. But what would he have done? Maybe in her situation he'd
have done the same thing. And how much had her hiding of the
truth hurt them?

Well, he supposed he would soon find out.

Ta'sus, now changed into robes of authority, walked to the
front and center of the dais, and Shamara came and stood next to
him. The crowd quickly quieted. He looked across the sea of bodies
with a sad but stalwart expression on his face. Kael saw him swallow and could tell he struggled to hold back tears.

"My people of Me'arah." He drew in a breath and let it out
slowly. "No doubt you see before you strangers to our land. I will
waste no time with a lengthy explanation, and what I am about to
say will come as a shock to you. But please know . . ." He gazed
into many faces, and although Kael saw the affection they had for
their long-time lord, a patina of fear and worry lay over them.

". . . everything I am about to tell you is the truth. And, no doubt, it will be hard to fathom and hard to believe."

Kael watched the reactions alongside the other wizards as Ta'sus related all—starting with the attack upon Moreb millennia ago, then following with the details of how Shamara had created and sustained their world, to the reason for the dome light failing, to the arrival of the wizards and company, and to Meris's escape and subsequent capture. The telling took most of an hour, with not a word uttered in the crowd. Kael could only imagine the shock and confusion these people must be feeling. To the right of the dais stood a woman with her arms around two young women, who must have been her daughters. No doubt this was Ta'sus's family. When he spoke of Meris's capture, the woman had nearly swooned, crying and throwing her hand over her heart.

He tried to imagine what it would be like to be told his life was all an illusion. He'd felt that way upon waking on his death bed in Ethryn, after he had spent a lifetime in the past, only to learn he'd been in a twilight sleep for three weeks. But that was different. His life in the past—however magical its circumstances—had not been an illusion. The kingdom he founded from infancy thousands of years ago still existed in the real world. But what if one of heaven's messengers came to him and told him *his* world was merely an illusion, just as Perthin had said? That it only *appeared* to be a world under a bright blue sky and a canopy of stars? What if there was something else, something more real above that, and he was none the wiser?

The king of Elysiel's words spoke in Kael's head: *"What if—like this place—there is something above the heavens, just beyond the veil. A whole other world above us we know nothing about because we can't see it, aren't meant to see it. What if our time here on this world is like . . . living in this cavern? And everything is illusion, not real at all?"*

Maybe, Kael pondered, this dream we are in is going to end,
just as one wakes from sleeping. Maybe clinging to this life and
trying to stop evil from destroying the world isn't a mere ending
but a beginning—as Perthin had been told by his ghostly ancestor.
The time of the end, the ghost had said. *"Everything comes to an end."*

Kael let out a long sigh and turned to watch Ta'sus. The crowd
had begun stirring, the reality of their situation sinking in. He
noted Shamara's stricken face. She no longer tried to influence the
minds of her people. They now knew the truth. But they also knew
there was no time for dissention or complaint.

"We must hurry," Ta'sus urged. "There is no time to dally. But
please, do not panic. Pack only what is precious to you. Take only
one skin of water and enough food for one meal. Your needs will
be provided for." He gestured for Kael to come forward. "This man
is the king of a great kingdom—Kael of Ethryn."

Kael stepped to the front and looked into the many faces. The
people of Me'arah seemed like lost sheep, huddling together out
of fear. He tried to sound reassuring and confident. "People of
Me'arah, my heart is sorrowed at the news, that you must vacate
your land—a land your protector and creator has lovingly sustained for you all these centuries. She has kept you safe while the
world above has raged in countless wars and endless bloodshed.
While the greedy rulers of many lands sought to oppress their
people and take what was not theirs, you lived in peaceful ignorance, free of turmoil, tyranny, or want. Do not criticize Shamara
for the decisions she made, for she only had your safety and happiness at heart.

"And now you are about to enter the real world with its danger
and its beauty. My kingdom is a prosperous, thriving one, and my
people are warmhearted and generous. The wizards here will lead
you to Ethryn, and from there you may decide to stay or leave—that

is your choice. But it is no longer safe to stay here, as your lord has told you. We will all do what we must to keep you safe and help you adjust to life outside Me'arah, but we cannot say what dangers we might face upon reaching the surface. I only ask that you trust us and cooperate, and together we will find a way to live without fear or the threat of attack." Kael paused, trying to think what else he might say to allay their fears, but all had been said.

Ta'sus nodded in gratitude to Kael, then turned to Shamara. "Would you like to address your people?"

The old wizard hesitated, then made her way to Kael's side. She looked out at the crowd and said, "I have loved you all, each and every one of you, and only did what I thought right. I hope you will find it in your heart to forgive me for withholding the truth from you all these years. I knew no other way to ensure your safety."

A moment of respectful silence ensued as Shamara openly wept. Then, applause and cheers rose from the crowd and grew to a deafening pitch. Shamara mustered a smile, then nodded and hobbled to Valonis's side. Relgar took and squeezed her arm. Kael was relieved to see the favorable response to Shamara's words, but wondered if the warm feelings would last. Time would tell—if they had time.

Ta'sus spoke, his voice firm and loud. "Bring your families and your belongings to the shore of the great sea by dinnertime. Once we are all gathered, we will leave Me'arah together and travel as a group, just as our ancestors did when they came here to this hidden kingdom."

Kael noted the fear streak the faces in the crowd at the mention of the sea. Shamara had not yet removed their magically induced aversion to crossing the water, but they voiced no complaint. He admired her people and their courage. He knew many in his kingdom would not react with such trust. It attested to Shamara's loving rule, however unseen.

And what did that say about heaven's rule? He had spent years running from the hound of heaven, who chased him down and claimed him. Kael would never forget how it felt in that moment, when he had been dressed in rich robes, his filthy rags removed, and appointed Keeper of the site. How he'd finally understood how much he was loved and cherished, and how much God loved his creation and meant good, not harm, for his creatures. Yet, God had allowed evil to proliferate, and now it appeared as if the world was about to end and evil would finally hold sway. Was that truly heaven's will, or was there more going on, more they just could not see beyond the veil of the world?

Kael stood and watched as the people of Me'arah hurried to their homes. Soon the marketplace was vacated except for his group. Ta'sus had left with his family. The wizards spoke among themselves. With Justyn and Perthin gone, Kael was the only one among them who was a mere man. And he suddenly felt his many years—of both lifetimes—weigh heavily on his heart.

What would he encounter upon returning to Ethryn? Was his the last site standing? Or would he return to a pile of rock and his kingdom in ruins? His throat closed tight at the thought.

He supposed he would soon find out.

TWENTY-SIX

"K EEP MOVING, keep moving," Hinwor urged as the flood of people emerged from rock out into the moonless night.

They are terrified, Joran realized standing beside the frowning wizard, thinking how they had never seen their world drenched in such darkness. They all cowered, gazing with open mouths at the sky sprinkled with stars. Imagine never having seen night or stars. *Or the moon*, he added with a shudder. He wished he'd never met the Moon, and just being back on the surface of the world gave him the eerie sense she was watching him. The hairs on his neck tingled uncomfortably. Was she friend or foe? Would she be glad to see the Destroyer make waste of the entire world? Joran hmphed. Did it matter?

Joran watched his father leap up onto a high boulder, as deftly as a wolf. Would Joran see the wolf emerge again? He'd never asked his father all these years if he ever transformed back into his former guise, but Joran suspected there were times he had. Nights when Joran looked up at the Sawtooth Mountains and saw a shadowy shape perched under the stars, as if contemplating. Something told him that was his father, once more the wolf that used to eye him with his watchful, protective gaze. Or maybe it was just Joran's fanciful imagination.

Yet, even if the wolf emerged to battle Sha'kath, would his prowess and power help stop the destruction of the remaining sites? Of the world itself? Uneasiness grew in his gut thinking about his life in Tebron, of his sweet wife and peaceful life in the towering forest. He closed his eyes and drew in a long breath, letting his mind linger briefly on the comforting images of home. A tremor of fear rushed through him at the thought that he might soon lose his world and all that he loved. He had tried not to think of this possibility. *Inevitability?* He hoped it would not come to that, but he knew deep in his heart some end was coming. Perthin had been told "endings are merely beginnings." But where was the comfort in that? He didn't want a new beginning. He wanted what he had, the home and life he enjoyed in Tebron. He didn't like change.

He looked out at the hundreds of people gathered in front of his father, a tight mass of humanity huddling in fear and worry amid the prodigious beauty of the restored valley. He imagined these people didn't welcome change either. They'd been enjoying a peaceful and prosperous existence, only to be wrested from it and thrust into danger and uncertainty. Well. at least they had a place of refuge to run to for the moment.

Joran looked at Kael standing by Zev and the other wizards. His face was a mask of calm, no doubt for the benefit of Shamara's people. Zev was saying something to the crowd, but Joran could not make out his words. A loud commotion then arose around him, and people turned every which way, looking about with frantic expressions. He made out Shamara, standing just below the protruding rock platform his companions were standing upon. Horror engulfed her face, which caused Joran's heart to batter his chest.

He looked up into the blackness of night, expecting the Moon to emerge behind the cliffs, but then he chided himself for his stupidity. The Moon posed no threat. Then he heard shrieks in the sky, and his heart clenched. He knew without a doubt what flew above them all.

The ground started shaking, and people toppled. Rocks broke free from the surrounding cliffs. and avalanches of boulders skipped and thudded down to the ground. Screams rose above the sounds of crashing rock. As Joran sought purchase for his feet, he grabbed on to a man's arm and knocked them both to the ground.

Through the melee of panic and destruction, Joran caught a glimpse of two shadows circling overhead. He then heard Zev's voice, loud and penetrating, crying out the words of a spell. Dust choked the air, occluding Joran's vision. All he could do was grip the man's arm tightly as magic swirled and wrapped him up, like a string tightening around a parcel.

Amid the jerking and bucking of the ground tearing apart around him, water sprayed his face and dirt clods pounded his head. He ducked as best he could, muttering his own feeble spell of protection, but it was no use. He was powerless before the onslaught of the Destroyer's gryphons. And he could see nothing past his own fingers over his eyes. Terror raced across every inch of his skin.

To his horror, a familiar film of ice formed crystalline shapes at his feet, teasing his boots. Joran jerked and his throat closed up. He felt the icy tentacles before they touched him.

But then . . . the air thickened with a syrupy calm, and the roar in his ears softened to a dull thrum of power. The screams around him were sucked into a vortex and whisked away to a place of silence. Joran thought his head would explode, and clutching it tightly in both hands, he moaned as he felt his feet swept out from under him and his body lurch sideways. He was airborne, pulled violently from the world and the grasp of the Destroyer, then deposited with a hard thud to the ground.

His fingers found sand, which he sifted and rubbed, waiting for the emptiness around him to fill back up with substance. He drew in a shaky breath, remembering a similar sensation, of slipping into that twilight place he'd been taken captive years ago when Charris went missing. The strange realm the wolf had rescued him from, when he'd despaired and lost hope. Zev had saved him then, and it appeared he had saved them all now—from the Destroyer's attack—although he had no idea if any had been killed. Joran could now make out the hazy outline of buildings through the clearing dust and grit. Moans and groans told him the people of Me'arah lay alongside him on this hillside overlooking what Joran supposed must be the kingdom of Ethryn.

When he looked overhead, the calm of night greeted him, and a thousand stars winked at him, as if impressed with this grand entrance to the kingdom.

He remained prone, waiting, listening. The sounds of panic and fear shifted into murmurings of relief and reassurance. Mothers spoke softly to children, husbands to wives. They were safe—for now.

He felt a hand on his shoulder. Joran turned his head and looked into his father's eyes.

"We've arrived," he said, his face weary. He offered a hand, and Joran took it and got to his feet. It took a moment to get his balance.

"Come," Zev said, "we have work to do." He nodded at the former inhabitants of the hidden kingdom, who looked down upon their new home with wonder and trepidation.

Now with the air cleared, Joran gazed upon the land of Ethryn, the place his adoptive family had come from. His brother Callen had journeyed here many years ago, and had told him wondrous stories of this land, back before the insidious drought that had recently ended. This was Kael's kingdom, home of the first sacred

site, and Kael was the first Keeper, and the last, for there would be
no more sites and no more Keepers appointed.

A sad sense of poignancy touched his soul, as he pondered
what Kael had told him of Ethryn's beginnings all those centuries
ago. Of how heaven had established the sacred site in the middle
of the desert, to keep evil from ever taking over the world. He
saw Perthin's stricken face in his mind as the king and Keeper of
Elysiel lay dead, the scepter lifeless in his clenched fist. The images
from his nightmare passed silently through his thoughts, the sites
tumbling, the Moon raving, his terror something he watched with
a detached sight, as if he were watching someone else, someone he
didn't know.

Joran walked with his father through the crowd, and all eyes
followed them. He felt their need and worry and sadness trail
behind him as they joined the other wizards and the king of Ethryn. Valonis supported Shamara with her arm, and the old wizard,
the creator and sustainer of the kingdom of Me'arah, muttered
words, her face gazing in wonder and disbelief at the sight before
her. An entire history of the world had unfolded while she lived
underground, like a bear sleeping winter away in a cave. Like a
blind worm unaware of the brilliant sunshine and teeming life aboveground. What must she be thinking?

Joran's heart was a heavy lump in his chest. Here was the world,
a glorious new world, before them all, ready for their exploration.
If these people had emerged from their hidden kingdom at another
time, years earlier, perhaps it would be a joyous discovery, one they
all would have been eager to embrace. But now? How could they
kindle any spark of hope or excitement after what met them when
they came out of the rock?

He met his father's studious gaze as the large group, led by the
wizards and the king of Ethryn, began moving downhill toward

the sleeping city—a city unaware of the attack just suffered by this people. Joran had the horrible sense they were bringing the danger with them, as harbingers of doom for the unwary dwellers of this land. He sighed in resignation. Whether or not it was so, the Destroyer would come eventually, no doubt sooner rather than later. Aside from the enigmatic seventh site, it appeared that Ethryn held the last standing sacred site in the world. What hope did they now have of finding that seventh site? None, that Joran could see. And even if they could find it, what then? How would they be able to stop Sha'kath from destroying that one as well? What good could one mere ring of rocks do to rid the world of evil? What made that last, hidden site so important anyway?

It was almost as if he could feel it—in every bone in his body—the infiltration of evil coating the world, slithering over sand and rock and the hearts of mankind and seeping evil into every crevice and shadow, turning the world cold and dark. Was there any way to resist? It all seemed so futile.

With his head bowed and his thoughts running rampant, Joran fell in step to the rhythm of boots pounding the ground as the people of Me'arah trekked down the sand-blown slope of hill and into the sleeping city.

Ta'sus held tightly to his two daughters' hands as they entered the great city under the unfriendly black sky. His wife walked beside him, strangely quiet. He had managed to calm his pounding heart after the terrifying attack and then the magical way they had been whisked from the land and transported to this place. It was all too much to take in, so much happening, so shocking. Never in his long life had he experienced such fear; he was amazed he was still alive and breathing. Amazed they had all escaped with their lives. Everyone seemed accounted for—Ta'sus sensed no grief among his people, something he would quickly detect. No, he only felt their fear and sorrow and anxiety. And although he did not feel brave, or hopeful about what lay ahead, he put on a brave face. Yet his heart ached for Meris, now even more so at knowing he and Drayna and his other girls were somewhat safe for the moment, but who knew what Meris was enduring—if she was even alive.

But, yes, she was. He would know if she died. He felt the spark of her life inside him, in his very blood. And his own blood cried out to her, willing her to come, to find her way to him, to their new home.

He fanned that desire as they walked through quiet sandy streets, the small clay houses with their tiled roofs so foreign, it was as if he were walking in a dream, a place of imagination. He had to touch a wall as they passed to convince himself this was all real. How could this be? He still could not fix the idea in his head that he had lived his entire life ignorant of the truth. Lived underground all these centuries completely unaware there were other kingdoms—like this one—full of people, living their lives unaware of their existence. He likened it to waking from a long sleep, shaking off a dream. His whole life had been a dream.

"I'm tired, Father," Sapha said in a whiny voice, her feet dragging. She clutched his hand tightly.

"We'll be stopping soon. I'm sure the king of Ethryn will arrange a place for all to sleep. And then in the morning it'll get sorted out." He gave her his best smile of assurance and she sighed.

He wished he had the right words to comfort her. Comfort his family and his people. He hoped this place would provide a safe refuge, but he knew he was fooling himself. From what Shamara had told him, he discerned it was only a matter of time. Could they have lived in peace forever underground if the wizards had not found them? Would Meris have taken Shamara's place and sustained their world while the real world above them raged in war and toppled in destruction? He imagined all in the kingdoms spread across the world dead or suffering tyranny under the Destroyer's reign. A world they were now a part of. He bristled thinking how they could have been safe. Ignorant still, yes, but safe.

What did the truth matter? He would trade truth for security any day. But this was all moot and useless to ponder. They had been forced into leaving; he'd been given no choice. He no longer led his people. They were now being dragged by the hooks of fate.

Oh, Meris—what of your fate? He pressed forward, his head down. He didn't want his children to see his tears.

In her cold cell, Meris leaned against the rough stone wall, her body hurting all over and her head throbbing. Her face hurt where it had met rock when the guard threw her to the ground, and her throat ached in raw pain from the Destroyer's grip. How much time had passed since she was taken, or since she had been returned to this horrid room, she could not tell.

As much pain as she was in, it paled in comparison to the pain in her heart. Guilt and shame assailed her mercilessly, and she missed her family more than she could bear. She was a little girl once more, needing the comfort of her parents' arms and their soothing words assuring her everything would be all right, that there was nothing to fear. Tears had bloated her eyes, and her hands and clothes were streaked with dirt. Her hair was a tangled mess, but she sought to work out the knots with anxious fingers, needing something to do. She had tried over and over to summon her magic, but not even a tiny spark burned inside her. The Destroyer had snuffed it all out. She was nothing, a mere human, and her wizard's blood was impotent. Oh, if only she could die.

The small crack in the stone wall across from her told her it was night. She pictured the black canopy overhead with its prickles of light. Her world didn't have night like this. The dome dimmed softly for hours, soothing them while they slept. Darkness to her meant death and fear. She recalled the moment the dome failed and ushered in such darkness. It was the darkness she saw when she squeezed her eyes shut. And more so, it was a darkness in her heart, a place she now wallowed in, a place with blame and without hope.

She had tried to understand evil. Why some meant harm. Why some wanted to hurt others. Kill other people, and for what? They wanted power to control people and lands and treasure. Shamara told her Sha'kath meant to rule over the world. Rule and do what? Make others his slaves, to work for him? Where did this evil come from? If not from heaven, why did heaven allow it? Why was the God of the world letting Sha'kath have this power? And what was this sacred site he was looking for? Her head ached too much to think further. She just didn't understand, not at all.

As she sat there, forlorn and homesick, her father's face drifted into her mind. *Meris*, he called. She heard the sadness in his voice, and it only amplified her own. *Come to me. Come home*, he whispered. Tears streaked her cheeks as she let herself be drawn into the warmth of his voice. She looked into his loving brown eyes and felt a tingly warmth in her empty stomach. She recognized the little spark of magic, as if one of her fireflies was flitting around inside her. The thought made her smile, although it hurt her face and neck to do so.

Meris, Meris, the voice called out, louder now and stronger. And with each mention of her name, the spark grew warmer, bigger, and soon the warmth filled her belly and spread to her chest, coupled with a great longing to be with him, to wrap her arms around him and feel his beard tickling her face.

A laugh came out of her chest, unexpected and free, as if it had just escaped some cage and could now spread its wings and fly unhindered. The sound startled her, sounding strange, and yet it encouraged her, although she did not understand why. She shrugged off her despondency, realizing her fear and shame and hopelessness was dampening her powers—the most important power being her capacity to love. The Destroyer wanted to break her spirit and drain her of hope. *That is how he negates magic! Why I haven't been able to draw upon my power.*

She pushed everything from her mind but her love for her father. For her family and her people. In her mind she saw her father smile encouragingly as he urged her. *Come, Meris, come. I miss you. I need you. I love you.*

Warmth spread outward from her chest, into her extremities. Her hands and feet began to glow with heat. Rising, she braced the wall and felt the heat shoot out into rock. Her eyes widened as the rock melted like butter under her palm, causing her to sink into the wall. With a gasp she pulled back, then moved away from the wall, to stand in the center of the cell.

She pictured her mind as still as the great sea, keeping her eyes on her father's, her heart entwined with his heart. His words kept coming, one after another, growing in size and volume but not a scream in her head. More like the way sound echoed in a cave, bouncing off walls. Her whole body washed hot, as if she had a fever, but she never wavered, even as sweat poured down her forehead and neck and slipped down her back.

With closed eyes, she let the love for her father ignite her. She was aflame, burning but not incinerating. And the flame of love was hotter than any heat she could imagine, able to burn down walls and fortresses and any weapon fashioned against it.

Her laughter grew to a roar. She understood now the source and power of her magic, of all magic. Of all creation. Shamara had built an entire kingdom by the power of love. God in the heavens had fashioned the entire world out of love for his creation. Love was greater than evil, a mighty weapon that could not be destroyed—not even by the Destroyer. Love was indestructible, for an enemy could strip you of everything you owned, even your very life. But he could not take away your love, or prevent heaven's love from showering upon those God chose to love.

Love was the key. The key to everything. And it was something she held, within her. Even though it felt like the biggest thing in the entire world, and as bright as the orb that shone in the sky of this strange new world, it fit into her heart, like a key in a lock. All she had to do was turn it just so . . .

In an instant of time, the cell she was in exploded in a blinding light, but noiselessly, as if someone had erased all sound from existence. With eyes wide, Meris saw a vast landscape spreading so far in the distance, it melted into the horizon. Somehow she could see in all directions at once as the love within and outside her radiated in heat waves that shot out from her body. She felt weightless, swimming in air, as she watched armies of the enemy march over hills like hordes of ants, ravaging kingdoms across time. Tall, majestic palaces tumbled to the ground, slowly, as if made of dust, and the armies marched on, city after city, village after village crushed. It pained her to watch, but her gaze riveted on all that presented before her.

Meris then saw the two gryphons circling over an open plain, dusty and surrounded by sand. A wide river wended slowly further away, and then she spotted it. A ring of rock rising from the sand. Huge slabs of rock, a dozen or two, with some flat pieces connecting a few. She knew this was the sacred site Sha'kath was speaking about, searching for.

Then, suddenly, she was on the ground, in the center of the site, with the sun burning hot overhead and the gryphons winging toward her.

She shut her eyes but still saw them speed toward her but she felt no fear for she wielded something greater than any magical onslaught. Alone, empty-handed, she threw her head back and laughed, and her laughter shattered the silence smothering the world. The gryphons shattered into tiny pieces that fell to the earth, and then the slabs around her fell too, crumbling to dust, and for as far as she could see, wildfire burned the vast expanse, sweeping across the open land and devouring everything, even the sand, until there was nothing left. Nothing but stark emptiness and a vanishing horizon.

A shiver raced down her back. Meris threw her eyes open to blackness and cool air. Her bare feet dug into soft sand. She looked up and gasped. Stretching out above her was the black sky, dotted with a million shimmering lights, so tiny, like pinpricks, but she felt their warmth, even from this unimaginable distance. She envisioned them as hot, burning orbs, like the one that moved across the daytime sky, that had burned hot upon her shoulders when she blasted through the rock and came out into the world above Me'arah. Into Moreb.

She knelt and felt the ground. This place was real, but where was she? Then she felt the spark in her heart. The tiny tinder of heat that was her father's love. That is what had set the world aflame, she now understood. What had whisked her from her cell and out from under Sha'kath's power to this place.

The magical power of love had brought her here. She could only guess this was where her father must be, now. Her people must have fled Me'arah, she realized with a start. The wizards had brought them here.

Meris stood and looked out across the sand. In the distance she made out structures. Buildings. Some small with tiled roofs. Others taller, rising above the smaller abodes. Her jaw dropped in wonder. She had no idea how far away she was, or that magic could do such a thing as move her from one place to another. The thought of seeing her family again set her heart pounding and her feet running.

She sped toward the city before her, her bare feet racing across cool sand, her heart overflowing with laughter and love.

• PART FIVE •

WHY DID Shamara hide from everyone?"

"Hmm?" Alia said, looking at Aron's sleepy face and wondering if he would be able to keep his eyes open tonight.

"Momi, you're not listening," he said, pulling Big Pig into his chest for a crushing hug.

Alia smoothed out the bedcovers so that the pig was neatly tucked in with her son.

"Well, it wasn't so much that she was hiding. They all knew her. She would go to the marketplace on occasion to buy food." She smiled at Aron and raised her eyebrows. "She was very fond of berry tarts, and so when she ran out of flour or honey or ber-ries, she had to shop."

Aron scrunched up his face. "I don't get what a marketplace is. And what's shopping?"

Alia tousled his hair. "Not everyone has all they need all the time. On some worlds, people trade for goods. Like, say you made chairs and someone needed a chair. And you wanted—"

"Momi," he sighed, "can't we just get back to the story?"

"You asked me about why Shamara was hiding."

He threw his hands into the air. "Okay, she wasn't hiding. She was shopping."

Alia laughed, but Aron clearly didn't understand why. "All right," she said. "But to answer your question, Shamara was old and tired, and it wore her out to walk all the way to the center of town. And talking to all those people was tiring too. When you're old—"

"No one gets *old* anymore, not like that," he argued.

Alia chuckled and stroked Aron's cheek. He pushed her hand away.

"You're right, sweetling. But she was old, and back then, being old made you very tired all the time. And Shamara had work to do. She had to sustain the whole kingdom, and that took a lot of energy and concentration."

"I could do that." He sat up abruptly, his eyes bright. "I could create a world. I have a big 'magination."

"You do. And that is very important when you are creating worlds. Just think of all the things God has created in the entire universe—all the millions of animals and birds and fish and plants."

"The story, Momi!" Aron blew out an exaggerated breath.

"My, you're a bit impatient tonight."

"I just want to get to the best part of the story. The final attack of Sha'kath the Destroyer!" he said with a hiss and an evil gleam in his eye.

How odd, she thought, that she could relate this story as if it were just a fairy tale. As if it had never happened. As if she hadn't seen it all with her own eyes—the end of the world. The memory burned as the world had burned, but was now relegated to a tiny flame in her heart. A flame that would never go out, that would serve as a reminder, a beacon that kept her course true.

She had felt a jolt that night, while lying, her energy spent, in a strange bed—the first time she'd slept in any bed other than her own, in some unfamiliar cottage in the kingdom of Ethryn. They'd arrived that night, after her second escape from the Destroyer. Words could hardly be found to describe the anguish twisting her heart. What she had felt seeing those gryphons in the sky after all those centuries, as if they had lain in wait for her to emerge from below. As if they had known all along she was there, with her people. The thought struck her with great pain as she mulled over how helpless she'd been to do anything to save them—again.

She lay under clean cool sheets and berated herself. For putting her people in danger again. For entrusting a young girl with the truth, and expecting her to do her bidding without question. She had done everything wrong. She could not undo her terrible mistakes. With tears pouring down her face and wetting her pillow, she tossed and turned in the quiet, empty room Kael had taken her to in this wholly different place. But sleep would not come. She could not bear to think of the lives that would soon be lost, all because of her.

And then, a strange sweep of magic encircled her. She sensed it coming from Ta'sus in a nearby cottage. No—outside one of the dwellings. He was standing under the stars, unable to sleep. She heard him calling for his daughter. Shamara groaned thinking of Meris taken by the gryphon to its master. She sat up, then went to the small round window set deeply in the brown clay wall. From there, in the dark night, she made out the Lord Na'tar, his head tilted back, pleading with heaven.

But suddenly his anguish shifted into something else. Shamara felt a blast of emotion emanate from Ta'sus, which shot out across the night sky in all directions. A quintessential surge of love, the seed of the universe, tiny but oh so potent. She had no idea Ta'sus knew how to summon it. But then she shook her head. Anyone who knew true, selfless love had this seed within, even though few knew how to germinate it. The power of love was easily diluted by self-interest and fear and need. But when a person wielded love in its pure form, it was powerful indeed. Love was at the core of creation, and nothing could ever exist—or endure—without it. Worlds would come and go, and stars explode, but love could never, ever be destroyed or vanish from existence. Love was the stuff of heaven: incorruptible, unfailing, imperishable.

And because of its indestructible nature, the Destroyer had been unable to prevent what happened next, although Meris's actions triggered his fierce retaliation, and from there . . . well . . . that was the rest of the story. The part Aron had been eagerly awaiting, through the telling over many nights, to hear.

She turned to Aron, who was staring at her with sleepy eyes. She had only indulged in a few seconds of remembering, but it had taken everything out of her. Exhaustion hit her, and she lay down alongside Aron and stroked his head.

"Aren't you going to tell the rest of the story?" he asked.

"Momi's too sleepy, sweetling."

His small hand patted hers. "That's okay. Grown-ups get tired a lot."

"Oh?" she asked, chuckling and nuzzling close. "And why is that?"

"Because they have frisky kids to take care of. And that poops them out."

She leaned over and gave him a kiss somewhere on the vicinity of his forehead, which he promptly wiped off with the back of his hand.

"Thanks for understanding," she said. Then she shut her eyes and fell asleep.

TWENTY-SEVEN

A POUNDING AT his door jerked Ta'sus from his strange sleep. He forgot where he was for the moment, then realized he had dozed off in a chair near the door to this cottage he and his family had been given by Kael upon entering Ethryn. He leapt to his feet as Drayna sat upright in the bed across the room, her face full of alarm. His daughters stirred and moaned in the small bed but didn't wake. No doubt fending off night terrors.

Who could be—? No, was it possible? Blood pounded his ears as he ran across the room.

He had no doubt who was knocking.

He threw the door open with a cry that caused tears to pool in his eyes.

"Oh, Meris!"

She stood, radiant under a glowing light streaming from the night sky, happiness spilling from her eyes. Ta'sus threw his arms around her and grasped her tightly, as if he would never let go.

She wept into his shoulder. "Oh, Father, Father, I love you so much. I was so afraid—"

"Hush, you're safe now, shh." He closed his eyes, his gratitude to heaven pouring from his heart as he rocked her in his arms in the doorway. He heard Drayna give a cry and throw the covers off. Then her arms were around them both, and together they sobbed and wept in joyful reunion. Abrella and Sapha, alerted by the noise, woke and came over, and Ta'sus stepped back to let his three daughters embrace and exchange their words and affection. He pulled Drayna to his side and stroked her hair.

"My baby is back," she said, wiping tears of relief from her face. While the girls talked excitedly, Drayna turned to face Ta'sus. "How? How did she escape those . . . creatures and find her way to us?"

"Her magic is great," Ta'sus said. "Greater than mine, and perhaps greater than any who has ever lived in Me'arah—except for Shamara." He thought for a moment. "Maybe the wizards had found a way to free her and bring her here."

"No, Father," Meris said, turning and pulling from her sisters' embraces and coming to stand before him. Ta'sus took her hands in his and studied his daughter's face. She seemed to have aged years in just these few hours she was away. Grown up. Her gaze bespoke a wisdom that wasn't evident before.

"I heard you calling me," she said, nodding. "And I felt your love." She put her hand over her heart. "In here. And it was like a spark that set the world on fire."

More tears filled his eyes and blurred his sight. She said, "You told me to come to you, and I did. My love grew into a power I . . . I don't even know how to describe what I felt."

Ta'sus saw a great weariness come over her features. He hated to think what had happened to her after she'd been taken. In the dim light streaming through the cottage window, he now could make out bruises on her face, and he stiffened.

"Did they hurt you?" he asked, barely able to get the words out.

"I'm fine, Father." Her visage darkened, and Drayna grasped Meris's arm.

"What is it? Tell us," his wife pleaded, her voice quavering.

"The Destroyer . . . he is sure to come after us, to find us." She glanced around at the small room they stood in. Her sisters sat on a narrow bench against the wall, huddled and listening, worried.

"What is this place?" she asked.

"It is called Ethryn," he told her. "A kingdom in a vast desert, ruled by Kael. He was among the wizards that came to Me'arah, and offered refuge to us."

"To our family? What about the people of Me'arah? Are they still underground?"

"They are all here as well," Drayna said. "The wizards . . . brought us all here."

"With a magic spell," Sapha added, her face lit up. "It only took a few moments, but somehow they transported us all"— she grimaced with fear—"when those terrifying things began to attack." Abrella wrapped her arms around Sapha, tears dripping down her cheeks.

Meris's face fell. Ta'sus knew her thoughts, that she blamed herself for the attack. For going to the surface and alerting the enemy of their existence.

Ta'sus stroked Meris's hair and led her to sit on the edge of the bed. "Do not blame yourself, Meris. What's done is done. The Destroyer may have found our hidden kingdom in time. The wizards' arrival may have alerted him. There is no way to know for certain." He tried to sound reassuring, but Meris stiffened under her self-reproach. "What matters now is that we are together, and whatever happens, nothing can separate us from the love we share."

Meris nodded, but Ta'sus could tell she did not believe him. And he understood why. If Sha'kath meant to ravage the world, they would never be safe. There was no longer a safe haven for them anywhere—not underground or aboveground.

Kael rode hard in the early morning dawn, alone and on horse-back. Usually a morning ride cleared his head and soothed his worries, but not this morning. Although he was assured the site still stood, untouched, and that there had been no unusual events taking place in Ethryn during his week's absence, he had to see for himself. More, he had to immerse himself in a place of worship, to seek heaven's face and favor, and most importantly, to know God's will. His heart was heavy with worry and responsibility, and he had never in his life been so unsure of what he was meant to do.

He had sent forces north to battle, and messengers had returned telling of bloody engagements and loss of life. As warm fall wind whipped his face and hair, he thought what a waste it was to have sent his men to die on foreign battlefields. Now that he understood more about Sha'kath and his intent, he concluded any attempt to fight the enemy was a fool's mission. He had called his messengers to him late last night, after he appointed servants to find lodging for all the refugees and could relax knowing their needs were presently being taken care of. He instructed the men to return to his soldiers and tell them to come home. The messengers had questions in their faces, but Kael gave no explanation. He was beyond tired, although sleep remained just beyond his reach all night.

He thought back to the discussions he'd had with Perthin and Justyn here in Ethryn, not all that long ago, but the memory seemed dragged up from years in the past. Time had moved dif-ferently underground, in the hidden kingdom, Kael realized. Each minute like an hour, each hour like a day. But now time was crawl-ing, as he waited. Waited for whatever storm was to come upon the world. Come to his land.

As he crested the final ridge overlooking the great wide river glistening under the pink-streaked sky, he was reminded of the sky in Me'arah, and of Shamara and all she had done to save and protect her people. They would still be safe now, had he and his companions not found them. Kael grunted and urged his horse faster up the sand dune. Now the people of Me'arah looked to him to keep them safe, and he was powerless to do so. Maybe, he hoped, the wizards would come up with a way to pool their power together and defeat him. He'd heard they'd battled him in the past, and often successfully.

But more was at stake now, and never before had mention been made of an end of things. He thought of Perthin and how the ghost had told him he would be the last king of Elysiel. And how he himself would be the last Keeper, and that he held the key to the kingdom. But what did that all mean?

He pulled back on the reins at the top of the dune. Below him, the majestic slabs of rock reached for heaven, standing as silent sentinels in a circle. Seeing them from afar took his breath away; it always did. The way they rose from the sand in the middle of nowhere attested to their purposeful placement. And Kael's memories of the night he had been appointed Keeper played in his mind and heart, as if it had been just yesterday and not five thousand years in the past. He would never forget how heaven had opened and the blast of power had struck the ground and spread out in massive undulations across the landscape, scattering the builders of the great tower and all their evil allies, and confusing their language so that they could no longer speak one to the other. No, there was nothing heaven could not do, no evil it could not repel or vanquish.

Soon, the others would arrive. He had given the order to his chief archivist, Avad, to strike the gong and gather his entire kingdom at the second hour. He wanted everyone in the land to come to the sacred site, just as they had not long ago when he'd had excavators dig for hours until they uncovered the buried rocks, and heaven cracked open the earth and water gushed out, ending the insidious drought. There they celebrated joyfully, together. Today, he needed to speak to his people, and this was where they needed to be: on holy ground.

Kael smiled at the memory of the moment he had been shown by God where the site was buried, and had been promised water would flow in the desert. He had been swept away in visions, into the past, where he had encountered the one who chased him down relentlessly.

And now, Kael would gather his people together, and together they would turn their faces to heaven and ask for favor and deliverance. Kael now understood. Heaven had a plan, and for some reason it was part of the plan to allow the Destroyer to tear down all the sites and let evil run rampant across the world. Why? He had no idea. But it was clear to him—a lesson he thought he'd well learned by now—that there was no way to thwart heaven's will. *We lead the best lives we can, do the most good, embrace honesty and kindness and generosity. We try to be faithful in all things, hardworking, honorable. Heaven asks for nothing more, other than to have faith. Only believe . . .*

He galloped down the sandy embankment to the site, then slid off his horse and dropped the reins. A few soft clouds floated overhead, the only thing visible in the vast blue sky. Kael drew in a long breath and straightened, then entered the circle of rock and stood in the center.

As always, a sense of awe and humility overcame him. The stones were ordinary rock, roughly hewn—but not by human hands—and stood in their places not perfectly aligned or of equal size. There was a simplicity about them, much like the stone altars the faithful had built over the centuries, to mark sacred places or covenants with God. Kael felt the reason for such plainness was to divert attention away from the structure itself and instead toward the symbolism and purpose of the site: to turn one's heart and face to God and to be reminded of man's utter dependency upon heaven for everything in life.

He let his gaze drift across the stones and felt a sublime peace wash over him, reminding him that, although he was a great ruler of a great kingdom, he was a mere man, a mortal, his years numbered and few in the broad sweep of time. What little he knew about life was little indeed. He was like a grain of sand in the universal hand. So very small.

And yet, as he dropped to his knees and lowered his head, he felt that same gush of love coat him that he'd felt so many times before, throughout both his lives, during trials and moments of stillness as well, when the world seem right and fair, and hope sprang wishfully from his heart and soared to the sky.

If it all ended now, did it matter? He had lived a more full life than he could have imagined, and had been drenched with countless blessings. From what he'd experienced and learned, he knew he should not fear death or what was to follow, but still, he had regrets. Things he wished he'd done or said differently. Places he longed to see but would never have the opportunity. He thought of his wife and children he'd left behind in his life in the past, when he journeyed with heaven's messengers to place the gemstone in the altar atop the great tower, and then died. He had loved them so much, and even now missed them, although truth was, they had died more than five thousand years ago.

Kael let the tears fall as he rested his forehead on the warm sand. He wasn't sad, not really. Just aware of an emptiness inside, a hunger that needed abating. But he knew nothing in this world could ever sate such a hunger. If he could describe it, he'd call it a hunger for life, for real life—not this semblance one called life. He wanted more, needed more. This hunger seemed situated at the very core of his being, as if he'd been created with it.

Life was just an exhale, a mist appearing and then disappearing. *We are here one day, and the next, we are gone, and in a short time, all memory of our existence will fade. All the thousands who have lived before me—who remembers them? They have slipped into an irretrievable past that drifts so far behind, no one can see them any longer. That is the legacy of humanity.*

Kael raised his head. He sensed something. Something on the wind, something coming. He searched the skies, but they spread thickly over his head in dazzling blue, undisturbed. Like a calm moment before a raging storm.

But there was no denying it. The storm was coming.

TWENTY-EIGHT

WHERE ARE we going?" Joran asked his father, trying to keep up with the wizard as he hurried through the Great Scroll Room with its massive marble arches and polished floors and impossibly high ceiling.

"To the king's chamber. There is something we need to bring to Kael."

As they passed the endless rows of shelving stacked with scroll upon scroll, Joran was awed. The vast amount of knowledge stored in this building was astonishing. He imagined on any ordinary day, the room would be filled with scholars and students and visitors from all over the world, but this was no ordinary day, and their footsteps rang out through empty halls. Joran had arrived in the open courtyard shortly after dawn to find the other wizards flanked by the entire population of Ethryn, which numbered in the thousands. And behind them were the hundreds from Me'arah, appearing numb from the confusion and changes wrought upon their lives in just a matter of hours.

A young man with authority, dressed in some kind of royal garments, stood upon a dais and spoke to the crowd, and although only those in close proximity heard his words, the listeners, spread the news back through the crowd until they all understood the king's command. Everyone had been told to eat a quick meal and journey to the sacred site, where the king awaited. What he planned to do there was not disclosed, but his people were quick to obey, and Joran noted all were readying to leave and making their way out of doors and walking or riding north through the city. Joran imagined he wouldn't have to ask where the site was; they would just follow the throng of citizens.

He thought about his nightmare, the one he'd had right before his father had roused him from sleep and bade him to go with him to Sherbourne. He'd seen the sites topple: at the house of the Moon, in Wentwater, in Rumble. He hadn't dreamed of this one, here at Ethryn, but he imagined it would look much the same as the others. The one he'd personally visited at the steps of the Moon's house was inspiring, yet forlorn and ignored. Joran had no idea at the time that Cielle was its Keeper, but no wonder it had been neglected.

A strange feeling had come over him when he stood in the center of the circle and moonlight sliced through the spaces between the slabs of stone and formed a perfect star of light on the ground around him. He'd thought little of it—or of the site—at the time; he was consumed with finding Charris. But now he wondered why heaven would set one of the seven sites there, and under the care of such a lunatic. He doubted he'd ever get an answer to that question.

When they arrived at what Joran presumed was Kael's private chamber, a guard nodded and allowed them entrance. Zev went directly to an old ornate trunk that rested at the foot of the king's bed and opened it.

As Zev rummaged through the contents, Joran asked, "What are you looking for?"

His father mumbled something, then pulled out a robe dyed in deep purple, then grabbed something else, but Joran couldn't make out what it was. After a moment of more searching, Zev bundled up the things he'd gathered and put them in a knapsack slung over his shoulder.

"We're meeting the others at the stables. Come," Zev instructed, moving at twice the speed as before.

"What's the hurry?" Joran asked. Zev stopped abruptly and faced Joran, who took a startled step back.

His father studied him and frowned. "We have to get to the sacred site before it is too late."

"Late?"

Zev spun back around and continued his rush through the halls and then out the door. Joran saw the stables ahead of them, and the other wizards standing alongside horses that were saddled and bridled and anxiously pawing the ground.

Joran sensed great agitation when he neared the others.

"Did you find them?" Hinwor asked Zev.

"Yes," Zev answered, swinging the knapsack off his shoulder. Relgar took the sack and strapped it onto the back of the saddle of the horse nearest him, whose reins he held.

Shamara stood warily eyeing the horses. Relgar turned to her. "Let me help you up."

Shamara made a face Joran interpreted as disbelief. "I haven't ridden one of those for five thousand years," she said to him.

Relgar chuckled. "You just hang on to these straps of leather. And if you fall off, you get back on." He helped her mount, then handed her the reins.

Joran noted the smiles of his companions seemed forced. He wished someone would tell him what was going on, but he didn't feel he should ask. The mood was thick and morose. And already the day was becoming uncomfortably warm, with a real sun glaring from a real sky.

"Tell me," Hinwor said to Zev, "what do you hope to achieve by having Kael petition heaven?"

Before his father could answer, he said, "We still haven't found the seventh site." Joran wondered if he should just keep quiet. But he was confused and couldn't hold back. "The Moon said we needed to find the site. That the kingdom was hidden, in our midst. That the seventh site was the key." He looked at his father.

Zev answered, a bit irritated, "Perthin was told that Kael was the key. He is the first and the last—the first and last Keeper, of the last standing sacred site. This site is the last stronghold against Sha'kath. Kael told us that when the first site was erected and he was appointed Keeper, a powerful energy surge shot down from the sky and spread throughout the whole world. That was the moment heaven created a covenant with mankind, to keep evil from taking over, by means of the sites and their Keepers. Perhaps heaven means to give a repeat performance there."

"Kael also said he was told he was a symbol of things to come," Hinwor added. "But does that refer to something still to come in the future? It could just mean he was the first Keeper, and the other Keepers' roles would be patterned after him."

Relgar then mounted his horse, and urged the others to do likewise. "When I spoke one evening to Justyn, he told me about a scroll he'd found. It too spoke of the seventh kingdom, and how it was 'in our midst.' But he also said the scroll mentioned something about living stones, and judgment against the wicked—"

"But that too could be referring to the past," Joran argued, "when Kael was first set up as Keeper."

Valonis, who had been quietly standing beside her sister, said with a sad expression, "We cannot second-guess heaven, my friends.

All we can do is trust. And try our best to protect those under our care."

Joran noted her expression, then looked in the other wizards' eyes. "You have a plan," he said.

"Well," Relgar answered, "not really a plan, Joran." He clucked at his horse and moved to position himself in front of the other horses. Everyone had now mounted except Joran.

"If not a plan, then what?" Joran asked.

His father chortled. "You can either ride with us and find out, or you can walk. But it may take you some time to get to the site if you choose the latter. And I know how much you hate being left out of things." He gave Joran a sly smile.

With a huff, Joran swung up onto the saddle of his patiently waiting horse.

I thought you were never going to get going, the horse mindspoke him, his tone a bit snarky.

Why are you in such a hurry, eh? Bored standing around? I'd trade places with you any day—especially now, Joran answered.

The horse merely snorted, and Zev laughed. But the light-hearted moment was snuffed out as all the wizards suddenly looked to the east.

A tingle of panic raced through Joran's limbs. He craned his neck to identify what they were seeing, but all he could make out was a faint gray cloud off in the distance.

"That's no cloud," his father said softly. Too softly for Joran's liking.

Joran turned to his father, who rode up alongside him. The others sat their horses with stiff posture, as if expecting something. Something fearsome. Then the horses threw their heads and danced in fear.

"Ride!" Zev shouted. "Ride hard!"

Before Joran could ask why, a flurry of movement erupted, and the horses with their riders galloped away from the stables down the wide road to the north.

As he hung on to his horse's wild-flying mane, he had a terrible feeling for what was to come.

Meris cringed as she watched the whirlwind of dark clouds gather overhead. The bright orb that had been beating down hot on her head was now blocked out, and a cool stream of air whipped about her face. The gray patches of wool she had seen on the animal hide matted together in the sky, but they looked ominous—nothing like the innocuous shapes that floated peacefully in the painting she'd studied. She grasped her father's arm tightly as they pushed through the huddling mass of frightened people.

"Can you see it?" she asked. "The site?" She was shorter than the people around her, but her father could see over most heads.

"Yes, we are almost there."

She detected the worry in his voice. *He knows. He knows what is coming.* Her legs ached from trudging so many miles. The people of Ethryn seemed accustomed to such trekking, but she had never walked across sand. She would collapse and rest if her need wasn't pressing her forward.

"Why must you talk to King Kael?" her father asked her, elbowing through more people to make headway.

"I have to tell him—" She stumbled, then righted herself. Her mother and sisters were somewhere in the back of the great river of people flowing toward the site, but they could not keep up this pace, and she told her father she needed his help to reach Kael before it was too late.

"There is no time to explain, Father," she said, out of breath. "Please, just trust me."

He pulled her close as they hurried downslope. She could see it now—at least the tops of the stones. Her heart pounded as she glanced at the sky, knowing any moment the Destroyer might arrive.

She had seen him in her fitful dreams last night—marching with an army of immeasurable size toward Ethryn. From what Meris gathered when talking to Shamara early this morning in the palace garden, Sha'kath knew where all the sites were, and had destroyed all but this one—and one that was somehow hidden from sight. This seventh site, she was told, was the key—the key to the *other* hidden kingdom—the one the wizards had hoped to find in Me'arah. And Kael supposedly was the one who held the key, being the first and the last Keeper of the first and last site. And yet, the kingdom was also in their midst.

Little of what Shamara told her made sense, but now Meris understood why the wizards had come to Me'arah—thinking the seventh site must have been in her kingdom. And that was why Sha'kath hurried to attack her land, in his eagerness to find that site, only to discover her people had fled it.

But he would find no underground kingdom. Shamara told Meris how she had used every last vestige of magic to destroy all trace of the beautiful land she created. When she said that, she touched Meris's wrist, and images flitted through Meris's mind. Of the woods melting like wax and the great waters of the sea turning to mist. Of the dome overhead sagging and collapsing until sky met with ground and folded up into rock. What were once dells and springs and wildflowers and deer had turned formless and gray and finally dissipated. And then her fireflies stopped flitting, and their tiny lights went out, and all turned dark and cold.

Pain shot through Meris's heart as she turned and looked into Shamara's milky green eyes. The wizard gave Meris a weak smile and said, "It is finished," and then with effort, hobbled away from

Meris as they stood under the eave of the palace wall. Shamara's great sadness and loss, though, was tempered by joy—by knowing what she had accomplished. Meris remembered how she spoke to her that first day of training. *"All that heaven asks is we be faithful. And believe."* Surely Shamara felt a measure of joy and reassurance that she had truly been faithful—beyond what any could have expected from her. Me'arah may have been a construct of a wizard's mind, merely a fantastic illusion, but it had been Shamara's home—and her own home—for years.

And then later, after the order had been given for all to journey to the site and her family prepared to set out, an understanding came over her, like a cold wave of water hitting her in the face, waking her up and showing her what was so obvious. Why didn't the wizards see it? With all their wisdom and magic, had they not been able to understand? Or was she mistaken?

No, there could be no mistake. There could be no other answer. A smile rose to her face as her father abruptly stopped and gestured with his arm.

"We're here." Meris saw that the crowds kept back a respectful distance from the site. A dozen or more huge slabs of ochre-colored rock stood at attention before her—gigantic rectangular rocks that formed a circle on a wide plateau. What looked like a group of religious men in white robes with hoods stood chanting beside the rocks, their heads hanging and their eyes closed. Off to the west, water spewed from the ground and spilled down a deeply creviced rock face to a majestic river in a lower valley. No doubt this river supplied all the water Ethryn needed, and she marveled at the way it shone like pounded metal under the thick gray clouds that matted overhead.

A great surge of peace entered her soul, lifting her in a joy she could hardly contain. Her father spun to face her, and he studied her inquisitively. Then he paled and his jaw dropped.

"Meris, what . . . what is happening to you?"

His voice sounded as if it came through a long tunnel, as if drifting up to her ears from under the ground. She couldn't reply. The warm glow circulating through her body made her skin tingle and her throat constrict.

She knew now what this sensation was. It was the same thing she had felt in her cell in the Destroyer's fortress—the wellspring of love that had grown from a spark into a wildfire. But this wasn't just the love she felt for her father, or that which she felt from him, however deep and pure and strong and enduring. No, this was another's love, and it was far more pure and strong than any human's love could ever be. It was more powerful than the burning orb in the sky. More powerful than a pounding waterfall or an avalanche of rocks. This was the source of all creation, what fueled and sustained not just the world around her but the whole of life, of existence. Every tiny particle of everything in and under heaven had this spark of life. Yet it was not only everywhere outside of her; it was also within.

The wellspring of her life. The key to the kingdom.

She tore her gaze away from her loving father's eyes and spotted the king of Ethryn standing inside the sacred site, in the middle of the circle. She pulled from her father's grasp.

He looked at her with awe but said nothing as she walked toward the king.

As the sky exploded in fire and storm and the gryphons shrieked overhead, sending everyone around her into chaos, tripping and falling and running away in the all directions, she heard nothing but the quiet beat of her heart as she took one surefooted step after another toward her destination.

TWENTY-NINE

THE STORM raged overhead, but Kael knew it wasn't any ordinary storm. A presentiment of doom hung so heavy on his shoulders, he buckled and fell to his knees, hearing the screams of his people echo in his ears. The cry of the gryphons overhead rushed him back to the past, when he was a slave building the tower. When those horrid manifestations dove and swooped and lifted terrified men from the ledges and tossed them like unwanted scraps to their deaths.

His heart pounded hard at the memory, the taste of fear metallic in his mouth. He tried to draw strength and courage from the images of his escape, reminding himself of heaven's deliverance, how he had burned down the great gates keeping them all imprisoned, and how he had led his friends to freedom, but not by his own doing. Not by any means. How many times had heaven intervened? More than he could count. And he had been given a great gift of healing, and through that gift saved his mother's life—and the lives of dozens more.

And now, the lives of thousands depended upon him and what he would do. But all he could do—kneeling humbled under heaven in the only appropriate place, with empty hands—was to wait. And trust.

Heaven had led him to this place five thousand years ago, and then led him again to uncover the site from under mountains of sand and pervasive hopelessness. And it had now led him here for a final time. This had to be the end—the end of all things. This was the last site, as far as Kael understood. And once it was destroyed, there would be no stopping Sha'kath. The Destroyer would destroy them all, and any in opposition would crumble under his wrath. Kael had seen such destruction in one of his visions—the one in which he himself had been reduced to a charred piece of timber, and the whole world burned around him, burned to ash.

He heard the messenger's voice in his head. *"I have snatched you as a burning stick from the fire. You are a symbol of things to come."*

And yet from that ash, he had been rescued, delivered. That was the hope he now clung to—that heaven meant to deliver them somehow. He couldn't bear to believe God would abandon mankind, however undeserving they all might be. For no one deserved God's grace and mercy. God had every right to wipe all creation from existence, if he so chose. Perhaps mankind was a mistake—an experiment gone wrong. There was so much evil in the hearts of men, even without influence from Sha'kath or his servants. And yet, Kael knew God to be merciful. He'd experienced such mercy and grace firsthand—how could he ever forget? Or deny God's nature? He could not. Would not.

He heard someone calling his name in the midst of the growling, snarling wind that had now stirred up the sand and threw it about in reckless abandon. He turned and saw Zev and Joran hurrying toward him, carrying something. When he realized what they'd brought, he smiled, and more memories flooded him.

"Here," Zev yelled over the noise, holding out the purple robe he kept in his trunk, similar to the one heaven had dressed him in that night in his vision, when he had arrived dirty and in filthy rags. The angelic messenger had cleaned him and given him white garments and put the robe around his shoulders. Zev said something to Kael, but he could only hear the sonorous tone of the angel, repeating what he'd uttered back then.

"The Lord never lets the guilty go unpunished. He displays his power in the whirlwind and the storm. The billowing clouds are the dust beneath his feet. At his command the oceans dry up and the rivers disappear. Who can survive his burning fury? His rage blazes forth like fire, and the mountains crumble to dust in his presence."

Across the expanse of desert, even amid the cacophony of ear-shattering noise around him, he heard mountains crumble and fall, snapping like bones. And in his mind's eye he saw oceans of water turning to steam, sizzling and hissing as if the world itself were smoldering like a bed of hot coals, burning everything upon it. Was this heaven's raging against the world—or the Destroyer's handiwork? Did it matter which? Either way, heaven would not allow it if it was not willed to occur.

What would remain once the cinders cooled and the ashes were carried off on the wind? Anything? Could anything rise up from such annihilation? Was anything salvageable?

Then Zev handed Kael the silver censer, burning too, with a sweet-smelling fragrance that wafted up his nose. He looked into the wizard's expectant face, and then into the face of Zev's son, whose fearful expression moved Kael to lay a hand on his shoulder.

He knew what they hoped would happen. They expected heaven would open up and send a blast of light and power down, a beam of divine retribution or salvation. But how could that be? When such a thing happened five thousand years ago, heaven had just set up the first site, and appointed the first Keeper, with six more to follow. But the sites had served their purpose, and now they were all being destroyed. And soon this one would be as well.

Perhaps they had failed. They were sent to find the seventh site, the key to the hidden kingdom. And here he was, purportedly holding the key to the kingdom. He looked at the censer dangling in his hand and smirked. This couldn't be the key—or the way to unlock the hidden kingdom. They'd failed to find it. They'd hoped it was in Me'arah and it wasn't. And even if it had been there, how would they have used it to stop Sha'kath?

He'd been over and over this in his mind, but it was a circle with no end. Like the site he stood in. An ending within a beginning.

As if to prove his point, he turned in a circle, within the circle, holding out the censer and looking to the skies, but the squall intensified and rain pelted him and dirt flew in his face. He caught glimpses of Zev and Joran, now joined by the other wizards, huddled against stone, watching expectantly. From the shrieks of the gryphons and the screams of his people, he knew they were under attack. He felt the ground tremble from the falling bodies, and then the stones began rocking. He moaned with the wind, sadness tugging him down.

He stopped circling and watched as the great slabs of rock crashed to the ground, one after another, each one hitting the next and creating a chain of collapse.

The wizards rushed toward him and away from certain death, but one toppled, and to his horror, crushed Valonis and Shamara, and he could see them no longer. As if time came screeching to a stop, he saw Relgar and Hinwor throw their arms in the air and run to their fallen companions, the anguish frozen on their faces as each step they took moved through air as thick as sorghum. Kael jerked. Another slab hit the corner of its neighbor and careened off to land on Relgar's leg.

Kael, standing motionless, unblinking, saw Relgar's mouth open in a scream, but the cry was sucked up into a vortex, a whirlwind not unlike the sandstrom that had sucked sand from the world and deposited it into mounds in Ethryn's past. Days and weeks and months passed as Kael watched the mighty rocks fall and pile up around him. He could not move, not even flinch, as the world shattered around him and time hung in a precarious freefall.

Then a gryphon overhead turned its fierce gaze in his direction and came toward him, although hours passed and Kael watched as its wings moved, barely perceptibly, up and then down, and finally some weeks later knocked Hinwor and then Zev and finally Joran to the ground.

The whirling vortex dropped down upon Kael, and he watched this too, as it crept his way and engulfed him, fluttering his robe and hair and spinning and spinning him until the world around him dissolved in a great hiss as if all the air had escaped. He steadied his heart and calmed his nerve, giving up all his will and resolve and surrendering to heaven. The sky turned to black ink, blotting out existence and smothering history—past and future.

And then a great calm suddenly ensconced him, muting the storm that raged and snapped and circled around him. His clothes fell back into place, and he pushed hair from his wind-battered face. He stood in a pool of utter silence, under a dome that was blacker than any night. It was naught but emptiness, yet this emptiness did not hurt him or make him sad. In fact, he felt nothing at all, caught in this eddy of waiting.

And then something caught his eye and he turned. He swallowed and blinked. Blinked again. Something or someone seemed to take shape just outside the whirlwind.

And then a hand appeared, poking through the wall of wind and dirt and madness, and then a foot.

Kael's eyebrows rose in surprise. The censer dropped from his hand to scorched sand. He'd assumed the world was gone.

Apparently not.

Joran opened his eyes and saw the last thing he wanted to see.

Above him in the blackness of night hung the Moon—full and bright and hovering over the edge of the world.

He glanced around him and saw flat terrain void of life in all directions. He was alone—except for her.

He watched as her form took shape way off near the horizon. The ground wavered like the sea, even shimmering from moonlight as if waves rippled upon its surface. The glow in the air around him was otherworldly, reminding him of the light he'd seen that night when Ruyah the wolf had used the magic stone. Then, a bright blast of light had shattered the night, but it had been more than light. Like this light. It wasn't just something visual; it was . . . more. The essence of joy.

He had forgotten how it felt, but now, oh now he remembered, as he reveled in the feeling, as joy rose from his toes and filled him to his head, like being wrapped in a warm blanket on a cold night.

And on its heels came a ponderous peace that pushed all questions from his mind. He chuckled. If his father were here, he would have been amazed. Joran—without a question? He then wondered why the wolf was nowhere in sight.

He waited, and it took her a while to reach him in those ridiculous shoes with their pointy heels that sank into the soft ground and caused her to trip. Although, Joran recalled she tripped practically over everything, including her own feet. She bumbled along, tripping and straightening, and now Joran heard her singing. The same scratchy-throated voice as always, and he recognized the tune as one she had sung the time he sat in her kitchen and she prepared him soup. Something about an owl and a cat and a runcible spoon. He never did figure out what ditty that was, something from his childhood that his adoptive mother used to sing to him.

Remembering his family in Tebron, Joran wondered at how long ago it seemed. Yes, it was decades, but the years has passed like a watch in the night, like mere hours. Where had the time gone? Just what was time anyway? Such a strange fluid thing we go through as we live out our lives, he thought. The more you tried to grasp a moment and capture it, the quicker it slipped through your hands.

He craned to see something, anything in the distance, but his eyes only met with emptiness. What was this place? Why he was alone? Where was everyone? The other wizards, Kael. He had been right beside them.

The air was dead calm, neither hot nor cold, and although it was night, in some odd way it wasn't. He looked again at the Moon sitting on the edge of the world. She hadn't moved, and her face was expressionless. He sensed no malice from her, only a similar expectancy. No stars dotted the sky. He must be back in his dreams, the ones from long ago. But where was the sea, and the sand castle?

Now he felt confused. He reached down and touched the ground, rubbed dirt between his fingers and smelled it. It should have smelled like something. *I am dreaming.*

"No, sweet potato, you're not," Cielle said in her singsong voice, coming up and tickling him under the chin.

Joran jumped back. "I wish you wouldn't do that."

"Oh, now, little mincemeat. Why are you always so unpleasant?" she asked with a frown. "Just what have I done to annoy you?

I took care of you when you came calling, didn't I? I washed your clothes and even let you sleep in my favorite bed." She leaned in closer and her many silver bracelets jangled in his face. Then she hmphed and raised her pointy chin at him. "I even made you my soup."

"You did," Joran said, relenting and giving her a smile. His annoyance thinned. "The best soup I ever had."

She threw back her head and chortled loudly. "I knew it! It's a secret recipe though, so don't bother asking for it."

"I know. You told me that."

"Hmmm. I see you are here without your wolf." She looked him over. "So, now what?"

Joran frowned. "What do you mean, now what?"

She gestured in an exaggerated way as she turned in a circle. "Here we are, at the beginning—or the ending. I suppose it all depends upon one's perspective, wouldn't you say?"

Joran didn't know how to answer that, so he just stood there, knowing she would probably get around to explaining herself.

"And you aren't dreaming," she said.

"I'm not?"

"No, my little pomegranate. This is *real*."

"Then where are we?"

"I already told you. We are at the beginning. Or the end." She flicked her wrist and tilted her head, eyeing him curiously. "Whatever."

"Those aren't places. They're . . . I don't know what they are."

Cielle batted her lashes in rapid motion. "You're just confusing the issue."

"What issue?" He could feel one of his headaches coming on. They seemed to be a certain side effect of being in close proximity to her meandering logic.

She blew out a hard breath. "We are circling around."

"We certainly are," he said, which was par for the course with the lunatic Moon.

"You misunderstand me, pumpkin. I am not speaking metaphorically." She stopped and put on a puzzled face. "Or is that figuratively? I always get those words mixed up."

Among others. "So, what do you mean?" Joran asked, pushing down his impatience. He wished she would get to the point, but that was harder than pulling a horse's teeth.

She waved a hand in the air. "Life is circular. Seasons follow seasons, the worlds spin and circle one another, night follows day in a circle across the heavens. There is no end." She scrunched up her face. "Didn't I tell you this before? The end of time only looks like the end, but it's just part of one big circle. Time loops around and comes back and here we go all over again." She gave him a big toothy smile that crinkled her eyes.

His headache throbbed in his temples.

She flicked a wayward strand of hair from her forehead. "Now you understand why the Moon is mad. Not angry—insane. Circling is a kind of madness." She turned thoughtful. "But then again, there's a very pleasant symmetry in it." She looked over at the Moon perched on the horizon. "Every story has an ending, Joran. Otherwise, how can it ever begin?"

He startled at the mention of his name. She had never used it, and she sounded lucid for one brief instant.

She added, "An ending and a beginning. You came into the story late, near the end of time. But no matter, my little bumblebee! Everyone has a part to play, and at the end, the players all gather on the stage and have a curtain call. Lots of bowing and—oh! Roses!"

"What?"

She grunted and flicked her hand at him. "Never mind." He shook his head.

A long silence ensued. Joran finally said, "Now what?" He was getting tired of all this circling and getting nowhere.

"We wait," she replied decisively.

"For what?"

"Silly. For Kael to use the key to the kingdom. So we can all get there already."

"Huh?"

She pointed at the Moon. "See, she's watching him. He's in the center of the circle, circling, waiting for the end of time. But voila! Here it comes. The inevitable ending, what you've all been waiting for."

Joran rubbed a hand over his face. *I give up.*

"Exactly. You can't get into the kingdom unless you do that."

"Do what?"

Cielle let out a raucous laugh. "Oh, dear muffin, you can be so funny at times. Give *everything up*. You can't *enter* the kingdom otherwise. What? You think you can take it all with you?" She came over and tickled him under the chin again. This time he didn't even flinch.

She fluttered her lashes at him. "Just a few more minutes, and then we can leave."

Joran was about to ask where, but she put a finger over his lips. He clamped his mouth shut.

"You know where, silly wombat. The hidden kingdom."

THIRTY

THE SHAPE turned out to be a girl. Meris, to be exact, although how he knew that, he wasn't sure. Kael frowned. The wind outside his circle of utter calm droned on, like the moaning of a sick man on his deathbed. The world itself was groaning and churning in pain, but all Kael felt was an unemotional emptiness. Her glowing presence dispelled the absolute dark of his strange sanctuary, cocooning them in a warm golden light.

"Your Highness," Meris said, a beatific smile on her face as she graced him with a bow.

He shook his head, trying to clear the fog from his senses. "What are you . . . How are you here, alive . . . ?"

"The same as you, King Kael." She came up close to him and looked up into his face. He marveled at the way her entire countenance glowed with ethereal light. Maybe they weren't alive. Maybe he was dead, and she was now a heavenly messenger sent to speak to him. He rubbed his face. *Maybe this is just another of my visions.*

"I don't understand," he said to her, pleading, a strong need rising in him for this confusion to end. He dropped to the ground.

The girl or angel laid a very real, human hand on his arm as he knelt on the hot sand. He looked into her innocent eyes and studied her young freckled face. He saw a resemblance to Ta'sus, her father. Why was she here, and why was she so . . . happy?

"It's really quite simple, Your Majesty," she said, squatting beside him. She took a finger and mindlessly began to draw something in the sand, still smiling. She then stopped and looked at him. "The kingdom you are seeking—it's here."

"Here?"

"Yes. Here."

He gestured to the whirlwind around them, held at bay somehow by magic. Why wasn't it devouring them the way it had devoured everything else? "There is nothing left," he told her. "Everything has been destroyed."

She chuckled and sat cross-legged to face him. She leaned close. "Not everything. But it all has been burned down to its essence."

Kael waited for her to explain, wondering how such a young girl could be so sure of herself, of what she knew. The older he got, the less he felt he understood—about the world, about life, about everything.

"When you burn something up," she said, "really burn it, there is nothing left. But when you burn . . . *everything*—all creation—there is something left, some essence that cannot be destroyed. The essence that is the spark of existence. The thing that is the seed of all life, all creation. It is the only thing that truly does exist, and once everything is gone, truly gone, it alone remains."

She must have noted his confused face, for she then said plainly, "Don't you see? It is love."

"Love? But that's . . . an idea . . . a feeling, a concept. It's not—"

"But it is! When everything else is gone, it remains. It *is* life and creation and existence. It is . . . God, to put it simply. God is love. And as simple as it sounds, it is more profound than anything at all. How can you define love, or put a face to it? Can you?"

Kael thought for a moment. Thought of all the people he had loved, and then thought of how God had chased him through the years and days and wrapped him in love, claiming him, saving him, defining him.

"How else could anything—everything—come into existence if not by love?" she said, searching his face. "Every tiny and great thing." She sifted sand through her fingers. "Every grain of sand."

He thought of the creative force of love. How love moved humans to conceive and birth and raise children. God had given birth to the world, to the heavens—an eccentric and prolific expression of love. For he didn't have to do it, do anything, make anything. He didn't have to care. Yet, he did.

And he'd seen the power such love had. The way it moved people to face tremendous obstacles and suffer pain and even sacrifice their lives for others. Why? Why would someone give his life—all that he had and was, his very essence—to save another? Was there anything in existence greater than that? Could anything destroy the love one felt for another? Anything in heaven or in the world? No. It was the only indestructible element in existence.

"You make good points," he told Meris, "but what does this have to do with the hidden kingdom? The end of the world? God so loved the world that now he's decided to wipe it away?" He brushed the sand and smoothed over her random scribblings.

"Yes," she said evenly. "but it's like a baby in the womb." She looked overhead to the black canopy blotting out heaven. "For a time, the child exists in darkness. She floats in a world of warmth and comfort, but it is not the life she was meant to live. It's a temporary home, and when the time comes for her to leave, her world convulses and amid great pain and turmoil she is thrust out of the safety of her dark home in terror. Yet in order for her to live, to *truly live*, she must be expelled from that safe shelter and into one that is bright and big and perhaps frightening at first. But that is the real life she was meant to experience. She can't stay in the womb forever."

Kael nodded, his thoughts swirling, swirling. "We are like babies in the womb," he said, envisioning his entire life enclosed in obscurity, seeing only what was immediately before him, understanding little—no, nothing—about the true world or the meaning of his life. He had spent his entire life in such darkness, without answers. And now he realized that underneath it all he'd had a yearning to leave, to reach his true home. To understand finally and fully this love that had created him. He'd always had this yearning. He knew the words she spoke were true. This life was only a temporary shelter, not *real* life. A preparation.

Just the thought made an ache, a painful one, well up inside him. It spread through his whole body as a horrible need—a need to be loved, to be wanted and protected and cared for. Tears pressed at the corners of his eyes, and he felt so small, so tiny, so helpless.

He dropped his head in his hands and wept, although he didn't understand what was happening to him. It was as if he was emptying out, like water draining through a sieve, leaving his heart yearning in such a way that he thought his heart would break.

He felt Meris's touch again, a hand resting on his back. And she waited patiently, saying nothing, as he kept crying until the last tear made its way down his cheek. Until there was nothing more to him, nothing left inside. He was a hollow shell.

He then heard the messenger's voice, and his eyes flew open. But instead of Meris standing before him, it was the youthful dark-skinned angel, whose malachite eyes shone with such radiance, Kael had to squint.

"Kael, you have to become empty to be filled. Emptied of hate and anger and striving and worry and fear. Love needs a vacuum, an empty space to fill. God spoke into the black emptiness of nothing and brought everything into existence. Entire worlds—yes, the heavens—were formed by the word of God and wrought by his love."

Then the angel touched him, and Kael jerked backward, his mouth open, astonished. A surge of love, unlike anything he had ever felt in his meager human body, gushed into him to overflowing. He knew without this angel's help, he would not be able to contain such a feeling. He could come up with no words to describe the humbling and elevating sensation that made him fall once more to the ground and drop his head to the sand. Every nerve in his body tingled—with joy.

And this joy exploded in a brilliant light from his body and cracked the black dome overhead. A million sparkling stars fell about his face as he stared upward, and as the whirlwind outside vanished, erased by the light, and the calm of his tiny sanctuary spread like honey across the open expanse of nothingness, filling it with luminous light for as far as his eyes could see.

"Look." Meris was by his side again, and the messenger was gone. She was pointing to the sky, or what seemed to be a sky. The air shimmered and light glinted off something afar. But whatever the object, it was approaching them, and soon Kael could make out the shapes of the sacred site's stone slabs. He had seen this reflection in the heavens eons ago, he now recalled, right before he was led to the site—the real site—and then appointed Keeper.

"But this is not a reflection, King Kael," Meris told him, as if knowing his thoughts and his past. "The other six sites—*they* are the reflection. Do you see?"

Swimming in a sea of love and warmth, bathed in divine love, Kael did see. Finally. And Meris was right. It was simple and made clear sense. He was emerging from the womb of this dark world into something better, something amazing.

Something real.

The yearning and need he'd felt moments before pressed him to raise his arms heavenward, beckoning this kingdom to come. He understood it all now—how the kingdom was within him, within everyone, in their midst and in every grain of sand. He only need reach out and grasp it . . .

Suddenly a shaft of light shone down upon him, and he was in the center of the slabs, but these were not made of stone. Or of crystal, like the one in Elysiel, as Perthin had described to him. These were made . . . of pure light, or perhaps of love itself, of that divine essence. They were living stones, throbbing with life, more real than anything Kael had ever seen or touched. A kingdom truly not made by human hands. A magical kingdom.

He realized then that all magic had a meaning, and that meant *someone* had to mean it.

He heard words in his head. *"Come, enter the kingdom prepared from the founding of the world. For you, Kael . . ."*

Tears clogged his throat as he laughed a great releasing laugh and spun in a circle, his arms waving overhead. Meris clapped her hands and laughed too, and danced around, carefree. He understood now how he held the key that opened the gate to the kingdom, but then realized everyone held such a key within them. The seventh site—the hidden kingdom—was truly in their midst, and had been all along.

He looked down and watched what was left of the world fade away under his feet as he was transported. To where, he had no idea. He only knew that he was finally going to the one place he wanted—needed—to journey to.

He was going home.

THIRTY-ONE

CIELLE CLAPPED her hands and bounced up and down on the balls of her toes. "Oh goody! Now we can go!"

Joran shook his head at her antics. He looked around him at the empty landscape, at the Moon still sitting complacently at the edge of the world, and shiny as a polished tea kettle.

"All right," he said resignedly, a bit amused and—he had to admit—stirred by curiosity. He felt as if they'd been waiting out here—wherever here was—for years. He wanted to get back home to Charris and his little cottage and make himself a nice hot cup of tea and put his feet up. The thought shook the tiredness from his limbs. "So where are we going?"

Cielle came over to him and *tsked*. "You should know better than to ask! We have to go to the end of the world—"

"Again?" Joran huffed. That was one long, exhausting journey he did not want to repeat. "Do you mean back to your . . . house?"

She threw back her head and chortled. "Ha! Very funny. Now why on earth would we want to go there?"

"Because . . . it's . . . where the world ends?" He remembered the eerie feeling he got when he peeked behind her shack and saw nothing beyond. The memory gave him shivers.

She gave him a pathetic look of disdain. "Silly boy. Really. With all the questions you ask and all the answers you've been given, one would think you would be the smartest person in the world. I guess not."

With that, she started off in a trot, away from the Moon and toward . . . somewhere. Joran couldn't see that any one direction led anywhere in particular. But he trotted after her and soon, to his surprise, he actually started seeing some formation off in the distance. And before he could voice his complaint about how long they would have to walk to get to that far-off place, the shape suddenly grew taller and wider and quickly turned into huge battlements and stone walls and towers, resembling a little like Sherbourne but more like a mirage. For the structure itself seemed ethereal, made of light, and it shone the way gold did in the sunlight.

Joran was reminded of Sola's house—the house of the sun. He followed Cielle in silence as they passed through the glimmering open gates and into a vast courtyard. He looked down and even the ground was sparkling like gold and felt soft and smooth under his boots. His eyes widened as his mouth dropped open. Where were they?

Cielle guffawed. "Really? You have to ask?" She gave him a little push and then smiled and waved. "Ta-ta, my cream puff. I'll be seeing you." And with that she skipped back out the gate, dropping pearls of moonlight as she went.

Joran looked around him, awed by the sight. Tall jewel-encrusted columns of marble rose around him—twelve, he counted, whose surfaces gleamed in the light that seemed to come from everywhere at once. He held out his hands, and they glowed in the same golden light. Even his clothes, which he noticed were now fine white linen, shimmered radiantly.

His excitement tingled too, for there was something special about this place. It felt so very familiar, but he was sure he had

never been here before—not in any of his dreams. It felt more like
. . . home than his cottage or town felt. It was as if he had been
here all along.

That was it! What an odd thing to realize. As if he'd lived one
whole life in Tebron, shoeing horses and eating meals with Charris
and walking through the Sawtooth Mountains, and yet, all the
while, he had been here. Not in a dream, either.

And it wasn't like there were two of him, no. He was . . . outside of time. Just as he had been when searching for Charris in his
dreams. Time had stood still. Or rather, time had been . . . different. After his long journey to rescue her, he had returned home
and had only just left. Yet all those months he had traveled, and
everything he had felt was certainly real. He'd experienced hunger
and sickness—and homesickness—and sadness and grief. Every
range of emotion in his journey had been as tactile and real as his
real life. And yet . . . There were those who would say dreams were
not real. That they were just fancies of imagination.

He took in the majesty of the place he now stood in. Then
what was this? It was not a flight of imagination. Not by any
stretch. Was it possible, then, that time was merely a matter of
place and perspective? Could one live an entire life as if in a dream,
only to "wake" and find out there was a *real* life, outside that one?
Was his life a dream?

He was back to the same musings he'd had when he came back
from his arduous journey to the ends of the world. He was still
the dreamer and the dreamed. Someone had dreamed him—and
everything in creation—into existence. So . . . did this mean he
was now awake? Had he died?

He sucked in a breath at the thought. And at first, it scared
him, and his pulse quickened. He didn't want to die. Dying meant

losing everything and everyone he loved. Charris! He rubbed his face and considered the gates. He could run out—

"But why would you want to do that?"

Joran spun around at the voice. His heart leapt. Charris! She looked beautiful, young! How was that possible? And what was she doing here? She should be in Tebron, awaiting his return from his "quest" with his father. She glowed as well, and her face with lit up with joy. As she ran to him, he suddenly remembered that he had been in Ethryn, standing alongside Zev, with the world reeling, watching the king of Ethryn in the middle of the circle . . .

The memories flooded his mind, along with the terror of the gryphons and the screams of the people around him. They had been attacked! He gasped. *And I saw Valonis and Shamara crushed . . .*

Just then the two wizards came out from between two of the towering pillars toward him. Valonis looked much the same, but Shamara had a youthful countenance and a lively step. What was happening?

Charris threw her arms around him and nuzzled his neck. "Welcome home, Joran," she said.

"What? I don't—"

Just then his father, accompanied by Hinwor and Relgar, came out of the shadows of the pillars and walked toward him with welcoming arms. His father's smile stretched across his face.

"Joran, I know you will be happy here," he said, his voice laced with a bit of mockery. "For now, every question you have ever had will be answered. Truly and to your satisfaction." He grabbed Joran and pulled him in for a big hug, then pulled back to look him in the eyes. "No more riddles."

Joran let out a grateful breath, letting the joy spill into him and pour out from him as he embraced all those he loved. And more people poured into the courtyard. Villagers from Tebron—even those who had died many years ago. How strange. And then . . .

He startled at the sight of his adoptive family. Oreb and Shyra—the mother and father that had raised him. And in came Maylon and his wife Malka, and—Bella, their daughter, who was now a young woman instead of the old woman she'd become. And his other brothers—Callen and Felas—they were young men as well. Oh, it was too much to take in. And there was Justyn—and Perthin! Very much alive, much to Joran's relief. His mind swirled in excitement and joy. He would claim this all was a dream, a wonderful dream, but he knew it was not. It was the real world. Real life. This, he now understood, was the seventh site, the hidden kingdom.

His mother, Rhianne, came up to Zev and took her husband's arm, smiling at Joran. And there, waving at him from across the courtyard were his sons, and his many grandchildren. Everyone he'd ever known and loved was here. They had always been here.

His father had said "no more riddles, no more questions," but now Joran seemed about to burst with them. He took his mother's hand, and although he was eager to speak to Oreb, who had died when he was young and whom he had so much he wanted to say to, he had to understand just one thing.

"Mother," he said as she look so lovingly upon him, "will I ever wake up from this dream and find it is all an illusion?"

"No, Joran," his father said to him, sharing a look of mirth between him and his wife. "No more dreams."

Joran spun around, barely able to contain the joy that filled him. He grabbed Charris's arm and spun her around too, and she let out a hearty laugh. He caught smiles on the wizards' faces as they all watched him dance with his wife under a bright golden moon that had made a sudden appearance overhead. He was so happy to be home with everyone he loved. He couldn't wait to tell his stories, and hear all of theirs. Why, it would take a lifetime—no—an eternity to hear them all. And to create new stories. *No more dreams?*

He caught his father's sparkling eyes as he danced by the light of the moon. Who needed dreams when this was waiting for them?

EPILOGUE

"OH, MOMI," Aron said with a big yawn. "I love that ending. That's the best story in the whole world."

Alia glanced out the window at the dusky sky. Somehow morning had come without her knowing. Had she really spent all night telling Aron the rest of the story? How had he stayed awake? But then, nights were short on this world. She still hadn't gotten used to that. And yet, she needed little sleep. It took some time, on each world they'd lived on, to adjust to the rhythms of the planet.

She heard Glynn rustling about in the kitchen. It was his morning to cook, and already she smelled the wonderful aroma of bentroot coffee and butter browning in a skillet. That would usually be enough to get Aron dashing out of bed to the table, but he'd fallen fast asleep, Puppy clutched tightly against his face.

Alia smiled as she smoothed his hair off his forehead and gave him a little kiss. He didn't like to be kissed much anymore. He was growing up so fast. And soon, he would be a man and married and off raising his own family, on this world or perhaps another.

She loosed a big sigh. Time was a strange thing. The longer you lived, the more nebulous it seemed. Thousands of years had gone by since she uttered the spell that erased Me'arah from existence, since she last walked the grasslands and deserts and woods of that world. She had raised many children and loved them all. And now they were scattered throughout the galaxy, and one day she would visit them all, or they would come visit her. But there was no rush. They had all the time in the universe. There was no end of time, and no end to life. Endless, flowing life that moved like a river, taking them with them as they floated along, sharing in their journey.

She closed the curtains to keep out the morning light, to let Aron sleep awhile, and the Ganari crystals caught the pale pink light and splintered it around the room, reminding her of the pink light in Me'arah. For a brief moment she felt wistful, remembering those many years she had lived underground in the hidden kingdom, keeping secrets and protecting her people. Doing her best to care for those who needed her. Until the day the wizards arrived and Meris fled, and the Destroyer attacked yet again.

But it all turned out fine, as every great story does. She thought how excited and frightened Aron got as she recounted the scary parts of the story to him, his hands gripping his blankets and his eyes wide. But as frightened as he was, he loved hearing the tale, for he knew what was coming: the happily ever after. There was something magical about story.

And all stories lead us home, she concluded. Our lives are journeys, and we wander seeking something, unsure of what it is, and stories tell of that wandering and that longing. But they never give us the true answer we seek—the answer to the question hidden so deep inside us, we hardly know it's there, and because it is hidden, we don't know what we want to ask.

She heard Glynn calling her, so she left Aron's room and went into the kitchen awash in candlelight.

"Here you go, my love," he said, setting down a plate of steaming hotcakes and a cup of coffee. She gave him a kiss and took her seat.

"Thank you, Glynn. This looks delicious." She took some bites as he watched her. She cocked her head. "You're not eating?"

"I already ate. I've been out in the glen. Some new people have moved in."

Alia's eyebrows rose. "Shall I pay them a visit this morning?"

"By all means," he said. "They have a young girl. Perhaps four or five."

Alia loved little girls. She had a few dozen daughters, but it had been many years since she'd raised the last one, and that was three worlds ago.

Excitement stirred in her chest. She hurried through her breakfast. "Aron's fallen back asleep. I'm afraid I kept him up too long, telling him the rest of the story."

Glynn sat down beside her and drank from his steaming mug. "Was he scared?"

"Of course. But he's a boy. He loves that."

Glynn nodded knowingly. He then grew thoughtful. "Does it bother you much, to relive those days?"

Alia set down her fork. "It's important to remember, isn't it? If we forget the stories, how can we live rich lives?"

"We can't," he said, pecking her on the cheek and taking her empty plate and fork to the sink. "We need the memory of sadness and pain to remind us of what we have now. Of the joy. You can't have one without the other."

"My, we're being a bit philosophical this morning," she said with a wink.

"I know. That's your domain, sorry."

"Apology accepted." She chuckled. "You know, a wise man once said, 'stories of magic alone can express my sense that life is not only a pleasure but a kind of eccentric privilege.' We must never forget the stories so that we never take life for granted."

It was her duty to make sure that never happened.

Imagining the little girl waking and eager to explore her new home, Alia gathered up her things, gave Glynn a quick kiss over at the sink, where he was filling the basin with soapy water, and hurried out the door. The warmth of the day sank into loamy earth, releasing the rich aroma into the air around her as she wove her spell and transformed arms into wings.

With a leap, she flew into the sky, reveling in the cool morning mist that lingered on the breeze and dusted her with fat drops of water. The giant blades of grass reached up and tickled her as she flitted through branches that now seemed larger than her house. Soon, she arrived at the overgrown and untended garden fronting the house where the new family had moved in. A place they would soon settle into. She hoped the family liked to garden, for she so loved flowers.

On this world, there weren't any small red deer, like the ones in Moreb, but she happily took the form of a close cousin—what people on this world called a rabella. It was a small creature with soft pale fur, very shy and quite skittish. But she never ran from children. Just as when she was fairy to Moreb, children trusted and befriended her. They never knew she was a fairy—actually, a great and mighty wizard—but they didn't need to know. They just needed to know they were loved and treasured and protected. And that was her job. It had been her job since the beginning of time, and would for as long as time existed, even forever.

THE END

A DISCUSSION OF
THE HIDDEN KINGDOM

The *Hidden Kingdom* is the seventh and final installment in my Gates of Heaven series, one I hope has taken readers on an enchanted and enchanting journey into the heart of fantasy and the heart of our Creator. Although I had read fantasy and sci-fi my entire life—hands down my favorite genres to read—I had never considered writing fantasy until I gave my heart to God and asked him to show me what I needed to write—not just to express myself creatively but, more importantly, to find a way to glorify and honor him through this amazing creative privilege he granted me.

And what God led me to was a thin book written more than one hundred years ago by an author I'd never heard of—G. K. Chesterton. The book was *Orthodoxy*, and it changed my life. Never had I seen (nor since) a small book so chock-full of insightful and delightful wisdom. Chesterton's way of looking at the world mirrored and amplified the yearning in my heart to know, love, and rejoice in my Creator. When I came upon the chapter "The Ethics of Elfland" and read how "this world of ours has some purpose; and if there is a purpose, there is a person. I had always felt life first as a story, and if there is a story, there is a storyteller," I knew then that I had to be a storyteller, too, in like manner.

Chesterton asked: "How can we continue to be at once astonished at the world and yet at home with it?" Throughout *Orthodoxy* he wonders at the sad truth that most people have lost their wonder—their awe and astonishment of existence. We get so caught up in daily, mundane things that we forget how miraculous life is, and how precious each day is. Our lives are a perilous, thrilling journey full of mystery, and although we long for all the answers to the questions gnawing at our hearts, we do well to heed Chesterton's wisdom and trust that "the riddles of God are more satisfying than the solutions of man" (as Ruyah, the wolf in *The Wolf of Tebron* tells Joran). I believe, as shown to Joran at the end of *The Hidden Kingdom*, that one day all those riddles will be answered to our satisfaction. But, in the meantime, we have to be content with the mystery.

I hoped to explore and elucidate as best I could this mysterious journey into the riddles of God through the books in this series. In all seven stories, characters struggle with their faith, questioning heaven's ways, seeking God's will for their lives—or trying to run from him. Arnyl in *The Crystal Scepter* admonishes: "Accept the way God does things, for who can straighten what he has made crooked?" (Ecclesiastes 7:13 NLT). We are taught that his ways are not our ways (Isaiah 55:8–9). Job asks: "Can you fathom the mysteries of God? Can you probe the limits of the Almighty? They are higher than the heavens above—what can you do? They are deeper than the depths below—what can you know? (Job 11:7–8 NIV).

In *The Hidden Kingdom*, Perthin, king of Elysiel, speaks with Kael, king of Ethryn, and wonders about this hidden kingdom they've discovered. All the people in Me'arah have lived underground for thousands of years, unaware of "the real world" above them. I have often looked out at the stars on a dark night, perplexed at the idea that the universe might be boundless, stretching for eternity. Perthin embodies the questions and amazement I have held my entire life at this astonishing truth of our existence.

He says to Kael, "Perhaps we are just like these people of Moreb. Day after day, they live their lives, completely unaware there exists another world above them. Just out of reach, as if separated by a thin veil. . . . We live on the face of the world, under a dome of heaven. But it could be an illusion. Don't you ever stop and ponder how the heavens stretch out endlessly, without boundaries? How perplexing that is! What if—like this place—there is something above the heavens, just beyond the veil? A whole other world above us we know nothing about because we can't see it, aren't meant to see it. . . . What if our time here on this earth is like . . . living in this cavern? And everything is illusion, not real at all?"

In *The Unraveling of Wentwater*, the characters are reminded how, with a word, God fashioned out of nothing all worlds (Hebrews 11:3), and Joran, in *The Wolf of Tebron*, realizes at the end of his journey that he is both the dreamer and the dreamed— he only exists because God imagined and brought into being all life. We are reminded by the apostle Paul that God "gives to all life, breath, and all things" (Acts 17:25 NKJV).

This, to me, is what is at the heart of wonder and astonishment at this life we have been gifted—that God chose, out of love, to create us and give us a world on which to live, and a hope of a better world outside this hidden cavern in which we dwell. Just as Me'arah is hidden under tons of rock, we live beneath a veil that keeps us from seeing what's beyond, what's outside this human life. But we don't live in the dark, for we have been promised very great and precious promises of a "real life"—an inheritance reserved in heaven for us that cannot fade, rot, or perish (2 Peter 1:4; 1 Peter

1:4). Therefore, we are admonished to not live our lives as if in the dark but to cling to the hope God gives us—the hope of a kingdom not made by human hands (Hebrews 11:16).

This precious gift of this heavenly kingdom is at the heart of this seventh book in the series. Each of the prior six books took readers to one of the sacred sites that heaven established on earth to keep evil in check, but although the first six sites could be found on earth, the seventh could not—for it represented the true "sacred site." Jacob dreamed of the gate of heaven when he saw angels ascending and descending a ladder. And Kael, in *The Sands of Ethryn*, saw what he thought was the reflection of his sacred site up above him, in the sky. He did not realize until the end of all things that what he saw was not a reflection but the true kingdom.

Two works inspired the storyline for *The Hidden Kingdom*. One is a Russian folktale called "Evening, Midnight, and Sunrise," which tells of a king who built an underground palace in order to keep his three daughters safe from the evils above—a place where the harsh winds and angry sun could not beat down on them. Yet, by protecting them he, in effect, imprisoned them. This made me ponder our existence, and how we are imprisoned now by sin, and although, like the daughters, we have the freedom to move and breathe and live, we are not truly free. Not until we can get to the "surface" and return "home" can we be free.

As wonderful as this underground world is, the daughters find a book that tells them of the true world, which is magnificent, and they yearn to go topside. They beg their father, but he refuses to take them there, fearful of all the evil they will encounter. You can guess what happens next, and in *The Hidden Kingdom*, Meris cannot resist the temptation to see the real world. Nor can she hold back from questioning the wisdom and mercy shown by Shamara to keep the truth hidden from her people.

The other source of inspiration for this novel was The Chronicles of Amber series by Roger Zelazny, written in the 1970s. In his books, all the worlds are shadow worlds of the true world—Amber. Only the princes and princesses of Amber can enter the real world and know the truth about the shadow worlds. I have to admit, too, that I was a bit inspired by the last episode of the TV series *Lost*. Especially the moment when Christian Shepherd says to his son, Jack, "There is no . . . now . . . here," explaining that heaven is outside of time, and showing that everyone we have ever known and loved has always been there with us. A little surreal and perplexing, but an intriguing concept.

I could write an entire book on all that inspired me while writing this series over the last seven years, but I'll spare you and instead leave you with these study questions to consider—and Jesus's invitation to those who are seeking the true kingdom: "Come, you who are blessed by my Father, inherit the Kingdom prepared for you from the creation of the world" (Matthew 25:34 NLT). May we all one day, soon and forever, gather together in his glorious kingdom to the praise and honor of our Creator and our Savior, Jesus Christ.

1) Characters in the book learn that the kingdom of God is "in their midst." They are puzzled by this, for they are also told the kingdom is within them (see Luke 17:21). How does Kael, the first and the last Keeper of the sacred site, understand this to mean at the end, when he is taken to the seventh site—the true kingdom?

2) The prophecies in the book tell of the end of time and a new age coming. How does this parallel what believers are told in the Bible of God's coming kingdom? This new kingdom is to

be made up of "living stones" instead of actual rock (1 Peter 2:5). How is this symbolized in *The Hidden Kingdom*?

3) Meris and some of the visitors to Me'arah questioned Shamara's right to keep all the people "in the dark" and not inform them of the truth about the real world. She created and sustained their world, believing they would be happier if they lived in ignorance. How do you feel about that, and what would you say to someone who feels God has done wrong by keeping humans in the dark (in sin) without freeing them from their prison all these centuries?

4) In *The Hidden Kingdom*, the seekers of truth are told that the world was meant to be destroyed or brought to an end. As distressing as the news sounded, the characters were told not to be overly distressed by this. Why? What happens at the end of the book to show this is a good thing? We are told this world as we know it will come to an end (2 Peter 3:5-10), but why should we rejoice?

5) The first covenant God made with his people had commandments etched into stone. The new covenant was foretold to be etched on hearts (Jeremiah 31:31). Can you make any comparisons of this to the sacred sites in the books and how they symbolically represent a covenant between God and mankind? How is this prophecy fulfilled, in a manner of speaking, in *The Hidden Kingdom*?

6) How is the power of love used in this book to portray salvation? See what the Bible says about love in 1 Corinthians 13.

"Love never fails." How is this shown in the scenes with Meris escaping her prison, and near the end, when she speaks with Kael? What does Meris realize is the true key to the kingdom and why?

7) How does Kael use the key to the kingdom so that everyone can be reunited? Can you think of how this is similar to how Jesus will use the key to God's kingdom? (compare Revelation 3:7).

8) The Moon tells Joran at the end of the story that he can't get into the kingdom unless he gives up—gives everything up. What does she mean, and how is this true for believers? (See Mark 8:35; 1 John 2:17.)

9) Meris compares our lives to a baby in the womb, saying we live for a short time hidden in darkness, but through turmoil we come out to real life. How does this parallel to the plans God has for mankind? In what way do you see this life as being a preparation for the "real life"?

10) How does Joran's experience in the kingdom at the end of the book reflect what the apostle John sees in the revelation given to him by Jesus? (See Revelation 21.)

11) Alia is telling the story of *The Hidden Kingdom* to her son Aron, which is her personal story. What does she say about the power of story and the need for us to remember stories?

12) How does the last scene in the book explain the "legend" of fairies, and show that this story, as with all stories, is a fairy tale?

When you buy a book from **AMG Publishers**, **Living Ink Books**, or **God and Country Press**, you are helping to make disciples of Jesus Christ around the world.

How? AMG Publishers and its imprints are ministries of **AMG** (*Advancing the Ministries of the Gospel*) **International**, a non-denominational evangelical Christian mission organization ministering in over 30 countries around the world. Profits from the sale of AMG Publishers books are poured into the outreaches of AMG International.

AMG International Mission Statement

AMG exists to advance with compassion the command of Christ to evangelize and make disciples around the world through national workers and in partnership with like-minded Christians.

AMG International Vision Statement

We envision a day when everyone on earth will have at least one opportunity to hear and respond to a clear presentation of the Gospel of Jesus Christ and have the opportunity to grow as a disciple of Christ.

To learn more about AMG International and how you can pray for or financially support this ministry, please visit **www.amginternational.org**.

CPSIA information can be obtained at www.ICGtesting.com
Printed in the USA
LVOW07s1708080715

445447LV00003B/453/P